Demon

The Cosantóir (Protectors) MC | Book 4

Michael Geraghty

Hold Fast Publishing

Chapter 1

The wheelbarrow filled with mud and crushed rock clanged along the ruddy floor of the tunnel as Darryl Garvey reached the far wall of the tunnel. He grimaced as he bent to toss another load aside, letting a guttural groan escape his lips as he spied the contents added to the pile.

Darryl reached into the back pocket of his jumpsuit to retrieve one of his extra bandanas so he could wipe the dirt and dust off his face and the back of his neck. He pulled the cloth up and over his bald head, regretting not wearing his usual head covering under his work helmet. Darryl breathed deeply, feeling the slight ache in his chest that had become commonplace over the last few weeks. His right hand instinctively touched his front pocket, and he gripped the inhaler his doctor had given him during his last appointment. He removed his hand, avoiding the temptation of pulling the device out and using it, knowing his fellow Sandhogs might notice and ask prying questions or give him a hard time.

Ribbing was a given working in the tunnels with a crew, and Darryl could dish it out and take it, no matter how personal it got. Of course, nothing proved to be off-limits, but the last thing Darryl wanted was to have to explain what was going on. The badge of honor of toughness he wore made him proud and carried over from his professional wrestling days. Any sign of weakness left you open to rivals, and even though the men Darryl worked with were his family—his brothers—he knew their joking eventually would bleed over to concern and might affect the way he worked.

Darryl returned the empty wheelbarrow to the area he was working. He reached down and plucked one of the bottles of water set aside for himself. He used his all-purpose bandana to wipe the dirt and dust off the bottle before twisting it and guzzling half of it. A quick look down at his work boots revealed inches of caked-on mud. It would take some scrubbing and chiseling to get down to where the laces were supposed to be when he returned to the Hog House on the site.

The job siren blared, signaling the end of today's shift. Darryl watched as his crew of five came to a halt, almost in unison. They all turned to face Darryl, chests heaving as they rubbed aching muscles from hard labor.

Duff Kennedy sauntered up and stood facing Darryl. Although Duff was a large man himself, Darryl dwarfed him easily.

"Calling it a day already, Demon?" Duff scoffed. "Jaysus, you didn't even show up until an hour into our shift. Put in some real work, man."

"Why do you think I was late this morning, Duff?" Darryl quipped. "Your wife just didn't want me to leave her. I put in plenty of real work with her."

The other team members guffawed as Duff's smile slid from his face.

"He gotcha with that one, Duff," Whitey added, slapping Duff on the back as he walked past him.

Darryl grinned, his white teeth showing through the dirt and dust on his cheeks and face. He slowly followed his team, putting his arm around Duff as they made their way toward the elevator to ascend to ground level again.

The elevator jolted to a halt as it reached the top. Immediately as Darryl stepped out, he felt the cold wind strike his face. Remnants of the latest February snowstorm were evident on the job site. Piles of snow had been cleared off to the sides, and frozen ground and mud areas were slick with ice patches. More than once, laughs echoed through the dusk as someone slipped and skidded or fell before they reached the trailers.

Darryl reached the Hog House, making his way to his locker. He stomped along the way, hoping to knock some of the crusted earth off his jumpsuit and boots. Instead, a chunk slid off right at the beginning of his locker row. It failed to go unnoticed by Kearney, the grizzled veteran who oversaw the house.

"Feck, Demon," Kearney yelled. "Now I'm gonna have to mop the floor again. Take your feckin' boots off before coming in here. It's not a barn, despite all the animals around."

"Sorry, Kearney," Darryl replied, "but it's five degrees outside. A little cold to be shedding the boots outside, and mine are pretty bad today."

Darryl followed Kearney's gaze as his eyes shifted down to the boots. Kearney sighed deeply.

"Give 'em to me," Kearney answered. I'll have them ready for you tomorrow."

"You're the best, K," Darryl smiled. "I'll drop them by your desk."

Darryl sat on the wooden bench in front of his locker, kicking off his boots while trying to minimize the piles of dirt around him. He stripped out of his work clothes, deciding to shun the shower tonight to get home sooner. He grabbed a t-shirt and pulled it over his head, feeling soreness in his shoulders as he got it into place. Once it made it over his head, he noticed Liam O'Farrell standing next to him, wrapped in only a towel.

"Hey, brother," Darryl said with a nod as he grabbed his jeans. "Long day today?"

"I doubled," Liam answered. "I started overnight and kept going until now. We needed to straighten out some of the night shift crew to move this project. We're supposed to be done by May, but it will never happen if they drag their feet like this. I was here crackin' skulls all night. I wouldn't be surprised if they slashed my tires. I kicked two asshats off the job for slacking."

Darryl finished putting his belt on before turning to his locker and grabbing his bike boots.

"Shit, you rode in today? You're going to freeze out there tonight."

"It didn't seem that bad this morning," Darryl answered. "I was kind of rushing anyway. Taking the bike was easier."

Darryl paused, hoping Liam wouldn't ask why he had to rush. Instead, Darryl veered the conversation off in another direction.

"I don't suppose you heard anything about the super job yet," Darryl inquired.

Liam shut his locker door, tossing his towel and putting on his boxer briefs.

"Actually, I have," Liam answered as he continued dressing.

"Oh yeah?" Darryl answered hopefully.

"Yeah. Here's the thing, Demon," Liam began.

"Don't even go there," Darryl said, holding his large palm. "I already know how this ends."

Darryl slammed his locker door loudly, turning heads.

"I'm sorry, brother," Liam acknowledged.

"Who did they give it to this time?" Darryl snapped.

"Does it really matter?"

Liam pulled back his long dark hair before splashing on some cologne.

"It does to me."

"Zach Russell," Liam told him. Darryl shot a look toward Liam.

"Are you serious? I trained that baby! He worked on my crew for two years. He could barely wipe his ass, let alone lead a project. Not to mention I have more experience than him. Why him?"

"Demon, we shouldn't get into this now," Liam answered, placing a hand on Darryl's shoulder.

"Who did he know?"

Liam shook his head before sitting on the bench next to Darryl.

"His uncle is Jeff Russell. He's a bigwig that the state gets a lot of jobs from. I guess he called in a favor or two. I'm sorry, man."

"This day just gets better and better," Darryl ranted. "I need a drink or ten tonight. You heading to the House?"

"Are you crazy, man?" Liam laughed. "You know what today is, right?"

Darryl sat staring at Liam, awaiting an answer.

"It's Valentine's Day," Liam snapped. "Olivia and I have... plans," Liam grinned salaciously.

"Damn, I forgot that was today," Darryl answered as he snatched his dirty boots off the floor. "I need to go pick something up for Annie."

"You still buy your daughter a Valentine's Day gift?"

"Of course I do," Darryl boasted. "She may be 22, but she's still my baby girl."

"Very sweet," Liam mocked. "You better get going then." Liam glanced at his watch. "It's after 6 already. You'll be lucky if you can get her a candy bar at QuickChek. I promise we'll have a few pints tomorrow."

Darryl made his way to Kearney's desk, dropping off his boots with the old man.

"Any chance I can get some new laces too?" Darryl asked.

"Christ, man, why not just ask me to cook you a nice meal too?" Kearney growled as he grabbed Darryl's size 15 boots.

Darryl pulled a twenty out of his wallet and slid it into Kearney's tip jar. Kearney beamed at Darryl.

"Get outta here before you ask me for something else," Kearney laughed.

Darryl zipped his leather jacket closed and pulled his gloves and hand-knitted scarf on before he ventured out of the trailer and into the cold. When he reached his custom Harley, Darryl winced at the thought of riding home with the freezing gusts he would face. He roared the engine before slipping his helmet on and flipping the faceguard down.

The frigid ride up 17M toward Harriman did little to ease all that ran through Darryl's thoughts. Fighting the cold, the disappointment of getting passed over for a supervisor position again, and what he would find to get Annie occupied space in his head until he headed left into Harriman and toward Monroe. Then, one glance at the cars crowded into the tiny parking lot of Greenery Plus, the local florist, let Darryl know that he was not going to get any flowers today.

He raced through the yellow traffic light and moved down the road past the jammed lot of the Captain's Table. Darryl didn't want to resort to one of the local supermarkets to pick up whatever was left for flowers or a box of Whitman's chocolates. Instead, he recalled a jewelry shop in Monroe and decided to give them a try.

Turning to Lake Street, he parked his bike in one of the empty spots in front of Macha's Treasures. Lights shone brightly inside, and Darryl hopped off his bike and entered, keeping his helmet on. The bells on the door jingled, and Darryl immediately felt all eyes on him. Peering through his visor, he saw the shocked look on the faces of the older female customer and the sales associate. The gray-haired customer stuffed the nicely-wrapped gift box into her purse, and she clutched her purse tightly before moving past Darryl. Darryl nodded and smiled, realizing he probably frightened the old woman with his look.

Darryl was alone with the sales associate in the store and gazed at the nicely decorated display cases filled with rings, bracelets, necklaces, and more. Soft classical music echoed through the air as he browsed. Darryl knew he was closely watched at this point as he saw the tall, lithe clerk looking at his every move. When he moved over to the case with diamond necklaces, the woman shot over to his location.

"Is there anything I can help you with?" the woman's voice cracked with a tinge of an Irish accent.

"I'm just looking right now," Darryl answered, his voice muffled by his helmet.

"Well, we close in about five minutes," glancing at her watch. "Perhaps you want to come back tomorrow when you have more time to browse or ask questions."

Darryl knew the not-so-subtle cues she gave him. It was nothing he hadn't heard before, especially when he was dressed in his club jacket. He deftly removed his helmet so he didn't have the haze in front of him, allowing him to see the jewelry clearer and better look at the saleswoman.

Darryl saw clearly that she looked all business. Dressed smartly in a red blouse and black skirt, her dark hair was pulled back tightly and slicked, allowing him to view her prominent cheekbones and chestnut eyes that widened as he looked down at her. Yet, surprisingly, he didn't need to look down as far as he often did with a woman.

"I'm looking for a Valentine's gift for my daughter," Darryl said. "I know I'm a little late. But, I promise I won't be long." He continued looking at the necklaces.

"These might be much for a little girl," the woman indicated. "We don't really carry anything suitable—"

"She's 22," Darryl interrupted.

"Oh, I see," she answered cautiously .

"That one looks nice," pointing at a silver necklace with the Tree of Life. Diamonds studded the leaves of the tree.

"Yes, it is nice. It's hand-designed," the woman answered. "It's... quite expensive," she hesitated. Darryl saw her eyes scan over him again, going from his bare head, over his sweaty, dirty face, down to his leather jacket decorated with a Cosantóir logo.

"How much is quite expensive?" Darryl quipped.

"Are you sure you wouldn't rather look at some quartz or zircon items? They are in the case over there," she pointed at the small stand nearer to the front door.

Darryl took a deep breath, keeping his cool.

"Can I see the Tree of Life, please?" Darryl asked, pointing a giant index finger down and tapping on the case.

Darryl saw the surprise on her face when he identified the necklace's design. She warily unlocked the case and pulled the box out. She held it in her palm in front of Darryl. He reached forward quickly, and she recoiled a bit.

"May I hold it?" he asked. "I promise not to run out the door with it."

The woman gingerly stretched her hand toward Darryl. Her palm shook as his large fingers took hold of the box, and he held it close to his eyes.

"Very nice indeed," Darryl crowed. "It's beautiful." He peered at the small tag attached to the item to scan the price.

Darryl whistled as he handed the box back to the woman.

"You weren't kidding about the price," Darryl added. He watched as the saleswoman took the necklace back, fussing with it in the box so it would look just right. Then, finally, she bent to start to put it back in the display case.

"I tried to tell you," the woman added, getting ready to lock the case.

"Is cash okay?" Darryl said as he pulled his wallet out.

"I'm sorry?" the woman questioned. Darryl spied her eyebrows raise, and he smiled.

"Cash," Darryl said. "I can use my card, but I have the cash."

Darryl removed several crisp hundred dollar bills from his wallet.

"I assume there's a tax too," Darryl added as he counted ten bills. "And can you gift wrap it for me? I saw that other customer's item, and it looked perfect."

"Sure," the woman answered as she hustled the box over to where the gift wrap lay. Darryl looked on as she quickly wrapped the box in heart-covered paper and used expert skills to tie a ribbon.

"Perfect," Darryl beamed as he handed the bills to the woman.

"You gave me too much," she stammered, trying to hand one of the hundreds back to him.

"That's for you," he added. "For all your help and hard work. I know I kept you past closing. I'm sure you have somewhere to be on Valentine's Day."

"I can't accept it," she said, trying to refuse the generous tip.

"Please," Darryl insisted, placing the bill back in her hand and holding it there for a moment before he curled her fingers around the money.

"I will give you one piece of advice, though," Darryl said as he placed the gift in his jacket pocket.

"What's that?" she asked.

"I'm sure you know it already, but the whole judging a book by its cover thing makes a difference. If I wasn't such a nice guy, I could have made life hell for you."

"Is that so?" she replied with surprise. "What makes you think I was judging you?"

"Seriously? I'm surprised you didn't trip some silent alarm to have the cops here two minutes after I walked in. You saw a big burly dude with a motorcycle helmet and club colors with a dirty face and jeans and assumed I was here to rob the place. Do you know how often I've heard the 'it's very expensive' speech from salespeople? All I'm saying is don't jump to conclusions next time."

"No offense, sir," the woman said, getting her back up. "But don't pretend to know anything about me or what I was thinking. Now, if you don't mind, I need to close up. Have a pleasant evening."

Darryl's eyes widened before he chuckled and shook his head.

"I don't think I caught your name," Darryl said as he walked toward the door. The woman followed close behind him, ushering him out.

"That's because I didn't give it to you," she answered.

Darryl stepped outside the door, and she shut it quickly, turning the locks on it.

"Are you planning on giving it to me?"

The woman stood on the opposite side of the thick glass, reaching up to grab the shade on the door. She pulled the shade halfway down before peering out to see if Darryl still stood there. She cracked a small smile when she saw him staring back at her.

"Rose," she answered.

"Thank you, Rose," Darryl grinned as he turned toward his bike.

Chapter 2

Working quickly, Rose Boyle locked the front door and drew the shade, flipping the leading overhead lights off and turning the open sign to closed. She leaned and walked behind the counter, switching off the interior lights of each display case and double-checking to ensure everything was locked and secure. Rose rested against the back counter and gave a big sigh of relief, thankful the workday finally ended.

A quick glance at her wristwatch let her know it was 6:15, leaving her plenty of time to walk down the street to the Plum House, where she would meet Walter for their Valentine's Day dinner. Rose went into the restroom in the back by the manager's office to freshen up. She loosened the bun in her hair, letting the long dark tresses fall down to her shoulders. Walter always complimented her when her hair was down, comparing her to Jennifer Hudson. She never saw it herself, but the thought of it made her feel sexy as hell. Rose tossed her hair a bit and looked in the mirror to see if she was ready. She undid the top two buttons of her red blouse, figuring to give Walter a big smile when she sat down at the table and took her coat off.

Rose set the alarm by the front door and exited, locking up and tugging on the door to check it. She turned to walk up the street, the cold wind slapping at her face as she moved. She crouched her head a bit to fight it off and moved quickly, her heels clicking on the sidewalk as she stepped. All the shops on the street had closed for the night, with the only lights shining from the sign over the sushi restaurant she neared. As she got closer, Rose noticed a man in a dark suit step out of the restaurant, holding the door open for a woman in a dress short enough to be obscured by an overcoat. A familiarity flashed across Rose's mind as the man walked over and opened the car's back door idling out front.

It was only when the woman wrapped her arms around the neck of the man that she got a side view and saw the unmistakable profile of Walter. The pointed chin and close-cropped hair stood out, even as he leaned in and gave a deep kiss to the woman with him. Initially, Rose stopped in place and watched, stunned by inaction. Then, as the kiss lingered more and more, Rose moved, her shoes echoing loudly on the pavement until she reached the couple. She shoved Walter, pushing his shoulder so that the kiss broke, and the woman stared wide-eyed back at Rose.

"What the hell are you doing?" the woman crowed.

Walter looked on, dumbfounded.

"Apparently interrupting my boyfriend kissing you," Rose snapped.

The woman gaped at Rose and then smiled and shot a look at Walter.

"This is her?" she asked. "She doesn't look close to Jennifer Hudson, Babe."

"I don't know who you are," Rose said with rage, "but I don't care either."

Rose turned to walk away before Walter reached out and grabbed her shoulder.

"Baby, wait," Walter pled.

"Don't call me Baby," Rose said through her gritted teeth. "In fact, don't call me at all. Two years of my life wasted on you, Walter."

"I didn't mean—" Walter began before Rose put her hand up to hush him.

"You didn't mean for me to see you kissing her, or you didn't mean to get caught cheating? Which is it? You know what? I don't care either way. You would just dump her in a car and then have another dinner with me and spend the night like nothing had happened."

Rose looked toward Walter's face, but he quickly shifted his gaze to his highly polished shoes.

"Or were you going to wait until I fell asleep and then go over to her place?"

"Now you're catching on there, girl," the woman cackled.

"Shut up, Denise!" Walter yelled.

Rose gazed at the woman, waiting to get in the car, before turning to Walter again.

"Denise? The receptionist from your office Denise? The one you hired a few months ago? How long has this been going on?"

"A lot longer than a few months, honey," Denise laughed. "I had to beg him for the job."

"Christ, Denise, shut the fuck up," Walter shouted.

"I can't believe this."

Rose's body shook as she clenched her fists. She badly wanted to punch one of them; it was just a question of who would be first. It took all her strength to resist before she turned on her heels and marched away, down the alley toward the back of the buildings, so she got to where her car sat.

She heard Walter give a cursory shout or two, trying to get her to stop and listen, but Rose marched on until she reached her car. She fumbled for her keys in her purse, dropping them onto a small patch of black ice next to her Subaru. She bent to reach for them before slipping in her heels and landing with a thud on her backside.

"You've got to be kidding me with this!" She yelled as she grabbed the keys, now taunting her from inches away. Rose grabbed the door handle and gingerly pulled herself up to get into the auto. She started up the car immediately, turning the seat warmer on with the hopes of warming up her now-wet behind. A glance down at her right leg gave her a view of the long run in her black stockings.

Rose smacked her palms onto her steering wheel several times. She felt the urge to swear more than ever, something she never gave into after growing up with her grandmother always telling her to mind what she said because God is always listening. Instead, she drove the car and tore out of the parking lot.

"You will not cry over him, Rose!" she told herself repeatedly as she waited for the traffic light to turn green.

Within minutes she was in the parking lot of her condo complex, exiting her car carefully to avoid a repeat fall. Rose trudged across the pavement and up the wooden steps that led to her second-floor dwelling, swinging the door open and getting hit by a blast of music over the speakers in the living room. George Michael was crooning "Careless Whisper," and the living room was dark, with only a string of heart-shaped red lights over the sliding glass door illuminating the space.

Rose stood near the living room before seeing a head peek over the high couch cushions. Her roommate Liz did a double-take before sitting up straight, revealing she was shirtless with just a black bra.

"Jesus, Rose, what are you doing here? You're supposed to be out all night," Liz said with her Manchester accent.

"Yeah, well, Walter wasn't supposed to be cheating on me with his receptionist either," Rose bemoaned.

"Oh, I knew he was a no-good fuck," Liz said. "Sorry, Rob. Night's over," Liz looked down before Rob's head popped up from behind the cushions.

"Hey, Rose," Rob said sheepishly. Liz rose from the couch and told Alexa to pause the music, leaving the sound of Rob's belt jingling followed by his zipper going up as the only sound in the room.

Liz picked up her red sweater off the floor and put it on before walking over to Rose to give her a hug.

"You don't need that prick anyways," Liz told her as they embraced.

Rose held firm, fending off tears she knew were building inside.

"So, that's it then?" Rob asked as he looked on.

"You two can enjoy your night," Rose said. "I can just go in my room or back out. Maybe I can catch a movie—"

"You will not be by yourself right now," Liz insisted. "Rob can take a raincheck, right?"

Liz's eyes widened as she stared at Rob, prompting him to answer.

"Yeah, of course," Rob answered. He walked over to the coat rack hanging by the front door and grabbed his winter jacket.

"I'm sorry," Rose apologized.

"No worries, Rose," Rob answered as Liz followed Rob to the front door.

"I'll make it up to you, love, I promise," Liz added before giving Rob a peck on the lips.

"When?" Rob asked softly as Liz closed the door on him.

Liz clapped her hands and walked back toward Rose, taking Rose by the hand.

"So Galentine's Day it is!" she said, leading Rose over to the small bar cart they kept in the corner of the room. "What will it be?"

Liz waved her hand across the cart like a model on a game show showing the latest available prize.

"Red wine for me," Rose said as she took her coat off and tossed it onto the chair nearby. Rose walked over to the couch and plopped down, kicking off her heels before propping her feet on a nearby ottoman.

"Valentine's Day sucks," Rose groaned. Her index finger grazed the long run in her stockings. "And I ruined my favorite pair of stockings because of him!"

Liz handed Rose a well-filled glass of Pinot Noir before she popped open a bottle of Peroni for herself and sat down next to Rose, putting her feet next to hers on the foot stool.

"Are you gonna tell me what happened, or are we just drinking to forget about him completely? Either way is okay with me," Liz added as she sipped her lager.

Rose explained the events to Liz regarding how she discovered Walter's cheating.

"Want to go over and egg his house?" Liz asked. "I just bought a dozen yesterday. So we can put them to good use."

"No, I don't think that will help much," Rose answered.

"I can go key the fucker's car if you want," Liz laughed.

"Is there anything that won't get us arrested?"

"Nothing fun or worth doing," Liz replied.

"Then drinking my sorrows away will have to do it," Rose added as she lifted her wine glass and clinked it on Liz's beer bottle.

Liz drained her Peroni before she got up from the sofa and took Rose's empty wine glass.

"No worries, Rosey Posey," Liz said as she walked toward the bar cart to refill the wine glass. "There are much nicer guys out there that are perfect for you than stodgy old cheater Walter."

Liz handed the topped-off wine glass back to Rose before moving to the kitchen to get another beer for herself.

"Yeah... where?" Rose asked aloud before swigging more of her wine.

Chapter 3

Darryl's bike rumbled into the driveway, kicking up some loose gravel and bits of ice left over from his latest shoveling efforts of the storm a few days before. Annie tried to get him to hire a plow service several times, but Darryl always balked. He often shoveled as part of his job, and taking care of snow never seemed more difficult than moving massive piles of dirt, clay, mud, and sludge by hand.

Darryl's only insistence was that he always had a spot in the garage for his bike. This meant Annie had to make sure he could always get in there and park her little car far enough to the left so he could pull in quickly. Tonight, Annie had placed her car right in the middle of the driveway and close to the garage door, so Darryl couldn't get around it. He parked his bike right behind her, blocking her in, before he climbed off and marched into the house, pulling the door closed behind him loudly enough that it rattled the front windows.

"That you, Dad?" Annie shouted from upstairs in her bedroom.

"Of course it is! Were you expecting someone else?"

Darryl tried not to imagine who might have been expected before Annie sauntered down the stairs. Instead, he watched as his daughter maneuvered down each step in her heels, her midriff exposed by the crop top she wore to show off her recent belly button ring that Darryl hated to be reminded of.

"You know it's five degrees outside?" Darryl reminded his daughter.

"I'm aware," Annie said, matter-of-fact.

"You won't be cold, barely wearing what you're wearing?"

Annie placed her hands on her hips and stared back at her father.

"What's our deal, Dad?" she asked.

It was Darryl's turn to roll his eyes as he pulled off his leather jacket and tossed it over the back of the oversized leather recliner facing the television. Then, he walked toward the kitchen, trying to avoid an impending argument.

"Don't ignore me," Annie stated firmly. "What's our deal?"

Annie slid in front of the refrigerator and blocked Darryl from opening the door. Darryl sighed before lifting Annie by her elbows and moving her aside. He swung the door open and grabbed the half-empty bottle of orange juice, twisting the top off and drinking right from the container.

"To remind you, our deal is you don't question my wardrobe, where I work, or who I date, and I don't question what you do with the Cosantóir."

"I was just concerned about your health by reminding you how cold it is outside," Darryl said.

"Speaking of health, how did your doctor's appointment go?"

Darryl groaned, marched out of the kitchen to his recliner, and sat down, picking up the HD TV remote and turning ESPN on.

Annie stood in front of the recliner, obstructing Darryl's view of the TV as he craned his neck to see around her. Annie snatched the remote off the arm of the recliner and shut the TV off.

"Just tell me how the visit went so I don't have to break into your patient portal chart online," Annie asked.

"You don't know my password," Darryl said as he reached for the remote before Annie stepped away.

"I Pinned Chris Jericho 2," Annie retorted. "You use that for too many things, Dad."

"Give me a break, Annie."

"What did the doctor say?"

Darryl sat forward in his chair, forcing the recliner down with his legs.

"They did x-rays and a CT scan," Darryl admitted. "I don't know anything yet. The doctor prescribed me an inhaler when I saw her last week. I haven't really had to use it yet. I'm fine."

"Why didn't you tell me about the inhaler?" Annie complained.

"Because it's not a big deal, I didn't want to worry you, and I didn't want you nagging me about it. Can I have the remote back, please?"

"Dad, you need to keep me updated on what's going on with you. It's important."

"I'm not a doddering old man, Annie. I'm forty-two. I'm in better shape than 98% of the people you know, including those scrawny hipsters you date."

Annie glanced at her watch and then grimaced at her father.

"We're not done with this," she assured him. "I need to go, but I want more details tonight."

"Where are you going?" Darryl asked, standing up. "I got us a couple of nice steaks I was going to cook for dinner. You know, like a father-daughter Valentine's thing. Oh, I almost forgot," Darryl reached into his jacket pocket, pulled out the small wrapped gift, and presented it to Annie. "Happy Valentine's Day."

"Dad, you don't have to get me anything."

"You're still my little girl, no matter what you might think sometimes."

Annie opened the delicate ribbon by giving it a tug.

"I know you didn't wrap this," she scoffed.

"Not with these giant things," Darryl added while wiggling his fingers. "The lady at the store did it. I think I scared her into it."

"They don't know you're a gentle giant," Annie smiled. She opened the box and pulled out the necklace, looking at the diamonds sparkle in the light.

"It's beautiful," Annie said, holding it high. "You spent too much on this."

"What else am I going to spend my money on?" Darryl answered. He got up from the chair to try and help Annie put the necklace on, but his fingers were too large to deal with the tiny clasp of the jewelry.

"I got it, Dad," Annie told him, quickly hooking the necklace around her neck. "Thank you, I love it."

Annie stood on her tiptoes, and Darryl bent down so his daughter could reach to kiss him on the cheek.

"Okay, I gotta go," Annie said, moving toward the door where her coat was hanging.

"Where are you going?" Darryl asked.

"I'm meeting a few girlfriends at Mille Malone's. We're going to hang out and see how the night goes. Just a girl's night."

"Hmmm, maybe I'll come down too. Finn and Preacher are probably there already," Darryl stood up.

"You don't want to do that," Annie insisted. "I'm sure they are there with dates enjoying Valentine's Day. No offense, Dad, but I don't want my father sitting around watching me while I'm out at the bar."

"I get it," Darryl replied. "Go have a good time."

"Thanks," Annie beamed. "Do you think you could move your bike for me to get out of the driveway?"

"If you had parked how you're supposed to, I could have got in the garage."

"I didn't think you would be home before I left," Annie insisted.

"Where was I going to be?"

"I thought you might go to Hog House and hang out, or maybe you would have a date," Annie replied as she put her coat and gloves on.

"Ha! That's a good one. I think you would know if I was seeing someone, and I doubt there are too many of the Brothers hanging out at the house tonight."

Annie slid her pom hat over her hair and walked over to Darryl as he put his leather jacket on.

"You know, it would be okay if you told me you were seeing someone, or even if you didn't tell me and just went on a date. So it's not the worst thing in the world, you know."

"Don't worry about my social life, honey," Darryl assured.

"I just don't want you to be lonely," she told him as her gloved hand took his and quickly was enveloped in his large palm.

"I'm not," Darryl insisted. He twirled his keys and walked out the front door with Annie trailing behind him.

Darryl reached the driveway and then escorted Annie over to the driver's side of the black Prius, a car he had purchased for Annie last year for her birthday. He opened the door, so Annie could climb in.

"You should lock your car doors when you park," Darryl admonished.

"Alright, alright," Annie waved as she grabbed the inside handle. "I won't be too late since I have to open tomorrow at Dunkin'."

"Maybe you shouldn't go out if you have to work early," Darryl added.

"Go do something, Dad," Annie chastised as she started the car and closed the door.

Darryl reached his bike and started it up to back it out of the driveway. He gave Annie a casual wave as she took off down the street. Then, Darryl strapped his helmet on and drove off in the opposite direction.

He zipped along back roads until he reached Schunemunk Road and arrived at his destination. Darryl grabbed his worn messenger bag from one of his saddlebags and strode toward the entrance to the building. He pulled the door open, and the immediate sounds of cats meowing and dogs barking echoed through the room.

No one was stationed at the desk just inside the door, so Darryl walked over to the nearest row of cages to see a couple of the cats. He reached into his bag and pulled out tiny morsels to share with a small orange tabby in the first cage. Darryl held out the treat, and the cat came to him immediately as he got his fingers as far into the small bars as he could so the cat could take the gift from him. The cat snatched the food happily, going back to use its rough tongue to catch any remnants on Darryl's fingers before he pulled away.

Darryl heard a door close and footsteps moving toward him before seeing a thin girl staring back at him. Her eyes widened as she scanned up to his face.

"Who are you?" the girl stuttered.

"That's Darryl; he's fine," an older woman said as she entered the room from the same door. The woman grinned at Darryl as she walked over and hugged him.

"We haven't seen you in a few days, Darryl," she said as she patted his leather jacket. "Everything okay?"

"Yeah, just busy, Hannah," Darryl replied.

"Darryl is one of our biggest supporters," Hannah explained to the young girl. "Darryl, this is Courtney, one of our new volunteers."

Darryl smiled at the teenager, who seemed to be two feet shorter than him.

"Nice to meet you," Darryl said, offering his large hand for a high five. Courtney just stared back at him.

"I do high-fives instead of handshakes," Darryl told her. "They're a little less intimidating."

Courtney tentatively raised her hand and placed it against Darryl's palm before pulling away.

"Come on now, you can do better than that," Darryl told her. "Trust me, I won't break."

Courtney slapped his hand harder as Darryl laughed.

"That's better!"

Darryl looked at Hannah as he moved over to see all the full cages.

"Packed house tonight, huh?" he asked.

"Unfortunately," Hannah lamented. "We've had lots of animals to get out of the cold weather lately. Hopefully, we'll get some people in for adoptions this weekend."

"Is he still back there?" Darryl pointed to the door.

"He is," Hannah smiled. "I'm sure he'll be thrilled to see you."

Darryl opened the door that led to the back room where the larger kennels were for the big dogs. He moved straight to the end of the row, with dogs yapping at him for attention as he went until he reached the final cage. The brindle-colored dog lay on the bed and faced the wall, his back to the enclosure entrance. Darryl watched as the dog softly snored before he reached to lift the latch. Then, just as his fingers approached, Darryl saw the dog's snout go into the air and loudly sniff as he caught Darryl's scent. The dog's head spun around as he raced to Darryl, his backside wiggling as he whined.

"Hey there, Buddy," Darryl said as the dog jumped up and put its paws on Darryl's waist.

"Don't let him jump on you like that," Hannah scolded from the doorway. "We're trying to teach him good manners, and you spoil it whenever you come in."

Darryl sat on the floor and let the dog jump all over him before the two began to wrestle.

"He needs to have some fun," Darryl insisted as he pinned the dog beneath his massive arms and the dog mouthed on his arm.

"You know you're the only person he is like this with. He either ignores everyone else or scares them away."

"Who would be scared of this face?" Darryl said as he grabbed the dog's cheeks and held its face in his hands before giving him a kiss on the snout.

"I keep waiting for the day when you come in and say you're taking him home," Hannah offered.

"You know I would in a second, Hannah," Darryl lamented. "My hours are too unpredictable. I would hate to leave him home alone all the time."

"I know. I just wish someone would adopt him. He's been here for months now."

"Hannah!" Courtney's voice rang out from the front. "Two cats got out while I was giving them water!"

"I'll be back," Hannah told Darryl as she moved back to the front.

Darryl nodded and fished some treats out of his pocket to give to Buddy.

"I know exactly how you feel," Darryl said as he petted the block head on his leg.

Chapter 4

A light knocking on her bedroom door proved enough to get Rose to pry her eyes open. She resisted moving the blanket off from over her head, fearing the light would pierce her eyes and go straight to her hungover soul.

"Hey there, you party animal," Liz said softly as she flipped the light switch just inside the entrance to the room. "Time to get up."

"Ugh, it can't be morning already," Rose groaned. Even the light that filtered through her warm nest caused her head to throb an extra beat.

"Sorry, love, but it is."

Liz tugged lightly on the down blanket and fought Rose a bit to get it down to see Rose's face. Rose immediately ducked her head under her pillow.

"Christ, Rose, this is as bad as when we were in uni, and you drank too much," Liz argued, struggling to pull the pillow.

"I don't want to get up," she whined.

"Well, I have to leave to get to work, so it's on you if you call out and stay home or go in late," Liz stated. "There's coffee brewing, and I left a bottle of water, Advil, and Tums on your nightstand. So if you puke, you better get it all in the washer before I get home. I'm not dealing with it."

"Thanks, Mum," Rose moaned.

Rose heard Liz's footsteps leave her room and go down the hall, with the front door closing shortly after. Rose lay with her eyes closed tightly as she attempted to squint away the pain she felt behind them. Her left eyelid slowly lifted to see the clock of her smartphone glaring the time at her, mocking Rose with each passing minute. Finally, the numbers turned to 8 AM.

Rose calculated how long she had before she would have to get up to ready herself and get to work by nine. Finally, she sat up in bed, her head disagreeing with the quickness and drumming louder than before. She reached for her phone, getting ready to press the call button to ring Mr. Quinn, the shop owner.

Holding the phone in her palm, her thumb hovered over the dial button before pulling it back. Rose recognized that she never called out for anything, and Mr. Quinn would gladly give her the time off. However, that meant that his granddaughter Riley worked the shop solo. Of course, Mr. Quinn would be there, but he spent most of his time in his office these days, only coming out to wait on customers he has worked with closely over the years. Riley began working in the shop just after the holidays when she decided to spurn returning to college for the spring semester.

Riley can handle one day, Rose rationalized before pressing the call button.

Mr. Quinn picked up on the second ring.

"Good morning, Rose," he answered in his usual jovial brogue.

Rose immediately felt pangs of guilt before she even had the chance to say anything. The silence got Mr. Quinn's attention.

"Everything alright, Rose?"

"Yes, everything is fine," Rose stammered. "I was just calling to ask what Riley likes in her coffee. I was going to stop at Dunkin' to get something for us before I came over to the store."

"Oh, how nice of you," Mr. Quinn replied. "I think she takes half and half and two sugars."

"Anything for yourself?" she asked, knowing the answer already.

"Oh, no, thank you, dear," Mr. Quinn told her. "I've got my teapot at the shop. I'll make my Irish tea when I get in. See you at nine."

"See you then," Rose forced as she heard Mr. Quinn disconnect.

Rose placed her phone down and dragged herself out of bed and into the hall to the bathroom. The bright lights in the tiled room blinded her, and she rapidly reached to turn the shower on before returning to her room to down the Advil and water Liz had left for her.

Everything Rose did from there out seemed like a laborious chore. Standing under the hot water helped to melt away some of the hangover, but her body ached as she went through the motions of getting ready for work. Once she dragged herself out to her car, the day worsened when she saw the layer of ice on the windows. Prying the door open with some effort, she turned the car on, hoping a little warmth would thaw the windows, but weak air filtering through the front defroster only achieved annoying Rose more.

"Don't do this to me today!" she yelled in frustration at the car before pulling herself out with her ice scraper in hand. Rose went to work on the thick buildup in the windshield, clearing a small view at eye level. She scraped with fervor, only to have the plastic tool snap into pieces.

"Shit!" she yelled, immediately clapping her mittened hand over her mouth, expecting lightning to strike her dead.

She tried to make do with the shards of what she held but got nowhere. Resigned to dealing with it, Rose sat down on the front seat, grateful the seat warmer still worked, and began a slow drive down the hill from her condo.

She peered through the opening, praying for light traffic so she wouldn't have to deal with too many more issues this morning. She rolled the side windows down to see cars left and right. The wind whipped through, chilling her more before she could finally pull out onto 17M and move along. Luckily, Dunkin' Donuts sat just a mile down the road, and she pulled into the parking lot, shutting the windows and rushing inside, only to be greeted by a long line reaching the door.

Rose nervously tapped her left boot on the floor, willing the line to move faster. She craned her neck to see an older woman agonizing over the dozen donuts she was choosing, complaining about the look of each one as the clerk would change out her selections.

"Come on," she muttered under her breath, though the gentleman in front of her heard her and turned around, giving her a look with a shrug.

The line inched forward as another clerk took a register to assist. Rose stood a few people away, happy for the respite in the warm shop. Then, she noticed the young girl behind the counter in her obligatory visor and Dunkin' polo shirt hurrying through customers. Just as Rose was next to the counter and about to order from her, she saw the girl look beyond her and leave her post to grab a beverage.

"Uhm, excuse me!" she yelled, trying not to lose her cool.

"I'll be right with you," the girl answered politely as she poured a coffee and rushed back to the counter. Rose watched as the girl waited, holding the coffee until a large shadow moved past Rose and stood next to the counter. Rose gazed up and immediately recognized the man from last night in the jewelry shop.

"We meet again," he said with a grin, taking the cup of coffee from the clerk before passing the girl a thermos to fill with coffee.

"Yes, hello," Rose said curtly. "I was just about to order something when you cut in front of me."

"My apologies," the man said, nodding his head. "It's the perk of my baby girl being the manager here," he answered as the girl returned with the thermos.

"I'm twenty-two, Dad," she reminded him.

Rose glanced at the girl and saw the Tree of Life necklace dangling around her neck before turning back to the man in the leather jacket.

"What can I get you?" the girl asked Rose. Rose saw the nametag of 'Annie' pinned to the polo.

"I just need two large coffees, light and sweet, please."

Annie walked off to make the coffee as her father stayed at the counter, sipping his coffee and holding the thermos. Rose glanced up at him, wondering why he was still there as he smiled at her. Rose turned her gaze forward, examining the half-empty shelves of donuts.

Annie returned with the coffees, placing them in a holder before ringing them up.

"$6.50," Annie said.

Rose fumbled with her purse, looking for her wallet while having trouble finding it.

"You've got to be kidding me," Rose mumbled as she searched. She hurried along, making it more difficult to find anything as people behind her in line grew frustrated.

"I've got it," Annie's father stated, pulling out his wallet and plunking down a ten-dollar bill.

"I can pay for my own coffee," Rose snapped as she kept searching.

"I'm sure you can," the man replied. "It's just a friendly gesture. Pay it forward next time. See you later, baby girl."

He walked out without waiting for a reply from Annie or Rose. Annie looked at Rose and grinned.

"You're all set. Have a nice day," she grinned.

Rose snatched the coffee tray off the counter and moved through the crowd and back outside to her car. She climbed back in, staring at her ice-covered windshield while she turned on her car, knowing the heat and defroster would do little to help the auto.

She sat gripping the steering wheel, staring straight ahead through the clear window slot, on the verge of tears.

The knock on her window jolted her out of her self-pity party.

"You okay?" A muffled voice asked. She could barely see through the frost on the side window and rolled the window down to see the large man again. He had just removed his motorcycle helmet, and the bike sat in the parking spot next to hers.

"I'm fine," Rose sniffled, using her mitten to wipe her face.

"You know, it's not safe to drive around like this," he said, pointing at the windshield.

"I'm aware," she shot back. "My heat and defroster picked today to stop working, and my ice scraper broke, and I'm running late for work, but thanks for your concern."

"Hold on," the man said, disappearing for a moment. Rose watched as he walked off behind her car before returning and began to scrape the front of the vehicle, clearing away everything quickly.

"You don't have to do that," Rose yelled.

"Oh, I know," the man answered with a grin as he made short work of the ice. Rose watched as he pushed through the buildup without a problem, leaving the windshield clear in no time.

"You should get your car looked at," he offered. "It might just be low coolant and cost you a few dollars, but it could be your thermostat. Go to Freeman's next door and have them check it for you. In the meantime, keep the scraper. Annie has an extra in her car she can use."

"I'll be sure to do that when I have more time," she grumbled. Realizing how that sounded, Rose sighed. "I'm sorry; that was rude. You've been very helpful. Thanks."

"It's not a problem, Rose," the man smiled, placing a hand on the car's roof.

Rose stared back at him.

"How did you know my name?"

"You told me last night," he replied. "Remember?"

"Sorry," she apologized. "I... my brain has blocked out most of last night."

"We all have nights like that. I hope your day gets better," he told her, tapping on the roof as he walked away to his bike and put his helmet back on. Rose watched as he started up and pulled away, giving her a slight wave as he went off.

Rose shut the open window, looking over at the ice scraper as she drove on her way to work. She parked in the lot behind the jewelry store and hustled to the back door as she saw Riley standing there, waiting.

"I'm sorry I'm late," Rose huffed as she handed the tray to Riley. "It has been the morning from hell."

"No biggie," Riley chirped, anxious to get inside.

Rose opened the back door and turned the alarm off, happy to be at work. Riley turned all the lights on while Rose started up the computer in the office and the two registers in the shop. She opened the safe, pulling the cash drawers out, before walking into the shop. Riley checked over the displays to see if anything needed replenishing.

"You sold the Tree necklace?" Riley asked as she looked into the empty space in the case.

"Oh yes, I did," Rose answered. "Right before closing last night."

"That's the one you designed, right? That must have made you happy."

"You know, I haven't even had much time to think about it," Rose admitted as she picked her coffee out of the tray. "Yes, it does make me happy."

"Was it one of our regulars?" Riley inquired. "I'll bet it was Mr. Reilly. He's always buying nice things for his wife. He's looked at it a couple of times."

"Actually, it was someone I had never seen in here before," Rose admitted. "He came in, saw it, and plunked down cash for it."

"Wow, he paid cash?" Riley offered, raising her eyebrows. "He must have been one of the Richie Riches in town now."

"I don't know," Rose shrugged as she sipped her coffee. "He didn't seem like it. He wore dirty jeans, a leather jacket, and a motorcycle helmet. He was wearing Cosantóir colors."

"I don't know what that means," Riley replied.

"Cosantóir is a motorcycle club around here," Rose explained. "It's Gaelic for Defenders."

"Does that mean they're a gang?"

"I'm not really sure," Rose admitted. "They've been around here for a while. They have a house not far from the Harriman train station that they hang out in."

"Have you ever been there?"

"Me? No. Why would you ask me that?"

"I don't know. You're Irish. You lived in Ireland for a long time. I thought maybe you're connected to them somehow since they have a Gaelic name."

"You're grandfather is Irish and from Ireland too. Does that mean he's part of the motorcycle club too?" Rose asked.

"I don't know. I never asked him," Riley admitted. "He could be."

Rose laughed loudly at Riley's admission.

"I'm sure he's far removed from the Cosantóir," Rose answered. "He's owned the store for what, thirty years?"

"I guess," Riley shrugged. "It was before I was born. Mom never really talks about him or Grandma, so I don't know much about the family history."

Rose cringed a bit at the mention of Riley's mother. Rose knew Gemma Quinn only cared about herself and spending money and not much else. She guessed family history was pretty far down on her list if she ever considered it.

"Well, your mother has her priorities," Rose answered, busying herself by fixing some of the displays.

"You don't like her much, do you?" Riley asked as she sat on one of the stools behind the counter.

"What? Why would you say that?"

"By the look on your face when you talk about her," Riley smiled.

"I don't really know her very well, Riley."

"It's okay. Most people don't like her," Riley said seriously. "I know I have more than my share of days when I don't. She treats my Dad like shit. I'm sure that's why he moved to the other side of the country."

"Then why did you come back to live with her?" Rose pried.

"I felt guilty," Riley admitted. "She's here by herself all the time and would complain that I spend all my breaks with Dad in California. So when I decided to do a gap year at school, I knew that I would come back here and give her a chance. Grandpa said I could live with him when I asked for the job, but it didn't feel right. She's not so bad. She's just—"

The bells to the front door jingled as it opened, and Rose's eyes moved up to see Gemma Quinn striding toward the counter, decked out in her floor-length black fur coat, carrying her black Hermes handbag.

"Speaking of Satan herself," Riley said softly with a giggle. "What are you doing here, Mom?"

Rose spied Gemma give her a cursory glance and then turned her eyes toward her daughter. Gemma placed her leather-gloved hand on the counter and looked at Riley.

"Did you grab the keys to the BMW this morning?" Gemma barked.

"No, I took my car," Riley replied.

"I don't care about that heap," Gemma answered. " I couldn't find the keys this morning, and I had to take the Navigator instead. I hate driving that thing."

Rose quietly slid herself to the back office and away from the argument about the first-world problems of Gemma. She sat at the desk, printing out yesterday's closing report to leave for Mr. Quinn, though he rarely even looked at it these days. Rose had earned the implicit trust almost immediately, and now Thomas left most of the store's day-to-day operations to her.

Rose had slid the last piece of paper into yesterday's folder just as Gemma stormed into the office.

"What are you doing back here?" Gemma cackled.

"Just working on the reports," Rose said without looking up. "Can I help you with something?"

"Hardly," Gemma answered. Rose saw Gemma march past her and over to the safe. She quickly punched in the digital code to open it before Rose got up from the desk.

"What are you doing?" Rose questioned.

"None of your business," Gemma replied as she pulled out the cash bag destined for the bank. Gemma unzipped the bag and saw a large amount of cash in there.

"Oh good," Gemma said as she counted five hundred dollars and stuffed the bills into her purse.

"Gemma, you can't just take that," Rose stated.

"Number one, don't call me Gemma," the woman yapped. "You can call me Ms. Quinn if you have to address me. Secondly, don't tell me what to do. My family owns this shop. I can do what I want when I want. My father won't care or even notice. I just don't feel like going to the bank this morning, and I'm late for my waxing because I couldn't find my keys."

"You really should check with—" Rose began before Gemma cut her off,

"Not another word!" she yelled. "Why my father keeps you around, I'll never know. He should have closed this place years ago and just left the other businesses to me. This place is a pit. Trust me, this whole place is going once he's gone."

Rose never knew when to take Gemma seriously as she had heard the same speech before. However, in the back of her mind, she added one more concern to how her life moved right now.

Chapter 5

I t took more than a few days and several visits to the animal shelter to get him out of his funk. Getting passed over for the supervisor position stung, and the potential of health issues looming in the back of his mind proved unsettling. He worried more than usual but did his best not to let it show to anyone.

Friday night had arrived with a break in the cold mid-February weather, allowing Darryl to ride his custom Harley comfortably from the worksite over to the Hog House. His bike climbed the dirt road to the parking area outside the Cosantóir's private hangout. As expected, there were plenty of bikes everywhere. Most of the club took advantage of the facility on the weekends to blow off steam. Darryl needed some comrades today to help him forget about all that weighed on him.

When he entered the house, he was hit by the blare of the Allman Brothers over the speakers playing "Statesboro Blues." After that, raucous drinking and yelling appeared at every step he took to get closer to the bar. Once he arrived, Darryl was head and shoulders above everyone else and quickly got Rory, the bartender's, attention so he could get a pint of Guinness. Darryl squeezed between two brothers to grab his pint glass before walking over to a table in the far corner where Finn, Liam, and Preacher sat drinking.

"There he is!" Liam shouted over the music when he spied Darryl. He kicked an empty chair toward him with the toe of his black boot. Darryl grasped the sliding chair and sat, moving closer for conversation.

"We were wondering if you were coming out tonight," Preacher offered before sipping his stout.

"It's Friday," Darryl answered. "Where else would I be?"

"You just seemed a bit out of it lately, distant," Preacher replied. "Everything good?"

Darryl looked over at Liam, the only person he knew who was aware that he had been passed over for the job. Liam shrugged his shoulders.

"They asked about you, so I told them," Liam admitted. "Word would have gotten around eventually on the job site."

"It's okay to be pissed off about it," Finn interjected. "I know I would be if I were in your shoes."

"I'm over it, really," Darryl insisted. "I'm not gonna let that eat me up inside. I'll keep on doing what I do."

"That's the spirit," Liam shouted before letting loose a hearty laugh and finishing off his pint.

"Rory, can I get a round of Jameson shots, Black Barrel, for the table?" he asked the bartender.

Rory flashed a thumbs up and set about getting shot glasses for the four men.

Rory arrived at the table and placed the glassware down with the bottle of Irish whiskey before filling the four shots. He turned to leave with the bottle before Liam stopped him.

"Leave the bottle, brother," Liam insisted. "Put it on my tab."

"You got it," Rory replied before heading back behind the bar.

Liam lifted his shot glass before giving a toast.

"May the best day of your past be the worst day of your future," he toasted as the four men clinked glasses and downed the whiskey. Darryl wiped his mouth with his hand before placing the glass down.

"Honestly, I'm surprised to see the three of you here," Darryl told the brothers.

"Why is that?" Finn asked as Liam poured another round.

"Well, seeing as you all have women in your lives now, I thought you would be with them tonight."

Darryl picked up his shot glass and went to take a drink before Liam cut him off.

"To our women," he toasted as the men then drank.

"Easy for you three to say," Darryl gruffed. "And you still didn't answer my question."

"Bella and Olivia are working at Millie's tonight," Preacher answered. "They're too busy on Friday or Saturday nights to go out much."

All eyes then turned to Finn.

"Siobhan's home. We're meeting up later," he answered.

"So, at least one of us is getting something tonight," Liam laughed.

"Feck off," Finn added to his brother.

Darryl lifted the whiskey to his lips and sucked it down, feeling less of the burn with his second drink.

"You're not seriously moping about women, are you?" Liam asked.

"I'm not moping," Darryl defended. "But I get tired of being the fifth wheel around here."

"Man, we don't look at you that way," Liam scoffed.

"Even if you don't, I do. I don't want to be the extra guy around when you guys go out with your ladies. It's too weird, and then the girls feel sorry for me and tell me they have someone they can set me up with."

"So let them do it," Finn added.

"I don't want a pity date," Darryl told him.

"If you're just looking for a fuck buddy, I can set you up," Liam boasted.

"Nice, Liam," Preacher told him sarcastically.

"What? I don't do that shite anymore, but I still know some girls who might be open to the idea, especially with Demon."

"No offense, brother, but I'll pass," Darryl replied as he took a draw on his Guinness.

"How about speed dating?" Rory asked as he arrived at the table with more pints.

All eyes turned back to the bartender and stared.

"Sorry, I overheard what you were saying," Rory apologized. "Have you ever tried speed dating?"

"I don't even know what that is," Darryl admitted. "If it's anything like the online dating apps, I'm not interested. I want to meet someone face-to-face, not just text back and forth."

"No, this is in-person," Rory explained. "I've done it a couple of times and met some nice people. I've had a few dates that have worked out well for a bit, which is a big deal for me."

"What do you have to do?" Darryl asked.

"You fill out a profile sheet, show up at the event, and move from table to table, spending a few minutes with each person to see how you mesh. Then, at the end of the night, they let you know if anyone is interested in seeing you."

"I don't know, Rory. It doesn't sound like it's for me."

"You're not meeting anyone how things are going now," Finn asked. "Maybe this wouldn't be so bad to try."

"There's one next weekend over in Chester," Rory added. "I'm going. I can give you the link if you want to check it out. You just have to fill out the questionnaire before you go."

"I think I'll pass, thanks," Darryl replied, finishing off his Guinness.

"Get the info, Rory," Liam insisted before Rory went off to the bar.

Darryl looked over at Liam with shock.

"What? You need to do something, dude," Liam spoke. "I'm not going to spend months staring at your sadsack face because you don't have a date."

Rory returned to the table with a fresh pint for Darryl and handed him the flyer printout for the speed dating event.

"Here it is," Rory said. "Let me know if you're going."

"I won't be," Darryl resisted, folding up the sheet and shoving it into the pocket of his leather jacket.

Rose had her feet propped up on the couch as she pulled the throw blanket down off the back cushions and wrapped it around herself. Then, picking up the TV remote, she began to scroll through the streaming services, looking for something to watch to pass the time. When nothing jumped out at her on Netflix, Rose swapped to Amazon to find a movie. She stumbled across a listing of romcoms and decided to look at the list, hoping Sandra Bullock or Meg Ryan could pull her out of the doldrums. She settled on "P.S. I Love You," knowing she would get a combination of sadness, smiles, and warmth.

Halfway into the heart-tugging film and her second glass of wine, the front door to the condo swung open, and Liz walked in. Liz stared at the

TV and then moved over to stand in front of the couch, blocking Rose's screen view.

"You are NOT watching this!" Liz insisted, reaching for the remote.

"Why not? " Rose whined. "I love this movie."

"You just want to wallow in self-pity and cry about how you'll never have a man like Gerard Butler."

"And what's wrong with that?" Rose said, grabbing the remote and hiding it under her blanket.

"I've been putting up with this shit for ten days now," Liz protested. "You come home from work, put your pajamas on and watch sad movies all night without doing anything else. It's time for you to get back to the real world of the living."

"I'm out in the real world all day," Rose retorted, "and I don't like it. This couch world suits me just fine."

"You need to get out of this, Rose. I love you and all, but I can't take you being home like this. Besides, it just means I have to spend more time at Rob's, and, well, his place smells, and not the manly smell that makes your legs weak."

"You can bring him here," Rose replied. "Nothing is stopping you."

"Just you laying around sighing about how miserable your life is. It's a real turn-on."

"Fine," Rose said, sitting up and turning off the TV. "I can go to my room."

"That's not any better!" Liz yelled. "So, if you're not going to take any steps to change things, then I am."

Liz sat on the couch next to Rose and pulled a flyer out of her purse.

"Rob and I were just over at Rushing Duck," Liz said as she handed Rose the sheet. "This is next weekend at Meadow Blues Coffee, and we're going."

Rose scanned the flyer announcing a speed dating event with cocktails, snacks, and coffee.

"I'm not doing speed dating, Liz," Rose said, pushing the flyer back to her friend.

"Oh yes, you are," Liz said. " I already paid for it and signed us up."

"Why would you do that? You know I hate stuff like that. Besides, you already have Rob. So there's no need for you to go."

"I'm not going for me, you arse," Liz told her. " I'm just there for moral support and eye candy. It's a night out for you to meet some people. So put Walter in the rearview mirror and move on from that dick."

Rose scanned the seemingly happy faces in the flyer with all the enjoyment and conversation going on and knew in her gut that it would be nothing like this, especially for her. She hated wading out into the dating pool to start with, never mind putting up with an endless stream of men she had no interest in.

"This looks like a trainwreck," Rose insisted. "I don't want to do it."

"Rose, I love you dearly," Liz answered. But if I have to come home every night and see you laying around in your ratty nightie or sweatpants, I will have to strangle you. So please, let's just do this one time. You're not going to meet anyone locking yourself away in here, and you know I'm not going to leave you alone until you agree."

Rose stared back at Liz, knowing she would be pestered until she gave in.

"Fine," Rose huffed as she slumped back on the couch. "One time, Liz. If we get there and it looks cheesy, I'm not doing it."

"Fair enough," Liz said excitedly. "Just promise me you'll wear something decent, maybe even something new."

"What's wrong with my wardrobe?"

"Nothing, love," Liz told her, taking her hand. "It's just you often go to work looking a little... well, severe."

"What are you talking about? I dress nicely for business."

"Exactly," Liz nodded. "For business, it's perfect. For socializing and dating, not so much. We'll work on it."

"Geez, Liz, don't hold back," Rose told her friend. "Anything else? Maybe hair and makeup too?"

"Now that you mention it—" Liz said sheepishly.

"Come on!" Rose complained.

"Well, you pull your hair back like a sour schoolmarm. Remember Miss Givens from school?"

Rose thought back to their early days of school together in Ireland, when Miss Givens had her hair slicked back tight every day. Her perpetually awful demeanor and dowdy approach to life led to speculation about her sex life, or lack of one.

Rose looked up to see that Liz had disappeared from view and heard her rummaging through drawers before seeing her roommate heading back to the living room. Liz held a black and white composition notebook in her hand.

"Oh no," Rose protested. "Not the list."

"I think you need to see it," Liz demanded, walking to the couch to sit down next to Rose.

Liz flipped open the book to the first page, and Rose spied where she and Liz and scrawled their names originally back when Liz created the list when they were about 11. The list started out as a joke to note all the things they both got annoyed about in life. Liz periodically added to it over the recent years, but Rose hadn't seen it rear its ugly head in a while.

Liz turned a few pages until she found the entry she was seeking.

"Here!" she said, pointing a finger in the middle of the page. "October 5, 2002. Miss Givens' oil-slicked hair and frumpy dress. We both initialed it, Rose."

The rule was that the person entering the item on the list had to date and initial it, and the other would initial if it applied to both of them. The list took on a life of its own as the friends stayed together through middle school, high school, university, and beyond.

Liz turned to the page with the last entry on it, allowing Rose to see it was dated just before the recently passed Christmas. Liz detached the pen clipped to the book and handed it to Rose.

"What?" Rose asked.

"You need to make an entry," Liz stated firmly, "about Walter."

"Come on, Liz," Rose said, pushing the notebook away. "That's kid stuff. I don't need to do that anymore."

"Trust me, it will make you feel better," Liz said, waving the pen in front of Rose. "And you know I won't leave you alone until you do it."

Rose snatched the pen from Liz's hand and placed the notebook in her lap. She gazed at the page and then shut her eyes, breathing deeply. All she saw in her mind was Walter kissing that other woman, and it was enough to spur her on.

She scribbled into the book quickly and passed it back to Liz before she could change her mind.

Rose looked on as Liz read what she wrote and laughed.

"Walter Muser's lying, cheating soul. Nicely done," Liz grinned, placing her initials next to Rose's. "I think it just needs one tiny addition."

Liz wrote quickly in the book before passing it back to Rose.

"Walter's tiny, insufficient prick," Rose read aloud before bursting out.

"Don't forget to initial it, Reb," Liz chuckled.

Rose smiled as she put her initials—REB for Rose Emma Boyle—next to Liz's and shut the book with fervor.

"So what do we need to do for this speed dating thing?" Rose asked.

Chapter 6

A grueling week went by for Darryl, with work dragging on as the site had some equipment issues. His team spent extra hours digging and mucking manually as drills failed and new gear orders caught up in red tape. Darryl put in extra shifts more than once during the week. He chose to take the hours in comp time, giving himself additional paid days off instead of the cash in his paycheck. He then used some of the time for the doctor's appointment he knew Friday brought.

Darryl walked into the Crystal Run Healthcare building, checking in at the front desk. He ignored the looks he got from many patrons and staff, having grown accustomed to people in awe of his size when he traveled the world for wrestling. Luckily, people rarely recognized him these days, mainly because he wore a mask for his matches. It was only the genuinely diehards who knew who he was, and it wasn't often that he came upon rabid fans anymore.

Darryl made his way upstairs to just outside his doctor's office. He considered sitting down on one of the chairs but just from their look, he feared he would have trouble getting out of them because they were low to the ground and small. So instead, he paced the waiting area, drawing looks from the people waiting for their appointments.

A young boy played with his toy truck at the table near the waiting area and noticed Darryl. He walked over to Darryl and craned his neck up, his eyes widening.

"Wow, you're big!" the boy exclaimed.

"Am I?" Darryl replied, feigning surprise, "I thought you were big!"

"I am," the boy said proudly. "I'm three."

He struggled to hold up three fingers to show Darryl.

"Man, I thought you were twenty," Darryl told the boy.

The youngster broke out in a giggle.

A woman hustled over to corral the young boy.

"Come on, Anthony. Leave the man alone," she said, tugging on the boy's hand.

A nurse appeared from the hallway and called out.

"Darryl?" She asked, looking around.

Darryl raised his hand and nodded at the nurse.

"I gotta go, big man," Darryl said, putting his giant fist down for Anthony to tap it with his own. Anthony bumped fists and made an explosion sound as he pulled his hand away.

Darryl followed the nurse into the exam room, shedding his leather jacket.

The petite woman guided Darryl to sit on the exam table while she pulled over her blood pressure machine. She went to place the arm cuff around Darryl's bicep, but the cuff's velcro wouldn't reach all the way around.

"You'll need the extra-large one if you want to do that," Darryl smiled. The nurse looked in the drawers to find the larger size and took Darryl's pressure.

"104 over 64. Very good," the nurse said as she ripped the cuff off Darryl's arm.

"It always is," he boasted.

"Dr. Nicoll will be right in," the nurse said as she slid out the door on the room's far end.

Darryl sat quietly, with only the sound of the rustling wax paper that lined the exam table beneath him. He looked around the room, hoping for something to distract him from sitting around and waiting for answers. Instead, he felt the vibration of his phone in his jeans pocket and plucked it out to see who the message was from.

"Never heard if you were going to speed dating tomorrow," the text read from Rory.

Darryl had discounted the event entirely when talking about it with the brothers, but after a day or two of the flyer sitting on his dresser, he had picked it up one night after a long day of work and gone online to the site. He stared for a long time at the screen before entering his information, filling the basic form out, and paying his entry fee.

"I'll be there," Darryl typed out and sent back.

"Awesome! See you there," Rory replied.

The exam room door slid open, and Darryl rapidly stuffed the phone back into his pocket as Dr. Nicoll walked in. She grinned widely at Darryl as she entered, moving over to the desk where the computer sat.

"How are you, Darryl?" she asked as she sat down and pulled up his medical charts.

"That's what I'm here to find out," he answered.

"Well, I was just speaking generally, but if you want to get right into it, we can," she laughed.

"Sorry," he apologized. "I guess I'm a little nervous about the results."

"I don't think I've ever seen you nervous," the doctor answered, looking at the screen. "Your blood pressure sure doesn't show it."

Dr. Nicoll swiveled on her stool to face Darryl.

"Okay, so the x-rays and CT scan show scarring on your lungs," she began. "That, along with some of the symptoms you've displayed with coughing and shortness of breath, leads me to believe it's—"

"Silicosis," Darryl interjected.

"More than likely, yes," she said thoughtfully. "I want to do a bronchoscopy and sputum test to be sure, but I think that's where we're headed. We talked about it, Darryl."

"I know," he agreed. "I'm not really surprised."

Dr. Nicoll approached Darryl and stood in front of him.

"Can you take your shirt off?" she asked.

Darryl pulled the shirt over his head, revealing his muscular, toned torso. Tattoos covered both upper arms and part of his chest, relating to the Cosantóir. Dr. Nicoll placed her stethoscope in her ears and put the cold diaphragm on Darryl to listen to his breathing.

"Breathe normally," she asked. "Have you used the inhaler?"

"Once or twice at night, after long days at work."

"You haven't needed it on the job?" she questioned, moving the stethoscope to his back. Darryl knew by the placement that it was right in the middle of the demon head of the large tattoo from his wrestling days that enveloped his back.

"Haven't needed it or haven't used it?" he replied.

"Deep breaths, Darryl," Dr. Nicoll ordered as he inhaled and exhaled.

"You're supposed to use it when you're feeling trouble breathing, no matter when that is," she scolded, facing Darryl. "Any chest pain or fatigue?"

"Nothing I've noticed."

"Be honest with me, Darryl," Dr. Nicoll told him. "It's the only way we can track this and help you."

"Honestly, I haven't felt any."

"Okay. I'm going to schedule those tests for you. Use the inhaler when you need it most, Darryl. Seriously. Have you had a flu shot already?"

"Yeah, we get them on the job," Darryl responded.

"Okay, I'm going to give you the pneumonia shot. The extra protection will help you. Have you talked to your daughter about all of this?"

"Have you talked to her?" Darryl questioned.

Dr. Nicoll gave a small smile.

"You know I can't discuss anything about you with her. However, she has called here asking anyway. You need to tell her so she's aware. It's chronic and mild right now, but it will worsen. It doesn't go away. We talked about this and the dangers because of what you do. You're a higher risk."

"I'll talk to her, I promise," Darryl answered as he pulled his t-shirt back on.

"The nurse will be back in to give you your shot and set up the bronchoscopy with the pulmonologist. I'll see you after about a month, okay?"

"Got it," Darryl gave her a thumbs up and smiled.

Dr. Nicoll exited the room as Darryl waited for the nurse to return. He had avoided using the inhaler at work or in front of Annie to keep questions at bay, but he was unsure how much longer he could do that. Silicosis was common among Sandhogs, though not as much as in the past since the union enforced better preventative equipment.

The nurse returned, pulling the needle out to give Darryl the pneumonia shot. He winced when he saw it in her hand as she approached him.

She wiped his arm with an alcohol wipe and held up the needle. Darryl closed his eyes and turned his head away from the nurse.

"It's not going to hurt," she smiled. "You're not afraid of needles, are you?"

"Let's just say we don't get along nicely," Darryl replied, avoiding watching.

The nurse jabbed his arm and pulled it back as Darryl did his best not to cry out.

"All done," she quipped, plucking a Band-Aid from the drawer. Darryl looked down to see the Batman logo on his arm.

"I give one of those to all my brave patients," she smiled, her hand lingering on his forearm.

Darryl exited the exam room, working his back out to the waiting area. He encountered Anthony and his mother leaving simultaneously as they moved toward the elevator.

"Hey, I got a shot too!" Anthony exclaimed as he pointed to Darryl's arm. Anthony stopped and bared his arm, showing off his own Batman bandage.

"You were probably better than I was with it, Big Man," Darryl said.

"It didn't hurt at all," the boy stated proudly.

"You're the man," Darryl told him, fist-bumping Anthony again. Anthony put more strength behind the bump this time.

"You're strong!" Darryl said, shaking his fist. He watched as Anthony did a Hulk Hogan flex, causing Darryl to laugh.

"Take care, Big Man," Darryl told him as he moved to walk down the stairs. He moved down the stairs and out to the parking lot, getting on his bike and starting it up. He sat on the motorcycle, fastening his helmet.

What next? He thought.

Chapter 7

Rose stared at her reflection, eyes squinted as she tried to decide if she wanted to go through with the event or not. All week long, she stressed about speed dating. No matter how many pep talks Liz gave, Rose didn't sway from thinking it was all a bad idea. Now that the evening had arrived, her brain raced to come up with any excuse for her to take off her robe, put her pajamas on, and climb into bed to forget the entire thing.

The creak of the bedroom door had Rose's head spin to the right to see what was going on. Liz peeked in, already dressed to the nines and ready to go.

"You're still in your robe!" Liz exclaimed. "We have to leave in thirty minutes. So what are you waiting for, Cinderella?"

"I keep hoping you'll forget about this, and we'll do something else," Rose replied as she brushed her hair back, getting it ready to put up in her customary tight bun.

"As you can see, love, I'm not forgetting about it," Liz gave a twirl in her black jeans. "And you are NOT wearing your hair that way."

Liz marched over to where Rose sat and pulled Rose's hair out of the bun. Then, she began running the brush through her hair.

"You promised me," Liz reminded her. Rose looked on as Liz brushed away and grabbed the curling iron out of the vanity drawer, going to work on Rose's tresses.

"Fine," Rose pouted, "but don't go crazy with the curls. I don't want to look like Shirley Temple."

Within minutes, Liz had transformed Rose's look, giving her dark hair beautiful loose curls that came down just short of her shoulders.

"What are you planning to wear?" Liz asked skeptically.

"Sweatpants and a muumuu," Rose groused as she got up from the vanity.

"Har har," Liz snarked. "Wear a dress."

"You're not wearing a dress," Rose shot back.

"I'm not the one this outing is for, remember?" Liz opened Rose's closet door and began to scroll through the hangers. "How about this one?"

Liz held up a black dress with a v-neck.

"I wore that one to Walter's sister's wedding last year," Rose lamented.

"Okay, never mind that one. "How about this?"

Liz held up a short silver dress with fringe.

"Liz, that was my flapper costume from Halloween two years ago."

"For feck's sake, Rose, where are your nice clothes?"

"What are you talking about? I have plenty of nice clothing that I wear to work," Rose defended.

"Your work clothes are fine for work, not for fun. You want to make a good first impression, don't you?"

"Not really," Rose added. She flung herself back on her bed and grabbed a pillow, hugging it tightly. "I'd rather just climb in bed and curl up with a book."

Rose stared longingly at the small stack of romance novels on her nightstand.

"Enough living in the fantasy world," Liz insisted, tugging Rose's limp arm so she sat up. "Come back to the land of the living. Look, this doesn't have to be anything serious. It's all just for fun so you can meet some new people. Remember what we used to do in secondary, college, and uni? We went out every weekend and did something and met people. Think of it that way tonight. It's just for a good time. We'll have some drinks, look at some guys and head home. No expectations."

Liz batted her eyelashes and widened her eyes, showing off the flecks of green, brown, and gray.

"Ugh, you know I am a sucker for that."

"Okay, enough laying around. Get dressed in something so we can get going," Liz said. "I'll give you ten minutes, and then I am coming in here and finding something for you, and I'm not ruling out the flapper dress."

Rose trudged over to the closet, considering what to wear. She eventually settled on a gray pleated skirt and white short-sleeved blouse. Next, she grabbed a yellow cardigan to wear and a pair of yellow flats. Finally, after dressing and putting on a pair of charcoal tights, she felt satisfied with the look.

Rose emerged from her room and walked down the hall to the living room, finding Liz sitting on the arm of the sofa, waiting patiently for her. Liz made a twirling motion with her hand, causing Rose to slowly spin so her friend could get a look at her attire.

"Nice choice," Liz smiled. "Let's go."

Rose insisted on driving, giving her the out of avoiding alcohol for the evening, so she knew just what she was doing and who she was with for the night. Liz more than happily agreed to the terms.

"More for me to drink then!" Liz laughed as Rose drove toward Chester.

Shock came to Rose's face when she saw the number of cars parked outside the coffee shop.

"It's too crowded. I don't see any parking left here. Let's just go home," Rose rushed.

"There's plenty of space down on the end," Liz pointed. "You're not getting out of this that easily."

Rose sighed as she drove to the far end of the parking lot and found space to pull in.

"It's not too late to change our minds," Rose said as she stepped out of the car. "We can just walk over to Rushing Duck, have a couple of beers, and go home."

"Maybe after," Liz said, grabbing Rose by the hand and dragging her to the front door of the coffee shop.

"What if it's all guys in there, and we're the only females?" Rose asked.

"Then you have more to choose from," Liz answered as she swung the door and pushed Rose inside.

Rose scanned the room rapidly, noticing to her dismay that it seemed to be equal numbers of men and women. A young woman approached the duo as they entered, asking to see their registration forms.

"Oh, I forgot mine," Rose replied. "I guess we need to leave."

"Don't worry," Liz said, grabbing Rose's arm. "I have them."

Liz pulled out two folded pieces of paper from her back pocket and presented them to the hostess.

"I knew you would try to pull this," Liz scolded. "I printed extra copies this morning."

Rose mumbled under her breath as the hostess grinned and handed each woman what looked like scoresheets.

"You can use these to rate the people you meet. Then, at the end of the night, you turn them in to us, and we send you the info of anyone you may have matched with so you can make contact afterward."

"Really? Do we have to rate people? Sounds a little too sexist for me," Rose protested, handing the paper back to the hostess.

"Wait, poor choice of words on my part," the hostess stammered. "You're not rating people like that. You're just letting us know whether you would be interested in contacting that person through email, phone, or chat. So it's not like a one to ten scale or anything."

"Too bad," Liz said, craning her neck at the crowd. "I see a few eights and nines in there already."

"We're going to start in about five minutes if you want to get a drink before we begin," the hostess remarked, pointing to the front counter.

Rose moved toward the counter, avoiding eye contact with any of the men who happened to look in her direction as she waited in line. She quickly ordered a café au lait and turned to find Liz. She spied her friend chatting up a couple of men while staying at the corner bar for drinks. Liz waved for Rose to walk over, and Rose begrudgingly obliged.

"Rose, this is Felix and Oscar," Liz said, introducing the two men. "Felix is Ukrainian, and Oscar is from... I'm sorry, Oscar, where did you say you were from?"

"I'm originally from the Dominican, but I've lived in Chester for years now," Oscar added.

"Rose here grew up in Montserrat," Liz said, pushing Rose forward. "That's not too far from the Dominican Republic?"

"About three or four hours," Oscar added. Finally, he turned and smiled at Rose.

"I didn't really grow up in Montserrat," Rose downplayed. "I lived there until I was seven, then I went to Ireland to live with my father and lived there until about ten years ago when I came to New York."

"When WE came to New York," Liz interjected. "We've been mates since we were kids."

"Well, it's a pleasure to meet you, Rose," Oscar said politely, raising his pint glass of craft beer. "Can I buy you a drink?"

"Oh, no, thank you," Rose politely nodded. "I have my coffee. I'm the driver tonight."

A loud clang pealed through the air, causing everyone to grow silent and turn toward the front door. Rose gazed as two prominent men walked through the door, wearing leather jackets. One of the men was unrecognizable, with long brown hair and badly in need of a shave, while the other stood out to her immediately.

Rose slid over next to Liz and whispered in her ear.

"That's the guy from the store and Dunkin'," she stated.

"The grubby-looking guy with the long hair?" Liz said as she spied the men speaking with the hostess.

No, the other guy," Rose hinted, trying to point with her head without bringing too much notice to herself.

Liz looked twice and then smiled at Rose.

"Wow," Liz said with admiration. "He's worth paying attention to. So he's the guy who bought the necklace?"

"And helped me with my car," Rose answered. She turned her back toward the door in an attempt to go unrecognized.

"So he's got money, takes care of his daughter, is chivalrous, and looks hot in a leather jacket. Yeah, he's not worth your time," Liz added.

"I don't know anything about him," Rose hushed.

"Well, it's too bad you're not in a place where you would get a chance to talk to each other," Liz said with an eye roll.

Oscar had stepped toward Rose to get her attention.

"Is everything okay?" he asked.

"Oh, yes, I'm sorry," Rose hurried. "I just... I just need to talk to my friend for a bit. I'm sure we'll chat at some point."

Rose guided Liz away from the bar area, moving quickly to avoid the bikers moving closer to order drinks.

"Jesus, Rosie, what are you doing?" Liz yanked her elbow from Rose's hand as they now stood in the far corner, Rose having her back to the crowd.

"I don't know. I guess I don't want him to see me here."

"Do you know how ridiculous you sound? You're here to meet people, remember? And you already kind of know him. So this is your chance to find out a little more about him and see if he's into you."

"I don't know if I want someone to be 'into' me. So let's just go home."

"We're too far in to just leave now," Liz told her.

"We can slip out the back door here and disappear," Rose insisted.

"You want to just Irish goodbye like that after we spent money to be here? Rose, you need to chill. Let's stay for just a little bit longer."

"I want to go." Rose began moving toward the back door when a loud alarm clock buzz sounded, causing most of the room to jump.

"Good evening, everyone!" the hostess yelled before shutting off the alarm. "My name is Rachel Vail, and I'm the owner of DateDash, the speed dating service putting on this evening's event. I'm so glad all of you decided to come out tonight to have some fun and meet some new people. I will go over a few of the ground rules before getting started. Once you sit at a table, you'll get 5 minutes with the person opposite you. There are some conversation prompts that you can use at each table, or you can talk about whatever you want. The men will rotate to the next table when you hear the alarm. Each person has a worksheet to mark the name of the person you spoke with, and you can decide whether you want to share your contact information or not. People who both agree with each other will be connected so they can chat or meet outside of this evening. Sounds easy, right? Okay, ladies, if you could please grab a seat at one of the tables, we will get ready to start."

Rose stood still as women began to move towards the empty spots throughout the room. Liz tapped her on the shoulder to get her attention.

"Time to shine, Rosie," Liz smiled as she guided Rose toward an empty table.

"I think I'm going to be sick," Rose grumbled as she sat down.

Darryl sat on his motorcycle outside of Meadow Blues for several minutes, helmet in his hands, working to decide if he wanted to bother going inside or not. Judging by the number of cars in the parking lot, the event looked to be filled, but even that wasn't an incentive for him to get off his bike. His head turned back toward Rushing Duck Brewery, and the temptation was strong to forgo his registration fee and just go next door, drink a couple of oatmeal stouts, and return home.

The pat on the back of his leather jacket prompted Darryl into action. He spun around and saw Rory standing there grinning.

"I figured you were gonna bail on me," Rory laughed.

"Another thirty seconds, and you would have seen dust kicking up," Darryl answered. "I'm still not convinced about this, man."

"It's no big deal, Demon—" Rory started.

"Call me Darryl through this," he insisted. "I don't want people freaking out more than they already do when they see me."

"No problem, *Darryl,*" Rory emphasized. "Sounds weird to say it."

"You'll deal with it," Darryl added, climbing off his bike and locking his helmet on.

Darryl pulled the door open and heard the chimes bong. He peered into the large room and saw all eyes focus on him before entering.

"Think of it as one of your wrestling entrances," Rory joked as he stepped inside.

"Shut up, Rory," Darryl sneered.

The two men were greeted by the overly cheerful hostess, who stood nearly two feet shorter than Darryl. She checked them in and handed them their scoresheets.

"We are starting any second if you want to grab a drink quickly," she added, hustling the men inside and locking the doors behind them, putting up a 'Closed for a Private Event' sign.

Darryl squeezed his way over to the bar and ordered an Imperial Beanhead coffee porter, figuring it was close to Guinness. He had barely taken two sips of his beer when the hostess went into her spiel about the event and how it was starting.

All the men gathered in a group while individual ladies took their spots at available tables. Once everyone was seated, Rachel let out a "let's get started!" and each man ventured to an open table.

Darryl scanned the room, unsure of what to do until Rachel came up to him.

"There's an empty spot over there," she said, pointing to a table at the room's far end.

"Right, thanks," he said as he worked through the maze to get to his destination.

Darryl arrived at the table and pulled the wooden chair out before glancing over at the woman across from him. The blonde's eyes widened and trailed down from his face to his leather jacket and stopped.

"Hi there," Darryl smiled. "I'm Darryl."

He offered his hand across the table, but the woman sat frozen before she finally reached her hand out and placed it in his.

"Theresa," she answered shakily.

"How are you tonight, Theresa?" Darryl shifted in his seat, getting comfortable in the too-small chair.

"Good, thanks," she answered. "You're a large man." Theresa immediately brought her hand up to her face, covering her mouth. "I'm so sorry. That came out wrong."

"No worries," Darryl replied. "It's not something I can deny. So, what do you do for a living?"

"I'm a preschool teacher," she answered. "I work in the area."

Darryl waited, expecting Theresa to ask him a question or add something more to the conversation, but she seemed befuddled.

"Everything okay?" Darryl asked.

"Oh yes," she nodded rapidly. Theresa fidgeted in her seat and began to tap her fingers on the table.

"You just seem a little nervous or uncomfortable," Darryl said as his chair squeaked underneath him. He glanced around the room and saw others primarily engaged in lively conversation instead of awkward silence.

"No... I mean, maybe," Theresa added. "I don't normally do things like this. I'm just trying this out for the first time. You surprised me, is all."

"It's my first time here," Darryl told her, hoping to make her more comfortable. But instead, Theresa just continued to nod without adding more to the conversation.

Darryl spotted the index card on the table and picked it up, reading the prompt.

"Have you ever been in a food fight?" he said aloud.

"What?" Theresa raised her eyebrows. "Why would you ask me that?"

"It's... it's just the prompt question at the table. You know, a conversation starter."

"Kind of a dumb question," Theresa snorted.

Darryl sat back in the chair, experiencing the longest five minutes of his life as nothing else went on at their table. Then, when the alarm sounded, Darryl stood.

"Nice to meet you, Theresa," Darryl said, attempting politeness but failing to elicit a response.

With a deep breath, he moved onto the following table with trepidation. He sat in a similar chair, feeling even smaller than the previous one. He looked over and saw a young lady beaming back at him.

"Hello," she grinned. "I'm Liz."

Liz sipped her Bud Light before placing the bottle down on the table.

"Darryl," he said, offering his hand. Liz shook it enthusiastically as she looked at Darryl.

"How are you this fine evening, Darryl?"

"I'm alright, thanks. I detect a British accent. So you're not from around here?"

"Oh, I've lived here for about ten years, but I've lived in Ireland and Britain. It's still hard to shake the accent and some lingo, though. It never really goes away," Liz laughed.

"So, what made you try speed dating, Liz?" Darryl asked, feeling more at ease than in his previous encounter.

"Oh, I'm not looking for a date, Darryl," Liz answered honestly as she sipped her beer. "I've got a boyfriend for years now."

Darryl cocked his head and stared at Liz.

"Kind of an odd way to spend a Friday night if you're not looking for someone to date," Darryl said.

"A fair statement, Darryl!" Liz guffawed, slapping the wooden table. "No, I'm just here for moral support for my friend over there," Liz pointed. "I think you two already know each other."

Darryl turned to the left and saw Rose seated at the following table, having a small discussion with a man with a heavy Eastern European accent.

"You know Rose?" Darryl asked.

"Know her? Darryl, she's been my bestie since we were kids. We grew up together, went to school together, came to the U.S. together, and we live together. So you could say I know her."

"How were you aware that I had met her already?"

"Intriguing, isn't it?" Liz laughed. "She saw you walk in and pointed you out to me. She said she had met you at the shop, and then you were a knight in shining armor at the donut shop."

"So she mentioned me before tonight?" Darryl pried.

"Are you the kind of gent who leaves an impression on a lady, Darryl?"

"I like to think so," he said honestly.

"All I can tell you is that you made an impression on my Rosie there," Liz replied. "And she could really use a boost and some cheering up. She's had a rough go of it lately, dumping her dirtbag of a boyfriend and all."

"So, are you just here to talk her up to all the guys who come to your table?" Darryl inquired.

"Not all of them. Just you, Darryl," Liz said with a wink. "Something tells me you are the man she needs to learn more about."

Liz leaned forward, holding out her beer bottle so that she could toast with Darryl. Darryl picked up his glass of stout and clinked.

"Slainte," he said before pulling his pint glass back.

"Ah, and you know Gaelic too and can pronounce it correctly!" she added excitedly.

"I work and ride with many Irish guys, so more than a little has rubbed off."

"Another plus in your column, Darryl," Liz said softly. "Rose is Irish through and through."

"Good to know, Liz," Darryl smiled.

The alarm buzzed, and Darryl pushed himself up out of the chair.

"Pleasure to meet you, Liz."

"Yes, it is!" she laughed. "Don't have hurt feelings if I don't mark you down to contact, Darryl. It's nothing personal."

"Understood," he nodded as he moved off from the table.

Three steps later, Darryl got onto another small chair and sat face to face with Rose.

"Hello again, Rose," Darryl grinned as he unzipped his leather jacket.

"Hi there," Rose answered sheepishly.

"I'm a little surprised to see you here," Darryl began.

"And why is that?"

"I figured a woman like yourself was attached to someone already."

"What does that mean... I'm sorry, I don't think I got your name," Rose offered.

"Darryl," he introduced. "I just figured a woman like you—young, confident, attractive—had a boyfriend or at least men she could easily choose from if she wanted."

"Well, Darryl," Rose began sternly, "just as you said to me when we met in the jewelry store, you shouldn't be quick to judge someone by their appearance."

"My apologies," Darryl bowed his head. "You're absolutely right. That was unfair of me. However, you are single, correct?"

Rose sighed before answering.

"At this moment, yes, I am."

"I guess I can dispense with the usual questions because I already know what you do and live in the area, and I know how you like your coffee. So what else shall we talk about?"

Rose sat back in her chair and examined Darryl.

"What do you do for a living, Darryl?"

"I'm a Sandhog," he answered, fully expecting the blank stare he typically received when he said that to people.

Rose nodded at Darryl.

"That's hard work spending all that time underground," she replied.

"You know who the Sandhogs are?" Darryl said with shock.

"Don't look so surprised," Rose smirked. "I know some things, especially if it ties into Irish history and heritage. My father is Irish-born and raised. He still lives there."

"So you grew up in Ireland?" Darryl leaned forward to listen closely.

"Sort of," Rose stated. "I was born in Montserrat. That's where my mother is from and where my parents met. So I lived there until I was seven, and then I went to Ireland."

"Ahh, the Ireland of the Caribbean," Darryl grinned.

"Have you ever been there?"

"Sadly, no," Darryl lamented before sipping his beer. "I'm sure it's beautiful, though."

"Yes, most of it is," Rose frowned. "Many of the best spots were destroyed by the volcano. However, there is still great beauty there."

"When was the last time you were there?" Darryl asked.

Rose took a sip of coffee and sighed.

"About a year or two, I guess," she answered. "Too long. Time just kind of gets away from you sometimes, you know?"

"Oh, I know it," Darryl agreed. "Do you still have family there?"

"I do," Rose nodded. "My mother is still there, and my uncle, her brother."

"They didn't go to Ireland with you and your father?"

"It's a long, complicated story," Rose said as the alarm buzzer sounded.

Darryl locked eyes with Rose, staring into the dark brown orbs before him. Then, he felt a tap on his shoulder and looked up to see Rory standing next to him.

"My turn De- I mean Darryl," he said, catching himself.

"Killjoy," Darryl said to his friend. "I guess we're out of time," he mourned. "It was nice to meet you—again—Rose."

"Same to you, Darryl," Rose said shyly.

Darryl gripped Rory by the arm and whispered into his ear.

"Be nice to her, but not too nice," he warned.

"Got it, brother," Rory agreed as Darryl moved to the following table.

Even though Darryl moved on to six more tables, he paid little attention to what the women had to say. While a few were engaging and all were people plenty of men would happily be with, Darryl kept turning his attention to the table in the corner where Rose sat. He thought her eyes were following him more than once from table to table.

When the night's end arrived, he and Rory stood filling out their sheets. Rory peeked over at Darryl's and saw he had just one checkmark on his.

"You only want to meet up with one person? That hardly seems worth it," Rory told him.

"Why? How many do you want to connect with?"

"All of them!" Rory said proudly. "It increases my odds of getting a date with at least one person."

"You're too much, dude," Darryl said, shaking his head while handing his sheet to Rachel.

"I hope you guys had a good time," Rachel smiled. "We'll go through these and pass along your information to anyone who agreed to connect with you."

"Thanks," Darryl added. He lingered a bit by the front door, scanning what was left of the crowd, hoping to meet up with Rose as she was going. However, he didn't see her or Liz anywhere in the shop.

"I think she scooted out the back door," Rory said, sensing who Darryl was looking for.

"Did Rose turn in her sheet?" Darryl asked Rachel, hoping to catch a glimpse.

"I'm sorry," Rachel told him. " I can't share any information about any of the participants. It's all about privacy and safety. But, if she agreed to contact you, you would hear from her."

"Sure, no trouble," Darryl said disappointingly.

He walked out into the chilly night air with Rory at his side.

"That was fun, huh?" Rory encouraged.

"Yeah, I guess," Darryl agreed.

"Come back to the Hog House and have a drink. Then, we can compare notes."

"Nah, I'm headed home," Darryl admitted. "I'm beat. I'll catch you tomorrow."

Darryl climbed on his bike, put his helmet on, and took off down Greycourt Road to head back toward Monroe. All he considered on the ride back to his house was the look of those brown eyes.

Chapter 8

L ate February bled into hints of Spring with teases of warm weather
followed by blasts of cold in the evening. More than a week had
passed since Darryl met up with Rose at the speed dating event, but he
still had not heard anything from her or the dating service. Several times
he had picked up the phone, tempted to call or email the event coordi-
nator, Rachel, to see if she had sent the information out to everyone or
not, but he backed off.

When the weekend had rolled around again, Darryl found himself at
Hog House, walking up to the bar and grabbing a stool nearby a couple
of other Cosantóir idly watching a Mets spring training game. Darryl
spotted Rory and nodded, prompting the bartender to pour a Guinness
for him and shuffle it down the bar.

"How was your week?" Rory asked, placing the Guinness on a coaster
while glancing at the TV screen.

"The project down in Sloatsburg is getting ready to wind down,"
Darryl noted as he watched the cascading head of hist stout. "We're
pushing pretty hard to get things done, so it's been crazy."

"Man, sometimes I really miss doing that work," Rory offered as he
shook his head. "Then there are other days where I see how exhausted
you guys are, and I am glad I'm behind the bar and working in the house
now."

"I get it," Darryl nodded, putting his beer down. "Say, Rory, have you heard anything?"

"Heard anything about what?" he answered as he pulled a couple of bottles of Corona out of the ice and placed them in front of the other bikers at the end of the bar. Groans were heard as Robinson Cano struck out once again.

"Fuckin' Cano," Rory added. "Man, that was a raw deal."

"You know, about the thing we went to," Darryl said in hushed tones.

"What? The dating thing?" Rory bellowed, pouring peanuts into one wooden bowl and sliding it to the bikers who caught Rory's words.

"You're not still doing that speed dating shit, are you, Rory?" one of the younger bikers laughed. "That shit is a waste of time."

"Fuck off, Dutch," Rory shot back. "I've gotten a few dates out of it. Beats nights out with your Mom."

Darryl rued bringing the topic up, and stared into his beer.

"Never mind, man," Darryl mumbled.

"No, it's cool," Rory assured. "Don't listen to that clown. Dutch is here every Friday and Saturday, all day and night. If a woman fell on him, he wouldn't know what to do with her. I haven't heard anything from anybody. How about you?"

Darryl shook his head.

"Does it usually take more than a week?"

"Sometimes," Rory answered. "Could be we just didn't match with anyone. But, it happens more often than not."

"Why didn't you say that before?" Darryl raised his voice. "I wouldn't have gone if I knew it would be a waste of my time."

"Are you telling me he hooked you into that shit, Demon?" Dutch cackled. "Man, I didn't know you were that desperate for pussy that you'd follow his advice. Pathetic."

Darryl slammed his pint glass and leaped off his stool, lifting Dutch into the air like a rag doll and tossing him across the room so he hit the wooden floor with force.

"What the fuck, man?" Dutch groaned as he scrambled to his feet. "It was a fucking joke. Lighten up."

"Mind your fucking business," Darryl growled.

"You brought it up by announcing it," Dutch said as he straightened his jacket. "If you want to go—" Dutch said, pulling a switchblade out of his jeans.

"Don't go there unless you're ready to do something, Dutch," Darryl warned.

"I'm not like these other guys, Demon. I ain't afraid of you."

"You should be."

Darryl moved closer, circling Dutch and watching how he shifted his knife from one hand to the other. Others in the room dared not get in the way. Dutch lunged toward Darryl and missed, staggering as Darryl nimbly moved to the side and shoved Dutch away.

No sooner had Dutch hit the floor and skittered up against the bar when Darryl was on top of him. He grasped Dutch's wrist, twisting it to relieve him of the knife he held before pinning the arm behind Dutch's back. Next, Darryl forced his knee down on Dutch's neck while holding the biker in place.

"Which will it be, Dutch?" Darryl said, tightening his grip. "A separated shoulder or a broken neck?"

"Fuck you," Dutch gasped as he squirmed. Darryl glanced down as Dutch's face reddened.

"I can do both," Darryl gritted his teeth and pushed harder on Dutch's neck.

Darryl heard a voice echo lightly in his head before it came more into focus.

"Demon! Stop!"

Darryl's gaze shot up as he saw Preacher standing next to him, tugging on his jacket. Rory came over to assist Preacher as they pried Darryl off Dutch.

Color started to return to Dutch's face as he gulped for air. Dutch scrambled toward the glint of his knife on the floor, but as he reached for it, a large black boot came down on his fingers while another boot kicked the knife away.

"Fuck!" Dutch yowled.

"Leave it, Dutch," Liam growled before lifting his boot off Dutch's hand.

"He started it," Dutch defended as he struggled to get to his feet, rubbing his aching shoulder.

"I don't care about the schoolyard shit," Liam told him. "You know the rules. You pulled a weapon on a brother in the House. Take a walk."

"Christ, Liam, come on. I was defending myself. He needs to be taught a lesson."

"If you think you're the guy to do it, come on!" Darryl yelled as Preacher and Rory did their best to hold Darryl back.

"Enough from all of you!" a gravelly voice yelled. Everyone looked around to see Conor O'Farrell, founder and leader of the Cosantóir, come into the room, walking with his cane.

"Don't bring this shite into my house," Conor barked. Conor made his way over and stood in front of Dutch.

"We're brothers here, Dutch," Conor said sternly. "We have each others' backs, even if one of us acts like a shit. You broke the trust by pulling a blade. Give me your colors."

"But Ceannairre," Dutch pled. "It was the heat of the moment. It won't happen again."

"I know it won't," Conor said, stonefaced. All looked on as Conor held out his hands and waited for the jacket.

Dutch walked over to the barstool where he previously sat and jerked his leather jacket from the back of the chair. He handed it reluctantly to Conor as Darryl looked on, following Dutch's every move.

"We're not finished with this!" Dutch yelled at Darryl. "I'll be coming for you, Demon. I'm not bound by these fucking rules anymore."

"You know where to find me," Darryl said confidently.

Liam followed behind Dutch to make sure he vacated while Conor turned back to Darryl.

"Jaysus, Demon, what the feck are you doing? And right in the middle of my house!"

"He had it coming, Ceannaire—" Rory began before Conor held up his hand.

"I wasn't asking you, Rory," Conor stated, waving off the younger man.

"He pushed my buttons, Conor," Darryl said. "I let him get to me. I'm sorry, Ceannaire."

"He's had a lot of shit going on, Conor," Preacher said, coming to Darryl's defense.

"We all do," Conor answered. "And we all deal with it in better ways than that. You know it, Demon."

Darryl hung his head and waited to hear what would come next.

"Take a few days away from here," Conor bade. "Cool off a bit, get your head together, and then come and see me. We'll go from there."

Darryl nodded and gathered himself before walking toward the front door. Liam greeted him as he reached the front porch.

"He's gone," Liam said. "I watched him take off. I'm kind of glad, Demon. I never liked Dutch. I didn't trust him. You did us all a favor. One thing, though. The guy is a loose cannon. You need to watch your back. He won't just let it go."

"I know," Darryl agreed. "Thanks."

Liam drew on his vape pen as the smell of weed wafted through the air.

"What gives, man? Are you okay? I'm supposed to be the one with the short temper. Is it the job thing? This project is just about done. There might be another supe position opening up soon. It's mostly city work, but I can put your name in."

"It's not just that," Darryl admitted. "I've got a lot rattling around in my head right now. Conor's right. I think I just need some time to cool off away from the House."

"You've got a shitload of PTO, man," Liam responded. "Take some. Give yourself a week away from everything and clear your head. I'll square it on the job."

"Cool. Thanks, man," Darryl told him.

"Wow, that was too easy," Liam arched his eyebrow.

"You're right. I need to clear my head of work, the House...everything," Darryl admitted. "I'll work on it."

Darryl descended the steps and went to his Harley, starting it up and leaving the Hog House area. He had no desire to go home just yet and sped off into Harriman and went right to River Road. He pulled into Millie Malone's parking lot and headed inside, where a line of people waiting to be seated greeted him.

Darryl turned to leave before hearing his name shouted.

"Darryl!" he heard over the din as he looked back. He looked to his left and saw Siobhan waving to him, asking him to come to the table where she sat with Finn.

Darryl made his way past the line and over to the table. Siobhan smiled broadly at him when he arrived. She rose from her seat and hugged him.

"I haven't seen you in a bit. How have you been?"

"Good, good," he said, looking around the crowded room. "I just stopped in for a pint, but it looks a little crazy tonight."

"They have a band starting in a bit," Finn added.

"Sit with us," Siobhan insisted, pointing to the two empty chairs at their table.

"I don't want to interfere with your date," Darryl explained. "I can go over to the bar."

"Don't be ridiculous," Siobhan told him. "Finn, tell him."

"Bon is right," Finn agreed. "Sit here. There's no room at the bar, and you're always welcome."

"Thanks," Darryl sighed as he sat.

"So, where have you been lately?" Siobhan began. "Over at the House? Or are you spending all your free time at the dog shelter?"

"A little both, I guess," Darryl shrugged. "But I won't be at the House for a bit."

"Why not?" Finn asked.

"I got into it with Dutch," Darryl explained. "He pulled a knife on me and came at me."

"Oh my God," Siobhan gasped.

"I'll bet he's sorry he did that," Finn replied.

"Preacher, Liam, and Conor stepped in before I went too far," Darryl admitted. "Conor took his colors."

"That's what he's supposed to do," Finn added before sipping his Guinness. "And you?"

"I have to stay away for a few days," Darryl told the couple. "It was the right thing to do. I crossed a line, but he pissed me off."

"You think he'll retaliate?"

"I don't know. I'm not worried about that asshole... pardon me, Siobhan." Darryl sat back in his chair, looking around for a server.

"It might be a bit before you see anyone," Siobhan told him. "They're short-staffed. Olivia is running all over to cover tables. Even Annabella has been out here working."

"It's okay. I'll make my way up to the bar. You two need anything?"

"We're good," Finn responded.

Darryl edged toward the crowded bar. His height gave him an advantage, allowing him to see over everyone where the bartenders were. He noticed Darren Hughes, the owner of Millie Malone's, hustling to get drinks on the left end of the bar. Darryl waved his paw in Darren's direction and got his attention, holding up one finger to let him know he needed just one Guinness. Darren nodded and began a pour.

Darryl glanced further down the bar, paying little attention to the younger patrons there. His eyes stopped when he recognized a face near the corner. He saw Rose's distinctive dark brown orbs scanning the crowd while sipping a drink.

Darryl waded through the crowd until he reached behind where Rose sat, with an empty seat with a purse on it next to her.

"Is someone sitting there?" Darryl asked over the crowd noise as the band started to tune their instruments.

"I'm sorry, my friend is there," Rose answered without looking back and sipping her drink. She just went to the ladies' room."

"That's okay," Darryl said. "These barstools are smaller than the chairs at Meadow Blues. I'll never fit on them."

Rose's head spun around as she caught sight of Darryl. Darryl pushed a smile onto his lips.

"Hello there."

"Darryl, hello," Rose fumbled, placing her glass down. "What are you doing here?"

"Just enjoying a Saturday night, having a drink with friends, just like you."

"I mean, I thought you guys only hung out at the house over there," she added as her hands fidgeted with the thin red stirrer that had been in her drink.

"We get to wander out and mingle with the good people now and then," he told her.

"No, I didn't mean it like that," she blushed.

"I'm just teasing," Darryl admitted. Darren found Darryl and placed the Guinness in front of him.

"Nice to see you," Darren shouted.

"Do you need a drink?" Darryl asked Rose, spying her glass nearly empty.

"Oh, you don't have to—" she started.

"Get her another of whatever she's having," Darryl asked. "And put it all on Finn's tab."

"You got it," Darren laughed.

"I can get my own drinks," Rose insisted.

"I know. You keep telling me that," Darryl laughed. "You can get it next time."

"Oh? You're assuming there's going to be a next time?"

"We keep running into each other," Darryl told her. "Seems like fate to me."

"I'm not much of a believer in fate," Rose told him. "Coincidence, yes. Fate, no."

Darryl drank a bit of his beer before placing his glass down on the bar. Then, he moved closer to Rose, entering her personal space.

"So why didn't you choose me, Rose?" he asked boldly.

Rose coughed on her drink and then looked straight into Darryl's eyes.

"What are you talking about?"

"The speed date sheet. I never got your contact information. You had to know I would say it was okay for you to contact me. I thought we had connected a bit."

"What makes you think I didn't say okay as well?"

"I never heard back from you or got notified of your contact information," Darryl told her, staying close to her. He sensed her nervousness, but Rose pivoted on the barstool so that her face was inches from Darryl's.

"I didn't get yours either," she said coolly. "I'm guessing they didn't get around to it yet. Besides, I'm sure there were several other women you checked off that would want to contact you."

"You're the only one I agreed to give my information to," Darryl told her as he peered at her.

He watched as Rose gulped her drink and then turned her face back to Darryl as she grinned.

"Well, what should we do about this then?"

"How much have you had to drink?" Darryl questioned, lowering his voice.

"Enough to take the edge I've been feeling for weeks off, but not enough to compromise my decision-making," she giggled.

A rush raced through Darryl's body as he leaned ever closer to Rose, bringing his lips just in front of hers.

"So what do we do about that?" he asked hungrily.

Rose moved forward as if she were going to place her lips on his, only to graze past his stubbled cheek and go next to his ear.

"I go to the ladies' room," she whispered and laughed, getting off the stool and walking away.

Darryl groaned as he watched Rose move in the dark green dress, her hips swaying slightly so that Darryl saw nothing else but her. It took a slap on the back from Liz to jolt Darryl out of his trance.

"Fancy meeting you here," Liz laughed as she squeezed onto her barstool.

"Oh, hi," Darryl answered Liz, still looking off in Rose's direction.

"Where's Rosie?" Liz asked as she picked up her bottle of Peroni.

"She said she was going to the ladies' room," Darryl replied, looking back to Liz and pointing.

"Then she's really lost," Liz told him. "I just came from the loo. It's the other direction. I didn't think she was smashed already."

Darryl put his pint glass down on the bar and moved off quickly in the direction Rose went. He darted down the hallway, past rows of pictures of the Malone clan on the walls, before reaching two doors. One led to the kitchen while the other went out to the back of the building. Darryl stood deciding which way to go before the kitchen door swung open, grabbing his attention. Olivia burst through, carrying two plates with hamburgers on them.

"Geez, Darryl, you scared the hell out of me," she said as she skirted past him. "What are you doing back here?"

"Did you see someone just come through here?" Darryl asked hurriedly.

"Through the kitchen? Just the three of us back here. Do you need something? I've got to serve these."

"No, sorry, go," Darryl answered as Olivia scurried off. Darryl pushed open the back door and went outside.

He scanned through the darkness, turning to the left and seeing nothing but woods and trees still covered with some remnants of snow and ice. He switched to the right in the direction of Mary Harriman Park and spied a shadow walking along the gravel drive that led into the park. A light humming came from that direction, and the unmistakable sway of the shadow let Darryl know who it was.

He stepped carefully in the dark, working hard not to slip into the stream behind the building and into the park before reaching the driveway. He skirted past the bar that served to block off the park entrance to vehicles after dark and made his way over beyond the slides to the pavilion area but saw no signs of Rose.

The humming started up again, followed by the familiar creak and groan of the swing set in motion. Darryl twirled in that direction and saw legs pumping in the air as the swing moved higher. He made his way closer until he reached the side of the set and looked on as Rose played.

"I wondered how long it would take you to get here," Rose told him as her legs kicked forward.

"What are you doing out here?" Darryl asked. "Aren't you cold?"

"Funny, I suddenly felt hot in there," she purred. "I needed to get out for some fresh air, and then I felt like... playing a little."

"Rose, maybe we should go back inside," Darryl told her as he moved behind the swing.

"What's the matter, Darryl? You don't want to play with me? I thought the Cosantóir was all about having a good time."

"I'm all for a good time," Darryl corrected, "but not with someone who doesn't have a clear head."

When Rose swung back in his direction, Darryl reached out and grasped the two chains and held them tightly, keeping Rose in place. Rose leaned back against Darryl's chest, her hands reaching back and gripping his thighs.

"Think about this," Darryl said, doing his best to show restraint as Rose's hands wandered up to his legs.

"Oh, I have. Several times," Rose said as she pressed tighter against Darryl.

Darryl's hands slid down from the chains to Rose's sides as he lifted her off the swing, eliciting a gasp from her. He quickly spun Rose around so they were face to face.

"Look me in the eyes, Rose, and tell me you know what you're doing," he demanded.

Rose's left hand came up and touched Darryl's cheek. She ran the back of her hand down his face, her fingernails trailing across him with just a bit of pressure.

"I know," she whispered before pulling Darryl's face down to hers to kiss him. "I know what I'm doing and what I want. Do you?"

Darryl pressed his lips firmly to hers without a second thought, his hands gripping her tightly. When he broke the kiss, he saw that Rose's eyes were wide.

"We need to leave. Now," Darryl rasped.

Chapter 9

Darryl grabbed Rose's hand, pulling her along as he moved out of the park and back toward Millie Malone's. He reached the back door they exited and found it locked. Darryl gave a cursory tug on the door to no avail.

"Shit!" he mumbled. "It must only open from the inside. Did you drive here?"

Rose shook her head no.

"Liz is the driver tonight, so I could have a couple of drinks," Rose admitted.

"It figures."

Darryl sighed as disappointment filled the air.

"Have you ever ridden on the back of a motorcycle?"

"No," Rose replied. "It's a little cold for that tonight, don't you think?"

"It's a short ride to my house from here, and I have an extra helmet," Darryl pondered aloud.

"Maybe we should just forget—" Rose began before Darryl turned back to her. His right hand went to her face, his palm cupping her as he leaned in and kissed her deeply, leaving Rose gasping so her breath was visible in the cold night air.

"Is that what you want, Rose? To just forget about it? Because I sure as hell don't want to."

Darryl took her hand once more, walking her around the side of the building until they reached a bit of snow they would have to get through.

"I can't get through there in these shoes," Rose protested.

"Sure you can," Darryl said as he swept Rose up in his arms and carried her like she was two bags of groceries until they had traversed the snow and reached the parking lot.

Darryl didn't stop toting her until he reached his motorcycle, placing her down next to the bike while he removed his spare helmet from one of the cases on his bike. He assisted her with putting it on, gently placing it on her head and adjusting the chin strap, looking deeply into her eyes.

"All this trouble for—" Rose started before Darryl placed his index finger on her lips.

"Trust me, it will be worth it," he swore.

Darryl climbed onto the bike and bade Rose get on behind him. Rose just stared at the bike and then looked back at him.

"I'm wearing a dress," she protested.

Darryl hopped off the bike, looking at Rose in her short, tight green dress. His hands shot down to the hem of the dress as he slowly raised it, his fingers seductively grazing her stockinged thighs until the dress was around her waist.

"You can get on now," he told her. "You may find that you like it."

Darryl gave Rose a salacious grin as he took off his leather jacket and put it on her. The jacket was huge for her frame and left Darryl with his arms bare. He mounted the bike once more, and Rose reluctantly got on behind him.

"Get close to me," he told her. "Wrap your arms on me and hold tight."

Roe dutifully put her arms around Darryl's waist. His muscular torso prevented her from clasping her hands together around him as she pressed her head against his back before he started the bike. When he revved the Harley, Darryl felt Rose jump and get closer to him. He let it idle for a few seconds so she could get her bearings and feel the engine's strength beneath them.

"Keep your feet up on the pegs!" Darryl shouted insistently. "Ready?"

Rose didn't verbally reply, instead raising the thumb on her left hand from his waist so he could see it.

"Here we go!"

Darryl took off, trying to keep things slow so he wouldn't scare Rose with the speed and power. He let the bike idle a bit longer at stop signs so she could get accustomed to the way everything felt. When he reached the red traffic light leading to Harriman Heights Road, he felt Rose's hands moving in circles on his hips, and Darryl swore he heard her let out a light moan.

"You're doing great," Darryl said, maintaining his composure. "We'll have to give it some thrust to get up the hill ahead. I hope you're okay with that."

"Uh-huh," Rose gasped as her head pressed harder into Darryl's back.

The light turned green, and Darryl gave the bike extra gas, sending it through the intersection and up Harriman Heights Road, ascending the hill and navigating the curves expertly as he passed the Kingdom Hall before turning left into the driveway outside his home.

He stopped the bike, cutting the engine and reaching down to grip Rose's hands that held his hips. He felt her hands tremble slightly as he put his leather riding gloves over her fingers. He dismounted first, guiding Rose off the bike. Her legs wobbled a bit as she got off and stood under the glare of the motion light that had come on when they pulled in. Darryl spied her enveloped in his leather jacket, her arms and hands invisible in the sleeves as the jacket hung like a baggy dress, leaving just her black stockings visible.

"How was it?" Darryl asked as he led Rose up the front porch steps to the front door.

"Intense," Rose whispered.

"Should I consider that foreplay?" he smirked as they entered the house.

Darryl took the leather jacket from Rose, hanging it on the peg by the door. When he turned to her, her dress was still up around her waist, giving Darryl a view of the white panties she wore beneath her stockings. Rose caught his look and quickly started to roll her dress back down.

"Don't do that on my account," he said, watching her move.

"You seem pretty sure of yourself," Rose said, straightening her dress.

"It seems like a waste to spend time doing all of that," Darryl told her as he stepped in front of Rose. "Especially when I just want to take it off you anyway."

"Is that so?" Rose answered playfully. "You'll have to work harder than just talking tough. I'm no pushover."

"It's okay. I love a challenge."

Darryl bent down and kissed Rose and rapidly moved his lips to her neck, planting small kisses on the nape as he drove down. His left hand snaked behind her back, finding the zipper for her dress, and began to ease it down click by click. Rose rested her hands against Darryl's chest as his lips wandered up and down her neck and the zipper reached its end.

Darryl's left hand moved to Rose's right shoulder, easing the dress from there so he could kiss the bare flesh and let his fingers explore more of her. Then, in one move, his fingers relieved Rose of her dress entirely as she stepped out of the garment at her feet and kicked it aside.

"Mission accomplished," Darryl growled into her ear.

"You haven't done anything yet," Rose whispered back, nibbling Darryl's ear and tugging it before kicking off her heels, making her even shorter next to Darryl's imposing figure.

Rose slipped past Darryl and sashayed up the stairs, reaching the top and turning the corner. Darryl looked on in awe until he saw a white lace bra get flung onto the top step of the staircase. Darryl bounded up the stairs, taking two at a time until he reached the apex and turned toward his bedroom at the end of the hall. A small stream of light emanated from the door sitting ajar.

Darryl pushed the door open and saw Rose lying on his bed, pillows propped behind her head and back.

"That didn't take you long," she laughed.

"I can move quickly when properly motivated," Darryl admitted. He sat in the chair just inside the door and started to take his boots off while never taking his eyes off Rose. He watched as her left hand trailed down from teasing her hair to just across her nipple and down her stomach, letting out a sex-charged sigh as she did so.

"Does that motivate you more?"

Darryl got to his feet and pulled his t-shirt over his head. He made fast work of his jeans, leaving them on the floor, before crawling up from the bottom of the bed until his head reached Rose's waist. He lightly kissed Rose's stomach while his left hand glided over her silky stockings, moving from her calf to her inner thigh.

Darryl looked up to see Rose close her eyes and arch her back slightly as the palm of his hand came to rest just at the top of the hose she wore. He slid his fingers down, caressing her sex through the stockings as she mewled under his touch.

"I hope these aren't expensive stockings," Darryl told her as his hands rubbed against her.

"They're not," she gasped.

That proved all Darryl needed to hear as his fingers tore into the nylon, ripping the hose, so it seemed as if Rose wore a garter now. His fingers touched the damp lace of her panties before he slipped a finger just inside her, dabbing on her wet lips, so she moaned loudly.

"And these?" he said, toying with the lace with his right hand while his left teased her.

"They're—" Rose began before Darryl interrupted.

"Fuck it, I don't care," he roared. "I'll buy you new ones."

His fingers ripped the lace panties, allowing Darryl easier access as Rose gasped again. Darryl looked up to Rose's face and saw her eyes were slits, barely open, as her chest heaved. He slid his head over and between her legs, kissing her inner thighs as his fingers continued to work on her. The base of his thumb slid over her swollen clit, making Rose moan once more.

Darryl eagerly pressed further, slipping his tongue inside her and tasting her. He felt Rose place her hands on the back of his head, guiding his mouth to where it would give her the most pleasure. His tongue swirled up, around, and over her clit, hitting all her extra-sensitive spots in a frenzy of action.

Rose lifted her stomach as she groaned, and Darryl slid his hands to her waist to hold her and press his lips and tongue into her. Within moments, Rose was tensing as she came as Darryl kept his tongue in place, bathing in the wetness surrounding it.

Rose's breathing became more controlled as Darryl continued kissing her inner thighs before she calmed, and he looked up at her contented face.

"Don't get too comfortable," Darryl told her. "We aren't anywhere near done yet."

Darryl rolled to his right and sat up, opening the drawer to his nightstand before fishing out a box of condoms. He wasted no time removing a foil packet and then stripping out of his navy blue boxer briefs, allowing his cock to spring free. He opened the condom package and rolled the protection on as Rose looked on as Darryl worked it down his length.

He returned to his position between Rose's legs, teasing her with just the tip of his cock on her wet lips. Even though he portrayed the picture of strength and control at the moment, Darryl barely hung on. He knew inside it wouldn't take much to push him over the edge, but he wanted this experience to last for as long as possible.

He slid himself between Rose's lips, never entering her fully. He saw her gripping the sheets in her balled-up fists as he moved achingly slow to control the tempo.

"Please... I can't... I can't take much more," she panted.

"I hope you can take more than this," Darryl said as he slid the tip of his cock inside her. Rose moaned and bucked her hips, attempting to bring more of Darryl inside her."Yes, yes, I can," she gasped, her hands clutching at Darryl's back.

Darryl hungrily plunged deep into Rose's pussy as he picked up speed and thrust. Rose wrapped her legs around his waist, keeping him where he was as she ground against him in rhythm. Soon after, Rose was crying out again as her second orgasm hit.

Rose tightened on Darryl's cock as she rode out her orgasm, pulsing on him. Sweat covered Darryl's brow as he groaned, attempting to hold out.

"Let go," Rose gasped. "I want to feel you come." She tightened her legs on him again, keeping him in place as she clenched on him, pushing back.

Darryl let out a guttural groan as he came, tensing his body and pressing his hands tightly into the sheet and mattress beneath him. Then, as his orgasm subsided, he collapsed onto the bed, moving to Rose's right on the pillow next to her.

Both lay panting, their bodies damp and tangled in the sheets. Darryl turned his head to see Rose staring up at the ceiling, cheeks flushed and bliss on her face.

"Mission accomplished," Darryl whispered into her ear as he kissed her neck.

"I'll say," he heard her say breathlessly as she nuzzled her head against his.

Chapter 10

Rose pried her eyes open as she lay on her side and looked at the clock on the nightstand to see it was after nine-thirty in the morning. Panic raced through her as she thought she would be late for work before recalling that it was Saturday. She wriggled under the blanket, and Darryl pulled her close, so her bare body was against his. The initial shock of having a body next to her made her jerk until she felt the protective arm drape on her.

She had no desire to leave the coziness of the bed and closed her eyes again, recalling the intensity of the experience the night before. Unlike any sexual encounter she had ever been through, it made her time with Walter seem like a distant memory. Just thinking about what Darryl made her feel sent chills of excitement coursing over her body.

Naturally, those chills led her to realize she did need to get out of bed and use the bathroom. She pulled the blanket back and slid out of bed, remembering that she had shed her dress and bra around the house, and Darryl had made short work of the stockings and panties she wore. She paced the floor quietly, finding Darryl's t-shirt and jeans balled up on the floor near the bottom of the bed. Rose plucked the t-shirt off the floor and slid it on. The length went down almost beyond her knees while the shoulders and torso made it like when she would play dress-up with costumes when she was a child.

Rose pulled the bedroom door open slowly, hoping to avoid it creaking so Darryl wouldn't rouse before she walked gingerly to the bathroom in the middle of the hallway. She slipped in and shut the door, taking care of her business and then looking in the mirror. Her face had a glow that had been missing for weeks, and for the first time in what seemed like forever, Rose was happy with herself. She flushed and washed her hands before opening the bathroom, gasping when she practically walked right into Darryl's daughter, Annie.

"Good morning," Annie said with a wide grin.

"Oh, hi," Rose said meekly, unsure of what to do.

"I wondered who the dress and bra belonged to when I got home last night and didn't see a car in the driveway. They looked a little too small to be Dad's."

Rose let out an uncomfortable chuckle while she looked down at her feet. She felt the t-shirt sliding off her shoulders and pulled the fabric tighter around her waist, so it didn't fall off entirely, making an already embarrassing situation mortifying.

Rose shuffled down the hallway and back into Darryl's bedroom, shutting the door behind her with less care this time and causing Darryl to stir. Darryl lifted his head as he saw Rose standing by the door.

"Everything okay?" he yawned.

"I just had to use the bathroom," Rose said, frozen at the door.

"What's wrong?" Darryl asked as he sat up.

Rose paced over to the bed and sat next to him.

"I ran into your daughter in the hallway," Rose told him.

"Oh. I thought Annie would be working the opening shift today," Darryl stated, scratching his chin. "I'm sure she was fine."

"Well, she did find my clothes scattered on the stairs when she got home," Rose added with embarrassment.

Darryl stifled a chuckle, and Rose shot him a stern look.

"I'm not wearing anything under this, Darryl," she scolded as she pulled at the collar of his t-shirt.

"I'm sorry," he said to her. "It does look good on you, and knowing you have nothing on underneath it, well..."

Darryl attempted to lift the hem of the shirt before Rose swatted his hand away.

"Be serious," she said to him. "What is she going to think?"

"I'm sure she figured it all out, Rose," Darryl dismissed. "She's twenty-two, not twelve."

"I know, but still," Rose said, flustered. "It puts me in an awkward position."

"You want me to go talk to her?"

"God, no!" Rose exclaimed. "That would be worse. Maybe I should go."

"If you want," Darryl said. "Let me throw something on, and I'll give you a ride home."

Rose watched as Darryl climbed out of bed. Seeing his naked form in the light of day took her breath away, allowing her to go over every inch of his body with her gaze. Examining his muscles, tone, and definition made her stir as she saw him pull on a clean pair of boxer briefs and reach for his jeans.

Rose looked around the room and then turned back toward Darryl.

"We have a problem," she told him. "What am I supposed to wear?"

Darryl opened his dresser drawer and pulled out a black t-shirt.

"I can go grab your things," Darryl offered.

"That's fine, but... but I don't have any underwear, remember?"

"Oh, I remember very well," Darryl said as he approached Rose. He put his hands on her waist, sliding his left hand down to cup her buttocks."Darryl, stop playing," Rose chided as she moved his hand away.

"No one's going to know except me," he grinned. "I'll get your stuff and give you a ride back to your place."

"You have a car, right?"

"No, I just use the bike," Darryl responded. "I've never found a car or truck I'm as comfortable in. None are ever big enough for me."

"I can't ride your bike home in a dress with no panties on," she said quietly, recalling the ride she took yesterday and what it did to her.

"Hmmm, I hadn't thought about that, but now that I have..." Darryl's hands roamed over Rose's body.

"Darryl, come on," Rose said, barely trying to fight him off as his hands spun her around, so her back pressed against him. His lips went back to work on her neck as his right hand slid under the t-shirt and ran across her stomach, sending chills through her body.

"You can always stay here longer," he whispered, his fingers wandering up from her stomach to under her left breast.

"I need to go," she whined lightly as his fingers held her breast closely. Her whine transitioned to a whimper as Darryl caressed her more.

"Are you sure?" he asked. His fingertips trailed down Rose's stomach lower and lower, grazing across soft hair before lightly tapping around her clit.

"Darryl, you're making me crazy," she moaned. Her right hand got the initial message from her brain to stop Darryl from what he was doing. However, she soon found her hand holding his in place as it worked its magic.

"Tell me to stop, and I will," he said huskily. His hard-on in his jeans pressed against Rose's back while he touched her and held her close.

Rose's brain and body were on fire, and the words wouldn't leap from her mouth.

"Just tell me, Rose," Darryl insisted, slipping a finger inside her. Rose's knees began to buckle underneath Darryl's touch.

"Should I stop?"

Her eyes tightly shut, Rose shook her head to indicate no.

"I didn't think so."

Only Darryl's arm around her waist kept Rose from crumpling to the floor when she came.

Rose stayed in his arms, turning to kiss him continually with fervor before resting her head on Darryl's chest.

"Want to go home now?" Darryl joked.

"I think I need a few minutes," she gasped.

"You might need more than a few," he said as he lifted Rose up and carried her back to the bed, placing her down in the center before stripping his shirt off and moving over her.

After spending the rest of the morning in bed with each other, Rose looked into Darryl's eyes, placing her palm gently on her cheek.

"I just want you to know, I don't... I don't normally do things like this," she said to him.

"Why would you think you have to tell me that?" Darryl asked, taking hold of her wrist and kissing her fingers.

"I didn't want you to think I was the type of person who goes home with someone just on a whim."

"Did you think I was the kind of person who just takes every woman who presents herself in front of me to bed?" Darryl asked.

"No, I mean," Rose said, fumbling for words. "I know the reputation of the Cosantóir, but I'm sure not everyone is like it. You hear things…"

"Mostly rumors, Rose," Darryl reassured her. "Are there guys who just go around looking to have sex with everyone who comes along? Sure there are. I know it happens, but it happens with doctors, lawyers, judges, salesmen, you name it. Guys who will do that don't exclusively wear leather jackets, ride motorcycles, and have tattoos."

"I know. I shouldn't assume," Rose offered.

"You already made that mistake with me a few times," Darryl said seriously. "Don't get caught up just in the way things look. There's a lot about me you don't know, just like I'm sure there is plenty about you I'm unaware of."

Rose turned her back to Darryl, and he pulled her close to him.

"I think we skipped a few steps in the dating process," Darryl admitted. "Maybe we can go out somewhere, do something together to get to know each other. What do you say?"

"Are you asking me out?" Rose giggled.

"I guess I am," he laughed. "Are you free tonight?"

"I'll have to check my calendar," Rose added sarcastically. "Yeah, I'm free. What did you want to do?"

"I'm not sure yet. Leave that to me."

"Ooh, a man of mystery. I like that. How will I know what to wear if I don't know what we're doing?"

"I'll keep it simple. Jeans will work just fine. Or you can just wear what you're wearing now," he teased.

"You're hysterical," she added with an elbow to Darryl's ribs.

"I prefer insatiable," he added as he kissed Rose's bare shoulder.

"You are that for sure," Rose added. She began melting inside again under Darryl's touch.

"Okay," she told him, rolling back to face him. "We need to stop, or we're never getting on that date tonight."

"I'd be fine with that."

Darryl leaned in and began kissing Rose again. Just as their lips parted, a constant buzzing filled the air.

"Crap, I bet that's my phone," Rose said, darting up and out of bed. She knelt down and grabbed her purse, pulling her phone out and looking out. The display showed a stream of missed texts and phone calls from Liz, with the last text all in caps:

WHERE THE FECK ARE YOU????

Rose dialed her phone to call Liz back.

"It's about time!" Liz yelled into the phone. "I've been texting and calling you since last night! You disappeared, and I never heard from you. I know Darryl went looking for you, and that was it. I was getting ready to go over to the Hog House with the cops. Christ, Rosie!"

"I'm sorry," Rose apologized. "I just got caught up in... in some stuff. But, I promise you, I'm fine. I'll be home in a little bit."

"Where did you end up last night?"

"I... I can't get into right now, Liz," Rose added, hushing her voice.

"You better be ready to get into it when you walk through this door," Liz demanded. "Love you."

"Love you too," Rose sighed as she hung up. She turned back toward the bed to see Darryl watching her.

"Everything cool?" he asked.

"Just Liz," Rose replied, holding up her phone and walking back to the bed. "She was texting and calling me all night. I left my phone silenced. She was worried."

"She sounds like a good friend."

"She's more like my sister," Rose admitted. "We grew up together. She's helped me through a lot of stuff."

"So I guess I'm 'the stuff' you got caught up in last night?" Darryl inquired.

"I... I didn't want to get into all of it on the phone. I told you, I don't do things like this. I'm coming out of a long relationship, Darryl. I've been going through a lot."

"I get it," he nodded. "We don't need to dive into it. It's your business."

A knock on the bedroom door froze Rose in place as her eyes widened. Rose dove onto the bed, pulling the blanket over her body.

"What's up?" Darryl yelled, grabbing his briefs off the floor.

"Don't worry, I'm not coming in," Annie yelled back. "I was just letting you know I'm leaving for work. I'm closing tonight, so I'll be late."

"Thanks, baby girl," Darryl said as he pulled his jeans on. "Have a good day."

"You can let your friend know I left her clothes hanging in the bathroom."

Rose put her face in the palms of her hands.

"I appreciate it. See you tonight," Darryl added.

Rose heard the footsteps trail off down the hall and then the stairs.

Darryl slowly pulled the door open and peeked out.

"The coast is clear," he laughed.

"I feel like crawling under the bed," Rose told him.

"Whatever you prefer." Darryl approached her and sat on the bed. "It's more fun on this side of the mattress, though."

"God only knows what she's thinking."

"She's probably thinking, 'Thank God Dad finally brought a woman home. Then, maybe, he'll be out of the house more.' So stop worrying about it."

Darryl grabbed Rose's hands and placed a finger under her chin, lifting her gaze to meet his.

"Tell you what? I'll go grab a pair of sweats from Annie's room you can wear, and then I'll drive you home. Sound good?"

"I don't want to take her clothes."

"Well, you can wear your dress home instead," Darryl told her. He bent down to the floor and emerged, holding Rose's pair of ripped panties. "I don't know how much comfort these will provide you on the bike, though."

Rose snatched the panties from Darryl, holding the bits of fabric.

"Sweatpants are fine," she resigned. "Is it okay if I shower first?"

"Absolutely."

Rose hopped out of bed, padding over to the bedroom door before peeking herself to verify no one was looking before she dashed down the hall to the bathroom, quickly closing the bathroom door behind her. She spotted her green dress and bra hanging on a hanger on the back of the door.

She opened the glass door to the enormous shower stall and reached in to turn the water on. The giant showerhead began to sprinkle down before becoming a more robust hot stream that she stepped under. The water massaged her skin as she turned her back to it, looking at the selection of bath products that clearly belonged to Darryl's daughter.

Steam filled the chamber as hot water coursed through Rose's hair. She shut her eyes, enjoying the warmth and recalling the events of the night before and the morning. Her body tingled as she imagined Darryl's touch, his hands everywhere, exploring her and learning her desires. She got so caught up in her thoughts that she never heard the bathroom door open and audibly gasped when she heard Darryl's voice so near to her.

"Here are sweats and a t-shirt," he said over the running water.

Rose pivoted toward the glass door, her arms instinctively covering her breasts.

"I don't think you have anything I haven't seen already at this point," Darryl grinned. "And I certainly don't mind watching."

"I bet you don't," Rose added coyly.

Steam continued to fill the shower stall when Darryl tugged the door open and stepped in behind Rose.

"I don't remember asking for company," Rose said.

"How else are you going to get your back washed?" Darryl asked. He grabbed the loofah from the shower caddy and began washing the back of Rose's neck.

"I usually do just fine," Rose said as she moved her wet hair to one side so Darryl could continue his task.

"Trust me, this is much better," he told her as the loofah moved across each shoulder to the middle of her back.

She allowed Darryl to keep going as he washed her waist before reaching her behind. He took great care caressing her, and Rose made sure to wiggle a bit extra to tease him before moving on to her legs.

Darryl slowly moved the loofah up and down each leg, stopping short of her inner thighs each time. Knots formed in the pit of Rose's stomach as he moved achingly close to her most sensitive spots.

"Time to do the front," Darryl whispered in Rose's ear as she eagerly spun to face Darryl. He towered over her in the shower, his imposing figure glistening from the water beading off his shaved head and across his pecs. Her hands moved to his chest as he started to use the loofah on hers.

The material moved slowly across each of her breasts. The water and Darryl's touch had her nipples at heightened sensitivity. As his hand moved lower across her stomach, her hands mimicked his and went to his solid and firm abs.

Rose could barely control herself as Darryl s' hands dipped below her waist, washing across her sex. Her hands reached out, grabbing hold of the loofah and taking it in her hands.

"My turn for a minute," she said, looking into Darryl's eyes as she soaped her hands and then grabbed hold of his thick cock. Her hand glided up and down his shaft, causing him to groan like Rose had not heard yet. She smiled, enjoying the sudden surge of power she felt over him as her hand went down and she raked her fingernails across his balls. She went back to his cock, taking it in her fist and slowly twisting her way up, leaving her index finger to run under the swollen head.

"Rose," Darryl growled, his eyes closed.

"Oh, did you want me to stop?" she mocked. "All you have to do is ask me."

Her lone finger worked that same spot over and over deliberately until she saw Darryl raise his arms and place the palms of his hands, one on the wall and the other on the shower door, to brace himself.

"I don't have to keep going," she cooed, her finger mingling in the mix of suds and pre-come on the tip of his cock. "Just ask me to stop."

Darryl's eyes flung open, and Rose smiled at him as she kept stroking. He groaned again before reaching down and taking hold of Rose's hands. She gasped when he grabbed her, surprised by his quick movements. In one swoop, he spun Rose around so she had her back to him. His lips dove back to her neck while his left hand reached around to take hold of her left breast. Darryl's right hand quickly found its mark between her legs as Rose groaned with pleasure.

Darryl's fingers strummed on and around her clit repeatedly to the point where Rose used the shower facing her to hold herself up. Moments later, Darryl was easing inside her, taking her from behind as her fingernails clutched the tile wall. She held on tightly as Darryl moved in and out until his body tensed, his lips clamping down on her shoulder as he moaned. Rose shuddered as he surged in her, and she closed her eyes, riding wave after wave through her body as she came again.

Darryl wrapped his hands around Rose's waist, holding her as water continued to pelt both of them. Rose snaked her left hand up around Darryl's neck to guide his head from the small of her back where it rested to her neck again so he could kiss her. She turned to face him then, kissing him repeatedly before putting her arms around him.

"I'm sorry," Darryl offered as he kept kissing. "I got caught up. I know I didn't use—"

Rose lifted her index finger to cover his lips.

"Quiet," she hushed. "If I didn't want to, you wouldn't have. It's okay."

"Do you want me to let you finish your shower now?" Darryl smirked.

"If you move right now, I might just collapse to the floor," she said, regaining her composure. "Just hold me here for a minute."

"My pleasure," Darryl added, putting his arms around her again.

Rose snuggled into his damp chest as Darryl moved, so the hot water hit her again.

"Mine too," she added softly.

Chapter 11

Darryl drove Rose back to her condo, hardly a word passing between them as she rested her head on his back for the ride. He pilfered a t-shirt and sweat pants from his daughter's room, convincing Rose to put them on after some struggle of convincing her that Annie wouldn't mind or even know.

Darryl pulled his bike into the Lexington Hill complex, following Rose's guide to her building just up the hill past the pool area. She tapped his shoulder regarding when he should stop, and Darryl let the motorcycle idle as she hopped off. He pulled off his helmet and took the other from Rose's hands.

"Thanks for the ride... and everything else," Rose said shyly.

"Don't get all shy on me now," Darryl laughed. "What time shall I pick you up tonight?"

"Right, our first date," she chuckled. "It depends on where we are going."

"I'm not telling just yet," Darryl said, tight-lipped. "I'll be here around seven, though, so get ready."

"I think I need to nap a little first to recharge."

"Good plan," Darryl said, pulling Rose toward him to kiss her. "I'll see you later."

Darryl watched as Rose walked toward the condo stairs, watching her go up to the second-floor unit and enter her home.

Darryl sped off toward Monroe, pulled into a strip mall, and parked outside Daylight Donuts. He hopped off his bike and walked into the small shop, inhaling deeply as he walked in so he could take in the scent of the freshly baked pastries.

"Oh man," he roared, getting the attention of the young couple in front of him. "I hope you leave me a couple for myself," he laughed.

The couple smiled uncomfortably before turning back to the display case and selecting the confections they wanted before Darryl moved in front of the case.

"Hey there, Darryl," the woman behind the counter smiled widely. "How are you today?"

"Hungry," he laughed. "I'm getting a dozen this morning, Sarah."

"Wow, you are hungry!" she laughed.

"Not all for me, I promise," he added.

Darryl selected a dozen donuts he wanted before stepping over to the cash register.

"Annie doesn't get mad at you for buying our donuts?" Sarah asked as she rang up the purchase.

"Hell no," Darryl stated. "She knows you guys have donuts way better than what Dunkin' delivers. No harm done."

Darryl reached his hand into the box before Sarah could tape it closed, grabbing a glazed donut and taking a big bite out of it, getting the yeasty flavor right away and savoring the taste.

He slid a twenty across the counter and waved Sarah off when she tried to give him change.

"Until next time," he said through a full mouth.

Placing the donuts in one of his side compartments, Darryl rode a bit further into town before stopping in at Harold's Barbershop. He hopped off his bike and entered the shop, greeted by bellows and laughter by a few older men holding court while Harold cut hair.

"Hey there, stranger!" Harold let out as he stepped back from the barber chair and hugged Darryl. "What drags you in here?"

"Dropping these off for you gentlemen," Darryl stated, handing Harold the box of donuts.

"Damn, Darryl, you know just how to get to me," Harold laughed as he placed the box down. Two older men immediately made their way to the donuts, with one of them grabbing two jelly donuts.

"You better have left me a jelly, Robbie," Harold scolded.

"There's another one in there," Robbie said as he slunk back to his seat.

Darryl sat in the chair behind Harold as Harold looked into the mirror and finished up the customer he was working on. Darryl took off his leather jacket and placed it on the chair beside him as the barber chair was vacated.

"Come on over," Harold waved to Darryl, wiping the seat off.

"Damn, Harold, I've been sitting here for an hour," Robbie complained.

"You're sitting there stuffing your face anyway," Harold replied. "When you start spending some money and getting me donuts, you get preferential treatment."

Darryl sat as Harold draped the cape on him and positioned the chair toward the mirror.

"You don't have anything coming up here," Harold said, looking at Darryl's close shaved head.

"Just clean it up and give me a nice shave, please," Darryl asked.

"Wow, a shave too," Harold said in awe. "What's the occasion?"

"Gotta date tonight," Darryl said proudly.

"Whoa!!" Harold said, stepping back. "Who did you tie up in the basement and get to agree to that?"

Laughter filled the shop as Harold grabbed the skull shaver and went over Darryl's scalp.

"Come on now," Darryl added.

"Man, I haven't heard you say you have a date in years," Harold added as he eliminated any sign of hair from Darryl's head.

"I've had dates," Darryl protested. "I don't share everything with you clowns. But this girl, I think she's different."

"Oh man," Robbie said, licking jelly off his fingers. "The boy has it bad already. Don't scare her off too fast now by coming on strong. I've seen it happen."

"That's just your ugly mug scaring them off, Robbie," Harold told him. "Where you taking her?"

Harold put some warm shaving cream on Darryl's face, covering his chin, cheeks, and upper lip.

"That's the tricky part," Darryl admitted. "I don't know where to go. I don't want to just take her to dinner or a movie. I need some ideas."

The men sat around muttering under their collective breath without coming up with anything.

"Damn, you guys are no help," Darryl bemoaned.

"How about Happy Valley?" the young barber working the next chair over added.

All eyes turned to the young man, staring at him.

"Isn't that a massage parlor down on 17 in Jersey?" one older man asked.

"Shit, Ralph, get your mind out of the gutter," Harold chided. "That's Happy Ending, anyway."

"Go on, Winston," Darryl said to the young man. "What is it?"

"It's a bar over in Beacon. They have arcade games, old school stuff like Pac-Man, Asteroids and Space Invaders, and pinball machines. They have craft beer and cocktails. It's someplace fun. I've been there a few times."

"Now that's an idea," Darryl exclaimed as Harold began using his straight razor on Darryl's face. "Thanks, Winston."

"You might make it to the first chair someday," Ralph chimed in.

"Not while I'm still alive and standing!" Harold howled.

No sooner had Rose come through the condo's front door when Liz was upon her, giving her a hug.

"Don't ever do that to me again!" Liz yelled. " I was worried out of my mind about where you were."

"I'm fine, 'Mom,' don't worry," Rose said as she walked into the living room.

Liz stood behind Rose and watched as her friend collapsed onto the couch.

"Why are you wearing white sweatpants with 'Pink' across your arse?" she asked.

"Oh," Rose said, looking at the sweatpants and the t-shirt she had on under her jacket. "I... I had to borrow something. It's a long story, Liz."

Liz sat on the sofa next to Rose.

"I guess you better start it now, then."

"C'mon, Liz," Rose whined. "I'm exhausted. Can we do this later?"

"No, we can't," Liz insisted. "You disappear from the face of the earth for fourteen hours without a word, and I'm supposed to just wait until you want to tell me what's going on? I don't think so. Spill it."

Rose detailed her events over the last day, leaving out the specifics about her interactions with Darryl.

"Unbelievable, Rosie," Liz laughed. "I didn't know you had a tramp in you."

"What?" Rose exclaimed. "I'm no tramp."

"I'm teasing. Relax."

Liz put her arm around Rose.

"It is certainly out of character for you. You have to admit that."

"I know," Rose said, surprised at her actions. "I don't know what happened. There was just something about him."

"Raw animal hunger and good looks?"

"Stop," Rose told her. "Well, that was part of it," she said sheepishly. "But he makes me feel different when I'm with him. He listens. He talks to me. He has respect. I feel—"

"Safe?" Liz asked,

"I feel safe when I'm with him," Rose agreed. "I don't feel like he would hide anything from me. I know, it sounds ridiculous. We barely know each other."

"I wouldn't say barely," Liz replied. "I get the feeling you found out a lot about each other in the park, his house, his bed, his shower—"

"I'm not just talking about the sex," Rose said, facing Liz now. "It was... let's just say it was on another level. One I've never experienced before. We connected. How's that?"

"Not very satisfying for me," Liz said, frowning. " I didn't get any details."

"You'll have to live with what I told you."

Rose yawned and stretched before standing up.

"Now, I need to go nap to rest up."

"Rest up for what?"

"We're going on a date tonight," Rose paced down the hallway toward her bedroom, opening the door and plopping down on her bed. Her arms and legs ached from the activity of the night and morning.

"Oh, and just where are you going?" Liz asked, following her friend and standing in the doorway while Rose lay on the bed.

"I don't know," Rose shrugged. "Darryl said he was going to surprise me. So I have no idea what to expect."

"Ugh," Liz said, exasperated. "Does this mean I will have to chase you down again?"

"No, it doesn't," Rose said as she rolled to her side and put an arm under her pillow. "You know I'll be with Darryl, so I'll be—"

"Safe, I got it," Liz remarked. "Fine. Get some rest. But make sure you don't silence your phone this time. Even if you're rolling around in the grass somewhere."

Rose gave Liz a thumbs up and closed her eyes, grateful that Liz shut the door and darkened the room.

Rose let out a contented sigh, relaxing on her bed. She set the alarm on her phone to wake up by 5 PM and leave herself time to get ready for whatever Darryl had planned for them. She smiled to herself as she recalled the last 24 hours and how amazing they had been for her.

Chapter 12

Darryl busied himself as best he could, changing shirts several times, making himself a cup of coffee, and flipping the channels mindlessly through spring training baseball before deciding to get out of the house.

He had more than an hour before Rose expected him at her door. However, sitting idly at home made him stir crazy, and he went out to his bike to drive and kill time. So, naturally, he headed to the Woodbury Animal Shelter and pulled into the parking lot moments later.

A few vehicles sat outside the facility, and when Darryl walked in, he came face to face with a family adopting two cats. Holding one of the kittens tightly, the little girl stared at the giant filling the doorway.

"A new friend for the family?" Darryl spoke.

The little girl nodded in awe of Darryl's size.

"What's his name?"

"This is Ernie," she said softly, holding the kitten out while Darryl politely scratched the cat's chin. "And she's Bert," she told him, indicating the cat her mother held.

"Isn't Bert a boy's name?" Darryl asked.

"Yeah, but we're saying it's short for Roberta."

"Very nice," Darryl laughed. "Well, congrats on your new friends. I'm sure they'll love you."

"Thank you," the girl squeaked.

Darryl glanced at the girl assisting the family.

"Is Hannah here?" he asked.

"She's in the back," she indicated with her head. "You can go see her, Darryl."

Darryl opened the door to the back room and heard all the dogs yapping. He spotted Hannah sitting on the floor, petting a large chocolate Lab that sat next to her.

"Hey there," Hannah smiled as she stroked the Lab's head.

"New pup?" Darryl said, looking over the dog as he slowly approached.

"Yep. This is Ophelia," Hannah told him as Darryl put his hand down for Ophelia to sniff.

"She's beautiful," Darryl replied as Ophelia licked his hand before he pet her.

"Someone left her tied to our front door this morning. It's heartbreaking."

"How's Buddy?" Darryl asked as he stood over Hannah, extending his hand so he could assist her in standing.

"He's doing well," she added, dusting herself off. "We even had someone check him out today. Fingers crossed."

Darryl peeked into Buddy's pen, but Buddy was already waiting for him at the door, panting and wiggling.

"Hey there, pal," Darryl added as he opened the door, and Buddy leaped out. He barked and nipped at Darryl's hands as Darryl tried to pet him. Buddy then laid down on the floor flat, barking and ready to play. Instead, Darryl squatted and took the dog's head in his hands, playfully rubbing his ears.

"So, what are you all dressed up for?" Hannah asked as she guided Ophelia back to her pen.

"What? This isn't fancy," Darryl brushed off.

"Seriously?" Hannah scoffed. "You never wear a button-down shirt with a collar."

"I don't know what you're talking about," Darryl added. Buddy rolled onto his back, so Darryl could rub his belly.

"You have a date tonight, don't you?"

Darryl didn't answer, focusing his attention on Buddy.

"I'll take that as a yes," Hannah laughed.

"I do have a date," he admitted, sitting on the floor next to Buddy. Buddy crawled into Darryl's lap.

"Well, good for you!" Hannah exclaimed. "Someone finally broke through. Is it anyone I know?"

"Maybe," Darryl answered nonchalantly. "She works over at Macha's Treasures."

"The jewelry store in Monroe? I haven't been there in a while. If she's going out with you, though, I'm sure she's a saint."

"Hey now," Darryl defended. "I'm a good guy, right, Buddy?"

Buddy leaned over and burrowed her head into Darryl's arms.

"See?"

"Of course, he thinks you're golden," Hannah added, "You come and see him and give him treats."

"Well, don't get your clothes all dirty wrestling with him before your date," Hannah advised as she opened the door to return to the front of the shelter.

"I'm sure she'll be fine tonight, right?" Darryl asked, staring into Buddy's face. Buddy lapped his tongue on Darryl's cheek in agreement.

Rose emerged from her bedroom and moved down the hall to the living room where Liz sat. She gave a slight spin, showing off her black jeans and cream-colored sweater.

"What do you think?" Rose asked.

"Gorgeous as always, Rosie," Liz grinned. "You're not wearing anything else that you can't afford to get torn, are you?"

"Stop," Rose said as she considered what she wore underneath for a second.

"I'm just looking out for you," Liz added.

A thud was heard on the stairwell, followed by a loud knock at the door. Rose froze as she looked at Liz, who sprang up from the couch to answer it before Rose moved.

Rose watched as Liz flung the door open to greet Darryl.

"Good evening," Liz said with a proper curtsey, letting Darryl in. "Ms. Rose, Mr. Darryl is here."

Rose rolled her eyes as Darryl entered the condo.

"Don't mind her," Rose added. "She's insane."

"I prefer adorable and quirky," Liz chimed in.

"You look nice," Darryl said. Rose knew his eyes were scanning her.

"Thanks," she added demurely. "So, where are we going?" Rose reached for her coat, and purse slung over the back of a nearby chair.

"I told you it was a surprise," Darryl insisted.

"Is that code for 'I don't know, and we're going to Burger King?'" Liz asked.

Rose shot a stern glare at Liz as Darryl laughed.

"I can promise you it's better than Burger King," Darryl remarked.

"Is it far from here?"

"Not too far," Darryl spoke.

"Well, I'm driving then," Rose said, gathering her keys. "It's too cold out to ride on the back of your bike all night."

Rose pushed passed Darryl and went to the front door.

"See you later," she told Liz, opening the door. "Are you coming?" she asked Darryl.

"I guess so," he shrugged, following Rose out the door.

Rose marched down the stairs and toward where her car was parked. She spotted Darryl's bike just a few feet over in one of the guest parking spots. The car locks clicked open with a button press as Rose got in the driver's seat. She looked on as Darryl slowly opened the passenger door, examining the interior before attempting to get in.

"What are you doing?" Rose inquired.

"Seeing if I'll fit into this sardine can before I try to climb in."

Darryl reached down to adjust the seat, guiding it back as far as it would go on the track. He put one foot in the car and sat down, the chair creaking beneath him. Rose experienced the car lowering slightly as he attempted to fit himself inside.

"You all good?" she asked as she started the Subaru.

"More room than I thought I'd have," Darryl chuckled as he shifted his legs to fit appropriately. "Let's go."

"Um... you need to tell me where I'm going so we can get there," she reminded, gripping the steering wheel.

"Oh, right."

Darryl reached into the interior pocket of his leather jacket and pulled out his phone. He pulled up the directions and sat at the ready.

"Are you going to tell me?" Rose said impatiently.

"I'll tell you where to turn," Darryl said, pointing to the road. "I don't want to ruin the surprise."

Rose shook her head and sighed, backing out of her parking spot and following Darryl's directions to the New York State Thruway and then to I-84 in Newburgh, crossing the Newburgh-Beacon Bridge until they got off on 9D in Beacon.

Rose slowly made her way through Beacon until Darryl pointed to a nearby municipal parking lot where they parked.

"Nice driving," he told her as he opened the passenger side door to get out.

After locking her vehicle, Rose walked alongside Darryl as they moved on the sidewalk. It shocked Rose when she felt Darryl's fingers reach for hers, entwining them together as she looked at the windows of the different eclectic shops lining Main Street.

Darryl hustled Rose across the street until they reached a small garden area with picnic tables. He pulled the door open for her to walk through, and she saw the space filled with arcade machines.

"What's all this?' she asked as she heard Phil Collins singing "Sussudio" over the speakers.

"It's the Arcade Bar," Darryl said as they walked towards the bar at the far end of the room. Rose glanced up and saw *Saved by the Bell* playing on the TVs in the room's upper corners as they reached the bar.

"What would you like to drink?" Darryl asked.

"Oh, just a water, I think," Rose said as she took in the atmosphere.

Darryl ordered the water and a Guinness for himself as Rose looked at the arcade cabinets for Pac-Man, Space Invaders, Galaga, and others. People, young and old, filled the room, shouting while playing games.

Darryl turned and handed the water bottle to Rose as he raised his Guinness to the bottle.

"To our first date," Darryl toasted with a smile. Rose grinned back before she sipped the bottle.

"Do you play video games?" Darryl asked as they walked around looking at the games available.

"Not since I was little," Rose admitted. "We didn't have many options of places to play in Montserrat or in Ireland. My Dad got a used Nintendo from a friend when I was ten, but I think he played it more than I did."

"I loved playing," Darryl admitted. "I have a Playstation at home and still play. It's mindless fun. Well, not mindless. It takes skill and concentration for some games."

"Don't take this the wrong way," Rose said as they stopped in front of the Star Wars pinball machine. "But it seems kind of childish to me."

"That's the best part of it!" Darryl roared. "Don't you ever feel like doing something silly or being like a kid again?"

"I don't know. But, Darryl, my childhood wasn't exactly one I want to relive too much. It was a lot of stress."

"Well, now seems like a good time to start changing that," he insisted.

Rose saw him stride over to the change machine and come back with a fistful of quarters. He put a dollar's worth into the pinball machine, and the lights started flashing. He took a step back and bade Rose to play.

"Oh, I don't know how to play these," Rose balked.

"Then I'll help you," he replied, standing behind Rose.

Darryl pressed his body against hers, guiding her hand up to the button to draw back the spring for the ball.

"Now, let go," he whispered in her ear. The ball flung from its starting spot, hitting bumpers and bells along the way. Sounds of lasers and explosions filled the air as Darryl placed his hands over hers so they could both control the flippers.

"When the ball gets close, use the flippers, like this," he told her, pressing her fingers on the buttons to make the ball shoot back up the machine.

Obi-Wan Kenobi's voice rasped "Use the Force" as the ball moved. Darryl bumped his hips against Rose's to guide her in her movements. Rose found herself enjoying the play together as they moved.

They jumped from game to game, Darryl explaining how to play things like Ms. Pac Man and Gran Turismo. Rose got caught up in each one more than she had imagined before they finally sat at a table to relax.

She faced Darryl, spying as he drained the last of his Guinness, leaving a light foamy mustache on his upper lip. She giggled at the initial sight of it.

"You've got something," she told him, pointing to her own lip and smiling.

"Oh," he chuckled, wiping the residue away. "That's the sign of a Guinness well drunk."

Darryl's eyes peered beyond Rose before his look came back to her. He got up from the table and took her hand as the Greg Kihn Band could be heard playing "Jeopardy" in the background.

"Come on," he told her as they walked to the photo booth.

"We're never going to fit in here," Rose resisted.

"You'll just have to sit on my lap," Darryl told her as he pulled the curtain and put five dollars into the machine.

Darryl placed Rose on his lap as both turned toward the camera. Unfortunately, the machine took the first picture before either had a chance to react.

"Let's make sure we smile for the next one!" Darryl said hastily.

Rose turned toward the camera and grinned, assuming Darryl did the same. A quick glance to her side revealed a broad smile on his face.

Before the next photo snapped, Darryl placed his hands on Rose's hips and positioned his head on her shoulder. Then, he gave a light tickle to her ribs, causing her to burst out laughing and wriggle on his lap.

"Stop!" she yelled playfully, turning her face toward his. She looked directly at him, her gaze softening as she noticed the adoring way he looked at her. Then, without a second thought, she pressed her lips to his as the last photo snapped.

The two sat in the booth as Rose melted into Darryl's arms. She pivoted around so she straddled his lap, kissing him deeply. Darryl's hands moved up from her hips and slid to touch the strip of bare flesh between Rose's jeans and the sweater's hem, making her move closer to him.

Only the incessant banging outside the photo booth caused them to break their embrace.

"Hey! What the fuck, man? Let someone else in," the voice bellowed from outside.

"I guess we need to get up," Rose said softly.

Darryl lifted Rose from his waist and pulled the curtain open to see a young man with long, stringy dark hair staring back at them.

"Dude, come on," the young man barked. "There's a line waiting out here. Go get a hotel room if you need more time."

Darryl let Rose leave the booth first, and she muttered an apology as she moved passed the man. However, when Darryl emerged and towered over everyone waiting, the man took two steps back.

"Do you have something to complain about?" Darryl offered, straightening his leather jacket. "We were taking pictures. Sorry if you had to wait."

"No problem, man," the hipster uttered, backing up.

Darryl reached into one of the front pockets of his jacket, causing the man to cower. Then, Darryl pulled a five-dollar bill out and handed it to the black-haired girl standing nearby.

"Here," Darryl told her. "Your pictures are on me. Enjoy."

"Thanks," she smiled. Then, embarrassed, she tugged on her boyfriend's arm to drag him into the booth.

"Let's go," Darryl said, taking Rose by the hand and leading her out into the chilly air.

"That was... interesting," Rose said as she pulled her coat closed.

"You didn't think that was fun?" Darryl questioned.

"Oh no, I loved the experience," she answered. "I was just talking about that last bit there."

Darryl grasped Rose's hand and led her across the street so they could walk down the road on the other side.

"It happens to me a lot," Darryl confided. "It's funny how people are tough and gruff when they can't see who they are talking to. People are too willing to say stuff they wouldn't normally say to someone. That's why I hate social media. You want to tell me something, say it to my face."

"But it's not like you would do anything to that guy, right?" Rose asked.

"Of course not," Darryl agreed. "But he doesn't know that. He doesn't know me from a hole in the wall. He just wanted to act tough in front of his girl. My size, it's a blessing and a curse. Sometimes I can use that to my advantage."

Darryl stopped in front of a putty-colored building and pulled the door open, holding it for Rose.

"Do you like pizza?" he asked.

"Love it," Rose replied as she walked inside.

The aroma of a wood-burning stove filled the room, along with the fresh smell of Italian spices. A polite waiter greeted Rose and ushered the couple over to a nearby table, placing menus in front of them.

"Hmmm, this place smells amazing," Rose commented.

"I've heard good things about Enoteca Ama. I think we'll enjoy it," Darryl answered.

"So you've never been here before?" Rose asked.

"To be honest, no," Darryl admitted. "I'd never been to Happy Valley either."

"What made you decide to want to come here then?"

Rose spotted the sheepish smile creep across Darryl's face.

"I'm not much of a dater, in case you hadn't noticed," he began. "It's been a while since I've gone out with anyone, and I wanted to do something different with you. I didn't want to just go to dinner or a movie. So this was recommended to me."

"By who?"

"My barber," Darryl sighed.

Rose tried to stifle a laugh but couldn't hold it back. Her laughter caused Darryl to break out as well.

"I know. It's lame," Darryl admitted.

"It's not lame," Rose replied, still giggling. "I think it's sweet that you would go that far. It's funny that your barber gives you advice since, you know..." she pointed at Darryl's bald head.

"Who do you think keeps me looking so fine?" Darryl grinned.

"Well, he does an excellent job," Rose offered.

The couple sat and chatted over a thin crust margarita pizza topped with fresh basil and Kalamata olives, allowing Rose to learn more about Darryl and his past.

"I can't imagine you as one of those professional wrestlers," she said, biting into the last piece of crust left on her plate.

"Why not?"

"I don't know. I'm trying to picture you in a mask and a pair of those wrestling tights, and I just don't see it."

"Play your cards right, and I can break them out of the closet next time you come over," Darryl grinned.

"It must have been tough on your family being on the road all the time," Rose offered. She glanced over and saw the serious look on Darryl's face as he took a sip of his glass of Coke.

"I'm sorry," she apologized immediately. "That was pretty nosy of me."

"No, no," Darryl waved off. "It's fine. I'm an open book. It was tough on Annie and Marsha—Marsha is my ex. I was away from home for most of the year because of travel. Even when I was home, it was for a few days at most, and I spent the whole time sleeping or nursing aches and pains. Marsha was done after ten years of doing it, and I don't blame her. She wanted something more stable in her life. Hell, we got married at eighteen, had Annie at twenty, and she had raised her by herself. I wrestled for another year or two after the divorce and then gave it up. I could have been a champ and made considerable money, but it wasn't worth it."

"I'm sure that was a difficult decision for you," Rose added.

"Not as much as you think," Darryl said as he wiped the last of his pizza from his plate. "Getting thrown around and punched for a living isn't a great way to earn a paycheck."

"I thought all that stuff was fake?" Rose asked.

"Choreographed more than faked," Darryl admitted. "You learn to pull punches and not go all out to really hurt someone, but it still takes its toll. I had plenty of broken ribs, black eyes, twisted knees, you name it. It makes digging tunnels look like a picnic."

Rose fought Darryl when the check arrived, attempting to pay it, but he beat her. They left the restaurant, going back out into the cold. Rose shivered even in her winter coat, and Darryl put his large arm around her, pulling her close. They hustled to get back to where Rose had parked, jumping in and starting it up as Rose blasted the heat.

"I guess you got that repaired," Darryl chuckled.

"Yes, I did," Rose snapped back before easing her tone. "Thank you for your help that day. You've been one of the few things going right for me lately. You seem to always be there when I need rescuing."

"I try," Darryl said smugly.

"Don't get too high on yourself, mister," Rose teased.

Rose worked her way back to I-84 and then the Thruway as Darryl looked out the window.

"So, you haven't talked too much about your past. You got all the dirt on me already," Darryl stated.

Rose stiffened as she drove, focusing on the road ahead.

"I don't think you want to hear about that," Rose brushed off.

"I know you lived on a tropical island and then in Ireland. That's pretty exciting."

"Exciting isn't the word I would use for it," Rose admitted. "Traumatic is more like it. I try not to think about Montserrat a lot."

"You must have had good times there," Darryl replied.

"Sure I did," Rose acquiesced. "But running from a volcano eruption isn't one of them. Then being forced to leave my home and my mother behind wasn't great either. Or growing up as an outsider in Ireland. Don't get me wrong. I love my father, and I love Liz, and Ireland was great when I was older and going to uni, but before that, it was rough.

Coming to the U.S. was supposed to be another reboot for me, and it has been good for the most part, but my life is nothing to crow about. I have a job, pay my bills, and do what I need to do."

"Wow. I hope your life is more than that," Darryl stated.

"It's a nice job, and I love Thomas, the shop owner, but I would like to do more."

"So, what is Rose's dream?"

Rose sighed, glancing over at Darryl.

"My dream? I don't think anyone has ever asked me about that," she surprisedly answered.

"You must have one," Darryl replied. "We all do."

"What's yours?" Rose asked quickly.

"Don't dodge the question and turn it around on me," Darryl scolded. "I went after my dream when I was eighteen and got it. I have no regrets. Now, back to you."

Rose exited the Thruway in Harriman and headed back toward her condo, avoiding the question for as long as possible. Finally, she pulled into her parking spot and turned the engine off before looking at Darryl.

"My dream has always been to have my own jewelry shop," she admitted. "That Tree of Life piece you bought for Annie? I designed and made that with my own two hands," she said, wiggling her fingers. "I would love to have a shop where I could sell my own stuff."

"I didn't realize you made that yourself," Darryl said in awe. "You have real talent, Rose."

"I don't know if I would go that far," Rose responded.

"Don't sell yourself short," Darryl told her. "That necklace caught my eye right away. It stood out from the other stuff. You should make more."

"I have a few other pieces done to show, and I have some designs, but nothing I have shown Thomas yet."

"Why not?"

"They aren't done or fleshed out yet, and Thomas might not like them," Rose shook off.

"You won't know that unless you talk to him about it."

"I will. Someday," Rose said. "Thank you so much for a lovely evening," she said to Darryl, taking his hand.

"Your hands are freezing!" Darryl exclaimed, rubbing them between his large palms.

Rose looked down as Darryl caressed her hands and leaned forward to kiss him. Her lips met his, and the simple kiss quickly became more passionate. Darryl moved his left hand behind Rose's head, holding her lips to his. Rose finally moved back, her eyes slits as she looked at Darryl.

"Do you have to leave right away?" she said softly.

"Only if you want me to," Darryl replied.

"I don't," she whispered, kissing him again. "Let's get inside before the neighbors talk about me."

"Let them talk," Darryl grinned, kissing Rose more and placing his hands on her hips, sliding his index finger over to the top button of her jeans and undoing it.

"Darryl," Rose said breathlessly. His thumb and index finger had gripped the zipper and were easing it down before her left hand stopped his motion.

"Let's go inside," she said, her head resting on the headrest of the driver's seat.

"I think that's what I was trying to do," he told her as his hands rested on her inner thighs.

"You know what I mean," Rose said, attempting to regain control. She opened her car door and eased herself out of Darryl's reach, zipping her jeans up rapidly as she stepped out.

Darryl begrudgingly climbed out of the passenger seat with a bit of effort before Rose led him up the stairs to her condo. She unlocked the door and entered tentatively.

"Liz?' she asked loudly, receiving no reply. Rose walked in and turned the lights on, illuminating the hallway.

'She must still be out with Rob," Rose smiled. She took Darryl and led him down the hall to her bedroom, pausing before opening the door.

"Don't judge," Rose warned before allowing Darryl to enter her room. "It might be a little messy."

"I don't care a bit," Darryl said, pushing the door open and lifting Rose, taking her straight to the large bed in the center of the room.

Rose squealed as Darryl picked her up and placed her on the bed. He hovered over her, looking deep into her, as her hands roamed behind his neck, pulling him down toward her. She allowed his lips to roam wherever they wanted, and soon clothing flew about the room in a frenzy of action. Rose found herself in just her pale pink bra and panties, her hands reaching for Darryl's bare flesh.

"Try not to tear these," she huffed into his ear as he worked to unclasp her bra. "I like this set."

"No promises," Darryl growled, pulling her bra off before kneeling between her legs to ease her panties down.

Before long, Rose maneuvered herself so that she now straddled Darryl. She felt a surge of power other men never allowed her to have as he watched her move. Then, she stretched over to her nightstand, plucking a condom from the top drawer, before returning to her location between Darryl's legs.

"I like a woman who's prepared for anything," Darryl smirked.

"I hope that means you're ready for whatever I can dish out," Rose said, waving the condom wrapper back and forth.

"Do your best... or your worst. I can take it," Darryl challenged.

"Oh, we'll see about that," Rose answered.

She grinned widely before taking Darryl's cock in her hands, rubbing him up and down rapidly before slowing her pace. She spied Darryl looking on, staying in control of himself. It wasn't until she bent down and licked up his shaft, reaching his engorged head and the tip of her tongue underneath it, that she noticed his breathing intensify. Her tongue swirled around him before she took him deep in her mouth, repeatedly drawing herself back up to the tip.

Rose lifted her head and saw Darryl still attempting to hold on.

"I guess I need to step up my game," Rose said as her fist slowly rode over him again, causing Darryl to groan.

She locked eyes with him and tore the foil wrapper open with her teeth, pulling it from the packet and unrolling it slowly onto Darryl's cock. She moved deliberately, placing her hands all over his erection.

"I want to make sure this is on just right," she teased, squeezing the tip in her fingers.

"Rose... fuck," Darryl moaned.

"You said to do my best," she responded coyly.

"You're best is going to make my head explode."

"Isn't that the goal?" she rasped, bringing herself close to Darryl, so his cock rested outside her.

Darryl attempted to move closer, reaching for her, but Rose placed her right hand on his chest, pushing him down. She knew his heart pounded rapidly beneath her.

"My game right now," she said, relishing the control he allowed her.

She moved on top of Darryl deftly, taking him inside her quickly. She moved with purpose, finding a rhythm that sent chills through her and Darryl. Darryl's hands gripped her hips as she rode him. She gyrated on him, pulled off him, and then slowly back on him before neither of them could take it anymore. She stayed with his cock deep within, squeezing him tightly until she shut her eyes and gasped, letting her orgasm flood on him before he exploded.

Rose collapsed on top of Darryl, her head resting on his chest as her hands went to his sides. Rose listened to his heart pumping wildly before it began to slow. Suddenly, she also heard Darryl wheezing and coughing. His body began to convulse slightly, and she sat up in a panic. One quick look at Darryl, and she saw he was struggling.

"Are you okay?" she shrieked.

He nodded rapidly as he gasped.

"My inhaler," he croaked, pointing to his jeans on the floor.

Rose hopped off the bed and rummaged through his pants pockets before finding the red inhaler and bringing it to Darryl. He placed it in his mouth and gave himself two puffs. Rose watched on, placing her hand on his heaving chest as he struggled to get his breathing under control.

Rose rushed to her purse and grabbed her phone, preparing to call 911 when Darryl spoke.

"It's all good, Rose," he got out as his breaths steadied more.

Rose climbed back to the bed and sat next to Darryl as he slid over a bit. She rested her head on his shoulder.

"You scared the hell out of me," Rose said, slapping him. "Why didn't you tell me you had asthma?"

" I don't have asthma," Darryl told her as he held her close.

"Then why do you have an inhaler? You couldn't breathe, dammit! I was calling an ambulance!"

Darryl turned to his side to look into Rose's face.

"It's a little more complicated than asthma," he offered. "It's called silicosis. One of the drawbacks of working underground in tons of rock for years."

"Is it... serious?"

"I'm not gonna lie," Darryl answered. "It can be. It can't be cured. Once the silica is in your lungs, it doesn't go away. I just have to be careful about it."

"Are you getting treatment for it?"

"Yeah, the doctors want me to go for a bunch of tests and a lung biopsy. I'm in no hurry."

Rose sat up.

"Don't you think you should be?"

"Why? It's not going to change anything whether they poke and prod me or not," Darryl said casually.

"Does your daughter know?"

"No one knows," he admitted. "You're the first person I've told. The diagnosis wasn't that long ago."

"You just seem like you're being pretty cavalier about something so serious," Rose said with concern.

Darryl sat up and took Rose's hands in his.

"Look, I know it seems that way, but I am taking it to heart. I'm going to do whatever I need to do, don't worry. But, for now, can we please just keep it between us? I haven't figured out the best way to tell Annie, the club, my co-workers... anyone."

"It's not something you can hide," Rose responded with concern. "Suppose you have an attack or a coughing fit like you did while working?"

"Well, if it only happens during things like this, I don't think anyone has to worry about finding anything out," Darryl laughed.

"I'm being serious, Darryl."

Darryl pulled Rose toward him as they both laid down. Rose curled into him, resting her head on his chest to hear his heart and lungs settling down.

"I got this, I promise you," he assured her. I'm not going anywhere any time soon."

"You better not be," Rose whispered.

Chapter 13

Rose stayed close to Darryl, laying awake long after he fell asleep in her bed. Her head stayed positioned in the crook of his arm, letting her rest while listening to him breathe. He snored softly, with the occasional light wheeze mixed in that would cause her to stir. She had no familiarity with silicosis but resolved to find out as much as possible when she had the chance.

Rose battled with herself, trying to will herself to get some rest, but errant thoughts jumped in and out of her head, preventing it. For the first time in a while, she had started to feel good about herself and where her life was going. Even though it had only been a few days with Darryl, the connection she made with him was more substantial than any she had experienced in her lifetime. Never one to get too far ahead of herself, the notion that he could just disappear as quickly as he entered her life frightened her.

She had managed to drift off to a fitful slumber when she noticed Darryl stirring next to her. Rose flung her eyes open to see him sitting up on the side of the bed.

"Is everything okay?" she said in a panic.

"I'm fine," Darryl told her, looking over his shoulder at her. "I was trying to sneak out to the bathroom without waking you up. I guess me sneaking anywhere is not an easy thing to do."

Rose forced a laugh before pulling the blanket up to cover herself. She watched as Darryl pulled on his black boxer briefs and t-shirt before moving toward the door.

"You're going out there like that?" Rose asked, sitting up.

"Why? I'm covered," Darryl answered, looking down at himself.

"Liz might be up out there."

"I think she can handle it," Darryl chortled, giving a flex before he opened the door and paced to the bathroom.

Rose watched the doorway, looking for any signs that Liz might be awake, but she saw and heard nothing. Darryl returned to the bedroom and shut the door, walking over to Rose's side of the bed.

"No problems at all," he said proudly. "I'm going to run out and grab some bagels from Bagel World. Want anything else?"

"You don't have to do that," Rose insisted. "We can just stay in. I'm sure we have something." Rose knew there was little food-wise in the kitchen beyond coffee creamer and frozen waffles right now, having skipped going to the grocery store the last few days to spend time with Darryl.

"No big deal," Darryl told her. "I'm happy to do it."

Darryl donned his jeans as Rose spied him, pulling them up his muscular legs before slipping his boots on and grabbing his jacket.

"I'll be back in a few minutes," he promised, giving Rose a lingering kiss before he departed.

No sooner had the front door closed when Liz sprang from her bedroom, peeking her head into Rose's room.

"He's gone?" Liz smiled.

"He'll be back in a few minutes with bagels," Rose said, keeping the blanket around her to cover her naked body.

"Oh good, I'm famished," Liz said, entering Rose's room and sitting on the edge of the bed. "I was waiting for him to go so I could pop in and see you. I saw his bike here when Rob dropped me off last night."

"I didn't hear you come in," Rose answered.

"I tried to be quiet about it after I heard you two engaged in activity," she grinned. "You're louder than I expected, Rosie."

"Oh God," Rose said, pulling the blanket over her head.

"Nothing to be ashamed about," Liz said, tugging the blanket down to look at Rose. "I'm assuming you had a good night?"

"It was..." Rose searched for just the right word. "Wonderful," she beamed.

"Now that's what I want to hear!" Liz shouted, patting Rose's leg. "I guess I did hear it last night too, but this confirms it."

"How long will it take before I live that down?"

"Oh, weeks at least, Rosie," Liz laughed.

"Great," Rose bemoaned, pulling the blanket back over her head. "Can you get out so I can get dressed before he comes back?"

"I've seen you naked before, Rose," Liz joked. "We grew up together, remember? So I know what your tits look like and have for a long time now."

"Ugh, you're determined to make this as embarrassing as possible, aren't you?"

"That's my job," Liz crowed.

"Fine!" Rose barked, tossing the blanket aside and marching over to her dresser.

"I hope Darryl appreciates how nice your ass looks," Liz teased as Rose grabbed a pair of flannel sleep pants and put them on.

Rose plucked an oversized olive-colored t-shirt from the next drawer and put it on.

A knock on the front door echoed before the front door opened in the condo.

"Hello?" Darryl's voice resounded.

"We're having a hen party, Darryl," Liz yelled. "We'll be out in a sec once Rosie stops dancing around naked."

Rose planted her face in the palm of her hands.

"Okay, I guess,' Darryl said, confused. "I'll go make some coffee."

"Perfect! Thanks, love," Liz responded.

"Can I go out there now?" Rose said, trying to get passed Liz.

"Are you sure you want to, like that?" Liz asked.

"What now?"

"You might want to grab your cardigan, is all, because you look a little chilly," Liz added, looking down at Rose's breasts.

Rose pivoted to the mirror and spotted her nipples clearly erect under her shirt.

"I don't mind, and I doubt Darryl will either," Liz told her.

"I really hate you, you know that, right?" Rose said with a scowl as she picked up her Irish wool cardigan that her mother had knit for her years ago.

"Of course you do," Liz added, kissing Rose on the cheek. "And I wouldn't have it any other way."

Liz skipped down the hall ahead of Rose, who trudged until she reached the small dining table they had just outside the kitchen. She spied Darryl hard at work in the kitchen, putting bagels on a platter and brewing coffee. He smiled as Rose sat at the table.

'What did you get us, Darryl?" Liz asked excitedly. "I'll bet it's so good it's worth moaning about, right, Rosie?" Liz winked at Rose as Darryl carried the bagels into the dining room.

Rose rolled her eyes and gritted her teeth.

"I wasn't sure what you might like, so there's a little of everything—different bagels, cream cheese, lox, butter, you name it. The coffee should be done shortly, I think. You gals live pretty sparsely, huh?"

"Neither of us are good shoppers or cooks—at least not in the kitchen. But I think you already know that."

Before pouring a cup for Rose, Darryl brought the coffee carafe and a few mugs to the table.

"Don't mind her," Rose added, looking up at Darryl. "She's like this all the time."

"I'm learning that," Darryl laughed as he made a mug for Liz and passed it to her.

"So, Darryl," Liz said as she took a bite of a buttered plain bagel, "what are your intentions with our Rose here? I mean, beyond the occasional tumble in bed. Bravo, by the way."

"Here we go," Rose muttered. "You don't have to answer that," Rose said, looking over the rim of her coffee mug at Darryl before shooting daggers at Liz.

"No, it's okay," Darryl smiled. "I get it. My intentions are... a work in progress," Darryl answered. "But I can promise you I will treat her very well because she deserves all that and more. Is that a good enough answer?"

"Yes. For now," Liz warned. "Just know, Darryl, if you hurt her, you'll have to deal with me, and I'm pretty sure you see that I can be a royal pain in the arse."

"Message received," Darryl agreed.

"Now that we're done with the pleasantries, let's dig in," Liz said, taking a big bite of bagel.

Once breakfast was completed, Darryl made sure to take care of all the clean-up, even setting up the dishwasher to run and take care of dishes that had sat for more than they should have.

"You'll have to sleep over more often, Darryl," Liz offered, surprising him with a hug.

"Thanks, I think," Darryl answered, hugging her.

"Rosie will agree with me, but no doubt for her own selfish reasons."

Rose rushed into the kitchen, grabbing Darryl by the hand and towing him down the hall.

"Should I turn the music up to drown you out?" Liz asked after Rose.

"Shut up, Liz!" Rose yelled back, closing her bedroom door and locking it behind her.

"I'm sorry about all that," Rose apologized as Darryl sat on the bed.

"It's fine," he chuckled. "She's your best friend. It's what friends do."

"Don't take her too seriously. I know I don't. She's just—"

"Looking out for you. I get," Darryl replied, reaching out for Rose's hand and taking it in his so he could pull her to his lap.

Rose sat and smiled into Darryl's eyes. She leaned in and kissed him as she draped her arms over his shoulders.

"Thank you," she said softly.

"For what?"

"Hmmm... everything right now," Rose admitted.

Darryl turned so Rose was suddenly beneath him as his hands roamed across her stomach, sending shivers through her body. Only the ring of her cell phone on her nightstand interrupted the moment.

"Do you need to get that?" Darryl said as he kissed Rose's neck.

"I don't really want to," Rose sighed, praying it was a wrong number or someone who would just leave a message. But instead, the ringing came to a halt, only to be followed up immediately by the sound again.

"It better not be Liz messing with me," Rose huffed as she sat up and reached for the phone. Instead, she spotted that the call was coming from Riley.

"Riley, what's up? Did you forget the alarm code again? I told you to keep it on your phone."

"Rose, it's not the alarm," Riley said solemnly. "It's Grandpa. Something's happened."

Chapter 14

Rose recognized the fear in Riley's voice and heard some commotion in the background.

"Riley, where are you? What's going on?" Rose rattled out.

"I'm at the shop," she rushed. I came in like I always do on Sunday mornings, but the back door was open already. I thought maybe you had come in to work a shift or something. The alarm wasn't on or anything. When I reached the back office, I opened the door and—"

Riley's voice trailed off into sobs.

"And what?" Rose exclaimed. She spotted the look of concern on Darryl's face as she spoke.

"Grandpa was in the desk chair, slumped over the desk. There was a big gash and blood everywhere... oh God."

"Where is he, Riley?"

The ambulance took him to Good Samaritan already. The police are here now going over everything. I'm standing outside. I don't know what to do, Rose. I called Mom. The police are saying someone robbed the place. The safe was emptied. Why would someone hurt him? He loves everybody."

"Hold on, I'll be down there as soon as possible, okay?"

Thanks, Rose," Riley answered.

Rose hung up and looked around the room, unsure of what to do first. Finally, she hurriedly went to the dresser and grabbed some clothes, tossing items aside.

"What's wrong?" Darryl asked.

"The shop was robbed," Rose answered as she pulled her underwear on and picked up her jeans. "Thomas was hurt. They took him to the hospital. I don't know what's going on. I have to get down there."

Rose scanned the room frantically.

"Where are my damn shoes!" she yelled.

Darryl pulled them from the floor, halfway under the bed.

"Here," he told her as she snatched the shoes.

"I'll drive you," Darryl insisted, pulling his keys out of his jacket pocket.

"No, I can handle it," Rose said as her fingers shook as she attempted to tie her sneakers.

Darryl's fingers slid down underneath Rose's chin, lifting her face to look into his.

"You're all frazzled right now," Darryl insisted. "Let me help you."

"I can take care of myself," she huffed, standing up.

"I know you can,' Darryl said, taking hold of Rose's shoulders. "But right now, you aren't thinking clearly. You're worried about your friends. So it's safer for me to drive you."

"Okay," she reluctantly agreed.

"We'll be back," Rose shouted to Liz as the couple raced out the door.

Rose bounded down the steps and stood next to Darryl's bike, tapping her feet as he got down the stairs.

Darryl retrieved the spare helmet before putting his own on, handing it to Rose. She had it on and sat on the bike, hurrying Darryl along.

"Come on," she rushed.

Darryl jumped and the bike and started up as Rose wrapped her hands around his waist. Darryl tore out from the parking area and down to Route 17M, barely looking to see if any traffic was coming as he cut across the road and drove.

All sorts of possibilities went through Rose's mind as they worked through traffic. Finally, she coaxed Darryl to speed up through one yellow light and even got him to drive on the shoulder and make an illegal right on red to turn toward Lakes Road, where the shop was located.

The police had cordoned off each end of the street, preventing onlookers, customers, and shop owners from getting to where they wanted to go. Darryl parked his bike on the road, and Rose rushed off as soon as he stopped, tossing her helmet to him as she moved closer to where the police barriers were.

The officer standing near would not let Rose move forward, no matter how much she pled. Darryl finally caught up with her as she argued with the officer.

"I'm the other full-time worker at the jewelry shop!" she insisted. " I need to get there to see what's going on."

"Ma'am," the young officer said as politely and firmly as possible, "it's a crime scene. I couldn't let you in there even if I wanted to. You could contaminate evidence."

"He's right, Rose," Darryl agreed, putting his hands on her shoulders. "It might be better to just wait a bit and—"

Rose spun around with rage in her heart.

"Are you here to help me?" she shouted at Darryl. "Because that isn't helping anything!"

"Hey, I'm on your side," Darryl told her. "I'm happy to help you, but I'm not letting you get arrested."

Rose scanned the area quickly and spotted Riley standing in her winter coat, speaking to what looked like law enforcement.

"Riley!" Rose yelled, waving her arms to get the girl's attention. She spotted Riley's head swivel in her direction, and Riley began to walk toward where Rose stood. The plainclothes officer followed alongside, with Riley pointing at Rose.

"Rose!" Riley shouted as she ran and embraced rose, breaking down. "I... I don't know what happened. I should have never let him stay late by himself last night, but he kept telling me to go and enjoy my Saturday night."

"It's not your fault," Rose said as she comforted Riley.

The officer in the plain clothing looked at Rose and then Darryl behind her.

"You work at the jewelry shop, miss?" the officer asked.

"Yes, I'm Rose Boyle," she said as Riley stepped back from her. "I've worked for Mr. Quinn for about ten years now. What happened?"

"It looks like a robbery," the officer added. "Someone entered the building through the back door, surprised him in the office, and struck him before taking cash and jewelry."

"Is he okay?" Rose asked.

"The ambulance took him, and I haven't received an update on him, so I can't answer that," the officer said calmly. "I would like to ask you a few questions, though, if you don't mind."

"Sure, I guess," Rose answered. "I don't know what I can do to help."

"Ms. Quinn here has been informative regarding what she found this morning," the officer began. "Any insight you can give us regarding the shop and Mr. Quinn will be helpful."

A commotion occurred just behind the officers, and everyone turned to see a woman in a fur coat approaching Rose and Riley. Rose knew immediately that it was Gemma Quinn.

Gemma reached Riley and grabbed her immediately, putting distance between the police, Rose, and Riley.

"Riley's not answering anything else," Gemma insisted.

"And you are?" the officer asked.

"I'm Gemma Quinn. Her mother and daughter of Thomas."

"Ms. Quinn, your daughter is an adult. Therefore, we don't need you present to speak with her."

"Mom, really," Riley started before Gemma hushed her.

"Our lawyer will be here any moment, and then you can talk, Riley," Gemma spoke.

"Gemma, Riley might have important information that can help," Rose stated.

"You keep your nose out of this!" Gemma yelled. "It wouldn't surprise me if you were involved in all this somehow."

"What?" Rose said with shock.

"I never trusted her," Gemma said, ignoring Rose and speaking with the police. "And look who she's with!"

Gemma had pointed at Darryl, and all eyes turned to him.

"He's in a God damn gang!" Gemma shouted. "You know what those guys do all the time! I've read the papers and heard the stories. Trouble follows them. He's probably got the money on him still!"

"Now wait a minute..." Rose shot back.

"Of course, she's going to cover for him," Gemma said, getting louder by the moment. "They're as thick as thieves. She gives him the info, he does the dirty work, and then they split the take. You should arrest both of them right now."

"You're out of your mind," Rose yelled back. "I would never do anything to hurt your father."

'Sure you wouldn't," Gemma answered sarcastically. "Riley, let's go. We need to get to the hospital to see Daddy."

Gemma handed a card to the policemen.

"That's our lawyer's information. If you need anything else, talk to him."

Rose watched as Gemma stormed off with Riley, leaving Rose aghast. Then, the police turned their attention back to Rose and Darryl.

"Now, about those questions for you, Ms. Boyle," the policeman added. "If you could just come around the corner with me, we can chat at the station. I think your friend here should come with you," he said, pointing to Darryl.

"For what? He doesn't even know Thomas."

"We just need to account for everybody's whereabouts last night. This will make it easier for you and for Mr...." The officer looked up at Darryl, waiting for an answer.

"Garvey," Darryl said defensively. "My name is Darryl Garvey. And I don't see why I have to go anywhere with you."

"No one's going to force you, Mr. Garvey, but it would be helpful to us."

"This is ridiculous," Rose told the police. "You're not really buying into her crazy story?"

"I'm not buying into anything at the moment, Ms. Boyle. I'm just trying to investigate and gather facts. Shall we?"

The officer held his arm to allow Rose to lead the way. Rose reached over and took Darryl's hand as they walked toward the police station with all eyes upon them.

"Everyone is staring at us," Rose said quietly to Darryl. "God only knows what they're thinking after all that."

"It's all good, Rose," Darryl assured her, squeezing her hand. "I'm used to it. People gawk at me all the time, especially when I'm wearing my jacket. Who cares what they think? We know we didn't do anything."

"The police don't seem so sure about it."

"They rarely are," Darryl said as they arrived at the front of the police station. "Look, I can tell you how this will go before the cops get here, so listen closely. They will separate us and interview us to see what went on. Just answer them honestly. You'll be fine. I'll take care of it."

Three police officers, including the plainclothes detective, arrived to usher Rose and Darryl outside. Rose watched as they led Darryl to a room down the hall, just as he predicted. However, she was placed in a different room with nothing more than a sparse table and a few chairs.

"We'll be right with you," a policeman told her curtly before shutting the door behind her.

Left alone, Rose scanned the room, seeing a single camera up in the corner looking straight at her. She placed her purse on the table before her, rifling through it to occupy her time while worrying about what might be happening with Darryl.

Darryl knew the drill, having dealt with local, state, and federal law enforcement on more than one occasion. He sat at the table as the detective sat across from him with a legal pad out.

"Can I get you anything?" the detective asked. "Coffee, water, soda?"

"Nah, I'm good," Darryl answered. "You could tell me your name, though, since I already gave you mine. Maybe a business card?"

"Oh, sure," the detective added with surprise. "Detective Jackson," he introduced, pulling a business card from his wallet and passing it to Darryl.

"Thanks," Darryl replied, glancing at the glossy card stock.

The door to the room swung open once more, this time with a younger man in a suit and cropped haircut approaching the table. He passed a few printed pages to Detective Jackson before sitting at the table across from Darryl. The officer looked barely old enough to shave, let alone conduct an interview.

"So you're the new school guy in this scenario, huh?" Darryl asked, his chair creaking underneath his size.

"Excuse me?" the younger man said as he turned on the tablet he carried.

"You know, old school, new school. Like good cop, bad cop updated for the 21st century," Darryl grinned. "Your friend here doesn't seem to get it, Detective Jackson."

"This is Detective Myers," Jackson indicated as he read the papers in front of him. Darryl assumed it was the information they quickly gathered on him.

"So, Darryl," Detective Myers began.

"You can call me Mr. Garvey, Detective Myers," Darryl replied. "I respect you. You respect me. That's how this goes. Didn't Detective Jackson teach you that yet? How long has he been doing this?" Darryl asked as he crossed his legs.

"If you're going to be a smartass—" Detective Myers barked.

"Easy," Detective Jackson intervened, holding his hand to quiet his partner.

"Mr. Garvey," Jackson began, "we just want to ask some questions and verify your whereabouts last night."

"Why?" Darryl questioned.

"Because a crime has been committed, and you know one of the parties involved," Myers interrupted.

"I know many people, but I don't get called every time someone does something wrong," Darryl answered. "Rose asked me to drive her down here, so I did."

"So you just happened to be with a woman who has keys and access to the jewelry store and knows the combination to the safe?"

"That's right. Everyone has to be somewhere. Where were you, Detective Myers? The station is only just around the corner from the shop. You could have walked over and done it yourself."

Myers's face began to turn red as Darryl toyed with him.

"I'm not a gang member with a record," Myers yelled.

"I'm not a gang member either," Darryl corrected. "The Cosantóir is a social club. People with Irish heritage who ride motorcycles."

"Hah! Social club," Myers laughed. "That 'club' as you call it has been involved in all kinds of problems, including recently. You know Conor O'Farrell, don't you?"

"Of course I do," Darryl admitted. "He helped get me the job with the Sandhogs when I left my previous profession."

"Right... wrestling," Myers scoffed. "You were the Demon, correct?"

"Sure was," Darryl said proudly. "It bought my house and put my kid through college, among other things. Do you own a house, Detective? Or maybe you still live with your parents."

Myers slammed his fist on the table, but Darryl never flinched.

"There's no shame in living at home and taking care of family," Darryl said casually.

"How many times have you been arrested, Mr. Garvey?" Myers said, looking down at his tablet.

"You already know the answer to that if you looked me up," Darryl told him. 'Doesn't your little gadget there tell you that?"

"Three times," Myers stated. "All for assault."

"I've never been convicted of anything. Arrested, yes, never convicted."

"Is that because people were afraid of you or intimidated by the Cosantóir?"

"I wouldn't know about people being afraid of me. You'd have to ask them. I think I'm pretty easy to get along with most days."

"Do you know how many times Conor O'Farrell has been arrested over the years? Or other members of your so-called club?"

"I have no idea, but I'm guessing it's more than my three."

Darryl turned to look at Detective Jackson.

"Are you gonna say anything, or is this all's the kid's show or some training session?"

"He's doing fine," Jackson said, scribbling notes.

"Well, if you gents think I'm going to be here long, maybe I would like that cup of coffee, Detective. Oh, and if I'm being officially detained, I'd like to use the phone."

"We haven't officially done anything... yet," Myers said, rolling up his shirt sleeves.

"Then I'm free to go?" Darryl said, standing up.

Myers shot up from the table as Darryl stood and towered over the Detective, causing the young man to step back and put his hand on his hip.

"Easy there, Wyatt Earp," Darryl grinned. "If I'm not detained, I can leave, correct Detective Jackson?"

"How do you take your coffee, Mr. Garvey?" Detective Jackson said calmly, getting up from the table.

"Just black," Darryl grinned, sitting back down.

"Make your call," Detective Jackson indicated. "Come on, Detective Myers."

Darryl pulled out his cell phone and looked on as the two detectives left the interrogation room.

Darryl removed his phone from his jacket pocket when the door closed and pressed a button. Within one ring, Finn answered the phone.

"What's going on?" Finn asked.

"You busy?" Darryl said calmly.

"Not really," Finn replied. "Siobhan and I will head out to the Marketplace this morning and walk around."

"Don't bother," Darryl told him. "Lake Street is blocked off by police activity. Oh, by the way, I'm down at the station getting interrogated about it. Do you think you can swing by?"

"Christ, Darryl!" Finn exclaimed. "What happened?"

"Nothing really. My lady friend's jewelry store was robbed, and the owner was assaulted. They saw me with her at the scene. You can fill in the blanks from there."

"Don't say anything else," Finn advised.

"I'm just messing with them so far," Darryl countered. "I didn't do anything wrong, Finn."

"It doesn't matter," Finn answered. "Tell them your lawyer is on the way."

"Actually, before you come to me, I need you to tell them you're Rose Boyle's attorney. They have her in another room, and she's pretty shaken up."

"Sure. Anything I need to know about either of you that will surprise me when I get there?"

"We were together all night last night. There's proof and witnesses if needed. That's it. Just take care of her first. I'm fine."

"Fair enough," Finn agreed. "I'll be down ASAP."

"Thanks, Brother," Darryl said before hanging up.

He thought to himself, that's all I can do, hoping Rose was holding up.

Rose fidgeted in her chair, got up and paced, chewed gum, and counted ceiling tiles while she waited in the interrogation room. There had been no signs of anyone coming in, and she wondered how long she might have to stay. The free time gave her too much to think about where Thomas Quinn was concerned. Grateful that she hadn't come upon the crime scene herself, she also felt guilty about not being there to help him when he needed it most.

Rose worried about Darryl as well. Even though she knew he couldn't have been involved, she saw the way Gemma and the police looked at him, assuming the worst immediately. Like everyone else, she had heard the rumors regarding the Cosantóir over the years and what they may or may not have done. Even though she had known Darryl for just a short time, she had difficulty believing any of the stories were genuine or as severe as the allegations.

Two men walked into the room to confront Rose, one of them being the plainclothes cop she had come across at the scene. The other looked much younger, sterner, and more intimidating.

"Ms. Boyle," the older detective began, "I'm Detective Jackson, and this is Detective Myers. We just have a few questions we want to go over with you. Are you sure we can't get you anything?"

"No, thank you," Rose replied, looking at the younger man as he organized his papers and his tablet.

"Is it okay if we record this?" Detective Jackson asked. "This way, I'll know we didn't miss anything."

"Sure, I guess. Is Darryl okay?"

"Mr. Garvey is fine," Detective Myers said gruffly. "He's down the hall. We'll be speaking with him again shortly. How long have you known him?"

"Not very long," Rose admitted. "We met a few weeks ago at the shop."

"So he's been to the shop before?" Detective Myers said with interest.

"Yes, as a customer," Rose accentuated. "He bought a necklace for his daughter."

"Did you notice anything peculiar about him the first time he came in? Did he seem like he was examining things, figuring out security, things like that?"

"No, he just looked like someone shopping. Why would I think anything else?"

"You're saying you weren't afraid of him when he came in, with his size, his jacket, knowing he was with the Cosantóir?"

I don't know. I guess when he first came in, I might have been concerned because it was near closing, but—"

Detective Myers cut her off abruptly.

"So you did think he was someone to be concerned about. Did he linger around after he left the shop? Maybe walked around to the back of the building to check things out?"

"No, that's not what I'm saying. Again, you're twisting my words around. I didn't see Darryl anywhere after he shopped and paid for his purchase until a week later."

Panic seeped into Rose's tone as she spoke.

"So, when did you see him after that initial meeting?" Detective Myers asked.

"We ran into each other at Dunkin' Donuts," Rose stated, regaining her composure. "He helped me with my car."

"He just happened to be there when you were there?"

"Yes, he did. It's not unusual to run into people around here, Detective. The town isn't that big," Rose argued.

"True, but it does seem coincidental since there are several donut shops in the area, and he turned up where you were. And after that? You clearly socialize with each other based on this morning."

Rose felt the stares from both detectives as a knot formed in her stomach.

"Well, we did run into each other again at social events," Rose said uncomfortably.

"What do you mean by social events?" Detective Myers pressed.

"We met again at a speed dating event and at Millie Malone's," Rose answered.

"The Irish pub over in Harriman?"

"Correct," Rose said, hoping the older detective might jump in with something.

"Many of the Cosantóir are seen over there often," Detective Myers noted. "Did you know that?"

"I never really considered it," Rose defended. "There are a lot of people there all the time. It's a popular place."

"You don't think it's odd that you kept running into each other at these places? Do you know where Mr. Garvey was last night?"

Rose's eyes shifted back and forth between the two men as they watched her, awaiting an answer.

"Yes, I do," she sighed. "He was with me. We went out on a date and... and he spent the night with me at my place."

Rose's face burned hot with anger and embarrassment.

"So, you would say you're in a relationship together?"

"I don't know about a relationship," Rose admitted.

"Just a casual sexual encounter then?" Detective Myers asked, grinning.

"I don't like your insinuation or tone, detective," Rose said harshly. "And it's none of your business."

"It is my business if he used you to get information about the jewelry store before the Cosantóir decided to rob the place. Or perhaps you were in on it together to make some extra cash."

Rose sat with her mouth agape, stunned at the accusation and about to say something when a knock rapped on the door, and a uniformed officer entered.

"What is it, Gentry?" Detective Myers barked.

"A gentleman here says he is Ms. Boyle's attorney and wants to come in," Officer Gentry stated.

"Did you ask anyone for a lawyer, Ms. Boyle?" Detective Myers said, his attention returning to Rose.

"She doesn't need your permission," a voice echoed from the hall.

Rose watched the door to the interrogation room as a man entered, pushing his way passed the police officer to come into the room. Rose didn't recognize the light hair or the stubble, but his jacket clearly indicated he was with the Cosantóir.

"Did you know Mr. Garvey was a member of the Cosantóir before you slept with him?" Detective Myers yelled. "Or that he was arrested three times for assault? Or that they call him Demon?"

"Get your puppy under control!" the biker yelled back before looking at Rose. "Don't answer any more of their questions."

"You don't have to listen to him," Detective Myers insisted. "He's probably not even a lawyer!"

The biker handed a card to the detectives and then moved toward Rose. He leaned down to Rose.

"Darryl called me to come to help you. I'm Finn. I'm a brother, but I am a lawyer," Finn whispered.

"I'd like some time to speak with my client alone," Finn stated, staring only at Detective Jackson.

Detective Jackson nodded and stood from the table, putting his hand on Detective Myers to back him off.

"Let's go, Myers," he said.

"We'll go talk to Mr. Garvey again," Myers offered to Rose. "He may have a different interpretation of your 'relationship,'" he added in air quotes.

"Don't waste your breath on him," Finn piped up. "He's my client and has nothing else to say to you. So unless you're charging him with something, he'll be leaving."

Myers stormed out of the room, Jackson following behind him and closing the door. Finn took a seat next to Rose, who exhaled.

"Thank you," Rose said as she breathed. "What about..." she asked, pointing at the camera in the corner.

"They can film, but they can't listen," Finn assured her.

"Are you really Darryl's lawyer?"

"I am for the entire club," Finn answered. "He asked me to come to see you first."

"Is he alright?"

"Darryl will be fine," Finn noted. "I haven't spoken with him in detail about this, but he's smart. He knows what to say and what not to say. If anything, he'll say just enough to piss them off more. But, for now, let's concentrate on you. I want you to explain everything that has happened right up to now."

Rose told the story as she knew it, from the phone call from Riley to arriving at the shop and coming to the police station to the initial interview until Finn arrived.

"Are they arresting me?" Rose said fearfully.

"No," Finn stated confidently. "They don't have any reason to hold you. I think they were hoping to make an easy connection between the Cosantóir and the robbery and assault. Do you remember the places you went to with Darryl last night? I'm sure plenty of people can verify they saw you."

"We went to Beacon to the Arcade Bar and then went for pizza. After that, we... we went back to my place."

"Were you both there all night?"

Rose hesitated before answering.

"Rose, it's no one's business what the two of you did at your place. I just need to know that he was with you the entire time."

Rose nodded.

"He spent the night with me," Rose replied. "My roommate Liz can vouch for it."

Rose thought back to what Liz told her that morning about how much noise she made and blushed.

"Good enough. Sit tight for a minute. I'm going to go get Darryl, and then we'll be back for you so we can all get out of here."

Rose sat nervously when Finn got up to leave the room.

Wait," she said, halting Finn. Finn turned to face her. "Is what they said about Darryl true? About the assaults? And that they call him Demon?"

Finn banged on the door so the officer would open it for him.

"I think you should ask Darryl those questions," Finn told her as the door opened and he slipped out.

I think I should, too, she thought as she sat back in the chair, clutching her purse.

Chapter 15

The door to the interrogation room popped open, and Finn walked in to greet Darryl.

"It's about time," Darryl added, standing up and shaking Finn's hand. "That chair was killing my ass."

"Let's go," Finn said, waving Darryl out of the room and to the hallway.

"Rose doing okay?" Darryl asked.

"She's fine," Finn told him. "We're getting her now."

Darryl followed Finn down the hall to another room, where an officer stood outside. Finn opened the door while Darryl spied the officers at their desks, staring in his direction. Rose emerged from the interrogation, and Darryl immediately put his arm around her.

"You alright?" he said softly. Rose nodded as she held onto him.

"We'll be back in touch," Detective Jackson added, keeping Detective Myers at bay. "I think we still have a few questions for each of you."

"You can contact me first, Detective," Finn added. "I'll let you know when we are available for interviews."

"Don't disappear anywhere!" Detective Myers shouted toward Darryl.

"Dude, look at the size of me!" Darryl yelled back. "People notice when I come and go, so I'm sure you will see me."

"Count on it, Demon!" Myers barked.

Darryl squinted in Myers's direction, feeling anger welling.

"He's just trying to goad you, brother," Finn said, guiding Darryl toward the front door. "Don't give him what he wants."

The trio walked out to the street, Darryl's arm around Rose. He faced Finn as they stopped at the corner.

"Thanks, man," Darryl told his friend. "I owe you one."

"Hardly," Finn answered. "I'm still playing catch up for all you have done for me. They will be watching you until they figure out who did this. So stay out of trouble and call me if you need anything."

Finn handed Rose a business card. Darryl looked on as Rose shakily took it into her hand.

"Rose, that's my office number and my cell number. Call me any time you need something, okay? Don't let them rattle you. I'm sorry about your friend."

"Thank you," she said softly.

Finn made his way down the street toward his bike while Darryl led Rose back to his Harley.

"If you're not up to riding on the bike, we can walk for a bit before I take you home," Darryl offered, concerned by the sadness on Rose's face.

"Do you think you can take me to Good Sam?" Rose asked. "I want to see if I can find out more about Thomas."

"Are you sure that's such a good idea?" Darryl questioned.

"Why not?"

"Well, there's likely to be cops down there, and if they see you, they might wonder why you are there."

Rose took a step back from Darryl and stared into his face.

"So what? I didn't do anything wrong, Darryl. Neither did you."

"We know that Rose, but the rest of the world may not see it that way. Suppose Riley and her mother are there? You saw the trouble that

woman just caused for us. Do you want more of that? Besides, you may
not be able to get in to see him. So maybe it's better to wait."

"If you don't want to go, it's fine," Rose added sternly. "I'm going
whether you are or not. You can either take me there or take me home so
I can get my car. Never mind, I'll just get an Uber down there."

Rose whipped out her phone before Darryl reached over and took her
hand.

"Hey, I'm on your side in this, remember? You might not be thinking
with a clear head right now."

"Oh, is that so?" Rose yelled. "My friend is in the hospital in God
knows what shape, and I just spent hours holed up in a police station
getting accused of being involved in a robbery and assault and had my
reputation dragged through the mud. So pardon me if I'm not as calm
and collected as you are."

Rose tugged her arm away from Darryl's grip and marched away from
him, moving down the street before he hustled to reach her.

"What the hell, Rose?" Darryl added. "You think I'm thrilled about
all this? You know they're looking at me too, dredging up every little last
thing."

"And what about the past, Darryl? Were you really arrested three times
like they said?"

"Yes," Darryl said bluntly. "I've been arrested, but the charges were all
dropped. It was bar fights, mostly."

"Is it true they call you Demon?"

Darryl looked down at Rose's face.

"That's true as well," Darryl admitted. "It was my wrestling name,
Rose. It doesn't mean anything."

"But people still call you that?"

"Brothers in the Cosantóir do, and some guys on the job sites. It's not like I go around asking people to call me that. It's a nickname that stuck. It was a character I played as a job. It's not who I really am. You're not buying into what that cop was telling you, are you?"

Darryl watched as Rose hesitated for a moment.

"Rose, if you have any doubts about me, especially after the last couple of days, you should know something about me. I don't lie. You'll get the truth from me every time—good, bad, or indifferent. I am telling you I had nothing to do with this or any knowledge about it."

"I know you didn't," she said quietly. "I'm sorry. I'm just all turned around with everything that has happened. Please, can you take me down to Good Sam?"

Darryl nodded in agreement and led Rose back to his Harley. They both mounted the bike and headed off to the hospital. Nary a word passed between them on the ride. Darryl's mind pored over the facts he knew from the police as he tried to piece together what went on at the robbery. When they had arrived at Good Samaritan Hospital, he was no further along in his theories than when they left.

Darryl followed behind Rose as she went to the main lobby to talk with the concierge at the front desk. Darryl spotted the two security guards who were already sizing him up and wondering if he was going to be a problem or not. He politely nodded in their direction, causing them to rapidly turn away from him and talk closely with each other.

Rose paced back over to Darryl, looking distraught.

"They won't let me up to see him," Rose stated, on the verge of tears. Darryl held her to comfort her as he scanned the lobby. It was then that he spotted a familiar face. Darryl grabbed Rose's hand and moved across the hall.

"Cara!" he yelled, getting the attention of a woman in scrubs near the elevators. Darryl saw the confused look on her face at first as they neared her.

"Cara, right?" Darryl pointed. "I'm Darryl. I'm a friend of Finn and Siobhan's from the Cosantóir. We met a few times, remember?"

"Of course," Cara smiled. "You're not an easy guy to forget, Darryl. What are you doing down here?"

This is my..." Darryl hesitated, "my friend Rose Boyle," he said. "A close friend of hers is here, and we were wondering if there's any way we can get up to see him."

Cara pulled out her tablet.

"What's his name?"

"Thomas Quinn," Rose said hopefully.

Cara typed in the name and waited for the information to come up.

"He's up in the ICU," Cara indicated. "I don't know if you'll be able to get up there to see him. You know they limit access up there, Darryl. Remember when Conor was here? If you check with the concierge—"

"I tried that already," Rose said, dejected. "They wouldn't let me up."

"I'm sorry," Cara told her sincerely.

Darryl looked over to Cara.

"Can you get us up there?"

"Darryl, I'm really not supposed to do that. They limit who goes up there for a reason."

"Cara, I know it's a big ask, and you barely know me," Darryl said, taking Cara aside. "Rose is very close to him. She needs to see how he is. I promise you, it will just be for a few minutes."

"I could get in a lot of trouble for this," Cara answered.

"Please. I'll get down on my knees and beg if you want."

Darryl began to go down when Cara halted him.

"Alright!" she said, preventing Darryl from moving further. "You'll have security over here if you get on the floor. Follow me, and move fast."

Cara guided Darryl and Rose over to the staff elevator, using her badge to open the elevator doors. They entered and shut the doors as fast as possible before Cara pressed the button for the ICU floor. Darryl took Rose's hand and held it. She squeezed it tightly until the elevator came to a stop.

The doors slid open as Cara peeked out first before waving them into the hall. She moved until they reached room 602.

"He's in here," she indicated. "You get three or four minutes, nothing more," Cara stressed. "I'll stand out here. If you're not out in four, I'm coming in to get you."

"Thank you," Rose added emphatically.

"I owe you," Darryl added.

"Damn right you do," Cara replied. "Now go."

Darryl pushed the door open, so Rose could slip in. Rose approached the bed immediately as Darryl stood back, waiting in the shadows.

From his view of Thomas Quinn, things did not look good. The older man was on oxygen, and other machines beeped along to pump medication and monitor the patient. A giant bandage covered the left side of his head, going down over his eye so that only his right was visible and barely open. Rose could be heard quietly saying something before she took her friend's hand.

Darryl waited patiently, looking on, knowing the time they had was short. He saw Rose lean closer to Thomas as if she were whispering to him. It looked as though Thomas moved his hand to touch Rose's face. Darryl sighed in relief, hoping this was a good sign.

He glanced at his watch, knowing they were out of time. Darryl paced over to the bedside and touched Rose on the shoulder. A closer view of

Thomas Quinn let him know just how severe the injuries were. Bruising and swelling covered most of his face, where there was no bandage. His left hand was also in a cast, and there looked to be a large bandage on his left side near the end of his rib cage.

"Rose, we have to get going," Darryl said softly.

"Just one more minute," Rose sobbed, bending to kiss Thomas's forehead. "I am so, so sorry, Thomas. I'll come back when I can."

Darryl noticed Thomas's eye barely close and open. He caught the older man looking at him, and the blackened eye widened. Thomas' heart rate noticeably quickened, and his hand went from holding Rose's to grasping the sleeve of Darryl's jacket. The man tugged and made gurgling sounds, attempting to look toward Rose in a panic.

"Thomas? What's wrong?" Rose asked the frightened man.

His head shook violently before Darryl could pull his jacket sleeve away and step back. He then saw the man reach for the call button for the nurse as he jabbed at it with his thumb.

"Rose, we need to get out of here, now!" Darryl boomed. "He called the nurse's station. They'll be down here any second."

"What's wrong?" Rose asked again as Darryl led her toward the door. "He's trying to tell me something!" she protested.

Cara had already opened the door to the room as Darryl and Rose stepped into the hall.

"What's going on?" Cara panicked.

"I don't know," Rose rushed. "He started to act scared and pressed the call button."

"You two need to go, now," Cara answered, hustling them back to the elevator and opening the doors for them. She hurried Darryl onto the elevator, and just as the doors were closing, Darryl spotted other nurses coming in their direction, along with Gemma Quinn. Gemma stopped as the elevator doors closed, leaving Darryl to wonder if they had been seen.

"Shit!" Darryl exclaimed as he tried to will the elevator to move faster to the lobby.

"What's the matter?" Rose asked. "What's going on?"

"I'm not sure what's happening with your friend, but I think his daughter spotted me as the elevator doors closed. We need to get out quickly."

Once they reached the bottom, the doors opened, and Darryl led Rose out and passed several hospital staff members looking to get on. They looked surprised to see non-staff exiting, but Darryl kept moving, stepping fast toward the exit while trying not to draw too much attention to themselves.

Once they were in the parking lot, Darryl never looked back, hustling Rose to his bike and passing her a helmet so she would get on the motorcycle right away.

"Darryl, what—" Rose started to ask.

"Rose, let me get out of here before we try to decipher what's going on," he insisted.

Darryl started the motorcycle and sped from the parking lot, working his way back toward Harriman as quickly as he could without drawing too much attention to his driving. He pulled into the Lexington Hill complex and stopped outside Rose's condo building. Rose got up and took the helmet off, handing it to Darryl as he removed his.

"I'm sorry about this," Darryl offered, unsure of what else to say.

"You have nothing to be sorry about," Rose replied. "It's not your fault."

"Do you want me to come up with you? I can stay for as long as you want me to. I mean, I'm off work this week, and if you want company or whatever..."

"I think I just need to go inside and decompress for a while," Rose answered. "Thank you for everything today."

"Are you sure you're okay?" Darryl questioned. He took Rose's hand once more, bringing her fingers to his lips to kiss them.

"Yeah, I am," Rose assured him.

I'll call you later to check on you," Darryl said as Rose began to walk toward the stairs.

"You don't have to do that," Rose told him as she turned to face him.

"I know I don't have to. I want to," Darryl reminded her.

He watched as Rose smiled slightly before heading to the stairs and going up to her condo.

Darryl drove to the exit for the complex and contemplated going back to his house before turning right to go to the Hog House.

Chapter 16

Rose plodded up the stairs to her condo, opening the door and entering before settling down on the sofa and burying her head in her hands. She cried softly, letting the emotion of the situation overwhelm her. No sooner had the sobs echoed than Liz was out in the living room to see what went on.

"What's wrong?" Liz panicked, sitting next to Rose on the couch. "You were gone for a long time."

"Everything seems wrong right now," Rose cried. "Thomas is in bad shape. Very bad. He's in the hospital. I guess there was a break-in while he was there last night. Someone robbed the place and hurt him. Gemma showed up and basically accused me and Darryl of planning the whole thing. The police took us to the station and interviewed us for a long time before they finally let us go."

Oh, Rosie," Liz consoled. "They have to know you and he had alibis. People saw you. I knew you were here. I could talk to them."

"I think it will be fine for me," Rose admitted. "Darryl's lawyer friend came and got us out. I'm worried about Darryl, though."

"What about him?"

"I don't know. The police were telling me things about him and the Cosantóir. All the issues the club has been involved in over the years make it easy for people to consider them first when something like this occurs.

Then they told me he's been arrested several times for assault. They call him Demon, Liz."

"People call me a lot of things, Rose. It doesn't mean any of it is true or means anything."

"I know it doesn't. But everything the police told me and asked me has made me doubt myself—and Darryl. When you get down to it, I do hardly know him. We only went out once—twice if you count the night at Millie Malone's. And we did run into each other coincidentally quite a few times. He turned up almost as if out of nowhere several times, including at Millie's."

"You think he was stalking you? Or picked you out because you work at the jewelry store?" Liz asked. "I have to tell you, Rosie, he doesn't seem like that guy to me. Sure, he's in the Cosantóir, but I don't think that makes him a criminal or a threat. The police want you to doubt him. He's an easy target for them. There's no way he could have gotten there. He was here with you."

Rose sat hack on the sofa, staring up at the ceiling before looking at Liz.

"He went out this morning to get the bagels," Rose added.

"So? He wasn't gone long enough to get to the shop, rough up Thomas, rob the place, get bagels, and get back here without looking like he even broke a sweat or got involved in a struggle."

"What if it wasn't him but someone else in the Cosantóir?" Rose asked. "When Darryl came close to Thomas in the hospital, Thomas was frightened. He grabbed Darryl's jacket like he had seen him before, and he was trying to let me know that he—or I—was in danger. What if he didn't do it but knew about it, or was just keeping me busy or gathering information so they could pull it off?"

"That's a lot of suppositions, Rose," Liz emphasized. "You're stretching to find something because they planted a seed in your head. What does your gut tell you? Deep down, in here," Liz added, pointing at Rose's stomach. "And in here," she said, indicating her heart.

Rose rested her head on the back of the couch, still looking up, before turning her head to spy Liz.

"My gut tells me he wouldn't hurt or use me, and I want to believe that more than anything."

Darryl's motorcycle kicked up dust and dirt as he made the turn off of the paved road of Route 17M and onto the path that led up to the Hog House. He parked his bike out in front of the house, away from where some of the other vehicles were stationed and walked to the front porch. The noise level from the hangout was quiet for a Sunday when the house was usually full after the club's morning ride.

Darryl swung the front door open and entered, his boots trodding across the wood floor of the entertainment room. A few members were scattered around the room, playing cards or kicking back on one of the sofas. Darryl moved to the bar, where Rory busied himself, pulling glassware out of the dishwasher and storing it.

"Hey," Darryl said as he sat down on one of the stools.

"Demon," Rory said with surprise. "What are you doing here? I thought you were supposed to stay away for a few days."

"I know I am, but something came up that I need to talk to the Ceannaire about. Is he here or at home?"

"He's here in the back with Maeve and Liam, but—"

"Don't sweat it, Rory," Darryl told him. "I'll tell them you tried to warn me and stop me."

Darryl got up and walked to the hall that led from the bar to the room in the rear of the house. He reached Conor O'Farrell's room/office and knocked twice before opening the door. Darryl entered, spying Conor and Liam sitting together, enjoying whiskey, while Maeve sat in her oversized chair knitting.

"Hey stranger," Maeve smiled, rising to greet Darryl with a hug. "I haven't seen you recently."

"Because he's supposed to be taking a break from here," Conor scolded. "Darryl, don't force my hand by defying the club rules."

"I know, Conor, and I'm sorry," Darryl apologized. "But it's vital that I see you. Something happened this morning—"

"We already know about the jewelry store thing," Liam said as he kicked an empty chair over in Darryl's direction so he would sit down.

"How did you find out about that?" Darryl said, bewildered.

"I told them," a voice echoed from the bathroom. Darryl looked to the right and saw Finn walking toward the group.

"What happened to attorney-client privilege?" Darryl said with scorn.

"You know I had to tell them if it involves the Cosantóir, Darryl," Finn explained.

"It doesn't sound like there's much to worry about," Liam chimed in. "From what Finn said, they don't have anything to pin on you or your girlfriend."

"I don't know if I'd call her my girlfriend," Darryl added.

"Whatever," Liam waved off. "You went places and have alibis, right? You're clean."

"I think there might be more to it than that," Darryl said.

"What do you mean?" Conor asked.

Darryl sighed before he began.

"After we left the police station, I took Rose down to the hospital to see Thomas Quinn, the owner of the shop—"

"Christ, Darryl, why would you do that?" Finn exclaimed.

"She wanted to go and was going to even if I didn't take her," Darryl stated.

"You should have just let her go by herself," Finn replied, shaking his head.

"Well, we went up to see him in the ICU."

"How the fuck did you pull that off?" Liam asked.

Darryl looked over at Finn as he spoke.

"I spotted Cara in the lobby, and she got us up there."

"Jesus, Darryl, you can't drag other people into this. She could get fired or arrested," Finn retorted.

"Will you let me finish telling the fucking story?' Darryl yelled, getting everyone's attention. The room all placed their eyes on him.

"We went into the room, and I stayed toward the back while she spoke to him. He looks horrible. Someone messed him up big time. When it came time to go, I went up to Rose to get her to leave, and Quinn saw me. It was like he was looking at the Grim Reaper or something."

"No offense, Demon, but is that really a surprise? The guy was beaten half to death and saw this huge guy appear out of the shadows in his hospital room. No wonder he was scared," Liam added.

"It was more than that," Darryl insisted. "He grabbed my jacket sleeve and held it tight while he shook. It was like he knew me and was trying to warn Rose about something."

"Did he say anything to you?" Finn asked.

"Nah, I don't think he can speak right now," Darryl responded.

"Have you met him before?"

Darryl shook his head no.

"I've known Thomas Quinn for years," Conor entered. "We may not be best friends, but we know each other, and he knows who the Cosantóir are."

"Yeah, but what I saw on his face, Ceannaire, was not just recognition. It was like he was expecting me to do something bad to him - or Rose."

"People all over the area know our jackets, tats, and bikes, you name it," Liam spoke. "Maybe it's just the rumors and reputation that scared him."

"I don't know. It could be, I guess," Darryl agreed, "but I think it's more than that."

"Anything else we need to know about?" Conor asked.

"Well, there is one more thing, and you're not going to like it," Darryl told the group.

"Yeah, we loved hearing all this so far," Liam scoffed.

"Just tell us, Darryl," Conor stated firmly.

"When we were leaving his room, I think his daughter saw me as the elevator doors closed."

"This gets better and better," Finn said. "Do you know for sure she spotted the two of you?"

"Not for sure, but I'd say 90%," Darryl said. "She already let the police know she suspected the Cosantóir or me in the robbery."

"Fuck, Darryl, the cops will be all over this, you, her, and us!" Liam shouted.

"You think I don't know that?" Darryl yelled back.

"All this because you finally got a piece of ass you like? You know better!"

Darryl shot up from his chair, tipping it over, and got right in Liam's face. Liam was the one member of the Cosantóir who came even close to Darryl's size and height. The two stood chest to chest with each other.

"Don't talk about her like that, Liam. Just don't," Darryl warned.

"You get all twisted up with some woman you barely know, and now you're going to risk all of us for her! For all we know, she orchestrated the whole thing. She works there, knows the routines, the safe combination, security cameras, everything. She could have anyone do this and let us take the fall for it."

"No way, man," Darryl affirmed. "You have no idea what the fuck you're talking about."

Darryl's face was inches from Liam's as both men breathed heavily.

"Enough of this shite!" Maeve yelled, getting between the two men. "Don't bring this into my part of the house!"

Maeve walked Darryl back toward the door and away from Liam.

"Darryl, you know I love you like my own, but don't let your judgment get clouded right now. You have a job, a house, the club—a daughter—to think about."

"I know," Darryl said in a hushed tone.

Darryl looked over to Finn.

"Liam said something important," Darryl added. "Security cameras. "The store must have them all over the place."

"More than likely," Finn agreed. "I'm guessing the police are retrieving them if they haven't already. They might show something that helps you. You should also remember that the hospital has cameras everywhere too, and they'll show you going there and heading to Quinn's room. That doesn't help at all."

"Maybe we can check out the security footage? Find something that might get us out of all this?" Darryl posited.

"I can try," Finn responded. "They may not let me see them. It's not like they have charged you with anything."

"We might be able to get a look at them," Conor nodded. "I'll make some calls."

"Thank you," Darryl sighed.

"Until then," Conor began, "You need to keep yourself out of trouble. Stay away from here, stay out of work, and stay away from the girl. Keep your nose clean until we get this sorted out. Stay home and relax, watch TV, spend time with your daughter."

"But Ceannaire—" Darryl began.

"Darryl, it's the smart thing to do right now," Finn reiterated. "Let some of this die down without entanglements. Then, the police can do their job, and I promise we will be on top of it."

Darryl hung his head, nodding in agreement despite disliking the solution.

Maeve hooked her arm around Darryl's and began to guide him out of the room.

"Walk with me," she said as she shuffled him out the door, closing it behind them.

"I don't like this," Darryl gruffed as they walked down the hall and back to the entertainment room.

"Hopefully, it won't be for too long," Maeve soothed. "You like this girl, huh?"

"I haven't known her very long, but there's something about her, Maeve. We connect like I haven't with someone in ages. I can't explain it."

"You don't have to," Maeve smiled, patting Darryl's hand as they reached the front porch. "That's when you know it's good. Just be careful, for your sake and hers."

"I will."

Darryl bent down and gave Maeve a kiss on the cheek.

"Come to the house for dinner next week," Maeve told him as he walked to his bike. "I'm making shepherd's pie on Wednesday."

"I'll be there," Darryl waved.

He climbed on his bike, heading back toward town and his house. He pulled into the driveway, seeing it empty, indicating Annie was at work or out. He walked inside, heading straight to the kitchen. He found a note from Annie on the table:

I'm assuming you were with your friend last night. I'm working the day shift today. I'll pick up a rotisserie chicken for dinner tonight for us or me if you don't make it.

A

Darryl went to the living room and slipped into his chair. He pulled the lever on the recliner, lifting his feet up before kicking his boots off and letting them clunk to the floor. Then, closing his eyes, he thought back to how Thomas Quinn looked at him.

What did you see?

Chapter 17

The sudden slam of the front door jolted Darryl, causing him to sit upright and scramble in his recliner. He snapped his head around to see Annie freeze in her tracks as she moved toward the stairs.

"Sorry, Dad, I didn't expect you to be snoozing there," Annie apologized. She hung her coat up and tossed her Dunkin' Donuts hat next to it.

"It's fine," Darryl yawned, stretching out his arms and legs while staying planted in his chair. He glanced down at his wristwatch and saw it was nearly 8 p.m.

"I thought you were just working the day shift," Darryl said, stifling another yawn.

"Yeah, two people called out, of course. Just another weekend," Annie sighed as she sat on the couch. "What time did you get home?" she asked slyly.

"Oh, I guess it was around 2 or so," Darryl told her.

"I hadn't realized you were at the sleepover stage so quickly," she kidded.

"Very funny," Darryl mocked, getting up from the recliner to stretch appropriately.

"I'm just teasing, Dad," Annie added. "She seems very nice. I know it's a big deal for you."

Darryl walked off to the kitchen and opened the fridge, initially reaching for a water bottle and then spurning it for a nitro can of Guinness. He grabbed a pint glass and began his pour before feeling a grumble in his stomach.

"I'm starving," Darryl said, turning to the pantry and rummaging through to find a bag of Fritos.

"Shit, I forgot to pick up the chicken!" Annie blurted out. "I can see if Shop Rite still has one."

"Don't worry about it, honey," Darryl said as he crunched on the salty corn chips.

"Fritos isn't going to cut it for your dinner," Annie scolded.

"How about pizza?" he suggested. "Let's make it easy. I'll order a pie from Rrapi's, we'll get some garlic knots, and just hang out and watch a movie. Unless you had other plans for tonight?"

"No, no plans at all," Annie said, surprised. "Don't you have to get up early for work tomorrow?"

"Nah, I'm taking the week off," Darryl said, grabbing a handful of chips before Annie snatched the bag from his hands.

"Really? You never take time off. What's going on?"

"I have a lot of PTO coming to me, is all. "

"I wish you had told me. Maybe I could have changed shifts or taken some time off too. You'll be stuck here by yourself all day. Or will you be?"

"What does that mean?" Darryl asked, going back to the pantry to see if there was anything else for him to snack on.

"I was just wondering if you were going to have any company. You know, like a play date or sleepover," Annie giggled.

"Honestly, I hadn't thought about that. She's probably working."

"Didn't you say she works at Macha's Treasures?" Annie asked as she picked up her cell phone to order the pizza.

Darryl nodded as he sipped his Guinness.

"I'll bet she's not working," Annie said, waiting for an answer on her phone. "Did you hear what happened down there today?"

Darryl recognized where Annie was going with the conversation and sat down at the kitchen table.

"What did you hear?" he asked.

"There was a robbery down there. I heard they killed the owner. Can you imagine that happening around here?"

"The owner isn't dead," Darryl answered. "He's in the hospital in pretty bad shape."

"How do you know that?"

"Sit," Darryl said, pointing to the chair. Annie held a finger as she placed the pizza order and then sat at the table.

"They called Rose this morning about it while I was there," Darryl explained. "I took her down to the shop."

"Did you see anything?"

"No, not really," Darryl offered. "We talked to the police, though. Or, rather, they interrogated us until I got Finn down there to get us out."

"They arrested you?' Annie said, shocked.

"No, no," Darryl told her. "But they saw us at the scene, and then the owner's daughter saw us and freaked out, and they decided they needed to talk to us."

"Because your Cosantóir? Or because you're Black and look tough?" Annie asked angrily, slamming her hand down on the table.

"Maybe a bit of both," Darryl answered. "Who knows? It doesn't matter. We weren't involved in anything. There's proof to show we were elsewhere."

"It does matter!" Annie complained. "They probably figured it was easy to blame you, or her or both of you, so they could resolve it quickly and be done with it. It's not right, Dad."

Darryl reached across the table and grabbed Annie's hand.

"Nope, it's not, but I handled it. Trust me, Annie. I've been dealing with shit like this for a long time. So I know what to do and what to say without losing my cool."

"I know you do," Annie agreed. "It's just frustrating. Is Rose okay?"

"She was rattled, but I think she'll be fine. I'll check in on her to make sure. We should have ordered some wings to go with the pizza."

"How can you be so casual about this, Dad?" Annie said, rising from the table.

"Because I know I didn't do anything wrong and can prove it," he answered confidently. "There's nothing else I can do about it."

"Yeah, but people will still think you were involved somehow, especially because you are who you are. It's not right."

"People are going to think what they want, Annie. You know that. How many assholes do you come across each day that flip out over the way their coffee is made?"

"This is more serious than coffee, Dad," Annie replied. "There's a man in the hospital, and they are saying the place was robbed of tens of thousands of dollars in cash and jewelry. People will scrutinize you once the story shows that they think the Cosantóir are involved."

"They already do. It will be fine," Darryl assured.

A knock on the door got the attention of both before Annie moved to answer it. She saw the delivery person standing there, holding a pizza box.

"$28.50," the tall young man with glasses said. Annie grabbed the pizza box and pointed toward Darryl, who sighed as he pulled out his wallet.

Darryl pulled two twenties out of his wallet and handed them to the delivery man.

"Thanks for coming out on Sunday night, man," Darryl said.

"Any time, dude," the young man smiled, grateful for the large tip.

Darryl shut the door and saw Annie taking a slice of sausage pizza out and putting it on a paper plate. She kicked her feet up on the coffee table in front of the couch.

"I'm done arguing about it," she offered, taking the TV remote and sorting through Amazon Prime to find a movie to watch.

"Good. I'm too hungry to argue," Darryl answered as he returned to the kitchen to retrieve his pint glass.

"No rom-com!" he yelled. "I want an action flick."

"Fine," Annie pouted.

Rose spent most of the day attempting to find anything to take her mind off the robbery and what occurred at the police station. As confident as she was about the police knowing she and Darryl had no involvement in the attack, there was an itch she couldn't scratch in the back of her mind. It gnawed at her while she tried to nap, while she did laundry, and even while she ate dinner with Liz.

"Hey, space cadet!" Liz yelled across the table as she placed her fork down.

"Huh?" Rose answered, looking confused.

"I don't know what planet you're on, but you haven't listened to what I said."

"Of course I have," Rose insisted, piercing a piece of broccoli with her fork.

"So then you think it's okay if we have the orgy here this Friday?"

"What? I didn't agree to that!"

"I wasn't saying anything about an orgy, Rosie. Just testing you," Liz smiled, scooping up some brown rice.

"I'm sorry, Liz," Rose said, pushing her plate away. "You know I'm lost today."

"And for a good reason," Liz assured. "I get it. I wish there was something I could do to help you."

"I hate just sitting around here with all this running through my head," Rose said as she gathered her plate and took it to the kitchen to dump what was left on her plate.

"You want to go out and grab a drink?"

"No," Rose answered. "I have to get up for work in the morning."

"Actually, Rosie, you don't," Liz reminded her.

"You're right," Rose said glumly, placing her plate and utensils in the dishwasher.

"Want to watch a movie?"

"Not really."

"We can go run a lap naked around the building and see if anyone notices," Liz joked.

"Nice try," Rose added as she put the leftovers away.

"If you want to call him, just pick up the phone and call," Liz said as she wiped down the table.

"Call who?"

"Jason Momoa," Liz said snarkily. "Who do you think I mean? Darryl, of course."

"I don't think I need to phone him," Rose replied, stepping out of the kitchen.

"No, you don't NEED to, but you want to, and there's nothing wrong with that. He's your comfort zone right now, Rosie."

"I don't even know what I would say."

Rose walked into the living room and sat, staring at her cell phone in the middle of the coffee table.

"It's okay," Liz said, sitting down next to her. "I knew the day would come when I would be replaced," Liz sniffled, putting her head on Rose's shoulder.

"Stop," Rose shrugged, pushing Liz lightly. "No one's replacing you."

"Oh, that's for sure," Liz answered. 'But by its sound, he can make you feel like I never can."

"Ugh, do you have to keep bringing that up?"

"How about this? If he doesn't call you in the next thirty seconds, we go out to Millie's and get a drink? Just one or two, I promise."

"Fair enough," Rose agreed as she looked idly at her cell phone.

Liz glanced down at her watch.

"Okay, starting now," Liz said.

The words had just escaped her lips when Rose's phone rang and buzzed, startling both women.

"Wow, I'm good," Liz marveled.

Rose watched the phone move slightly on the table, reluctant to grab it.

"Are you going to answer it?" Liz insisted, reaching for the phone.

Liz plucked it up before Rose could get it and immediately turned to Rose.

"It's not him," Liz told her, examining the phone. "It's Riley."

Rose hesitated before taking the phone from Liz's hand and pressing the answer button.

"Riley?" Rose said hesitatingly into the phone. Unmistakable sobs came through the phone.

"Oh, Rose," Riley wept.

"What's wrong, Riley?" Rose insisted.

"He's gone," Riley cried. "They tried to save him, but they couldn't."

Rose choked up, her body shaking.

"I'll come down," Rose told her, fighting tears.

"No!" Riley shouted. "Don't come down here," she said in a more hushed tone. "Mom's already on the warpath. She's been talking to the police on and off all day and night. She keeps asking them more and more questions about... your friend and the club. If she sees you, who knows what she'll say or do. I'll call you and let you know what's going on and any arrangements we make."

"Okay," Rose agreed as tears streamed down her cheeks. "Let me know if you need anything, anything at all."

"I will. I'm sorry, Rose. I can't believe all this," Riley said, trailing off before hanging up.

Rose stood, dumbfounded, holding her phone.

"Thomas died," Rose said in disbelief.

"Oh, Rosie," Liz comforted. "I'm so sorry."

"I need to go," Rose said, moving to grab her coat and purse.

"Down to the hospital? Maybe that's not a good idea right now," Liz advised.

"Not to the hospital," Rose answered, turning to her friend. "I'll call you later, I promise."

Rose flew down the steps to her car and raced along the road, desperately wracking her brain to remember where Darryl's house was located. She made several wrong turns, pulled into driveways, and even stopped twice to let out yells and cries. She finally recognized the shadow of a parked motorcycle in a driveway with a dim porchlight and parked her car. Rose hesitated before stepping to the front door to knock lightly.

"Did you order those wings?" Rose heard Annie's voice echo as the door opened. Rose spotted Annie's eyes widen when she recognized her.

"Dad?" Annie called.

"I didn't order anything else, I swear," Darryl said as he walked to the door from the kitchen, carrying a bowl of freshly-popped popcorn.

Rose slid inside as Annie held the door open for her. She dashed to Darryl and threw her arms around him as she began sobbing.

"He's dead, Darryl," she wept, holding onto his chest.

"When did that happen?" Darryl said, wrapping his arms around Rose and holding her tightly.

"I just got a call from Riley," Rose told him. "It's horrible. I can't believe it."

"I'm so sorry," Darryl began to stroke Rose's hair as she cried more. "What can I do? Do you want to go down to the hospital?"

"Can I... can I just stay with you?" Rose stammered, looking up into Darryl's face.

"Of course, you can," Darryl said. He began to guide Rose over toward the couch where Annie sat.

Annie pushed a box of tissues over in front of Rose, plucking two out and passing them to Rose.

"Can I get you anything?" Annie asked sincerely.

Rose shook her head and looked at Darryl squatting down next to where she sat, taking Rose's hand.

The trio sat in silence for a bit before Annie spoke up.

"If he's dead, it's a murder," Annie stated.

"Annie now isn't the time," Darryl said sternly.

"It's something you need to be worried about, Dad. You both do. Suppose they decide to come at you with charges?"

Rose looked at Annie and then back to Darryl.

"Why would they do that? We had nothing to do with any of it," Rose emphasized.

"They already interrogated you," Annie added. "If they want to, they'll figure out a way to link things to make it look like you were involved. It's just a short leap to an arrest from there, especially for Dad."

"Do you think that will happen?" Rose asked worriedly.

"No, I don't," Darryl firmly replied. "Rose, they don't have evidence to link you or me to it. All they have is a lot of coincidences."

"But Annie might be correct," Rose added, drying her eyes. "They could turn all that into something."

"Let's not read too much into this just yet," Darryl said calmly. "Rose, are there security cameras in the store?"

"Of course," Rose spoke. "There are cameras everywhere, in the front and back of the store and outside."

"Good," Darryl nodded. "That should be all we need to acquit ourselves. Anything recorded will show who was there. Hopefully, the police already have the footage. So they can see who came in and did what."

"Dad, you know—" Annie started.

"Not now, Annie," Darryl scolded. "One step at a time."

Darryl held out a large hand for Rose to take as he helped her up from the sofa.

"Let's go upstairs," Darryl said as he led Rose to the staircase and up. Rose glanced back at Annie on the sofa, shaking her head.

Darryl brought Rose into his bedroom at the end of the hall and shut the door. Rose sat on the bed, watching Darryl.

"You didn't have to cut her off like that," Rose acknowledged.

"Anything she was going to say at that point wasn't going to be helpful," Darryl said before sitting next to Rose.

"What was she going to say?" Rose asked.

"We don't have to get into this, Rose."

"I want to know," Rose shot back. She got up from the bed and stood in front of Darryl. "I can just go back down and ask her."

"Wait!" Darryl halted her as she swiveled to face the door. "More than likely, she would tell you how the police will make things look the way they want, no matter what the camera footage shows."

"Do you think they would do that?"

"I would like to believe they wouldn't, Rose. But to be honest, anything is possible. Enough things are working against me already that if they want to tie the Cosantóir, you, or me to it, they probably can. So we have to work to protect ourselves. I'll call Finn to keep him up to speed on everything so he's aware."

"This is a nightmare," Rose said, sitting back down.

"Rose, listen to me. I'm not going to let anything happen to you. I promise you that," Darryl vowed.

Darryl placed his hand on Rose's neck and pulled her closer to him, kissing her.

"Can I stay here tonight with you?" Rose whispered.

"I wouldn't have it any other way," Darryl replied, guiding Rose to lay back on the bed in his arms.

Most of the evening passed with Darryl holding Rose in his arms. The few times they separated, Rose immediately moved near him again. Darryl pulled the down comforter up over here as she snored softly.

Darryl woke with a start when he heard his bedroom door open, and Annie whispered to him.

"Dad!" she said louder to get him up.

"What's wrong?" he asked, looking at the clock to see it was 4:30 in the morning and dark out.

"Someone's outside," Annie answered.

"What? At the door?"

"No," she said darkly. Annie waved to get him to come out to the hall.

All the lights were off in the house as Annie led her father toward her bedroom.

"I was just getting up to take a shower and start getting ready for work," she began in a hushed tone. "I went in the bathroom, turned the shower on, and returned to my room. I peeked out my window and saw a shadow standing in the backyard, looking up at our windows."

"How long ago?" Darryl said before moving closer to the window.

"Right before I came to get you," Annie replied. "Do you think I would wait to let you know?"

Darryl went to the edge of the window and looked through the gap between the curtains. He spied nothing immediately, but when his eyes adjusted to the darkness, he saw something toward the rear edge of the yard, staying just far enough away to avoid triggering any of the motion lights.

"I see him," Darryl whispered.

"I'm calling the police," Annie added, reaching for her cell phone.

"Don't bother," Darryl said as he stormed out of the bedroom. Annie followed closely behind him as he moved down the stairs toward the closet nearest to the front door.

"Dad, don't go out there," Annie warned. "You don't know who that is or if he has a weapon."

"He doesn't know that about me either," Darryl said as he plucked an aluminum baseball bat from the closet. "Lock the door behind me and don't open it unless you know it's me. If you hear anything bad or I'm not back soon, call Liam and the police."

Darryl went back to the kitchen and then out the door that led to the garage. Then, keeping the lights off, he went to the far side of the garage, flipped the switch to turn off the motion lights, and slipped out the side door, allowing him to move to an area outside the house without being noticed.

Darryl crept toward the rear of the house, reaching the corner where he could obscure himself behind some bushes. He spotted the shadow still at the periphery of the yard, looking back and forth between Annie's window and the windows for his bedroom.

Darryl knew once he tried to move with any speed, the noise would give away his location. He picked up several stones from the garden to his left and stuffed them in his pockets. He took one and held it in his right hand, feeling the smoothness of the oval rock before he tossed it several feet away from the intruder, causing the bushes along the back fence to rustle when the stone thudded in. The man's head spun around in that direction to look at what might have made the sound.

Taking the opportunity, Darryl sprang into action. He began his dash across the yard, his feet crunching on the bits of frozen turf he crossed so that the trespasser pivoted back in Darryl's direction. Darryl had built a good head of steam, and as he closed in on the man, he swung the bat around and let it go, sending it flying. The man had no time to react, and the bat caught him flush on the left shin, causing him to collapse.

"Fuck!" a muffled voice yelled. "Help!" emerged seconds later in a desperate tone.

Darryl was on the man at that point, lifting him off the ground with the hope of catching a glimpse of who it was. Instead, Darryl saw a face hidden beneath a ski mask that grunted when Darryl hoisted him up.

"What the fuck are you doing at my house?" Darryl growled, stepping further back on the lawn as the man was in his hands, struggling to escape.

"Fuck you," the man spat, his feet off the ground.

Darryl grabbed the ski mask as the man fidgeted, trying to pull away. Frustrated, Darryl pulled back and landed a head butt directly on the man's forehead. The crack was dulled slightly by the mask's fabric, but it was more than enough to put the intruder into a stupor.

Walking further, Darryl pinned the man against the fence surrounding the rear of the yard.

"I'm not asking you twice," Darryl said. "Next time I break your nose, and then another body part for every time you don't answer me."

A light groan escaped the man's lips as he struggled.

"Have it your way," Darryl answered, preparing to strike again when he felt someone hit him in the back. Darryl stood straight and turned, still holding the one man in his fists, when he spotted another masked person who attempted to hit Darryl with the bat.

Darryl hefted the stunned man above his head and tossed him over the back fence, hearing a loud thud as he crashed. Darryl then stepped forward toward the second man. The second man turned and ran toward the front of the house. Darryl chased closely behind him, slipping on the wet lawn to leave him a bit behind. Darryl caught sight of a car pulling up to the edge of the driveway with the passenger door swinging open and the driver yelling, "Move it!"

Darryl started to feel his chest tighten as he moved and slowed a bit, working to catch his breath. Then, realizing he wouldn't reach the runner, he pulled two stones from his pocket. He tossed the first rock and heard it strike the car's windshield. The driver implored his comrade to go faster.

Taking the last stone between his thumb and forefinger, Darry flipped the stone as hard as he could toward the escapee, hitting its mark. The shadow fell to the ground as the rock hit the top of his head. He staggered back to his feet before falling face-first into the open vehicle.

Darryl was on the move again with ragged breath, but the car squealed away with the door swinging open. Darryl put his hands on his knees, huffing and trying to see the car's license plate, but it had gotten too far for him to gather information.

He walked to the backyard again, picking up the baseball bat along the way, and reached the area where he had dumped the one man over the fence. He peered over the wall, but the only sign he saw of anyone there was the imprint in the soft sod and mud of where the body landed.

Darryl moved back to the front door, knocking loudly to get Annie's attention.

"Annie, open up," he gasped, wheezing a bit.

Hearing the door unbolt, Darryl leaned on the wooden door as it swung open. He saw Annie standing there, now flanked by Rose, wearing one of Darryl's t-shirts.

"Did you get him?" Annie asked.

Darryl struggled a bit before just nodding and looking at Rose. Rose recognized what was going on?

"Where's your inhaler?" Rose panicked.

"Upstairs," Darryl pointed.

Rose dashed up the steps while Annie guided Darryl over to his recliner. Darryl sat back, working to catch his breath between violent hacks.

"Dad? What's wrong?"

Fear coated Annie's voice as she knelt in front of Darryl. He looked down at her and shook his head slowly.

"I'm okay," he rasped. "I just need a minute."

Rose reappeared and handed the inhaler to Darryl. He quickly put it to his lips and squeezed the mist into his throat, feeling it hit his lungs. He followed it up seconds later with a second puff, allowing him to ease his labored breathing.

Darryl's eyes shifted back and forth across the worried gazes of Rose and Annie as his breaths regularly came again.

"They got away," Darryl answered.

"What happened?" Rose asked.

"There was more than one person?" Annie added.

"There were three of them," Darryl told his daughter. "Two around the house and one in the car."

"What do you think they wanted? Should we call the police?" Rose offered worriedly.

"I don't know what they were looking for," Darryl responded. "Calling the cops won't do too much."

"Okay," Annie said, attempting to calm herself. "Now, what's going on with you? Should we go to the emergency room? Call an ambulance?"

"Annie, I'll be fine," Darryl insisted.

"You're not fine if you look like this and need the inhaler," Annie said.

"It's silicosis," Rose said, drawing the attention of Darryl and Annie.

"Rose!" Darryl barked.

"She has a right to know, Darryl," Rose told him. "She's your family."

Annie looked over at her father. Darryl cast his eyes down to avoid contact with her.

"Why didn't you tell me? Why do I have to find out like this?" Annie asked.

"Because I haven't gotten a final diagnosis yet," Darryl explained. "The doctors still want to run some other tests, but they seem pretty sure that's what it is. I didn't want to worry you."

"Right, it's much better that I find out like this, or come home one night and find you laying on the floor, or I get a call from a job site telling me you collapsed."

"Annie, this isn't how I planned to let you know, but I don't think that's the most pressing thing at the moment. Someone is interested in one of us here, and that's what we should worry about."

"Well, what do you think they are looking to do?" Annie posited.

"Do you think this has something to do with the robbery, Thomas, or me?" Rose said, sitting on the arm of the recliner next to Darryl.

Darryl's hand covered Rose's while resting his head on the recliner.

"I wish I knew," Darryl whispered.

Chapter 18

R ose couldn't return to sleep after the commotion of the early morning. Darryl had walked Annie out to her car when she left for work and then returned inside, locking the doors and leading Rose back to his bedroom. Darryl had managed to drift off while Rose lay next to him, trying to put pieces together of what went on.

A future that seemed more certain for Rose just a few weeks ago no longer appeared that way. Now, everything hovered up in the air. The reality that a close friend had been murdered felt unreal, and the notion that people somehow thought she might be involved astounded her. Adding the morning events to that, Rose knew she may be in more trouble than she ever thought possible.

Spending time in bed made Rose more restless, and she pried herself away from Darryl to look out the window. She pulled a cushioned chair over to sit and look out onto the backyard. She spied the area Darryl had the confrontation in the far corner by the back fence. Rose puttered across the room, slipping out to the door and down the stairs. She looked around the kitchen to find all she needed to make a pot of coffee and got it started. As the smell of fresh brew permeated the air, Rose wandered around downstairs, examining the different pictures on the walls and tables.

Many were of Annie growing up, playing basketball, and at what Rose assumed were different vacation spots. Darryl appeared in some photos, and a woman Rose believed was Darryl's ex-wife Marsha. When Rose walked over to the far side of the living room, she spotted some items on a table with a few pictures.

The area served as a small shrine to Darryl's wrestling days. There were a couple of small trophies and ribbons commemorating his days as a high school wrestler, but photos were all of his professional days. Rose, never much of a wrestling fan, didn't recognize any of the faces other than a couple, including guys like Hulk Hogan and Ric Flair. However, one set of pictures caught her eye. Darryl stood tall, flexing his muscles and growling while wearing a black and silver luchador mask. His muscles strained and glistened thanks to sweat and oil on his body. It was hard to miss the bloodstains on the mat beneath him, along with streaks spread on his bare chest.

The beeping of the coffeemaker pulled Rose away from the photo gallery and back to the kitchen. She poured a cup for herself before making a mug for Darryl and bringing it upstairs. She carefully placed the one steaming cup on the nightstand next to where Darryl slept while she curled up in the chair near the window. Her pursed lips lightly blew on the coffee before taking her first sip of the Partners Coffee Brooklyn she had chosen to brew.

Rose pulled her legs up and under the immensely oversized t-shirt of Darryls she wore. Her knees were nearly under her chin as her gaze settled on the now-sunny yard before her. The weather had started to warm slightly now that it was early March, leaving areas thawing out and mud-riddled. One lone, last icicle resided just at the edge of the eave, and Rose watched it rhythmically drip from the gutter to the patio down below.

Eyeing the dripping sent an involuntary shiver through Rose's body. Goosebumps coursed over every inch of her body, causing the mug to rattle lightly as she placed it on the window sill. The noise caused Darryl to stir, and Rose spotted his eyes open and stared at her in the chair.

"You okay?" he muttered, his head resting on the pillow.

"Yeah, I just needed to get out of bed," she answered. "I'm sorry if I woke you."

"It's all good," Darryl yawned, stretching his burly arms out to the sides.

"I made you some," Rose said as she picked up her mug.

Rose returned to mindlessly staring out the window until Darryl got out of bed and stood next to her. She instinctively put her coffee mug down and wrapped her arms around his waist, holding herself as close to his body as possible. Her fingers walked their way up his back as she touched each defined muscle before sliding back down to Darryl's waist.

"You sure you're okay?" Darryl asked, running his fingers through Rose's hair, sending tingling over her body.

"About as good as I can be right now," Rose admitted. "Darryl, I'm scared."

"You have nothing to be frightened of."

"How can you say that?" Rose asked, choking up. She pulled her head back from resting on Darryl's stomach so she could look up at him. "Thomas dying is a horrible loss. He was more than just my boss. Thomas was a mentor and a friend. He's always what I imagined my grandfather on Dad's side was - kind, funny, caring, and honest. He gave me chances to work at the business, learn it, and sell my jewelry. And now, just like that, he's gone. Who knows what happens next. With the police and goodness knows who else watching us all the time, I think I have good reasons to be scared."

Darryl knelt on the floor, bringing him closer to being face-to-face with Rose. She looked into his piercing brown eyes and found the comfort she sought.

"As long as I am around, you have nothing to be afraid of," Darryl vowed.

"You can't be around me 24/7," Rose replied.

Darryl rose from his knees and quickly scooped Rose out of the chair, cradling her in his arms. Rose gasped as Darryl hoisted her into the air.

"I think I can," Darryl offered. "At least for right now. I'm on PTO starting today. I can be your protector."

Darryl leaned in and kissed Rose's neck before kissing her lips. Darryl's lips pressed to hers firmly, and Rose got lost in the moment.

"I like being in your arms," she sighed, placing her hands on his shoulders.

"Glad to hear it."

Darryl moved slightly until he could place Rose down in the center of the bed. He crawled up toward her, taking the hem of the baggy t-shirt up along with him until it was bunched around her waist. His fingers grazed across her stomach before settling on her hips and hooking inside her panties so he could tug them down her legs.

"Darryl, what—" Rose began before her breath was taken away by the movement of his fingers back up her legs to the tops of her thighs. Rose opened her legs wider as her head rested back on the pillow.

In an instant, jolts ran through Rose as Darryl's tongue found its mark. His tongue slowly went horizontally across her clit, back and forth, in a pattern Rose did not want him to stop.

"Right... right there," Rose gasped, holding Darryl's head so his tongue hit the most sensitive spot she had now.

"As you wish," he hummed, returning to work.

Rose's hand worked to the back of Darryl's head to keep him in place while he pleasured her. Her pelvis thrust off the mattress slightly to meet his mouth as he fed on her hungrily. Finally, Darryl's tongue pressed hard on the underside of her clit, proving all he needed to do to push Rose over the edge and make her come.

Rose's legs quivered as she laid them straight out on the bed. Darryl propped himself on his elbows and stayed between Rose's thighs, kissing her up and down as her orgasm began to subside.

"Shall I keep going?" Darryl growled. His fingers toyed with the damp strip of hair covering Rose's sex.

"Only if you want to turn me into a puddle here on your bed," Rose panted, still riding the end of the last wave.

"I think I'm okay with that," Darryl grinned as his left index finger lightly dipped inside Rose, making her moan again.

Only the buzzing of a cell phone could interrupt Darryl from achieving his goal. When Rose heard the familiar tone, she knew someone was calling her. Darryl continued to caress Rose outside and inside before Rose began to tremble again.

"Darryl, I should get—" Rose began to blindly reach for the buzzing phone, wanting to answer it but not wanting the pleasure to end.

"Get it if you want, but I'm not stopping," Darryl instructed.

"Please," Rose begged, reaching with her left hand for the phone while she balled up the sheet in her right palm, attempting to hold on.

"Please what, Rose? Please stop and let me get the phone? Or please, don't stop making me come again?"

Rose closed her eyes tightly, lightning bolts crisscrossing inside her eyelids while the phone's ringing became fainter and fainter in her ears.

Darryl's fingers hovered just above Rose's wetness, awaiting further instructions.

"Please," Rose uttered softly, "don't stop."

"That's what I thought," Darryl answered. His index finger grazed across her swollen clit before it plunged into her.

Rose found herself grinding against Darryl's fingers. Once he curled inside and tapped her most sensitive spot, Rose's orgasm flowed throughout her body. She clenched Darryl's digits, holding them in place as she groaned loudly.

Darryl sat up and moved to the top of the bed, sitting next to Rose while she worked on composing her body. Every inch of her flamed and flushed as she peered at Darryl. Darryl casually sipped his mug of coffee, smiling the entire time.

"Can I get your coffee for you?" Darryl asked.

Sweat coated Rose's brow and soaked through the t-shirt she wore. She turned to Darryl and cracked a smile.

"No thanks," she huffed. "Water would be better. Puddles need water."

"I'll go grab you a bottle," Darryl laughed, climbing from the bed.

Rose placed her hand on her chest, and her breathing calmed. She pushed the t-shirt down from her waist to cover her body. Bliss reigned the moment until Rose looked to her left and saw her cellphone flashing, letting her know she had a message.

She scooted over on the bed, so the phone was in reach and pulled it toward her. The missed call was from a local number she did not recognize, but they had left a message for her. Rose laid her head back on the pillow, put her phone on speaker, and pressed play on her voicemail, shutting her eyes and expecting it to be more nonsense about extending her car's warranty. But, instead, a gravelly voice kicked in almost immediately:

Good morning, Ms. Boyle. My name is Victor Gunderson. I'm an attorney over in Highland Falls. I represent the estate of Thomas Quinn. I know it's unusual since Mr.Quinn just passed, but his daughter has asked for the reading of his will later today. Since you are named in the will, I called to see if you wish to attend. It will take place at my offices at 4 p.m.You can contact me at this number if you have any questions. Thank you for your attention, and I hope to see you later today.

Rose sat up and grabbed the phone. She pressed the button to replay the message to be sure she heard it correctly. Darryl walked into the room with two water bottles as the recording finished.

"What was that?" he asked, passing her a bottle and climbing onto the bed with Rose.

"It's a message from some lawyer," Rose indicated. "They're reading Thomas' will this afternoon and want me to attend."

"Reading his will already? That seems pretty quick to me," Darryl answered.

"Me too. I can't believe I'm even in it."

"Had Thomas ever mentioned anything like that to you?"

"Never," Rose admitted.

"Well, it's weird that they are doing it today. The man just passed away yesterday. His daughter probably can't wait to get him in the ground," Darryl added. He put his arm around Rose and pulled her close, resting her head on his chest.

"Darryl, that's not nice," Rose scolded.

"It's true," he defended. "You said yourself Gemma's selfish and greedy. She's anxious to get her hands on his money."

"Even so, if that's the way he wanted it, then that will happen. It probably means the end of my working at the shop, though. That breaks my heart. I loved that shop. I don't know what I'm going to do now."

Rose snuggled in with Darryl as he kissed her forehead.

"It may not seem like it right now, but maybe this is fate telling you that you have a chance to do what you want now."

"I told you I don't believe in fate," Rose scoffed. "Coincidences, yes. Fate, no."

"Whatever you call it, Rose, I think it's in front of you now. You just have to decide what you're going to do about it."

Rose lightly kissed Darryl's bare chest before closing her eyes.

"I'm not ready for that yet," she sighed.

Rose initially considered going to the lawyer's office alone to avoid further entanglement with Gemma and Darryl, but as the hour grew closer to leave, fear built in her stomach that she would not hold up under Gemma's scorn and scrutiny for just being present. She didn't need to get the words out of her mouth as Darryl was prepared to go with her from the start. She acquiesced to riding on the back of his bike since it was a warmer March day. However, the ride up the steep Route 6 that led to the nearly-deserted road leading back through West Point property to get to Highland Falls sent more than one chill through her.

Darryl parked his bike in the small driveway just outside the office of Victor Gunderson, Esquire. Rose took off her helmet and grasped Darryl's hand as the couple made their way toward the entrance at the lower portion of the house marked as an office.

Rose looked around at the small waiting area and spotted an unmanned desk.

"I'll be right there!" A voice echoed from the back office.

An older gentleman emerged, silver hair slicked back. He greeted Rose with a welcoming smile.

"I'm sorry. My receptionist had to leave early today, so I'm running around getting things done. How can I help you?"

"I'm Rose Boyle," Rose stated as the man eyed her before turning his gaze to Darryl.

"Oh yes! Ms. Boyle. I'm glad you could make it on such short notice. I'm Victor Gunderson. I'm Mr. Quinn's lawyer. Thank you for coming."

"I must admit, it was surprising to hear that they were reading his will so soon," Rose said skeptically, "or why I'm even included."

Rose spied Victor looking at Darryl with trepidation before turning back to Rose.

"Do you want to speak privately about this?" Gunderson indicated, giving Darryl a side glance.

"This is my friend, Darryl Garvey," Rose said, unsure what to call Darryl. "It's okay to speak in front of him."

Darryl grinned widely, clearly unsettling Victor, bringing out a smile and titter from Rose.

"Okay then," Victor coughed. "Well, Ms. Quinn, Thomas' daughter, wanted to complete the paperwork early. It's not conventional, but Thomas didn't specify anything about a timeline in his will. As to you being in the will, I can tell you that Thomas thought very highly of you when I spoke with him personally, so it's not a surprise to find you mentioned."

The outer office door swung open abruptly, with Gemma Quinn marching through and Riley following a few steps behind her. Gemma removed her sunglasses once in the dimly lit office. She came to a screeching halt when she spotted Rose and Darryl in attendance.

"Gunderson, what are THEY doing here?" Gemma said snidely. "They don't belong here."

"Ms. Quinn, your father's will includes Ms. Boyle, so she is entitled to be here for the reading. I explained to you on the phone that anyone in it would be contacted."

"I can't imagine why Daddy would include you," Gemma spat at Rose.

Rose noticed Darryl grip her left hand tightly.

"I see you brought your thug boyfriend with you," Gemma sneered. "He has no reason to be at this."

"Ms. Quinn," Victor interrupted. "Ms. Boyle can bring anyone she wishes with her. That's her decision."

Gemma snorted with derision, turning away from Rose and Darryl.

"Fine. Let's get down to this, then."

Victor led everyone into his wood-paneled office, pointing to a round table at the room's far end. Gemma muscled her way to the seat nearest the head of the table where Victor had his portfolio laid out. Rose sat at the opposite end, guiding Darryl to the chair next to her. Rose spotted Riley sitting across from her with a mournful face. Rose stretched her hand across the table toward the young woman, and Riley did the same as their fingers touched.

"I'm so sorry, Riley," Rose uttered softly.

"You don't need to speak to her," Gemma scowled, pulling Riley's hand back.

"Okay then," Victor stated. "Let's get started with this."

Victor opened his portfolio and took out the folders and envelopes.

"Most of Thomas's will is straightforward," Victor began, looking through the paperwork. "You will each receive a copy. However, the bulk of his estate is left to his daughter, Gemma."

Gemma smiled broadly upon hearing the statement. Rose caught a glare from her as Victor continued.

"A few specifics are excluded from that part of the estate," Gunderson continued, clearing his throat. "His house in Monroe and its contents are left to his granddaughter, Riley Quinn."

Riley's eyes widened before she began to cry.

"Well, that was nice of him," Gemma said curtly. "At least you have a place to go now."

"While the bulk of Quinn Fine Jewelry belongs to Gemma Quinn, there is a stipulation that Macha's Treasures in Monroe and all of its debts and assets are left to Ms. Rose Boyle. The other facilities in New York belong to you, Ms. Quinn."

Rose sat dumbfounded as Gemma erupted and slammed her hands on the table.

"What?" Gemma screamed. "He can't do that!"

"I'm afraid he can and did," Victor stated, looking at the documents. "Mr. Quinn owned the building on Lake Street outright. So he can specify who he wants to inherit it."

" There's no way I will let that happen," Gemma insisted.

"I'm afraid Mr. Quinn was quite clear about the document, and it is perfectly legal, I can assure you, Ms. Quinn. Now you can hire your own attorney if you wish to."

"You can bet your ass I will," Gemma yelled. "No doubt this one here had undue influence over my father to make him do that."

Gemma pointed an accusatory finger at Rose, who recoiled as Gemma yelled.

"What?" Rose replied. "I never did anything. I had no idea I was even in his will."

"Sure you didn't," Gemma laughed. "I'm sure it wouldn't take much for you to get him to go along with anything. Wear a tight, low-cut dress to work, be extra friendly, and voila! You get what you want. First, you use a gang to rob the place so that you can take the store over. Then you can do what you want with the money and everything else."

"None of this is true!" Rose spoke. "I never asked for anything or wanted anything from Thomas beyond my job. I certainly wouldn't do any of the things you described."

"This isn't the end of this!" Gemma slammed her palms on the table again. "You'll be hearing from my lawyer, Gunderson! Come on, Riley."

Gemma grabbed Riley and tugged the young woman from her seat, pulling her out of the room as Rose sat aghast.

"I'm sorry for that," Victor said, straightening his tie as he pulled a manila envelope from his pile. "Here is a copy of the will and the paperwork related to the property. There is also this envelope," he said, holding it up. "Its contents are for you."

Victor passed the items to Rose, who sat still with everything in front of her. She glanced down at the manila envelope and saw her name in Thomas's distinctive cursive across the front. Her eyes welled as she gazed at it.

"What happens next?" Darryl asked the lawyer.

"Well," Victor said, removing his wire-rimmed glasses and using a tissue to wipe them, "if Ms. Quinn chooses to contest the will in probate, it's hard to figure how long it might drag out. If you need any advice or representation, please contact me. Thomas was a good man. He was my friend for many years. It devastated me when I heard about him. He always spoke highly of you, Ms. Boyle. I think he knew you would make the right choices for that shop."

"Thank you," Rose said sincerely. She stood up from the table, with Victor and Darryl rising also.

Rose emerged from the meeting in a daze. Darryl led her out the door and toward his bike. But, before they could get there, Rose spotted Gemma emerging from behind the wheel of her Cadillac Escalade.

"Now what?" she muttered, but loud enough for Darryl to hear it.

"I don't know what you think you're up to, Rose," Gemma shouted, "But I can guarantee you that you will not end up with that store. You can have your enforcer here intimidate me all you want, but it will not work."

"Look, lady," Darryl began. 'I've been quiet and polite every time I have come across you. I don't know what you think is going on here, but trust me, if I was going to intimidate you, you would know it."

"Is that a threat now?" Gemma retorted. "See what I mean?"

"Darryl, please," Rose said, standing before him. "Gemma, I'm not up to anything other than trying to mourn the loss of your father and my friend. I never expected or wanted anything from Thomas."

"Good," Gemma nodded. "then you'll have no problem giving up this ridiculous claim to the store."

"I... I didn't say that," Rose added. "I need to look at everything and think about all this. Thomas obviously wanted to keep the store going after he was gone. If that's what he desired, I will respect his wishes."

"Have it you're way," Gemma responded. "This is far from the end of this."

Gemma marched back toward her vehicle, slamming the car door loudly as she got in. The tires squealed loudly as Gemma backed out of the driveway and sped off.

"Never a dull moment with you, is there?" Darryl asked Rose as he passed her the extra helmet.

"Can we go home, please?" Rose asked, waiting to climb onto the bike.

"Your home or mine?" Darryl asked as he sat on the motorcycle.

"Yours, if I'm still welcome there," Rose sighed. She leaned her head against Darryl's back.

"Of course you are," Darryl told her.

Rose hugged him tightly as Darryl maneuvered the bike back toward Route 293. Rose watched the blurs of the bare trees whizz by as they moved along the road and reached Route 6. Dusk closed in around them, and Rose looked down as they crested the top of the hill, examining the recent sprawl of the area with stores, malls, and homes of all shapes and sizes below.

Rose gripped Darryl's waist, getting closer to him as the bike idled at the traffic light.

"You okay?" Darryl asked loudly.

"I don't know. I feel like I'm not sure about anything right now."

Chapter 19

The ticking of the kitchen wall clock echoed throughout the room as Darryl and Rose sat silently at the table. Darryl sipped from his pint glass, enjoying his Guinness while he watched Rose stare down at the sealed envelopes in front of her. Her lithe fingers fiddled with the edges of the manila, threatening to open them but never acting on it.

"Are you going to open them?" Darryl asked, polishing off the rest of his beer. He stood up from his chair and paced to the refrigerator, grasping another nitro can. He waved a second can in Rose's direction.

"Got anything stronger?" she asked.

"That's my girl!" Darryl beamed. He opened a cabinet to the right of the fridge and looked at the liquor bottles before him.

"Irish whiskey, Scotch, bourbon?"

"Do you have the makings of a White Russian?"

Darryl scoured the cabinet to find the half-used Kahlua bottle and a closed Grey Goose bottle. He quickly mixed the cocktail with some cream and ice and poured it out into a rocks glass before placing it in front of Rose.

Rose lifted the glass and sipped it before sighing.

"The Dude abides," she smiled.

Darryl broke out in laughter as he put the cream back in the fridge.

"What's so funny?" Rose asked him.

"I never would have pegged you as a 'Big Lebowski' fan, is all," Darryl said.

"It's a guilty pleasure of mine," Rose blushed as she took another drink.

"Mine too," Darryl admitted. "We can watch it later if you want. But, for now, you need to decide what you're doing with those. You're making me crazy just fiddling with them like that."

"I don't know," Rose answered, pushing the envelopes more toward the middle of the table. "Part of me doesn't want to open them. I don't want to see what Thomas had to say. It makes it all seem so... final."

"I get it," Darryl consoled. "You don't have to do this tonight."

"The other part of me really wants to see what's in that envelope," Rose added, tapping the table with her index finger.

Darryl placed his fingers on the two envelopes, sliding them on the table.

"The one here," Darryl indicated, spinning the item under his right hand, "is the will. You pretty much already know what it's going to say. Gunderson told you what Thomas left you. So it's this one here," he said, imitating his movement with his left hand, "that's the mystery."

"It might be nothing more than a simple note from Thomas that will make me cry," Rose offered.

"True," Darryl nodded. "But you'll never know until you open it."

Darryl pushed the packet with Rose's name on it closer to her and watched her tap on it repeatedly until he reached his hand across and stopped her.

"You want me to do it?" he asked.

Rose nodded and passed the envelope back to Darryl.

Darryl carefully slid his finger under the sealed flap to peel it open. He reached inside and pulled out two smaller, white envelopes and placed them on the table. One was labeled "Read Me First." He glanced at Rose, who sat watching his every move, hands on her face as if anticipating a jump scare during a horror movie.

Darryl tore open the "Read me" envelope and removed the single sheet of paper. He found a note written in classic calligraphy with an old ink pen.

"He's got nice handwriting," Darryl commented as he looked at the letter.

"It was something Thomas prided himself in," Rose answered. "He even had an old quill and ink bottle he would sometimes use to write special notes for gifts. So, what does it say?"

Darryl cleared his throat before he began reading aloud.

My dear Rose,

Unfortunately, if you're reading this letter, I am no longer with you. Please try not to be sad about my departure. We all know it is an inevitable part of life. If you have received this letter from Victor Gunderson, you are also aware that I have left ownership of the shop from top to bottom. Macha's Treasures was the first jewelry shop I opened many years ago with my beautiful wife, and it has always been dedicated to her. I know the business may not be as profitable as the other shops I have had, but it is the one that has always meant the most to me.

From the moment you came into my shop, I knew that you were the ideal person to work with and train and the one that would take the best care of our little treasure. You have the passion and respect for the customers, the heritage, the history, and the jewelry just like my beloved had, and I know you will continue with that.

It all belongs to you now, Rose. Follow your heart and do what is best. You will know what that is. Continue to be the wonderful person I have known you to be. I know you will find all that you are looking for in life. Embrace

every precious moment and make the most of it. I'm sure I'll see you again
someday.

Thomas

Darryl looked over at Rose, tears streaming down her face before she buried herself into the palms of her hands and wept.

Darryl picked up the second white envelope and opened it. Inside, he found a single key and another note.

"There's more, Rose," Darryl said, looking down at the note before passing it to Rose. "I don't know what this one says."

Darryl watched as Rose took the note and examined it, wrinkling her brow with a puzzled look.

"Teacht ar an crann na beatha," Rose said softly.

"I know it's Gaelic, but I only know a few words. Do you understand it?"

Rose nodded.

"I understand the words. It says, 'Find the Tree of Life.' I'm just not sure what he means by it."

"Maybe he was just being philosophical," Darryl offered.

"Maybe," Rose said as she placed the note down. "He knew I always felt the Tree of Life was meaningful and important."

"Okay, then do you know what this is for?" Darryl asked as he held up the key.

Rose reached over and plucked the key from Darryl's hand so she could examine it. She turned it over and over before looking back at Darryl.

"I have no idea," Rose shrugged. "It's not one of the keys to the shop doors. I already have those from the past. I don't recognize it."

"That's odd," Darryl pondered. "It wouldn't make sense for him to give you a key that had nothing to do with the shop. It could be for anything."

"I know there's a locked drawer on the desk in the office, but these don't look like a desk key."

Darryl looked closer at the key, attempting to figure out what it could be. The key was of an odd shape and size, not like a standard door lock but too large to fit into something like a locker or safety deposit box.

"Well, the only way we will find out is to go to the shop and try it out," Darryl said, pushing himself back from the table and standing up.

"As soon as the police clear it as a crime scene, we can do that," Rose answered. "But who knows when that will be?"

Darryl reached for another can of Guinness but eschewed it and went for a water bottle instead.

"Then maybe we don't wait," Darryl stated.

"What?"

"Maybe we don't wait. You have the keys to get in and out, and you can turn off the alarm, assuming it's even turned on right now. So we take a quick look around and leave."

"Darryl, I'm not doing that," Rose refused.

"Why not? Don't you want to know?"

"I do, but I don't want to break the law either. We already have the police suspicious enough about both of us. The last thing I want to do is go to a crime scene right near the station so they can catch us entering."

"Rose, someone broke into the shop and killed Thomas for a reason," Darryl spoke. "Sure, it could have been a case of a robbery gone bad, and they didn't expect him to be there, but it could also be something else. Maybe someone is looking for whatever this key opens."

"If that's true, we should just let the police find it," Rose reasoned. "Why give them more reason to suspect us of something?"

"It's your decision, Rose," Darryl. "We don't have to do anything you don't want to do."

Darryl moved behind Rose and began to massage her shoulders. Darryl worked to loosen the tension in her neck, and a sigh escaped from Rose's lips.

"That feels so good," Rose said.

"I aim to please," Darryl offered as his thumbs rubbed at the base of Rose's neck. First, he lifted her hair hanging down to her shoulders and moved it so he could gently kiss her neck. Next, his hands moved to her biceps and kept massaging.

"We can move this from the kitchen, you know," Darryl whispered into Rose's ear before nibbling on her ear lobe, eliciting a giggle.

"Oh? And where do you suggest we go?"

"Your choice," Darryl said, placing his hands at Rose's waist. "The bedroom, the couch, the kitchen floor, whatever."

"Hmmm, how about the couch?" Rose asked as she stood up. Darryl wrapped his arms around her waist and pulled her to him so her back was against him. "We can relax and watch 'The Big Lebowski.'"

Darryl pulled back from Rose and spun her around to face him.

"You really want to watch a movie right now?" he asked, exasperated.

"Why, don't you?"

"It wasn't my first choice of activity."

"Oh, and what was your first choice?" she asked coyly.

"Do you need me to spell it out?" Darryl reached for Rose's body, but Rose playfully pulled away from him.

Rose dashed to the couch, throwing herself on it as Darryl came behind her. She rolled over beneath as Darryl went to work tickling her ribs and waist until she laughed hysterically.

"Okay, I give!" she squealed.

"I had no idea your body was so sensitive to touch," Darryl added as his hands caressed the bare flesh exposed just above the waist of the black linen pants Rose wore.

"Hmmm, I'm sure you already knew that," Rose purred.

Darryl's hands moved up further, reaching the base of Rose's bra before he moved them deftly to undo the front clasp.

"What are you doing?" Rose said, gasping as Darryl's thumbs grazed across her pert nipples.

"Picking up where I left off," Darryl growled into Rose's ear.

"We shouldn't," Rose added. "Annie might come walking in at any moment."

Darryl took a quick look at his watch and realized Rose was correct.

"I guess we need to move faster then," Darryl grinned. He leaned back down and kissed Rose as she put her hands on his waist and fumbled with his belt buckle.

No sooner had Darryl completed unbuttoning Rose's blouse, exposing her breasts to his hungry hands and mouth, when the creak of the front door opening filled the air. Darryl jolted upright off of Rose and peered his head over the arm of the couch to see Annie walking in. Rose hustled to close her bra and began to button her shirt.

"Oh, geez. Really, Dad?" Annie said, turning away from the scene on the sofa.

"I didn't expect you home already," Darryl mumbled, fastening his belt.

"You have a more private spot than the living room," Annie said, avoiding turning around. "I'm going up to my room. Nice seeing you, Rose."

Annie's feet pounded up the steps, and Darryl heard her bedroom door close before he looked back at Rose. Rose sat on the couch, blushing with several of her blouse buttons still undone.

"Perhaps I can come to your house one day without her finding me barely dressed," Rose added in embarrassment.

"I'm so sorry," Darryl apologized. "It's been a very long time since I've had a girlfriend, let alone someone who has spent the night."

Rose stood from the couch and stared at Darryl.

"So, I guess that makes me your girlfriend," Rose smiled. "That's the first time you've said that."

"I know. It sounds kind of corny."

"What?" Rose added, putting her hands on her hips.

"It's just that... I don't know. It seems kind of high school to say the whole boyfriend-girlfriend thing. You're getting my brain all mixed up, I guess."

"I like that I rattle your brain," Rose said softly as she moved by Darryl, purposely giving him a clear view of her cleavage while her fingers grazed his chin to shut his partly open mouth as he gaped at her.

"Where are you going?" Darryl asked as he watched Rose move.

"I'm going up to your more private spot," Rose said, looking back over her shoulder. "I'm hoping my boyfriend will join me."

Rose took three steps up before turning back toward Darryl.

"Just in case you weren't sure, that means you," she grinned as she turned to go upstairs.

Darryl stood in awe for a moment before his brain reminded his feet to get moving and follow Rose upstairs to the bedroom.

Rose woke with a start, sitting up in the bed, panting. She looked to her left and saw Darryl sleeping soundly. She climbed out of bed and peeked out the window, checking the backyard to see if she spotted anyone spying on them this evening. The moon illuminated the backyard, and Rose saw nothing, not even the wind moving the branches on the trees or bushes. She sat down in the chair facing the window but turned her attention toward Darryl.

Peaceful, low snores escaped his mouth as she watched his bare chest move up and down. She reflected on all that had occurred recently and what it might have been like had Darryl not been there with her. Relief washed over her knowing that he was.

Rose got out of the chair and walked to her side of the bed, grabbing the blouse and panties she had tossed on the floor earlier to put them back on. She quietly left the bedroom and moved downstairs, going to the kitchen to grab a water bottle from the fridge. She unscrewed the top and took a sip before her gaze turned to the kitchen table. There she saw the letter from Thomas, along with the key. Rose paced over to the table and reluctantly picked up the letter, reading it herself for the first time. Tears formed once more as she took in Thomas's words. She wiped them away before taking the key off the table and walking back toward the living room.

Rose sat on the couch, flipping on the floor lamp next to the sofa and rereading the note.

"Find the Tree of Life," she whispered aloud. "What are you talking about, Thomas? And what is this key for?"

Rose examined the key closely, running her thumb over each notch and curve to figure out what the key might open. She closed her eyes and scanned her memory for all the places locks existed in the shop. The key looked nothing like the ones for the front or rear doors, the office door, or even any display cases in the shop. The safe had a keypad on it and was entirely digital, and the desk drawer lock seemed too small for this key.

The heavy thud that echoed in the room had Rose flinging her eyes open. She spied Darryl working his way down the stairs and coming toward her.

"Everything alright?" Darryl asked as he approached. He sat down on the sofa next to Rose, placing his hand on her bare knee.

"Yeah, I just couldn't sleep," Rose replied. She placed the letter and note down on the arm of the couch and turned the key over and over in her hand. "I didn't mean to get you up."

"No worries," Darryl answered. "It seems the world wants me up at four in the morning even when I don't have work."

"I'm sorry." Rose placed a light kiss on Darryl's lips. "I've just been thinking about Thomas, this whole mess, and this key."

"I get it," Darryl told her, putting his arm around Rose so she could rest her head on his shoulder. "He means a lot to you. So it's natural to be upset about it."

"It's more than being sad. It's terrifying, unbelievable, crazy, and mysterious all at once. There are so many unanswered questions. Why would someone kill that man? Thomas would have given them anything they wanted. I'm sure of it. We talked about what would happen if someone tried to rob the place while either of us was there. We had a plan just to let them take whatever they wanted. It's all covered by insurance anyway. The jewelry and cash mean nothing in the big scheme of things. There would be no reason to hurt him. I just can't put it together."

The two sat silently together for several minutes, the only sound coming from the wind calling at the windows. Then, finally, Rose cuddled in with Darryl, burying herself in his arm.

"Let's do it," she murmured, her eyes still closed.

"Do what?" Darryl asked.

"Go to the shop. I need to see it and figure out what happened and what that key is for."

"Are you sure, Rose?" Darryl questioned. "You may not want to see what's there. It might make sense to just wait a bit for the police to clear the scene and for you to get cleaners in there before you step into it. It's not going to be pretty. I never should have suggested it to you."

"It's a little late for that now," Rose answered. You planted the seed in my head."

"There are risks involved in this, Rose. If the police show up while we're there, we're screwed."

"I guess we'll have to make sure that doesn't happen," Rose said, rising from the couch and looking at Darryl. "I'm going to get dressed and get in my car. If you're joining me, you might want to put some pants on."

Rose walked upstairs and pulled her pants on as Darryl filled the doorway. She eyed him as he moved to his closet and grabbed a pair of jeans off the shelf. Once he had a t-shirt, he looked over at Rose.

"I'm not going to let you go down there by yourself," Darryl insisted. "You just have to promise me one thing."

"What's that?" Rose replied as she slipped her shoes on.

"If anything goes down with the police or anyone else, you get out of there as fast as you can and let me deal with the fallout."

"I wouldn't let—"

Darryl cut Rose off immediately. He stared down at her with a severe look.

"I'm not kidding around, Rose. You haven't dealt with anything like this before. If the police are there, just let me take the heat for it. If it's anything else or anyone else, you get out as fast as you can and call Finn."

"You made it sound like it would be no big deal to do this," Rose replied.

"It might be, but there are no guarantees. Whoever robbed the place initially might go back to grab anything they didn't get the first time. The point is, you don't know and need to be prepared for that. Promise me, Rose. I won't let you go if you don't."

"You won't let me?" Rose said, shocked. "I hate to tell you, Darryl, but no matter how big you are doesn't matter. I haven't asked for permission to do anything since I was twelve and living with my father. I'm not going to start now. I thought you would have figured that out about me."

"Just promise me, and we won't have to deal with the rest of it," Darryl implored.

Rose reached and put her hand on Darryl's chest.

"I'm promising because I know you're trying to protect me," Rose told him. "That's as good as you're going to get."

"I'll take it, I guess," Darryl resigned. "We're taking separate vehicles, though. Just in case you need to get out of there."

"Whatever you say, boss," Rose saluted.

"You're acting pretty casual about something you were against completely hours ago," Darryl said as he made his way out of the room and down the hallway.

Rose spied Darryl reach the top of the staircase and saw Annie's bedroom door swing open. Annie stood gaping at Rose and Darryl.

"Why are you two up and being so loud at this hour of the morning? Somebody has to get up and get ready for work in fifteen minutes!"

"Sorry, baby girl," Darryl told her. "We're headed out for a bit. If something happens and you don't hear from either of us..."

"Yeah, yeah, call Liam," Annie waved off as she walked down the hall toward the bathroom. Finally, Annie reached Rose and gave her a hug.

"Good morning," Annie said, surprising Rose. Annie patted her back and looked at Rose. "Thanks for taking care of him," she whispered.

A small smile crept across Rose's lips as Annie broke the embrace and turned toward the bathroom.

"You two kids have a good time," Annie added as she closed the bathroom door.

Rose trailed to the stairs and followed Darryl down and out the front door. The air was crisp and cold, leaving just a trace of ice on the windshield of Rose's car.

Rose started up her car, letting the warmth filter up to defrost her windshield before backing out of the driveway. She spotted Darryl following behind on his motorcycle. The short trip down to Lake Street seemed faster in the early morning, with barely any cars on the road. Lake Street sat deserted, causing Rose to park in the rear parking lot to avoid her vehicle being detected by anyone who might pass by. Darryl pulled his bike alongside her car and hopped off, opening the car door for Rose.

"Are you sure you want to do this?" He asked, his breath visible in the cold air as they stood under one of the halogen lampposts. "It's not too late to change your mind. We can go back to my place, or go somewhere for breakfast, or—"

"We're here. Let's do this," Rose interrupted. She walked toward the rear of Macha's Treasures. Rose spotted the yellow police tape crisscrossed across the back door. The blockage sagged loosely in the doorway so that Rose could easily pull it down and out of the way so she could unlock it.

Rose stepped inside, moving quickly to the alarm keypad to shut it off. Darryl stood close to her, closing the rear door and locking it behind them.

"The alarm was on," Rose said softly. "No one's in here right now except for us."

Rose turned toward the office door just a few steps away from the back entrance. A light emanated from behind her as she swung around, startled. Darryl held a flashlight in his right hand, shining it on the corridor.

"I always have a flashlight on me," he admitted. "It's a work thing."

The light reflected off the silver-colored doorknob of the office as Rose gingerly stepped in that direction. She had her keys in her hand, poised to unlock the door. Instead, however, a twist of the doorknob had it open with ease.

Rose pushed the door open but did not walk into the room's darkness. Instead, she stood, staring into the space, recalling the previous positions of what she knew was in there before the robbery.

"Let me go in first," Darryl said. As he moved Rose from the doorway to the side. Rose allowed him to go by as she waited nervously outside the room. She saw the light from the flashlight spread around the room several times.

"Can the overhead light in here be seen from outside the shop?" Darryl asked.

"It shouldn't, especially with the blinds on the front windows and doors closed," Rose answered.

The light escaped barely beyond the doorframe when Darryl turned it on.

Rose moved back to the doorway to peer into the office. She spotted Darryl standing in the center of the room, trying to move among the evidence markings around the room without disturbing anything.

"Just watch where you step if you come in," Darryl warned.

Rose glanced at the floor and saw patches of dried blood scattered by the desk. The desk sat in quiet disarray, with papers usually placed neatly in folders spread out everywhere. The laptop that typically sat on the desk was missing. Easily spotted, however, were the blood splotches on the desk. Rose moved nearer and saw bits of dried skin and hair stuck in the pooled blood on the desk. She winced and turned away from the sight.

"It looks like whoever attacked Thomas bashed his head against the desk," Darryl said mournfully.

Rose's attention turned to the open safe on the floor. She looked in, swinging the heavy door with her foot to open it widely. The cash envelopes were gone, and the trays that held various jewelry pieces lay tossed aside and empty.

"They cleaned out the safe," Rose spoke.

Darryl bent down and examined the keypad on the door of the safe.

"I don't see any blood or marks on the keypad. Whoever opened it wore gloves, or it was opened before they did anything to Thomas. Did he usually leave it open?"

"Sometimes when it was the end of the day if he was putting cash in or any jewelry. But that door was almost always shut," Rose remarked.

Rose wandered out of the room toward the front of the shop. It was difficult to see anything in the blackness, but Rose used her memory to move around the display cases. She noticed several of the doors to the counters torn off their hinges, with items missing or scattered on the floor. The drawers to both registers were open, with the tills emptied of what little cash likely resided in them.

Rose glanced around the room but did not see anything else suspicious. She looked up at the ceiling and saw the security cameras, but none of them were lit to indicate they were active. She walked back to the office to see Darryl still looking around, moving items carefully before placing them back down to get them exactly where they were.

"What are you looking for?" Rose queried.

"Anything out of the ordinary," Darryl answered. "Or anything that key might open and gives us some guidance."

Rose clutched the key in her pocket before pulling it out and holding it up. She walked over toward the desk to look at the locked drawer. The key was nowhere near the shape to fit it, but looking proved pointless since the drawer had been pried open and the contents went through.

"It's not for the desk," Rose answered, dejected. "Looks like someone got into it anyway."

Rose leafed through some of the papers in the drawer, finding invoices she did not recognize. The invoices were written in various languages that Rose was unfamiliar with. In addition, the dollar amounts were higher than any purchases she typically saw coming to the shop.

"What have you got?" Darryl asked as he came up behind Rose.

"Invoices," Rose added, shaking her head. "But not what I usually see. These are from different places than we customarily do business with. I can't even read most of them."

Rose passed a couple to Darryl for him to examine.

"These are written in different languages," he commented. "This one is Portuguese, and this one is French. I'm not sure what language this one is," he said, waving one small piece of paper. But, whatever they say, those dollar amounts are enormous. It looks like hundreds of thousands of dollars of merchandise."

"All the inventory we have in the shop wouldn't add up to what's on one of those," Rose told him.

"Maybe he was buying items for his other shops," Darryl posed.

"I guess it could be, but why would he keep the paperwork here, locked up in a desk, instead of the merchandise stores? It doesn't make any sense. I had no idea Thomas had this kind of money."

Rose went back to looking through the drawer, finding a few baubles and what looked like samples or personal items. At the bottom of the drawer was a false bottom lifted out. When Rose removed the panel, all she found was a box of bullets.

"Darryl," Rose said as she pulled the bullets out and held the box.

"Where were those?"

"In the drawer, under the false bottom."

"Was there a gun?"

"If there was one, it's not there now," Rose stated. "Thomas never told me there was a gun in the store. So why keep it locked away where you wouldn't be able to get to it quickly if you needed it?"

"There's no reason to keep ammo around unless there's a weapon to go with it," Darryl added. "Someone found the gun when they were looking for whatever they wanted. Maybe he didn't want to scare you by letting you know he had a weapon here."

Rose silently looked around the office, hoping to find anything that might give her a better clue who was in the shop or what might have been taken.

"Do you think the police took the laptop?" Rose asked.

"If it was here, I'm sure they did," Darryl replied as he looked behind the pictures hanging on the walls.

"The laptop had access to the security camera footage," Rose told him. "The only other way to get it would be to contact the security company."

"You think whoever robbed the place knew that and took the laptop? If it was really just a robbery, they might have taken it just because it's a computer, or they hoped to get banking or financial information they could use to steal more money. Or it could be the police took it as evidence."

"Or," Rose said, "they knew it could access the recordings, and they didn't want anyone to find out who was in here."

"So, who knew about the cameras?" Darryl asked.

"Thomas, me, the security company, maybe Riley, but that would be it," Rose answered.

"Do you think Riley could be involved?" Darryl responded.

"Riley?" Rose said, aghast. "She's just a kid and Thomas's grand-daughter. Why would she want to hurt him? He loved her dearly and gave her whatever she wanted."

"But how much do you really know about her, Rose?"

Rose thought back to what she did know about Riley. Thomas had talked about his granddaughter a lot over the years, and she had visited the shop several times before she began working with Rose.

"I know she lived with her father and went to school out west. We never talked much about her personal life. I assume she lived pretty well, judging by Gemma. Outside of that, I guess I don't know a lot."

"I'm not saying she was involved in all this, but let's not completely discount the possibility."

"Like the police thought we were part of it?"

"It sounds hypocritical, I know, Rose," Darryl rationalized.

"Cynical too," Rose added.

"Hey, I get what it looks like, but I have to constantly deal with shit like this," Darryl spoke. "People take one look at me and make up their minds about my guilt, innocence, involvement, and attitude without me even saying a word. You were guilty of doing that same thing to me when I walked into this shop on Valentine's Day. I try to turn the other cheek most of the time, but you see it often enough in life that cynicism creeps in. You have to do what you can to protect yourself sometimes, Rose, and I'm going to do whatever I have to so we're both protected from whatever is happening here."

"I get it," Rose nodded. "And I know I've misjudged you... more than once. So I'm trying to get better at it."

Rose watched as Darryl looked around the room once more. Finally, he glanced up at the light in the middle of the room, and Rose spotted his gaze freeze.

"Do you see that?"

"What? I don't see anything," Rose added, looking up at the drop ceiling panels.

"There's a little shadow to the left of the light there," Darryl pointed. "I think you have to be my size to see it."

Rose looked on as Darryl reached up and pushed the panel to the right of the light up and out of the frame. His hand moved toward the light, scratching until his fingers poked against something. Rose now saw the shadowy outline of a box.

Darryl used his left hand to push the clear panel covering the fluorescent light out of the way and grabbed the box, pulling it down. He handed the package directly to Rose.

The small gray security box rattled lightly as Rose moved it.

"Ever seen it before?" Darryl asked.

"I had no idea it was up there," Rose remarked.

"I'm guessing whoever broke in didn't know about it either," Darryl answered.

Rose examined the box and checked its lock before pulling the key out of her pocket. The key easily slid into place, and she turned the latch, popping it open. Inside lay a small manila envelope, just like the others Rose had received from the attorney. She placed the box on the desk and held the envelope, looking at Darryl before opening it.

Inside the envelope was a small sheet of paper and a black velvet bag.

"What does it say?" Darryl asked.

Rose flipped the paper over towards Darryl so he could view the calligraphy.

"Teacht ar an crann na beatha," she spoke. "Find the Tree of Life."

"Again with the cryptic shit?" Darryl asked.

Rose pulled the strings on the velvet bag to open it and held it over the palm of her hand to dump out the contents. Another key and a single green gem fell out into her hand. Rose moved the rock between her fingers, feeling its delicate smoothness.

"What is it?"

"It's an emerald," Rose answered. "Fairly large and uncut."

"Is it real?" Darryl asked.

"I can't really tell in this light," Rose said as she held up the emerald. "From first glance, it's pure green. That tells me it's probably real. I'd have to have my loupe to check it for sure. Darryl, if it's real, this emerald is probably about nine or ten carats. We're talking about $100,000 stone."

"Holy shit!" Darryl exclaimed.

Rose went back to the damaged drawer and grabbed the invoices there, flipping through them quickly until she found one dated about six months prior. The invoice language was French, but the total cost came in at $92,000.

"This is the invoice for this stone," Rose said, holding up the paper. "It's probably from a dealer in Madagascar. A lot of emeralds come from there. So these other invoices are likely for emeralds as well."

Rose skimmed through the invoices, just looking at dollar amounts.

"Over a million dollars invoiced for these," Rose said to Darryl.

"Where do you think the rest of them are?"

Rose held the new key up to Darryl.

"Good question. Wherever the lock is that this key fits, I'm guessing. Or whoever robbed the place already has them. Unfortunately, there's no way for us to know if someone else has them without the security footage."

A rattling sound emanated from the front of the store, causing Rose and Darryl to freeze in place and hold their breath.

"That sounds like someone checking the front door," Rose whispered.

Darryl quickly shut the light in the office and pulled Rose behind him. He peeked around the door jamb as Rose moved behind him. She looked out toward the front door and spotted a shadow beyond the blinds. There was another tug on the door before the shadow moved off to the right and headed back up the street.

"We need to get out of here," Rose said, tugging on Darryl's jacket.

"Let's wait a few minutes first," Darryl indicated. "Whoever checked the front may come around and look at the back. We don't want anyone surprising us at the back door."

Rose looked on as Darryl replaced the ceiling panels before leading her out of the office. Darryl gripped Rose's hand and led her toward the rear of the shop, just inside the rear door.

"You have to set the alarm," Darryl told her. "We need to leave things as close as they were when we got here."

"What about the invoices? Someone might notice they are gone if they come back."

"If they weren't important enough for them to take the first time around, I doubt they will be missed. Besides, I hate to tell you this, but whoever did all this is probably already aware of us and what we do. So if the thieves want something, they will come looking for us before coming back here."

"And that doesn't scare you?" Rose rushed.

"Let 'em come," Darryl grinned. "I'll be ready for them."

"Easy for you to say," Rose answered.

As they rushed out the back door and locked it, Darryl pointed to the alarm, getting Rose to turn it back on. Darryl looked both ways before leading Rose through the parking lot to her car.

"Do you want to come back to my place?" Darryl asked.

"No, I think I am going to my condo," Rose told him, taking his hand. "I want to take a closer look at these invoices and that gem to figure this out."

"I can come with you if you want," Darryl answered.

"No, go home and get some rest. I'll call you later today. Maybe I can make you dinner tonight as a thank you."

"Does that include dessert?" Darryl smiled, putting his hands on Rose's waist.

"You're insatiable," Rose scolded.

"Yes, yes I am," Darryl admitted.

"Hold on to your appetite until tonight," Rose said, pushing Darryl back a step so she could slide into her car. She sat behind the wheel and started the car before rolling the window down and beckoning Darryl with her crooked finger. Darryl brought his face down to the window and kissed her.

"Thank you, again," Rose sighed.

"My pleasure. I mean that. See you later."

Darryl tapped on the car's roof before Rose drove off toward Harriman. When she reached the traffic light near McDonald's, she looked in the rearview mirror and saw the sizeable helmeted figure on the bike behind her. Darryl gave her a casual wave as he followed her to her complex, ensuring she arrived safely at Lexington Hill before speeding off toward his home.

Rose arrived at her front door, pushing her way in and heading straight to her bedroom, ignoring whatever Liz was shouting at her as Liz stood in her bedroom doorway. She flipped the desk lamp and sat down before pulling out the emerald and grabbing her loupe.

A closer examination of the emerald showed the unique green color, but Rose needed to look for other signs. One pass under her loupe gave her the irregular patterns and striations she hoped to spot. Just a couple of gas bubbles present made her heart race slightly.

"Did you even hear what I said?" Liz said as she entered the bedroom.

"Shh, not now, Liz," Rose hushed, poring over the gem.

"Is that real?" Liz said, snatching the emerald out of Rose's fingers.

"That's what I'm trying to figure out," Rose answered, reaching for the emerald before Liz stepped away from her, moving close to the overhead light attached to the ceiling fan.

"It doesn't look real," Liz pronounced, tossing it back toward a surprised Rose, who fumbled the gem and dropped it. "There's no sparkle."

"Real emeralds don't sparkle," Rose said, picking the gem up and polishing it with a cloth on her desk. "Can you put some water in this?" Rose passed a small dish to Liz.

"I guess so."

Liz strode off toward the bathroom as Rose rotated the gem in her hands. She grabbed her Chelsea filter and her synthetic filter. The emerald still displayed no signs of any other color than green. When Liz returned with the water dish, Rose never broke her intense gaze from the gem.

"Rosie, I just wanted to ask—" Liz began.

"In a minute," Rose said, holding up her hand. She placed the stone gently into the water and looked at it for any signs of layering. Nothing.

Rose's hand shook as she picked up the emerald again. A final pass under her loupe with a trembling hand caused her to see the tiny wisps present.

"I can't believe it," Rose said softly, sitting back in her chair.

"Can't believe what?" Liz insisted.

Rose turned to face her roommate.

"It's real," Rose spoke. "This emerald is genuine."

"Where did you get it?"

"From the store," Rose said, placing the gem down on the desk and staring at it.

"How did you get into the store?" Liz said, flabbergasted. "It's a crime scene."

"Darryl took me down there," Rose stated firmly.

"What? Are you serious? Rose, you could get in a lot of trouble for that. What if the police had shown up? Or, even worse, whoever robbed the place and killed Thomas? What were you thinking?"

"There's a lot about all this you don't know, Liz. Thomas left me the store in his will and this cryptic note about finding the Tree of Life. I had to find out more, so Darryl took me down to the store and watched for me while we looked around. That's when I found this emerald and invoices for a bunch more, along with another note saying the same thing. Somewhere there are about a million dollars in gems."

Rose got out of her chair and started to walk toward the kitchen.

"So, what? Are you just some crime-solving duo now? The police already think you and Darryl might be involved in this, Rosie! I'm telling you as your best friend that maybe you need to back off a bit."

Rose noticed how Liz had furrowed her brow and crossed her arms at her.

"I can't back off of this, Liz. Thomas was hiding something—something someone was willing to kill him over—and he wanted me to know what it was about based on these notes."

"Rose, if he wanted you to know about it, why wouldn't he have just told you about the emeralds when he bought them? He kept it a secret for a reason. I don't like where this might be going."

"Darryl thinks that—"

"Will you listen to yourself?" Liz exclaimed. "Darryl seems like a sweet guy, Rosie, but you've completely upended your life since he walked into it, and you still don't know much about him. I wasn't worried too much about him at first, but now he seems to be dragging you into a dangerous situation. That's why I think you need to back off some—from the store, from Darryl, all of it. It's the safer thing to do."

"Well, I don't think that will happen," Rose said, opening the refrigerator to see what she might have available. "And Darryl's coming over tonight. I'm making dinner. Maybe I'll make some cottage pie," she bemused, lifting up a package of ground beef.

"How can you be so casual about all this?" Liz asked. "Aren't you worried about what will happen or if you are secure?"

"Because I've never felt safer, Liz," Rose added as she shut the refrigerator door to look at her friend. "For the first time since we were teenagers in Dublin, I understand things better. I can't explain it. Darryl makes me feel…"

"Like a smitten, horny teenager?" Liz joked.

"I wasn't going to say that," Rose scoffed before smiling. "But there is that part. He makes me happy, makes me feel protected, and loved."

"Love? Rosie, do you really think that's it? It hasn't been that long since you started seeing him."

"I don't know what else to call it, but that's sure what it feels like to me," Rose grinned. "Are you staying for dinner or going out?"

"Rose, I have to get ready for work," Liz stated. "Do you even know what day and time it is? You're really starting to worry me."

Rose placed her hands on Liz's shoulders.

"I'm sorry," Rose offered. "I know it's been crazy the last few days or so. I'm sorting through a lot of stuff right now. But, I promise you I am taking care of myself. You don't have to worry about me, I swear."

Rose's fingers traced the imaginary cross across her heart before she hugged Liz.

"Thanks for watching out for me."

"We're not done talking about this," Liz told her. "I won't be home for dinner. Rob and I are going out tonight. I'll check in with you, though."

"That's fine. For now, exhaustion is catching up to me. I'm going to sleep for a while."

Liz guided Rose down the hall toward Rose's bedroom, maneuvering Rose away from her desk and to her bed. She got Rose to lay down and pulled the blanket up to Rose's chin. Rose sighed as her head hit the pillow.

"No distractions, Rosie," Liz implored. "Just think about resting and forget about it."

Liz kissed the top of Rose's head before shutting the lights and exiting Rose's room. No sooner were the lights off when Rose's eyes flung open. She heard the distinct sound of the shower going on in the bathroom that let her know Liz had readied herself for the day. Rose sprang from the bed and went back to her desk, sorting through the invoices and looking at the emerald again.

Chapter 20

Darryl paced about the house, looking for anything to occupy his time. He finished three loads of laundry, emptied the fridge, and straightened up his tool bench in the garage. He walked upstairs and opened his closet, looking at the row of jeans he had on the shelves. When Annie interrupted him, he took two steps back from the area, still staring into the clothing abyss.

"Dad? What are you doing?"

"Hey, baby girl," Darryl answered, never breaking his gaze. "What are you doing home so early?"

"Early? Dad, it's three in the afternoon. I worked the morning shift, remember?"

"Oh right," Darryl answered, shaking the cobwebs out. "It's just been a lot going on, I guess."

"What are you expecting to jump out of the closet at you?" Annie asked.

"I was just looking—" he began before cutting himself off. "Okay, don't make fun of me or anything. Rose invited me over for dinner. I just thought it would be nice if I wore something that wasn't a t-shirt and jeans, but I don't think I own anything."

Darryl pivoted and looked at his daughter. Annie had her fingertips over her mouth, attempting to contain a snicker.

"Come on, now," Darryl chided.

"I'm sorry, Dad," Annie laughed. "I never thought I would see a day where you were worrying about what to wear on a date."

Annie stepped toward the closet to see for herself what it contained. Darryl watched as she turned away from the shelves of denim to the sparsely filled rod hanging on the other side.

"What did you wear on dates with Mom?" Annie asked, flipping through the few shirts that hung.

"I dated your Mom when I was eighteen," Darryl responded. "I wore jeans and t-shirts."

"You must have some dress clothes," Annie said, moving to the rear of the closet.

"Not that I know of. I got married in a rented tux, and I had a suit I used to wear for traveling when I was wrestling, but that was a long time ago. I ditched that stuff."

"Well, I don't see much in here," Annie told him. "What time is your date tonight?"

"I'm going to her place for dinner at seven."

"Okay, hold on," Annie answered, pulling out her cell phone. Darryl spied her walking down the hall toward her room, talking to someone in hushed tones. A moment later, she returned to Darryl.

"Okay, you're all set," Annie beamed.

"Set with what? Is my fairy godmother going to show up and magically put me in different clothing?"

"Almost," Annie said. "I talked to my friend Sandy. She works at DXL up in Middletown. She said if you come up now, she can fix you up with something. You have enough time to get there, pick out some clothes, get back to prepare and then go to Rose's."

"That's it?" Darryl asked.

"If you're waiting for me to turn a pumpkin into a coach for you, you're out of luck. You'll have to drive to Middletown yourself."

"Thanks," Darryl said, giving his daughter a kiss on the cheek.

Darryl lumbered down the steps, grabbed his leather jacket, and went straight to his motorcycle. The ride to the big and tall shop had Darryl weaving in and out of traffic to get to the store quickly, and the moment he walked in, he was greeted by the smiling face of Sandy.

"How are you, Mr. Garvey?" Sandy offered.

"I'm great," he replied. "Did Annie tell you what I'm looking for?"

"She did, and I think I have just the thing for you. A nice sports coat and slacks will do the trick. You look like you are about a 66 Long for the jacket. Is that right?"

Darryl stood silently and chuckled.

"You're asking me like I know the answer to that," he laughed. "I haven't worn a suit in many years, and even when I did, my ex-wife picked it out for me."

Sandy waltzed over to the rack of jackets and searched toward the far end. Finally, she pulled down an ebony jacket and passed it to Darryl.

"Try this one," she bade as she scanned the other colors.

Darryl removed his leather jacket and slid his arms into the suit jacket. He was astonished by its comfort and how well it fit him. He stood in front of the full-length mirror and admired what he saw. Sandy strode up behind him, but Darryl's size obscured her from view in the mirror other than her fingertips reaching up to adjust the shoulders of the jacket.

"Wow, this is nice," Darryl said.

"Okay, let's get you some pants to match," Sandy replied, sauntering over to the racks of dress pants to find the appropriate shade of black to match.

"Hmmm, I will say 52 x 40 for the pants," Sandy offered, grabbing pair and passing them to Darryl. "Go try them on and let me know how they work for you."

Darryl went to the dressing room to put the dress pants on. While they looked awkward with his plain navy t-shirt, the fit was ideal. A light knock on the dressing room door startled him a bit.

"How's it going?" Sandy asked.

"They look great. Thanks."

"I've got a dress shirt and a belt here for you to complete the look," Sandy offered. "They're hanging on the door if you want them."

Darryl pulled open the dressing room stall door and grabbed the shirt and belt. He pulled on the charcoal button-down shirt, tucked it in, donned the belt, and looked at himself again. Finally, he stepped out of the stall and walked out toward the shop where Sandy waited.

"Very nice!" she oohed. "Do you need some dress shoes? "

"I've got some at home," Darryl answered. "I think this will do it."

Darryl went back and changed before approaching the counter, where Sandy waited to ring everything up. She punched in the codes for everything, and Darryl's bill totaled close to $400.

"Yikes," he said under his breath as he handed over his credit card.

"Looking good isn't cheap, Mr. Garvey," Sandy grinned. "Annie said this is for a special date?"

Sandy placed the items into a garment bag behind the counter as Darryl watched.

"Yeah, it is," Darryl told her. "She's only seen me in my jeans and stuff. So I thought I would show her I can dress nicely too."

"Well, I'm sure she will be impressed," Sandy said as she handed the receipt and garment bag to Darryl. "I hope you enjoy your evening."

Darryl gathered his items and left the store, thanking Sandy profusely before storing everything on his bike to head home. He worried about clothing getting wrinkled in the storage compartment and dashed off his bike once he parked in the driveway to get his new wardrobe into the house.

He opened the bag as soon as he got home, looking at the shirt and pants and seeing what had happened.

"Shit!" he barked, examining his stuff.

"What's the matter?" Annie said, racing down the steps.

"Look at this!" Darryl groaned.

"Really, Dad?' she said, looking at his clothes. "You're yelling like a teenager about this. Go take a shower. I'll take care of this."

Darryl went upstairs to the shower to get himself prepared. The extra-hot water relaxed him, and he took special care to shave his face and head to keep his smooth look. When he emerged from the bathroom and went to his bedroom, he found his new attire neatly laid out.

Once dressed, Darryl made his way downstairs and saw Annie sitting on the couch, waiting for him to enter. Annie gave a whistle as he entered the room.

"Looking good," she admired. Annie rose and moved toward her father so she could straighten his lapel. "I don't think I have ever seen you this dressed up. It's like you're going to prom or something."

"Will you stop?" Darryl asked, fussing with Annie's hands. He lowered her fingers from the lapel and held her hand.

"Thanks for doing all this," he said sincerely.

"I'm just glad to see you this happy," Annie smiled. "I called Fran over at Greenery Plus. Stop in there and pick up flowers for Rose."

"Yeah? Flowers?"

"Yes, flowers," Annie scolded. "It's a nice thing to do, and women love to get them from their special person, so just do it."

"I will. Anything else?"

"I don't need to have 'the talk' with you, so I think you're good," Annie joked. She gave Darryl a kiss on the cheek. "Let me know if you're coming home tonight."

"I'll try," Darryl admitted before walking out the door.

Darryl mounted his bike, working on getting comfortable as he rode in his dress pants with his suit jacket under his leather. He reached Greenery Plus in moments, pulling into the near-empty lot. When he entered the florist, his senses were overwhelmed by the fragrance of the flowers. The salt-and-pepper-haired woman behind the counter greeted him with a grin.

"You must be Annie's father," she laughed. "I'm Fran. I have the bouquet ready for you."

Fran walked to the table behind her and grabbed the arrangement. The cellophane and paper crinkled loudly as she placed the flowers down. Darryl gazed at what lay in front of him, taking in the white roses, daisies, and baby's breath nicely put together.

"Does this work for you?" Fran asked. "Annie gave me a quick rundown of who they were for, and I thought this might be ideal."

"They look good to me. I'm sure my date will love them," Darryl responded, getting out his wallet to pay for the flowers.

When he arrived back at his bike, he stored the flowers gently to keep them safe on the short trip over to Rose's condo. Finally, he reached Rose's home and made his way up the stairs, straightening up before knocking on the door.

Rose opened the door, greeting Darryl with a smile.

"Right on time," she said as she ushered Darryl inside. Darryl walked in, going to the living room before presenting Rose with the bouquet.

"These are for you," he said proudly as he handed the flowers over.

"Oh, that's so sweet of you," Rose blushed as she sniffed the flowers. "I'll put these in a vase. Do you want something to drink? I got Guinness for you."

"That would be perfect," Darryl said as he removed his leather jacket and draped it over the back of the chair before sitting on the sofa.

Rose arrived back in the living room, bearing a nitro can and a pint glass. She placed the stout on the table in front of Darryl before looking over at him.

"Wow," she said with surprise. "Look at you."

"What?" Darryl asked, peering around.

"You're all dressed up."

"I thought it would be nice if you saw me in something besides jeans and a leather jacket."

"I have to say, you clean up nicely. It's pretty sexy," Rose grinned.

"Well, I'm glad you think so," Darryl chuckled.

"Now I feel underdressed," Rose said, looking down at her t-shirt and jeans.

"You can always take those things off."

"I said underdressed, not undressed," Rose laughed.

"I'll take either one," Darryl said as he got up from the couch. He took Rose in his arms and kissed her. The palm of her hand grazed Darryl's cheek as she held her lips on his.

"Hmm, you smell nice," Rose whispered. "You put cologne on, too? Damn."

Rose moved her lips against Darryl's again, pressing them tightly to his.

"Keep this up, and we'll never get to dinner," Darryl growled.

"I should go check on that," she sighed, staying in Darryl's arms.

"I think I have all I need right here," Darryl answered with another kiss.

Rose wriggled out of Darryl's arms, giggling and backing toward the kitchen. Darryl took a seat on the sofa and, with Guinness in hand, took a gulp of his beverage.

"I hope you like cottage pie," Rose shouted. "It was all I could put together with what I already had in the house."

"I love it," Darryl replied. "My mother used to make it when I was a kid. It was one of my father's favorites. You didn't have to go to any trouble. We could have ordered in."

"It's not often I get to cook for someone anymore," Rose said as she emerged from the kitchen holding a casserole dish. "Liz and I are often on different schedules. I used to cook for my Dad until I moved to the States."

Darryl walked to the dining room table, nicely covered with an Irish linen tablecloth and decorated with candles. He sat opposite Rose, looking across at her as the candlelight flickered and the reflection showed in her eyes as she smiled.

"I made some bread too," Rose said, jumping up from the table and hopping back in the kitchen.

"Boy, you went all out."

"It's just soda bread, nothing fancy," Rose shrugged as she placed the brown, round loaf on the cutting board positioned on the table. Darryl eyed the wisps of steam from the warm bread as Rose cut two slices.

"It seems fancy enough to me. Home-cooked meals aren't something I have seen much since my childhood. I was always on the road touring.

Once I got out of wrestling, and it was just Annie and me, it was more convenient to eat out than cook most nights. So this is a treat."

Rose served Darryl a portion of cottage pie. Darryl placed a pat of Irish butter on top of the mashed potato crust, watching it dissolve into a puddle of rich goodness before he dove into it. Forkful after forkful went down quickly as the combination of the savory beef, carrots, mushrooms, and peas made for a delectable meal.

Darryl returned for seconds, and as tempting as a third portion was, he refrained, even at Rose's insistence. Finally, however, he did agree to take some leftovers home. Rose got up from the table, starting to clear things before Darryl stopped her.

"No way," he insisted. "You cooked. I can clean up."

Darryl grabbed the dishes and set to work, putting items in the dishwasher and handwashing others as Rose pivoted her chair to watch.

"You want an apron?" she half-joked. "I'd hate for you to ruin your nice clothes."

"I doubt you have an apron to fit me," Darryl chuckled as he washed out his pint glass.

"I don't, but I'm sure you would look adorable."

Darryl completed his chore, wiping down the sink with a sponge, before turning to Rose, who applauded his efforts. Darryl obliged with a stage bow before moving back toward the dining room. He took Rose by the hand and led her to the couch. She curled up next to him. Laying her head on his chest.

"I didn't have anything in to make a dessert," Rose lamented, cuddling closer and draping an arm over Darryl's midsection.

"That's okay," Darryl answered. "I'm sure there's something to snack on," he added with a grin. He abruptly pulled Rose toward his lap, so her face looked up at him. His left hand snaked over to her stomach and slid underneath her shirt to touch the bare flesh there. Rose trembled a bit beneath his fingers.

"Maybe up here," Darryl suggested, his hand gliding up to graze across Rose's lace-covered breasts to cause her to sigh.

"Or perhaps down here," he inquired, his fingertips trailing down from under her shirt to the waist of her jeans and lower until he reached her zipper. Darryl toyed and played, undoing the button and clicking the teeth of the zipper down slowly until it reached its end. He placed his thumb just under the visible purple lace he found, rubbing back and forth.

"What do you think?" Darryl asked. "Where would be best?"

"Do I have to choose?" Rose gasped.

Darryl's fingers dipped lower, touching the front of her lace panties before he gently tugged them to the side, allowing his index finger to caress her and dabble in the wetness on her lips.

"I guess not," Darryl answered. "Sometimes, you want to taste a little of everything for dessert."

Darryl deftly took Rose in his arms, lifting her as he stood and causing her to squeal as he cradled her.

"Here or the bedroom?" he asked, bringing her close to his lips so he could kiss her neck.

"Wherever you want. You're in charge," Rose answered, closing her eyes again.

"The bedroom is it then," Darryl said as he carried Rose down the hall, turning as they crossed the threshold into her bedroom. Darryl laid Rose gently on the covering before pulling her jeans down and off her legs.

"Now, where to start," Darryl considered as his fingers traced back and forth over Rose's thighs, leaving them quivering.

He leaned forward, pushing her shirt up to bunch just under her breasts. His lips kissed her belly, and Rose inhaled deeply.

"I'm always happy to try a tasting menu," Darryl added, kissing his way up her stomach and pushing Rose's t-shirt ever higher until she leaned forward to remove it altogether.

Darryl's lips found their mark on Rose's breasts, kissing her cleavage before moving to her left breast and then her right. His fingers tugged on the fabric before frustration led him to slip the straps off Rose's shoulders so he could pull the garment down and free her from the lace guarding her body.

"You're going to owe me a lot of undergarments if you keep this up," Rose huffed. Darryl kept at her, taking her left breast in his hand, his thumb flicking across her nipple as his mouth drew her right nipple between his teeth.

"You're right, and I don't care," Darryl answered, his tongue circling her nipple before pulling it back into his mouth again.

Darryl's left hand moved down and found its mark inside Rose's panties, pressing his palm against her as he rubbed more.

Moans filled the room while Darryl continued his handy work, teasing Rose's body with his lips and fingers as he went along. Finally, he eased down, kissing her below her belly button before his fingers hooked into the waistband of her panties to peel them off.

"I think it's time for another taste," Darryl crowed. His tongue danced just outside Rose's pussy, forcing Rose to moan again before he dove in for a delicate morsel.

"I always save the sweetest for last. Does that sound good to you?" Darryl asked as his hungry lips hovered over Rose. Every breath Darryl took, he emphasized sending chills through Rose's body.

Darryl glanced at Rose's face. Her eyes were shut tightly, but she peeked at him when he halted his actions.

"Does it sound right to you, Rose?"

Rose nodded emphatically, begging Darryl to continue.

Needing no further instructions, pressed his mouth to Rose's pussy, using soft licks like enjoying an ice cream slowly melting down the sides of the cone. Darryl's tongue lay flat against her as he gently worked Rose into a frenzy. With each heavy breath Rose took, Darryl knew he had hit a sweet spot for her and would revisit it slowly. The rhythmic motion of his tongue circling around her clitoris had Rose placing her hands on Darryl's scalp to keep him in place. His tongue then pulsed on her, repeatedly hitting her most sensitive spot until she cried out.

Darryl lifted his head and laid it on Rose's thigh as she panted and recovered, her breathing becoming more controlled.

"I don't know if I'm finished quite yet," Darryl added as he placed light kisses on Rose's shaking thighs.

Darryl rose from the bed, stripping off his clothing as Rose fixed her gaze on him. He climbed back on the bed with her once he was naked, positioning the head of his erect cock just outside of Rose's pussy.

"I remembered this time," Darryl grinned as he held up the foil packet and tore it open with his teeth. He quickly rolled the condom on before easing into Rose achingly slow so that each thrust was electric.

Darryl spied Rose closing her eyes, and her palms glided across her breasts as he moved in her.

"Let me get that," Darryl offered, bringing his mouth to her breast as he thrust again and again.

Rose wrapped her legs around Darryl, holding him tightly in place as he kissed, sucked, and nibbled at her.

"Should I finish with dessert?" he asked huskily as he moved.

"Yes, yes, please," Rose gasped, pulling Darryl down toward her mouth to kiss him deeply. Darryl surged once more, his orgasm hitting just as her second arrived. Darryl grunted loudly as his body stiffened, and wave after wave of pleasure washed over them.

When their bodies separated, Rose worked to stay as close to Darryl as possible. The couple spooned on the bed as Darryl's arms enveloped Rose.

"Best dessert I've had in ages," Darryl whispered, nibbling on her lobe playfully.

"Sure beats the apple cake I was thinking about making," Rose sighed.

Rose rolled over to face Darryl, cupping his face in her hands.

"I think I'm falling in love with you," she said softly. Rose turned her face away, looking down and unable to stare into Darryl's eyes.

Darryl froze momentarily before placing his index finger under Rose's chin, so she looked at him again.

"Hey, why did you look away?" he asked.

"I don't know," Rose spoke. "I guess I was embarrassed or worried about how you would react if I said it. I know we haven't been together long, but I'm all frazzled like a schoolgirl."

Rose tried to look away again, but Darryl lifted her chin.

"Never be embarrassed about saying that—especially to me," Darryl answered.

Darryl leaned in for a kiss, softly pressing his lips against Rose's.

"By the way, I feel the same way," he whispered.

Chapter 21

Darryl dozed with Rose comfortably nuzzled in his arms. Her body pressed to his as she slept brought Darryl a comfort he had not experienced in many years. It wasn't until he woke in the middle of the night, unable to sleep any longer, that he got out of bed and watched as Rose pulled the blanket up under her chin and snuggled to her side.

Darryl moved to the bottom of the bed, pulling his boxer briefs on before looking around Rose's room. He spotted the desk where Rose had all of her tools scattered and the invoices they had taken from the jewelry store. Darryl spotted the emerald they had secured and held the gem in his hand. He picked up Rose's loupe, unsure how to use it properly. Unable to see anything in the dark, Darryl reached for the desk lamp and switched it on. The light blasting through the darkness caused him to squint immediately.

He turned and saw Rose stirring in the bed. She sat up, wiping her eyes as she attempted to focus on Darryl.

"Is everything alright?" she asked groggily.

"I'm sorry. I didn't realize the light would be that bright. I woke up and couldn't sleep and saw the stuff on your desk."

"No, no, it's okay," Rose answered as she grabbed her t-shirt off the floor and put it on. "I meant to tell you about this anyway, but we got caught up... in other things," she chuckled.

Rose walked to the desk and sat at the chair as Darryl held the emerald in his hands.

"It's the real deal, Darryl," Rose told him. "I checked it every which way for about an hour. I would guess that's a pure emerald worth close to $100,000."

"Damn," he said as he felt the sharpness in his hands.

"Somewhere, there are a dozen more, maybe just like it, if these invoices are accurate. I still can't believe it."

"Do you think Thomas was up to something illegal?" Darryl asked, passing the gem to Rose.

"I can't imagine he was," Rose said confidently. "Why create invoices for things if you bought them on the black market? He must have had some kind of plan for these, but I can't figure out what it might have been. Even the letter and notes he left don't make much sense, and who knows what lock that key fits. It could be a safe deposit box, a door somewhere in his home, a locker... I have no idea and may never know."

"So, what's next?" Darryl inquired, sitting on the bed and pulling Rose to his lap.

"I guess I just have to wait for the police to sort out everything at the store, and then there will be Gemma to deal with. I imagine she will contest the will, so I don't know where that will leave me. I'm stuck in limbo at the moment."

"I'm on vacation all week," Darryl answered, kissing the nape of Rose's neck. "We'll have time to spend together. Maybe we can have dessert together a few more times."

"Hmmm, that sounds nice," Rose responded.

Rose placed her hand on Darryl's bare chest as they kissed. The familiar ring of Darryl's cell phone was heard over their lips parting.

"Who the hell is calling me right now?" Darryl grumbled. "It's three in the morning."

Rose moved from Darryl's lap so he could find his phone in his suit jacket. Darryl dug it out of the inside pocket and saw it was Annie calling him.

"Annie? What's wrong?" Darryl answered.

"Dad," Annie began in hushed tones. "The police are here. They have a search warrant and are looking for you."

"Are you alright?" he said with panic.

"I'm fine, but I'm worried about you. What are the police looking for?"

"I don't know, baby girl," Darryl told her. "I'll be right over."

Darryl hung up and reached for his pants and shirt.

"What's going on?" Rose asked.

"The police are at my house with a search warrant. I need to get over there and make sure Annie is okay."

"Do you want me to come with you?"

"No, you stay here," Darryl insisted. "I don't want you to get mixed up in whatever they do there."

Darryl finished dressing and headed for the front door, grabbing his leather jacket as he left. He got to the door and turned to face Rose, kissing her once more.

"I'll let you know as soon as I find out something," he told her. "Don't worry."

Darryl had barely made it down two steps when flashing lights from two police cars speeding into the parking lot filled the area.

Two uniformed officers stepped out of their vehicles and reached for their holsters immediately.

"Hands on your head!" one officer yelled.

Darryl placed his hands slowly on his head, intertwining his fingers as he moved down each step. He spied Rose looking to move toward him.

"Rose!" he commanded. "Don't move! Just stay by the door or go inside!"

"Do not move, Ms. Boyle!"

Darryl shot a look over and saw Detective Myers moving toward the bottom step to greet Darryl. The detective had his hand on his holster, ready to draw his weapon at any moment.

"Let's go, Mr. Garvey," Detective Myers said, waving him down the stairs.

Darryl reached the bottom step, towering over Myers with a piercing stare.

"Turn around," the detective ordered as Darryl complied. Next, the detective took Darryl's hand, pulling it roughly behind his back. When the detective placed the handcuffs on Darryl's wrist, he realized Darryl's hands were too large to fit in the cuffs.

"You're coming up short there, detective," Darryl mocked.

"I didn't ask you to say anything!" Myers barked, calling other officers over. "Try to resist again, and we will user the Tasers on you."

"He's not resisting anything!" Rose shouted. Darryl saw nearby neighbors coming out of their homes to look at the commotion.

"Someone get me some fucking zip ties!" Detective Myers yelled as Darryl waited calmly. He looked at Rose, seeing fear on her face.

"It's all good, Rose," Darryl reassured. "Make sure you call Finn and tell him what's going on."

"You do that, Ms. Boyle," Detective Myers uttered with a scowl. "Let your lawyer know Mr. Garvey is being charged with first-degree murder."

"What?" Rose shrieked as Liz joined her at the front door.

"We found evidence at your house," Myers told him as he tightened black zip ties on Darryl's wrists.

"What evidence?" Rose shouted.

"Don't even talk to him, Rose," Darryl warned harshly. "Just call Finn and ask him to meet me at the police station."

"Go check the condo," Myers ordered two uniformed officers.

"Not without a warrant," Liz spoke, stepping in front of the officers coming up the stairs, halting them there. "Unless you fellows have one, you can march back down those steps."

Darryl grinned as Myers rolled his eyes, indicating there was no warrant for Rose's home.

"I'm glad you can smile through all this," Myers said as he roughly grabbed Darryl by the jacket and shoved him toward the unmarked police car Myers had climbed out of.

Darryl watched as they tried to figure out how to get him into the back of the car while Liz ushered Rose into the condo and closed the door. Moments later, as Darryl was easing into the back seat, he spotted Rose watching out the window of her room to see what was going on. Darryl simply mouthed, "It's okay." Before disappearing into the rear of the vehicle.

Detective Myers attempted a conversation with Darryl several times, but Darryl never spoke to him during the ride to the police station. As Myers pulled his car to a stop in the station parking lot, four uniformed officers came out and greeted him to assist in getting Darryl from the back seat and into the station.

Darryl was kept in zip ties and led to the same interrogation room he was placed in when the police initially interviewed him regarding the robbery. He sat back in the creaky aluminum chair and sighed.

Detective Myers eventually entered the room alone, carrying a folder and a bag in front of him. He sat across from Darryl and flipped through the folder before glaring at him.

"Got anything to say?" Myers asked.

"Nope," Darryl answered casually. "Where's your owner, Detective Jackson? Is he even aware you are doing all this or is this your own wild goose chase?"

Myers twisted his face before focusing back on the papers in front of him.

"I don't need his permission to do anything," Myers mumbled. "I follow the leads as I see them, and this one led me directly to you. We got an anonymous tip that a motorcycle was spotted in the shop parking lot early yesterday morning. So I went back over there, and it sure looked like someone had crossed the police tape and entered the premises, looking for something. It didn't take much for a judge to give me a warrant for your house after that."

"Good for you," Darryl said bluntly.

"We searched the place up and down. You have a nice place, and your daughter... hmph, she sure is pretty. She didn't seem to like me much, though."

Darryl narrowed his eyes and stared through Detective Myers.

"She has good taste and can spot an asshole a mile away," Darryl replied.

"Maybe," Myers laughed. "I guess I'll have to take another run at her and see how it goes."

Darryl did his best to maintain calm, controlling his breathing as he knew the detective was trying to bait him into reacting.

"Well, with our search of your place, we found something interesting in that locked shed of yours in the back. The usual stuff of lawnmower and tools and the like, but also this."

Myers reached down into the bag and pulled out a zippered pouch with a wad of cash.

"Look familiar?" Myers asked.

Darryl just stared at it and then back at Myers, not responding but knowing what it likely was.

"It's cash from the safe at the jewelry store. Not a bad little haul for yourself, huh, Darryl?"

"I wouldn't know," Darryl answered bluntly.

"I suppose you don't know anything about this either," Myers said, laying a clear evidence bag on the table for Darryl to examine.

Darryl brought his face closer to the bag and saw the knife inside, the blade streaked with blood.

"Can't say I do," Darryl responded as he lifted his head and sat back in the chair.

"This was in the shed too," Myers answered. "You really didn't hide them very well."

Darryl shrugged before a knock was heard on the door and a uniformed officer peeked his head in.

"Garvey's lawyer is here," the officer stated.

"Shit," Myers grumbled as Finn pushed into the room.

Darryl spotted Finn staring at his large form in the small chair before turning to the detective. "You can leave now," Finn said abruptly to the detective.

"He's not just walking out of here this time, Mr. O'Farrell," Myers spat. "We're charging him with robbery, assault, murder, and probably a few other things I'm still working on."

"Good, you go work on that," Finn told him, ushering Myers out the door and closing it.

Darryl exhaled as Finn sat down across from him.

"Darryl, I expect to have to come down here for Liam or some of the other guys, but not twice in a week for you. So now he wants to charge you with Quinn's murder?"

"It's all bullshit, Finn," Darryl answered. "I wasn't anywhere near that place when he was killed. All that stuff they say they found at my house wasn't there. There are many things Myers said that don't add up."

"Like what?" Finn asked.

"First, he said he went into the locked shed in my backyard."

"So, they would just cut the lock off if they are searching. You know that."

"Finn, I never put a lock on the shed," Darryl answered. "The door closes too tight as it is. I practically tear it off the hinges every time I open it. Sure, they probably pried it open, but it never had a lock."

"You think they planted evidence?"

"That's the other thing," Darryl said, leaning forward. "He showed me an evidence bag with a knife they say they found in the shed. It had blood on it. It wasn't my knife, Finn."

"Are you sure?"

"Absolutely," Darryl said confidently. "It was a slim switchblade. That thing would get lost in my hand. I have a hunting knife at home twice the size of that. I keep it tucked under the top drawer of my dresser. I've had it for years. I would never carry a blade like that."

"I'm sure they won't find any fingerprints on it anyway, and I'm betting it's the true murder weapon, so where did it come from?"

"I think I know that too," Darryl answered. Before he could say anything else, the door to the interrogation room burst open, and Detective Myers entered with two uniformed officers.

"On your feet, Mr. Garvey," Myers ordered.

"Darryl Garvey, you are under arrest for the murder of Thomas Quinn. You have the right to remain silent."

Darryl barely acknowledged the Miranda rights Detective Myers read as he was led from the room, with Finn following close behind. Eyes ogled him as he was directed toward the holding cell at the station. He stopped short in front of the jail cell, waiting for the door to open before leaning over to Finn.

"Make sure Rose and Annie are safe," Darryl whispered.

Finn nodded quickly, already grabbing hold of his cell phone.

"I'll start working on trying to get you out of here," Finn replied.

"Fat chance, counselor," Myers laughed. "He's getting charged with first-degree murder. They won't give him any bail."

"Don't listen to him, Darryl," Finn said, ignoring the detective as Darryl was locked behind the cell door.

Darryl placed his hands through the slot in the steel door so the zip ties could be cut from his hands. He then walked over to the lone cot in the cell and lay back, staring at the bare ceiling, his mind clicking through the facts like a slideshow as he attempted to decipher what went on.

Rose sat helplessly, watching Darryl get led into the squad car and away. Another marked car sat idly in the parking lot, monitoring her condo. She saw neighbors milling about outside, pointing and clearly gossiping about what went on.

A light knock on her bedroom door caused Rose to turn and see Liz standing in the doorway.

"They will come back with a warrant," Liz said. "Rose, don't take this the wrong way, but I have to ask, is there anything here that we need to worry about?"

"What? Of course not," she said, looking back out the window. "I mean, there's the stuff from the store like the emerald, and the invoices, and the key..."

"Gather it up," Liz said quickly. "We need to figure out what to do with it all."

"Why would the police care about that stuff?"

"Because it's stuff you took from the store while it was a crime scene, Rose. It's evidence and could show that there was a motive for the crime."

"But there wasn't. We didn't do anything."

"We know that. The police may not see it the same way if you went to a scene and removed things from it. It looks like you're trying to hide something. We can all go to jail."

Rose stacked up the invoices and grabbed the notes from Thomas, the key, and the emerald, and walked out of her bedroom, frantically looking about for a place they could hide these items.

"I have an idea," Liz told her, leading Rose to the bathroom.

"Remember when I used to hide my extra cash from my brother when we were teenagers?"

"Yeah, you had that old cigar box tucked under your bed in your room," Rose answered.

"Well, he figured that out pretty quickly, so I had to switch things up."

Liz bent down to the sink and pulled out a zipper-close storage bag. She took the items from Rose and placed them in the bag, rolling the papers like a tube before sealing the bag. Next, she opened the dryer and pulled out the lint trap, stuffing the package in there and packing the gray lint over the bag, hiding it before snapping the mesh basket back into place.

"Voila!" Liz said proudly, closing the dryer door.

"Your brother never found it?"

"Are you kidding? It would mean he would have to do laundry. This will be good enough for today until we can come up with something else."

A loud knock on the door had Rose and Liz frozen in place, unsure of what to do. The banging resounded through the condo again as the two moved slowly to the front door.

Liz peeked through the peephole and spun back to Rose.

"It's a guy in a leather jacket," Liz whispered. "He looks like one of the Cosantóir."

Rose moved Liz aside so she could look out. She spotted Finn standing there looking back at her.

"It's Finn," Rose answered, flinging the door open.

"Who's Finn?" Liz asked.

"He's my lawyer," Rose said as she waved Finn into the condo and shut the door. "Did you see Darryl? How is he?"

"Not for very long," Finn answered. "They charged him with Thomas Quinn's murder. They said they found evidence at his house. Money and a knife they think is the murder weapon."

"He didn't do anything!" Rose insisted. "He couldn't have."

"Calm down, Rose," Finn replied, placing his hands on her shoulders. "I'm sure he didn't. He explained everything to me. Right now, it's all circumstantial evidence, but it's enough to hold him in jail. I don't know if I'll be able to get him bail or not."

"I can't believe this is happening," Rose said, stunned. Liz put her arm around Rose and led her to the couch.

"Rose, is there anything I need to know that you guys haven't told me? Anything that might help Darryl's case? Now is the time to share." Rose looked at Liz and then back at Finn.

"We went to the store yesterday. We went inside," Rose admitted.

"Damn it, what were you two thinking?" Finn blasted.

"I thought we might find anything that might give us a clue about what went on and why."

"Did you?"

Rose nodded as Liz got up from the couch and went to the bathroom. She pulled the packet out of the dryer and returned, handing it to Finn. Finn pulled out the paperwork, the notes, and the emerald, looking at each item. He held the emerald in the palm of his hand.

"Is it real?"

"It is," Rose answered.

"And what's the key for? And the note in Gaelic?"

"The note reads 'Find the Tree of Life.' Unfortunately, I have no idea what the key is for. We couldn't find anything that it fit."

"Do the police know about any of this?" Finn asked.

"Not yet," Rose answered. "They said they were coming back with a search warrant."

"I doubt they will, at least today," Finn assured her. "They seem hyper-focused on Darryl and probably went over his place with a fine-toothed comb. I'm headed over to check on Annie now. Just so you know, there will be one of the brothers hanging around outside for a few days, just to keep an eye on the two of you to make sure you're safe."

"Why?" Liz asked.

"Because Darryl asked," Finn replied casually. "It's just a precaution. Whoever is involved in this might be looking for what you have already found, Rose. No sense in taking chances. There will be someone with Annie until we can get this all sorted out."

"This all seems too much," Rose added before slumping onto the sofa. "Why is this all happening?"

"Greed, more than likely," Finn told her. "Money does it every time. But, look, Rose, you need to do what you have to to keep yourself safe. I know it's not my place to tell you what to do, but it might be better for you—maybe for both you and your friend here..." Finn pointed at Liz, "to go somewhere else for a little bit. Do you have someplace else you can go?"

Rose turned to Liz, staring at her.

"I have a brother in England," Liz replied. "I'm sure we can both stay with him."

"I don't want to run away from this and leave Darryl to fend for himself," Rose stated firmly. "There's too much at stake with all this. If he's being framed, it's because of me. He didn't even know Thomas or have any involvement in this until we got together. I want to be able to help him."

"Honestly, Rose," Finn began, "I don't think you can do a lot for him at this point. Darryl has some information that he thinks might point to who is behind this. I will head up to Orange County Correctional in Goshen after seeing Annie. That's where they'll take him until we can get him bail. I'll talk to him and see what I can discover."

"Who does he think is involved?" Rose asked excitedly. "How long will they hold him there?"

"I'm not sure who, but he's got some ideas. As for how long he'll be there, it's hard to say," Finn nodded. "It might be a day or so before we get in front of the judge to discuss bail. If you're not going to leave, I just need you to sit tight and be aware of your surroundings. It doesn't hurt to be suspicious of everyone at this point."

Finn moved toward the front door as Rose remained on the sofa.

"I'll be in touch as soon as I can with information. Call me if you need anything," Finn added, handing Liz his business card as she followed him to the door. "Don't open this door for anyone not wearing one of these," Finn said as he gripped the lapel of his leather jacket. "Make them show you their colors and tattoo."

Finn exited the condo under Liz's watchful eyes, and she locked the door behind him before approaching Rose.

"Leaving for a little while might not be such a bad thing, Rosie," Liz uttered quietly as she sat next to Rose. "My brother would put us up, and we could escape all this until it's sorted out. Then, we would be safer."

Rose looked over at Liz with determination.

"I need to stay and help Darryl any way I can," Rose spoke. "You should go to Adam's place. Spend some time with him and your family. I'll be okay."

"I'm not going to leave you by yourself through this," Liz insisted. "We're sisters, remember?'

Rose took Liz's hand and held it.

"As your sister, then, I'm telling you to go. I couldn't take it if something happened to you because of what I'm involved in. So get yourself the first ticket out that you can. I'll be fine here until Darryl is back with me. But, Liz, please, you need to go."

Liz sat silently, gripping Rose's hand tightly.

"I can't," Liz sniffled.

"You can," Rose replied. "You know it's the right thing to do. Go call Adam and tell him you're coming."

Liz sighed before rising and moving down the hall toward her room. Rose sat, placing her head in the palms of her hands before taking a deep breath and looking up. She spotted the notebook on the table in front of her and picked it up, turning to the last entry on the list about Walter. She grabbed a pen, scribbled the date, and wrote:

Being apart from Darryl.

Rose initialed the entry and closed the notebook, hugging it close to her body.

22

Rose and Liz went back and forth for over an hour discussing the pros and cons of staying put before Rose convinced her friend that leaving would be best for her. Finally, they were able to book a flight for Liz out of Newark Airport headed to London that night, and Liz reluctantly packed a bag and had called for an Uber so she could get out of town. The two hugged, not wanting to part, before Liz moved to the front door and opened it. Rose stepped out with her, spotting the idling red Honda with a driver getting interrogated by a Cosantóir member.

"You better go before they pull your driver out of the car," Rose smiled through her tears.

"Be careful, Rosie," Liz said, hugging Rose again. "We'll have a hell of a story to tell when this is all over."

"Yes, we will," Rose answered. "Call me when you land and give my best to Adam. Love you."

Rose watched Liz walk down the steps to the Honda as she dropped her bag near the trunk.

"You mind getting that for me?" Liz grinned at the biker, moving away from the driver's window to open the car's back door for her.

Once situated, the auto pulled away, and Rose spied Liz waving to her as she left. The two Cosantóir went back to their bikes positioned in one of the guest parking spots, giving a casual nod to Rose as she moved back indoors.

Rose locked the front door again, plucked the plastic bag containing the invoices and emerald, and placed it back in its hiding spot in the dryer's lint trap. She did her best to occupy her mind for the rest of the day, puttering about, straightening up, and organizing and then reorganizing her room until there was nothing left to clean.

Checking her phone and texts became routine for her every twenty minutes, hoping she would hear news from someone about how Darryl was and what was going on. Each time there was nothing. Rose sat on the couch, pulling her knees up to her chest, and grabbed one of the throw blankets off the back of the sofa, covering herself. She kept her phone nearby and closed her eyes to block the anxiety coursing through her brain.

The sound of knuckles rapping on the front door startled Rose awake. She sat frozen on the couch for a moment, unsure if it was just a dream she had until the knocking occurred again with more force.

Rose slowly moved toward the front door, remembering Finn's words to her. She peeked through the peephole to see a prominent figure taking up the entirety of the circle.

"Can I help you?" she asked, trying to steel her voice.

"Rose? Hi, I'm one of the brothers on watch here. I'm just checking in on you. I just arrived a minute ago, so we're still here."

"Okay, thanks," she sighed.

"I don't suppose you have something to drink, like a soda or bottle of water?" the biker asked. "I forgot to grab something before I came over, and Preacher won't like it if I even leave for a minute to go to Quick Chek for something."

"Sure, let me take a look," Rose said as she moved to the kitchen. She grabbed one of the cold bottles from the fridge and returned to the front door, moving to unlock the deadbolt before stopping.

"I know this will sound weird, but can you show me your jacket?"

"My jacket? Oh yeah, sure," the biker replied.

He took a step back and turned around to display the rear of his coat with the club emblem on it. Rose watched as the man spun around and smiled.

"Okay?" he asked.

"I need to see your club tattoo also," Rose said through the door. "I'm sorry. I know it's a pain."

"Not at all," he offered politely as he took off his jacket. Rose could see the sleeves of ink on each arm. He pushed the shoulder of his t-shirt on his left arm up and turned to face the peephole, so Rose could see the authentic artwork.

She sighed as she undid the lock and opened the door. The biker's presence filled the doorway as he grinned and reached for the water bottle. Rose passed it over, and he quickly twisted the cap off and guzzled the water down, draining the bottle.

"Thanks so much," he gasped, wiping his mouth. "I don't suppose I could bother you for another one to save for later."

"Sure, no bother," Rose answered as she turned and moved to the kitchen, opening the fridge and reaching for another bottle toward the back of the shelf.

"I didn't catch your name," Rose said, her voice muffled by the refrigerator's interior.

She pivoted and saw the biker standing right behind her, grinning a broad smile as he had been eyeing her bent-over body. Startled, Rose dropped the plastic bottle on the floor and heard it bounce and roll as she stared at the imposing figure.

"The name's Dutch," he growled as his arm shot passed Rose and shut the fridge door.

Darryl went through the prison transfer process as he was brought to Orange County Correctional. He turned all his belongings over and waited for them to find an orange jumpsuit that would fit his build before being placed with the general population at the prison. A corrections officer led Darryl to the small cell he was assigned, where he spent more than a few hours staring up at the ceiling and attempting to sort out the facts of what brought him to his current state.

The cell doors slid open so that Darryl could get out and be led outside for some time in the small yard available to the inmates. He walked alone, glad for the warmth of the sun and the knit cap he had provided. He stood next to the chain-link fence at the far end of the yard and watched as a few inmates played basketball.

"You want in, big man?" A tall, lanky, bearded man asked. "We could use your size."

"I'll play for a bit," he agreed, joining a team of two others so they could play.

The game proved more intense than the casual pickup games Darryl would play at Mary Harriman Park on occasion. His height and muscles worked to his advantage as the much smaller players had difficulty defending him. A small crowd had gathered around to watch, with quite a bit of chatter going on among the inmates, including hoots and hollers anytime anyone tried to dunk on Darryl, and he blocked them.

As he guarded one of the other players, Darryl picked up bits and pieces of conversation. He heard a shrill voice echo above the others, bragging.

"The guy hit me in the head with a fucking rock," he heard the voice screech. "This was after he dumped one of the guys over the fence. Threw him like a rag doll, he said. All I know is I had to get five fucking stitches in my head, and Vinny broke two ribs, and then we didn't even get paid because the asshole said we didn't finish it."

Darryl froze and stared as he tried to pick out where the voice came from from the crowd. Then, his view became obscured by a tall player stepping in front of him and leaping high to go to the basket. The man dunked over Darryl, eliciting groans from the crowd and Darryl's teammates.

"Shit, man, keep your head in it," one of Darryl's team members shouted.

"It's all good," the tall man said, patting Darryl's chest. Whistles shrieked through the air to indicate time outside was up. Darryl tried to view who the inmate was with the shrill voice but had difficulty picking anyone out of the crowd. He heard the voice one more time, up ahead of him as they waited in line to get back into the jail. Darryl turned to his tall teammate behind him.

"You know who that is?" Darryl asked.

"You're going have to be more specific, man," the tall man laughed.

The shrill voice echoed down the line once again, this time with a hyena laugh following it.

"That guy," Darryl pushed.

Tall Man rolled his eyes.

"That asshole," he told Darryl. "His name is Mouth. Big surprise, right? His real name is Marcel Ruiz. He's in and out of OCJ. Usually, petty stuff that gets him right back out, it seems. Pain in the fucking ass, man. The guy never shuts up. He's always bragging about this and that, but he ain't done shit. Seems like he gets caught more than he works. Rumor is he's an ass-hat snitch. You know him?"

"Sort of," Darryl admitted as he spotted the smaller man bobbing up and down in the crowd. "He with anyone?"

"Nah, no one trusts him," Tall Man replied. "He just got back in yesterday. Odds are he'll be out tomorrow. He never stays long. He's got COs looking out for him. You got a beef with him?"

"You could say that," Darryl offered. "He's part of why I'm here, and I think his friends are messing with my lady."

The men made it back inside and were filing toward their cells.

"Hey, if you want time with him, I know where he's at," Tall Man answered. "He's next floor down in B7. I'm sure I can get you there."

"You got that kind of pull here?" Darryl asked.

"Dude, you know who you're talking to?" Tall Man laughed. "I'm Reggie Mason. I can get it done for you."

"Demon," Darryl said, offering his big fist to Reggie. Reggie gave him a bump and grinned.

"Name fit you?" Reggie asked.

"Sometimes it does," Darryl nodded.

"I'll catch you later, Demon," Reggie said with a point before walking into his cell.

Darryl slid into his cell a few doors down from Reggie and sat on the unforgiving mattress on his bed, listening to the groans underneath. Then, finally, he laid back, piecing things together and hoping to figure it out before any danger befell Rose.

"I... I would have brought it out to you," Rose stammered as Dutch's body took one step closer to her, pinning her against the refrigerator door.

"It's no bother, Rose," Dutch told her. Rose felt his eyes on her, scanning every inch of her body. Fear seized her, immobilizing her for the moment.

"Who knew Demon had such good taste in women," Dutch said, reaching out and grazing his fingers across Rose's right cheek. She instinctively flinched and turned her face.

"Oh, don't turn away from me, honey," Dutch's voice oozed. He turned her face back to face his, and Rose stared into his blank, dark eyes.

"What do you want?" Rose croaked. Her right hand gripped the refrigerator door handle behind her to steady herself.

"Well, first, you will tell me what you may have found in the jewelry store and where it is. After that, maybe we can have some other fun."

Dutch moved his right hand to Rose's torso, intent on snaking higher over or under Rose's shirt.

Frozen in place, Rose's memory flashed back to her teenage years when her father gave her and Liz self-defense lessons in the backyard. She remembered his distinctive voice telling them, "Eyes, ears, balls."

Dutch's hand moved under the hem of her shirt before reality came back to Rose. Her left knee shot up, striking Dutch directly in the groin and causing him to recoil and slump to the floor, groaning.

Rose scanned the kitchen quickly as she looked for anything to use as a weapon. Her hand shot over to the stovetop, where she gripped the tea kettle of still hot water she had put on to make some tea before nodding off to sleep. Then, flipping the spout open, she dumped the water onto Dutch's face, causing him to scream in agony. His hands moved from his aching balls to cover his face.

"You fucking bitch! You burned me!" he yowled.

Rose darted past Dutch's prone body, stomping on his crotch as hard as she could to make him howl louder. She raced to her bedroom, locking the door behind her, and searched her purse for her phone. Then she realized it was still on the sofa next to where she napped. Reluctant to go back out of her room, she scoured her desk and dresser to see what she could use to defend herself.

Footsteps lumbered down the hallway before she heard Dutch's body slam against her door, causing her to jump back.

"It's probably better that you're there," Dutch shouted. "Once I'm in there with you, I can get you on the bed and teach you some manners!"

The body slammed into the door again, making the wood creak and the hinges shudder. Rose spotted the few candles she had scattered on her desk and reached just as she heard her bedroom door splinter.

Light filled the room from the hallway behind Dutch as he faced Rose. Swelling and red peeling skin covered the left side of his face with his eye barely open.

"Nowhere left to go, Rose," Dutch cackled. "This is going to be sweet."

Rose grabbed the flexible lighter next to the candles just as Dutch seized her, wrapping his burly arm around her waist and flinging her to the bed. Her body bounced on the mattress, her head striking her headboard, stunning her. Dutch was on her immediately, punching Rose in the rib cage to knock the wind out of her.

"Now maybe you'll learn to listen to me and behave," Dutch roared. His hands unbuttoned the top of Rose's jeans and began to reach for his own belt. Rose gripped the lighter in her left hand as she turned her head to the right and saw the can of Lysol on her nightstand. She pulled the cane down and positioned it just as Dutch finished undoing his belt to look up at her. She sprayed the Lysol directly into his face and eyes. Dutch floundered off Rose's body and staggered back, striking the far wall with his back.

Curses flew from Dutch's lips as Rose kept spraying his face. Finally, Dutch attempted to flee, feeling his way down the hall with his palms on each wall.

"I can't see!" he yelled as he staggered back. Rose kept moving toward him, still spraying the Lysol feverishly until the can was emptied. Dutch tripped over the ottoman, his head thumping on the floor in the living room. Rose glanced at his face, seeing tears streaming from both eyes. His right swelled shut while his left barely opened and was bloodshot.

Rage surged through Rose's body as she breathed heavily and stood over Dutch. She turned and picked up her cellphone to call 911.

"Yeah, call an ambulance and the cops," Dutch laughed through the pain. "I need some help."

Rose stopped and slid the phone into her back pocket.

"Who sent you here? What did you want from the shop?"

"I'm not telling you shit," Dutch spat out. His left hand scrambled and reached to grab Rose's leg, but she quickly kicked it aside before stomping on his stomach, forcing all the air from his body.

Dutch gasped, struggling to breathe.

"Think about it for a second," Rose shot back. "Next refusal and I'm stomping those little grapes of yours into oblivion. After that, you'll never have to worry about being with a woman again."

"Okay, okay," he wheezed, working to cover his groin with his hand. Rose spied Dutch peer his one eye open and smile at her. Before she could do anything, his left leg swept across, striking her legs and knocking her down, so her head hit the sofa's cushions before hitting the floor. Her movements pushed the side table over, sending the lamp and everything else on the table crashing to the floor.

Dutch struggled to rise and move toward Rose as she regained her senses. He grabbed at her feet, pulling her to him as she shouted, "No! No!"

"I've been nice up to now, Rose," Dutch reminded Rose as his hands took hold of her calves and tugged on her. "Now it's time to get dirty."

Rose looked at the ceiling as she felt her body moving on the floor and Dutch's hands groping up to her denim-covered thighs. Her fingertips grabbed for anything as he tried to drag her, and she hooked her fingers onto the leg of the couch, putting up some resistance.

"You're feisty, I'll give you that," Dutch laughed as he tugged harder. Rose refused to give up, clinging to the couch leg until she spotted the crystal vase lying on the floor. She could just get the top of the heavy urn between her fingertips enough to grab hold of it as she slid closer to Dutch.

Gripping the vase in her hands, she looked down to see Dutch crawling up her body, pressing himself against her.

"Game over, Rose," Dutch hissed.

"You're right about that," she said back as she screamed and crashed the vase against his forehead.

A loud thud resounded through the room, and Dutch made no sound and just stared blankly at Rose. A small stream of blood trickled down his forehead as he slumped to the left and fell over, hitting the floor.

Rose pulled her legs from underneath Dutch's body and hoisted herself onto the sofa. She worked to control her breathing as she watched Dutch's body, looking for any sign of movement. She pulled her phone out of her back pocket, ready to call for help, before stopping herself again. Instead, she got up from the sofa and backed down the hall keeping her eyes on Dutch for as long as she could before she slipped into the bathroom. She flung the dryer door open and grabbed the bag, shutting the door quickly. She paced back to her room to grab her purse and then moved slowly back to the living room.

Rose had seen enough horror movies where she expected to see an empty space where Dutch's body lay. She moved with trepidation down the hall, peering into the living room. Relief washed over her when she saw his body lying on the floor. Even though the pool of blood around his head had spanned out, Rose noted he was breathing.

She dashed out the front door, down the steps, and to her car without a second thought. She spotted one lone bike parked out front before starting her car and racing to the development entrance. She came to a stop and the stop sign and then squealed the tires as she tore out into traffic. She sped along Route 17M, pulling over into the small strip mall just down the road and going to the back of the mall where no cars were parked.

Rose flung open the driver's side door and spewed vomit onto the ground. She gasped, got sick again, and then pulled herself back inside her vehicle. Her heart raced as Rose stared straight ahead, watching the parking lot entrance to ensure no one was looking for her. After a few minutes, she gained control of herself, pulled back onto the road, and began driving without a destination.

Chapter 22

Rose and Liz went back and forth for over an hour discussing the pros and cons of staying put before Rose convinced her friend that leaving would be best for her. Finally, they were able to book a flight for Liz out of Newark Airport headed to London that night, and Liz reluctantly packed a bag and had called for an Uber so she could get out of town. The two hugged, not wanting to part, before Liz moved to the front door and opened it. Rose stepped out with her, spotting the idling red Honda with a driver getting interrogated by a Cosantóir member.

"You better go before they pull your driver out of the car," Rose smiled through her tears.

"Be careful, Rosie," Liz said, hugging Rose again. "We'll have a hell of a story to tell when this is all over."

"Yes, we will," Rose answered. "Call me when you land and give my best to Adam. Love you."

Rose watched Liz walk down the steps to the Honda as she dropped her bag near the trunk.

"You mind getting that for me?" Liz grinned at the biker, moving away from the driver's window to open the car's back door for her.

Once situated, the auto pulled away, and Rose spied Liz waving to her as she left. The two Cosantóir went back to their bikes positioned in one of the guest parking spots, giving a casual nod to Rose as she moved back indoors.

Rose locked the front door again, plucked the plastic bag containing the invoices and emerald, and placed it back in its hiding spot in the dryer's lint trap. She did her best to occupy her mind for the rest of the day, puttering about, straightening up, and organizing and then reorganizing her room until there was nothing left to clean.

Checking her phone and texts became routine for her every twenty minutes, hoping she would hear news from someone about how Darryl was and what was going on. Each time there was nothing. Rose sat on the couch, pulling her knees up to her chest, and grabbed one of the throw blankets off the back of the sofa, covering herself. She kept her phone nearby and closed her eyes to block the anxiety coursing through her brain.

The sound of knuckles rapping on the front door startled Rose awake. She sat frozen on the couch for a moment, unsure if it was just a dream she had until the knocking occurred again with more force.

Rose slowly moved toward the front door, remembering Finn's words to her. She peeked through the peephole to see a prominent figure taking up the entirety of the circle.

"Can I help you?" she asked, trying to steel her voice.

"Rose? Hi, I'm one of the brothers on watch here. I'm just checking in on you. I just arrived a minute ago, so we're still here."

"Okay, thanks," she sighed.

"I don't suppose you have something to drink, like a soda or bottle of water?" the biker asked. "I forgot to grab something before I came over, and Preacher won't like it if I even leave for a minute to go to Quick Chek for something."

"Sure, let me take a look," Rose said as she moved to the kitchen. She grabbed one of the cold bottles from the fridge and returned to the front door, moving to unlock the deadbolt before stopping.

"I know this will sound weird, but can you show me your jacket?"

"My jacket? Oh yeah, sure," the biker replied.

He took a step back and turned around to display the rear of his coat with the club emblem on it. Rose watched as the man spun around and smiled.

"Okay?" he asked.

"I need to see your club tattoo also," Rose said through the door. "I'm sorry. I know it's a pain."

"Not at all," he offered politely as he took off his jacket. Rose could see the sleeves of ink on each arm. He pushed the shoulder of his t-shirt on his left arm up and turned to face the peephole, so Rose could see the authentic artwork.

She sighed as she undid the lock and opened the door. The biker's presence filled the doorway as he grinned and reached for the water bottle. Rose passed it over, and he quickly twisted the cap off and guzzled the water down, draining the bottle.

"Thanks so much," he gasped, wiping his mouth. "I don't suppose I could bother you for another one to save for later."

"Sure, no bother," Rose answered as she turned and moved to the kitchen, opening the fridge and reaching for another bottle toward the back of the shelf.

"I didn't catch your name," Rose said, her voice muffled by the refrigerator's interior.

She pivoted and saw the biker standing right behind her, grinning a broad smile as he had been eyeing her bent-over body. Startled, Rose dropped the plastic bottle on the floor and heard it bounce and roll as she stared at the imposing figure.

"The name's Dutch," he growled as his arm shot passed Rose and shut the fridge door.

Darryl went through the prison transfer process as he was brought to Orange County Correctional. He turned all his belongings over and waited for them to find an orange jumpsuit that would fit his build before being placed with the general population at the prison. A corrections officer led Darryl to the small cell he was assigned, where he spent more than a few hours staring up at the ceiling and attempting to sort out the facts of what brought him to his current state.

The cell doors slid open so that Darryl could get out and be led outside for some time in the small yard available to the inmates. He walked alone, glad for the warmth of the sun and the knit cap he had provided. He stood next to the chain-link fence at the far end of the yard and watched as a few inmates played basketball.

"You want in, big man?" A tall, lanky, bearded man asked. "We could use your size."

"I'll play for a bit," he agreed, joining a team of two others so they could play.

The game proved more intense than the casual pickup games Darryl would play at Mary Harriman Park on occasion. His height and muscles worked to his advantage as the much smaller players had difficulty defending him. A small crowd had gathered around to watch, with quite a bit of chatter going on among the inmates, including hoots and hollers anytime anyone tried to dunk on Darryl, and he blocked them.

As he guarded one of the other players, Darryl picked up bits and pieces of conversation. He heard a shrill voice echo above the others, bragging.

"The guy hit me in the head with a fucking rock," he heard the voice screech. "This was after he dumped one of the guys over the fence. Threw him like a rag doll, he said. All I know is I had to get five fucking stitches in my head, and Vinny broke two ribs, and then we didn't even get paid because the asshole said we didn't finish it."

Darryl froze and stared as he tried to pick out where the voice came from from the crowd. Then, his view became obscured by a tall player stepping in front of him and leaping high to go to the basket. The man dunked over Darryl, eliciting groans from the crowd and Darryl's teammates.

"Shit, man, keep your head in it," one of Darryl's team members shouted.

"It's all good," the tall man said, patting Darryl's chest. Whistles shrieked through the air to indicate time outside was up. Darryl tried to view who the inmate was with the shrill voice but had difficulty picking anyone out of the crowd. He heard the voice one more time, up ahead of him as they waited in line to get back into the jail. Darryl turned to his tall teammate behind him.

"You know who that is?" Darryl asked.

"You're going have to be more specific, man," the tall man laughed.

The shrill voice echoed down the line once again, this time with a hyena laugh following it.

"That guy," Darryl pushed.

Tall Man rolled his eyes.

"That asshole," he told Darryl. "His name is Mouth. Big surprise, right? His real name is Marcel Ruiz. He's in and out of OCJ. Usually, petty stuff that gets him right back out, it seems. Pain in the fucking ass, man. The guy never shuts up. He's always bragging about this and that, but he ain't done shit. Seems like he gets caught more than he works. Rumor is he's an ass-hat snitch. You know him?"

"Sort of," Darryl admitted as he spotted the smaller man bobbing up and down in the crowd. "He with anyone?"

"Nah, no one trusts him," Tall Man replied. "He just got back in yesterday. Odds are he'll be out tomorrow. He never stays long. He's got COs looking out for him. You got a beef with him?"

"You could say that," Darryl offered. "He's part of why I'm here, and I think his friends are messing with my lady."

The men made it back inside and were filing toward their cells.

"Hey, if you want time with him, I know where he's at," Tall Man answered. "He's next floor down in B7. I'm sure I can get you there."

"You got that kind of pull here?" Darryl asked.

"Dude, you know who you're talking to?" Tall Man laughed. "I'm Reggie Mason. I can get it done for you."

"Demon," Darryl said, offering his big fist to Reggie. Reggie gave him a bump and grinned.

"Name fit you?" Reggie asked.

"Sometimes it does," Darryl nodded.

"I'll catch you later, Demon," Reggie said with a point before walking into his cell.

Darryl slid into his cell a few doors down from Reggie and sat on the unforgiving mattress on his bed, listening to the groans underneath. Then, finally, he laid back, piecing things together and hoping to figure it out before any danger befell Rose.

"I... I would have brought it out to you," Rose stammered as Dutch's body took one step closer to her, pinning her against the refrigerator door.

"It's no bother, Rose," Dutch told her. Rose felt his eyes on her, scanning every inch of her body. Fear seized her, immobilizing her for the moment.

"Who knew Demon had such good taste in women," Dutch said, reaching out and grazing his fingers across Rose's right cheek. She instinctively flinched and turned her face.

"Oh, don't turn away from me, honey," Dutch's voice oozed. He turned her face back to face his, and Rose stared into his blank, dark eyes.

"What do you want?" Rose croaked. Her right hand gripped the refrigerator door handle behind her to steady herself.

"Well, first, you will tell me what you may have found in the jewelry store and where it is. After that, maybe we can have some other fun."

Dutch moved his right hand to Rose's torso, intent on snaking higher over or under Rose's shirt.

Frozen in place, Rose's memory flashed back to her teenage years when her father gave her and Liz self-defense lessons in the backyard. She remembered his distinctive voice telling them, "Eyes, ears, balls."

Dutch's hand moved under the hem of her shirt before reality came back to Rose. Her left knee shot up, striking Dutch directly in the groin and causing him to recoil and slump to the floor, groaning.

Rose scanned the kitchen quickly as she looked for anything to use as a weapon. Her hand shot over to the stovetop, where she gripped the tea kettle of still hot water she had put on to make some tea before nodding off to sleep. Then, flipping the spout open, she dumped the water onto Dutch's face, causing him to scream in agony. His hands moved from his aching balls to cover his face.

"You fucking bitch! You burned me!" he yowled.

Rose darted past Dutch's prone body, stomping on his crotch as hard as she could to make him howl louder. She raced to her bedroom, locking the door behind her, and searched her purse for her phone. Then she realized it was still on the sofa next to where she napped. Reluctant to go back out of her room, she scoured her desk and dresser to see what she could use to defend herself.

Footsteps lumbered down the hallway before she heard Dutch's body slam against her door, causing her to jump back.

"It's probably better that you're there," Dutch shouted. "Once I'm in there with you, I can get you on the bed and teach you some manners!"

The body slammed into the door again, making the wood creak and the hinges shudder. Rose spotted the few candles she had scattered on her desk and reached just as she heard her bedroom door splinter.

Light filled the room from the hallway behind Dutch as he faced Rose. Swelling and red peeling skin covered the left side of his face with his eye barely open.

"Nowhere left to go, Rose," Dutch cackled. "This is going to be sweet."

Rose grabbed the flexible lighter next to the candles just as Dutch seized her, wrapping his burly arm around her waist and flinging her to the bed. Her body bounced on the mattress, her head striking her headboard, stunning her. Dutch was on her immediately, punching Rose in the rib cage to knock the wind out of her.

"Now maybe you'll learn to listen to me and behave," Dutch roared. His hands unbuttoned the top of Rose's jeans and began to reach for his own belt. Rose gripped the lighter in her left hand as she turned her head to the right and saw the can of Lysol on her nightstand. She pulled the cane down and positioned it just as Dutch finished undoing his belt to look up at her. She sprayed the Lysol directly into his face and eyes. Dutch floundered off Rose's body and staggered back, striking the far wall with his back.

Curses flew from Dutch's lips as Rose kept spraying his face. Finally, Dutch attempted to flee, feeling his way down the hall with his palms on each wall.

"I can't see!" he yelled as he staggered back. Rose kept moving toward him, still spraying the Lysol feverishly until the can was emptied. Dutch tripped over the ottoman, his head thumping on the floor in the living room. Rose glanced at his face, seeing tears streaming from both eyes. His right swelled shut while his left barely opened and was bloodshot.

Rage surged through Rose's body as she breathed heavily and stood over Dutch. She turned and picked up her cellphone to call 911.

"Yeah, call an ambulance and the cops," Dutch laughed through the pain. "I need some help."

Rose stopped and slid the phone into her back pocket.

"Who sent you here? What did you want from the shop?"

"I'm not telling you shit," Dutch spat out. His left hand scrambled and reached to grab Rose's leg, but she quickly kicked it aside before stomping on his stomach, forcing all the air from his body.

Dutch gasped, struggling to breathe.

"Think about it for a second," Rose shot back. "Next refusal and I'm stomping those little grapes of yours into oblivion. After that, you'll never have to worry about being with a woman again."

"Okay, okay," he wheezed, working to cover his groin with his hand. Rose spied Dutch peer his one eye open and smile at her. Before she could do anything, his left leg swept across, striking her legs and knocking her down, so her head hit the sofa's cushions before hitting the floor. Her movements pushed the side table over, sending the lamp and everything else on the table crashing to the floor.

Dutch struggled to rise and move toward Rose as she regained her senses. He grabbed at her feet, pulling her to him as she shouted, "No! No!"

"I've been nice up to now, Rose," Dutch reminded Rose as his hands took hold of her calves and tugged on her. "Now it's time to get dirty."

Rose looked at the ceiling as she felt her body moving on the floor and Dutch's hands groping up to her denim-covered thighs. Her fingertips grabbed for anything as he tried to drag her, and she hooked her fingers onto the leg of the couch, putting up some resistance.

"You're feisty, I'll give you that," Dutch laughed as he tugged harder. Rose refused to give up, clinging to the couch leg until she spotted the crystal vase lying on the floor. She could just get the top of the heavy urn between her fingertips enough to grab hold of it as she slid closer to Dutch.

Gripping the vase in her hands, she looked down to see Dutch crawling up her body, pressing himself against her.

"Game over, Rose," Dutch hissed.

"You're right about that," she said back as she screamed and crashed the vase against his forehead.

A loud thud resounded through the room, and Dutch made no sound and just stared blankly at Rose. A small stream of blood trickled down his forehead as he slumped to the left and fell over, hitting the floor.

Rose pulled her legs from underneath Dutch's body and hoisted herself onto the sofa. She worked to control her breathing as she watched Dutch's body, looking for any sign of movement. She pulled her phone out of her back pocket, ready to call for help, before stopping herself again. Instead, she got up from the sofa and backed down the hall keeping her eyes on Dutch for as long as she could before she slipped into the bathroom. She flung the dryer door open and grabbed the bag, shutting the door quickly. She paced back to her room to grab her purse and then moved slowly back to the living room.

Rose had seen enough horror movies where she expected to see an empty space where Dutch's body lay. She moved with trepidation down the hall, peering into the living room. Relief washed over her when she saw his body lying on the floor. Even though the pool of blood around his head had spanned out, Rose noted he was breathing.

She dashed out the front door, down the steps, and to her car without a second thought. She spotted one lone bike parked out front before starting her car and racing to the development entrance. She came to a stop and the stop sign and then squealed the tires as she tore out into traffic. She sped along Route 17M, pulling over into the small strip mall just down the road and going to the back of the mall where no cars were parked.

Rose flung open the driver's side door and spewed vomit onto the ground. She gasped, got sick again, and then pulled herself back inside her vehicle. Her heart raced as Rose stared straight ahead, watching the parking lot entrance to ensure no one was looking for her. After a few minutes, she gained control of herself, pulled back onto the road, and began driving without a destination.

Chapter 23

Darryl sought out anything he could to help him pass the time. His mind raced obsessively regarding Rose and what she might be going through right now. Even with the protection that the Cosantóir provided for her, the fear of the unknown made him anxious. He spent time doing push-ups and crunches to the point where he stripped to the waist to avoid soaking himself in sweat.

Muscles tense and glistening in the light of the cell, a slow knock rapped on the cell bars, getting Darryl's attention. Darryl looked up from the last of his reps and spied a CO watching him.

"Enjoying the view?" Darryl asked sarcastically as he returned to his exercise.

"I heard you were here, but I had to see for myself," the guard remarked.

"Do I know you?"

Darryl ceased his crunches and stood up, facing the officer through the bars. Darryl sized him up, wondering if he was here to try and take him on.

"Nah, but I know you, Demon. I watched you on TV for years. You were always one of my favorite wrestlers."

Darryl sighed and sat down on his cot.

"It's not the best time to ask me for an autograph. Catch me another time."

"I get it," the guard nodded. Darryl's eyes turned to the nametag the officer wore.

"No offense... Turner, is it? I've just got a lot on my mind."

"Like how to get to see Mouth?" Turner asked.

"I don't know what you're talking about," Darryl spoke, putting his t-shirt back on.

"Okay, then I guess Reggie asked me to stop here for nothing. Have a good a one." Before Darryl sprang up from his cot, Turner began to walk away and went to the bars.

"What did you say?"

"You heard me," Turner said in a hushed tone. "Reggie asked me to see what I could do so you can get some time with Mouth. If you want to do it, it's got to be now. The dinner alarm is going to sound in a few minutes. When your cell slides open, you come with me. I'll take you down to him. He's in a protective custody cell now, but I can get you there. You'll only have a few minutes with him. Deal?"

"What do I owe you for that?" Darryl asked.

"Me? Get me a picture, and we're cool. Reggie is the one you'll be in debt to, not me."

"Fair enough," Darryl nodded, trying not to concern himself with what Reggie might ask for down the road.

"Be ready, and don't act like anything is up," Turner advised just as the buzzer sounded and the cell door opened.

Darryl stepped out of the cell as other inmates did the same. Turner nodded forward, indicating Darryl should move ahead of him.

"Down the first staircase," Turner barked as he pointed the direction for Darryl to move.

Once he was down the metal steps, Darryl entered the wider area where cells with locked doors sat with a small open space for inmates to sit at.

Turner pressed on the handset attached to his shoulders and spoke into it rapidly.

"Dave, open B7," he rushed as the door to B7 popped open.

"Three minutes, Demon. Don't make me have to come in there and taser you or something. When I say go, we go."

Darryl nodded again and slipped into the cell, which was larger and more comfortable than what he was assigned. He saw the shorter figure of Mouth facing the wall away from him, with his hands on the wall.

"Just leave the tray of food, man," Mouth ordered. "My potatoes better not be cold this time," he whined.

Darryl stepped up right behind Mouth and towered over him.

"We're fresh out of potatoes today," Darryl uttered, causing Mouth to turn around.

Darryl pinned him to the far wall.

"What the fuck, man?" Mouth said, scared and preparing to yell for a CO.

"Scream like a bitch, and I'll break your jaw, Marcel," Darryl warned.

"What do you want? I don't even know you."

Darryl looked over Marcel and saw the telltale signs of where the rock he tossed struck Marcel in the head. In addition, stitch marks were still present on the sizeable gash the stone had created.

"Nice scar, Marcel," Darryl told him as he eyed it.

"Look, man," Mouth started. "You don't want to mess with me."

"How'd you get the scar on your head?" Darryl asked, ignoring Mouth's warning.

"You came in here acting all tough to ask me that?" Mouth laughed nervously. "Christ, man, some dude hit me in the head during a job."

"Hmph," Darryl grunted. "Next time, I need to aim better."

The color drained from Mouth's face as he realized who he was trapped with.

"Whoa, look, man, I don't know who—"

Darryl's hand shot over and gripped Mouth by the throat. The smaller man struggled under tightening fingers.

"I will ask you questions, and you will answer them. Try to avoid answering me, and my grip gets tighter. It won't take much for me to strangle you, and I'm sure no one will be sad you're gone. Got it?"

Mouth nodded quickly as he choked.

"You were hired to come to my house that night and do what?"

"Fuck, man," Mouth gasped.

"That's not an answer, Marcel," Darryl said as his fingers pressed deeper into Mouth's throat.

"We... we were planting stuff, man. We were supposed to leave stuff there in the shed and get in the house if we could."

"What did you want in the house?"

"I don't know, man, I swear," Mouth croaked. "That wasn't my part of the job. I had the stuff to leave. Somebody else was supposed to go inside. You came out and fucked everything up, so we looked to get out of there. We went back when no one was around and planted the stuff. They just wanted to frame you to get you out of the way. It's the girl they were more interested in."

"Who's 'they,' Marcel?" Darryl asked.

"Shit, man, I can't tell you that," Marcel pled.

Darryl increased pressure on Marcel's throat. The chokehold pressed on Mouth's carotid artery as Darryl watched the fearful man's face turn red and purple.

"You won't be much good to anyone as a snitch after this anyway, Mouth. Who put you onto this?"

"Please," Mouth begged as he struggled to breathe.

"WHO WAS IT?" Darryl yelled into his face, striking the wall just to the left of Mouth's head.

"Myers!" Mouth croaked out. "I work for Myers!"

Darryl released his grip as Mouth collapsed to the floor, panting to get air into his body.

"Why would Myers want anything from the woman or me?" Darryl asked. He squatted down and lifted Mouth by his ragged mop of black hair.

"How should I know? Mouth asked. "I just do what he asks me. I give him the info and do jobs for him, and he gives me the cash and keeps me out of trouble. Look, man, I got no beef with you. It was just a job."

"A job that put me, my daughter, and my lady in danger. I should just choke the life out of you. You won't be missed."

Darryl reached for Mouth's throat once more, and the smaller man recoiled, scrabbling on the floor as his back hit the wall.

"Shit, I can't. I'll be dead as soon as he finds out," Mouth said, shaking his head.

"You're dead either way, Marcel. At least if you answer me now, you'll know you get a couple of hot meals before Myers kills you."

Mouth hesitated before answering, his eyes scanning all around the room.

"Have it your way," Darryl shrugged. He grabbed Mouth by the legs and tugged him to the floor, Mouth's head bouncing on the cement.

Darryl firmly placed his foot on Mouth's throat while grabbing his right arm and pulling it tightly.

"Wait!" Mouth gurgled. "It was some Irish bitch. I never met her, but I heard Myers complaining about her and then yelling on the phone. I never heard her name. That's all I know!"

"Demon!' Turner's voice echoed from just outside the cell door. "You gotta go."

Darryl looked down at Mouth and squinted.

Darryl applied extra pressure on Mouth's throat before he twisted the arm quickly. A loud pop sounded throughout the cell as Mouth attempted to scream, but nothing came out of his mouth. Darryl removed his foot and then released Marcel's arm, sending it flopping to the ground. Mouth lay on the floor in agony, his shoulder separated and his arm broken.

Darryl squatted down next to Mouth.

"Come near Rose, my daughter, or my house again, and you'll wish I killed you today," Darryl growled before standing up and striding toward the door.

Darryl stepped out of the cell and stood next to Turner. Cries and whelps were heard from inside.

"He'll need medical attention," Darryl said. "He slipped and landed on the floor. I think his shoulder is separated, and maybe his arm is broken."

Turner nodded as they took a few steps away from the cell before he radioed in.

"Medical to B7, Dave," Turner spoke as he prodded Darryl to move toward the cafeteria.

"Thanks," Darryl said as he reached the line to get food.

"For what?" Turner asked. "All I did was lead you from your cell to the cafeteria. Man's gotta eat, right?"

Darryl nodded and moved down the line as Turner drifted off. Once Darryl had placed the semblance of a meal onto his tray and walked across the room. He made his way toward an empty table before being waved over by Reggie. Reggie cleared out the seat next to him, so Darryl had a spot at the table.

Darryl sat as Reggie reached over to Darryl's tray and grabbed the dinner roll and pudding cup. Darryl just looked on as Reggie opened the pudding cup and dove into the chocolate.

"Everything good?" Reggie asked as he ate.

"All good," Darryl acknowledged as he went about picking at the leaden meatballs on his tray.

Reggie just nodded along as he polished off the pudding.

"So, what do I owe?" Darryl asked casually.

"Pudding and rolls for one," Reggie indicated. "Every day."

"I won't be here long enough for you to get much," Darryl replied. "My bail hearing is tomorrow. So I'll be out."

Reggie laughed as others at the table snickered.

"You know how many times I've heard that from people?"

Reggie split the dinner roll in half and dunked part of it into the bits of sauce remaining on Darryl's tray.

"It's not always as easy as you think making bail, man," Reggie advised. "You might want to get comfortable."

"Can't do it. I've got a good lawyer. I'll be gone. I have to be. Maybe I can put a word in with my lawyer and see what he can do for you."

"Don't bother," Reggie told him. "I'm not going anywhere. I'm doing my time just fine. Three squares, TV, Internet, and people got me what I needed, and all I had to do was kill someone. I should have done it years before," he laughed. "When you're still here after your bail hearing, we'll talk more about what you can do for me."

Darryl finished the rest of his meal in silence, comfortable in the notion that the information he acquired would be enough to get him free, away from Reggie and back to Rose.

Rose found herself instinctively driving to Darryl's home. It wasn't until she pulled into the driveway and saw the two motorcycles that she recalled Darryl would not be here for her. She climbed out of her car and approached the front porch, where the two bikers sat. One lolled on the porch swing while the other sat on the front steps. The white-haired biker on the steps stood up when she neared.

"Hey there," he said. The keys looped onto his belt jingled as he moved. "Something I can help you with?"

It wasn't until Rose reached the porch where the light illuminated her face that the man took a step back.

"You okay?" the biker said, reaching out to her.

"I need to see Annie," she trembled.

"Does she know you?" he asked as the other biker joined him on the steps.

"I'm..." Rose froze as she tried to focus on what she did.

"Rose!" Annie yelled.

Rose glanced up and saw Annie pushing open the screen door and coming outside. She raced to Rose, moving between the two bikers so she could embrace Rose. Rose felt the tension from her body release as she leaned into Annie and cried.

Annie led Rose inside and to the couch, with one of the bikers following behind. She tilted a lamp over to better look at Rose's face. Rose winced as the bright light hit her eyes, and Annie's thumb grazed the welt blooming on Rose's face.

"What the hell happened?" Annie asked.

"Someone came into my... my house," Rose stammered. "He was one of them," she said as she pointed at the biker. Rose watched as Annie spun and shot a look at the biker.

"It wasn't me, Annie," the biker added. "Pick and I have been out front for hours."

"What did he look like, Rose," Annie prodded.

"He was big. He had the jacket and the tattoo Finn said to look for," Rose said.

"Did you get a name?" the other biker asked. As he neared Rose, she flinched and pulled away.

"Whitey, go outside and call Finn and Liam," Annie ordered as she pointed to the door.

Whitey left the living room, allowing Rose to relax and lay her head back on the sofa.

"Let me get you some ice for that," Annie said, rising from the couch.

"No!" Rose yelled, grabbing Annie's hand. "Stay with me, please."

Annie sat back down on the sofa and took Rose's trembling hand in hers.

"Yeah, of course," Annie said calmly.

Pick entered the house and stood outside the living room, not wanting to get too close.

"Whitey got a hold of Finn. He and Liam are on their way. Do we know who it was?"

"No," Annie indicated.

"He said his name was Dutch," Rose blurted out.

"Fuck," Pick responded. "He's not Cosantóir anymore. The Ceannaire booted him and took his colors. Are you sure it was him?"

"How the fuck would she know, Pick?" Annie barked. "Ask for his business card before he attacks her? Jesus. Get me some ice."

Rose sat composing herself, trying to sort through her experience. She had barely the opportunity to take a breath when Finn burst into the room with another large biker behind him.

"Rose, are you alright?" Finn said as he knelt next to her.

"No, she's not alright," Annie insisted. "Some asshole attacked her in her house."

"Do you need to go to the hospital?"

"No, I don't want that," Rose replied.

"She said it was Dutch," Annie added.

"And you're alive to talk about it?" the other biker added.

"Christ, Liam," Finn said, shaking his head.

"All I'm saying is you're a tough woman if you faced off with Dutch and walked away with just a few bruises. I know plenty of men who couldn't say the same thing. So did you kill him?"

Rose shook her head no.

"He was unconscious at my place when I ran out."

"I'm on it," Liam said. "I'll take Whitey with me and check it out. Lexington Hill, right?"

Finn nodded, and Liam was off before Rose could utter another word.

"Rose, did he say anything to you?" Finn asked.

Rose took a deep breath and closed her eyes, focusing on Dutch's words.

"He said he wanted whatever I took from the shop."

"So he knows you have the keys and the emerald?"

"I never told him I had anything," Rose responded. "I think he just assumed I did."

"What are you talking about?" Annie interrupted.

"Later, Annie," Finn insisted. "For now, we need to figure out a way to keep you two safe."

"How's Darryl?" Rose asked.

"His bail hearing is in the morning," Finn answered. "I'll know more then."

"Can I talk to him? Maybe I can come to the hearing," Rose asked as she placed an ice pack on her swollen cheek.

"Rose, no," Finn told her sternly. "No one can speak to him while he's there, and there is no way you are going to that hearing. It's not safe. We need to get you out of harm's way. Where can you go?"

Rose looked at Annie for guidance.

"It might be safer for you, Rose," Annie admitted.

"But what about your father?" Rose said softly.

"Dad would want you to be safe first, even if that means going elsewhere. I'm sure of it."

Rose took a deep breath and then turned back to Finn.

"Montserrat," she sighed. "My mother lives there. I'm sure I could go there, and no one would look for me."

"Okay, good," Finn agreed. "Let me make a few phone calls and see if we can get you out tonight."

"What?" Rose said, shocked. "Tonight? I don't have any of my things—clothes, passport, anything like that."

"Where's your passport?" Finn asked. "I'll get one of the brothers to get it from your home. They can get you clothes too if you want."

"I don't want some stranger pawing through all my stuff."

"We don't have time to fight about this, Rose," Finn told her. "Annie, can you talk to her, please?"

Finn walked off as he spoke into his cellphone, and Annie retook Rose's hand.

"I know you don't want things to be this way," Annie began, "but it makes sense for it to happen. I can lend you some things to take with you. It's just for a little bit until Finn can figure it all out."

"I have to leave something with you then," Rose added.

"Sure," Annie replied.

"You have to promise me you'll keep it safe. Don't show it or give it to anyone but your father."

Rose reached into her purse and pulled out the plastic bag holding the keys, emerald, and documents.

"Promise me," Rose emphasized.

"I promise," Annie told her as she took the bag.

Finn moved to walk back into the living room. Annie quickly stuffed the bag between the cushions of the couch.

"Liam is grabbing your passport. He said Dutch wasn't in your condo. There's lots of blood and broken stuff, but no body. He got out of there somehow. All the more reason for you to get out of here tonight. He won't go easy on you if he comes across you again."

"I'll go," Rose said resignedly.

"Good. I'll contact Siobhan and Conor. They'll help make all the arrangements to see about flying out immediately."

"What about Darryl?" Rose asked.

"What about him?" Annie inquired.

"I don't want to just leave him without any word. I can't."

"I'll talk to him, Rose," Finn told her. "It has to be this way. We can't wait. It's too dangerous for you."

Finn left the room, leaving Rose alone with Annie again.

"I'll let him know," Annie assured Rose. "He'll understand."

"I hope he will because I sure don't."

Chapter 24

Morning arrived quickly for Darryl since his night involved little sleep. He was ushered to a transfer van early for his court appearance and arrived at the courthouse with little fanfare. Darryl sat in a locked holding room, awaiting his fate, until Finn strolled in, wearing a suit and tie.

"Wow, you clean up nice," Darryl commented as Finn sat across from him.

"Good morning to you, too," Finn greeted. "Are we ready for this?"

"I have something for you."

Darryl explained the situation to Finn regarding Detective Myers, Gemma, Mouth, and all he was told.

"I knew Myers was involved somehow," Darryl said as he put things together. "He's been in Gemma's pocket the entire time. We couldn't figure out why Gemma was so upset that Quinn left the shop to Rose. It was because she knew about the emeralds and wanted to find them. So all that evidence they supposedly found in my shed was planted."

Finn sat back in his chair as Darryl finished speaking.

"It certainly creates enough doubt to get you out of here so we can make our case," Finn told him.

A knock on the holding room door brought a court officer in.

"You're up next," the officer said, opening the door for Finn to leave. Finn walked away as Darryl was led by the officer into the courtroom and placed on the bench to await the judge's call.

"State of New York vs. Darryl Garvey," the court called.

Darryl was led to the defense table, where Finn stood by. He glanced over at the prosecutor's table and spotted Detective Jackson speaking intensely to the prosecuting attorney. Jackson pointed several times over to Darryl and waved his arms about before he was silenced by the prosecutor.

"What the hell's going on over there?" Darryl whispered to Finn.

"No clue," Finn shrugged. "Probably arguing over where to order breakfast from."

"O'Farrell," the prosecutor said across the courtroom, gaining Finn and Darryl's attention. "A word, please."

Darryl looked on as Finn animatedly discussed with the detective and the other attorneys. Finally, Finn turned and moved back to Darryl, taking his spot.

"What's going on?" Darryl said anxiously.

"Just wait a minute," Finn whispered and pointed toward the judge's bench, where Judge Montero sat speaking with the prosecutor before ushering him back to his place.

"Are we ready to proceed now? Mr. Albert?" Judge Montero asked as she looked at the prosecutor.

"Your Honor, based on news and evidence that came to light just this morning, the state is dropping the charges against Mr. Garvey," Mr. Albert stated.

"Are you certain about that, Mr. Albert?" the judge asked. "These are serious charges."

"I realize that, Your Honor," Mr. Albert offered. "However, some -egregious errors were made in this case that led us in Mr. Garvey's direction. We look to correct that now."

Judge Montero sighed loudly and turned to Darryl.

"Mr. Garvey, on behalf of the state of New York, I apologize. The charges against you are dropped, and the case is dismissed."

Judge Montero banged her gavel and stared intensely at Mr. Albert and his staff before she rose and left to return to her chambers.

"Is someone going to explain this to me?" Darryl said, bewildered.

"They'll have some paperwork to process for you, but you'll be free shortly," Finn answered as he filed papers into his worn satchel. "I'll wait for you outside."

"Not until you let me know what happened."

"Darryl, just go with the court officer for now, and I'll tell you what I know," Finn urged as the bailiff came up behind Darryl to lead him away.

Darryl went through the laborious process of getting released and finally met Finn outside the jail complex.

"Thanks," Darryl said, bumping fists with Finn.

"I didn't really do much," Finn added as they walked toward the parking lot. "They fucked up royally on this one."

"Can you tell me now?"

"Your information panned out before I even got to tell it to the police," Finn admitted. "Detective Jackson's been snooping around every which way regarding this case. He had a bad feeling about Myers before they even busted you. They had things pretty well planned out to frame you and Rose. Jackson is pretty sure Gemma Quinn is behind all of it. She arranged for the robbery, and once she saw you on the scene with Rose, she decided to turn it all on you in hopes of getting the store. They had a bunch of people involved, including Dutch."

"That bastard? What did he do?"

"I don't know for sure, but he was part of it. I'm guessing the one who roughed up Thomas Quinn a little too much. Then, once she and Myers didn't find what they wanted in the shop and Quinn died, she thought the will would leave her everything. Old Thomas Quinn threw a monkeywrench into that by leaving the store to Rose. They had no choice but to set you two up to get the shop and the emeralds. When they didn't find anything, Dutch got a little antsy and came after Rose."

"What?" Darryl yelled, stopping before they reached Finn's car. "What happened? Is Rose okay?"

"She's okay," Finn assured as he unlocked the car. "Get in."

Darryl folded himself into the front seat and waited patiently for Finn to get in and start the car.

"You better start talking, Finn," Darryl warned.

"Dutch showed up at her place after you were arrested," Finn said calmly. "We had brothers at your place watching Annie and a couple at Rose's. He caught Pilot before he could get settled in at Rose's place. You know Dutch. He roughed Pilot up pretty well and swiped his jacket. He was no fool to convince Rose to open the door for him. He had the jacket and the tats, so she thought he was one of us."

"Jesus, man, what did he do to her?"

"Chill, Darryl," Finn said as he drove. "Rose more than took care of herself. She fought him off, got out of there, and went to your place. She got a little banged up and scared, but she took Dutch down. Unfortunately, he got away. I'm not sure where he's at. The Ceannaire put some feelers out to see if we can track him, Myers, or Gemma Quinn."

"Just get me home to be with Rose," Darryl commanded.

"Well, that's another issue for you," Finn said before taking a big breath. "She's gone, Darryl."

"Gone? What the hell does that mean?"

"We thought it would be safer to get her out of the area for now, to get her somewhere people wouldn't be looking for her. I got her on a flight last night."

"To where?"

"Darryl, I know you can't see it right now, but it was right. It's too dangerous for her to be out there. We don't know what lengths they'll go to so they get what they want."

The car stopped at a traffic light just as Darryl slammed his fists on the dashboard of Finn's Lexus.

"Where is she, Finn?" Darryl spat.

"She went home," Finn said calmly.

"To Ireland?"

"No. Rose went to Montserrat, where her mother lives. She'll be safe there. Let her stay there for a while. She's out of harm's way, and that's what is most important."

"Are you sure about that?" Darryl asked. "Myers, Quinn, and Dutch are all still out there. You think they'll stop with all the money that's involved?'

"They must know the cops are after them by this point. I would think they'll have disappeared from view."

"All the more reason for them to go after her," Darryl surmised. "Especially if they think she has figured out Quinn's riddle about the Tree of Life and knows how to use the keys."

"Let's not jump to conclusions," Finn answered. "Once we're back at your place—"

"Once we're back there and I know Annie is okay, I'm calling her."

"Yeah, about that," Finn said, scratching his stubbled chin as he drove. "She didn't bring her cell phone. It was too risky that they would track her signal. Siobhan gave her a burner phone. We don't have the number for it unless she calls and gives it to us."

"For fuck's sake, Finn!"

"It's how we protect, Darryl," Finn insisted. "Siobhan does this all the time with women in need. She knows what she's doing to keep Rose safe. Trust the system."

"My trust in any system was gone long ago. Get me home."

The rest of the ride to Darryl's place occurred without a word between the friends. Darryl gazed out the window, trying to come up with the steps to take next. Once they arrived at his driveway, he was greeted by several Cosantóir with smiles. Darryl, however, scowled and marched right into the house. He spotted Annie sitting on the couch next to Preacher.

"Dad!" she exclaimed as Darryl walked in, racing toward him to give him a hug.

"Are you okay, baby girl?" Darryl said as he embraced his daughter.

"I'm fine. I'm just glad you're home. Are you out and free?"

Darryl nodded as he looked at Annie.

"I'm done. The state dropped the charges against me."

"Thank God," Annie said softly, hugging her father again.

"Dad, Rose... she..."

"I know, honey," Darryl answered. "I'm gonna fix that next."

Darryl stepped back from Annie and looked around at the Cosantóir in his home.

"I appreciate what all the brothers have done to help keep Annie and Rose safe," Darryl announced. "It means a lot to me. Now get the hell out of my house. I have to pack."

A few brothers laughed uncomfortably until they realized Darryl wasn't joking.

Darryl scanned the room once with peering eyes before turning and going up the stairs to his bedroom. He pulled a duffel bag out of his closet and packed quickly, paying little attention to what went into the bag. A knock on the doorframe had him spinning around to see Conor standing there.

"I heard your little speech while in your kitchen," Conor told him. Conor limped over to the chair by the window, using his blackthorn shillelagh to guide him there. "Nice to have you home."

"Conor, if you're here to try and talk me out of going after her, don't waste your breath."

"Take a step back for a minute, Darryl," Conor advised. "Let's see what information we can get about all this before you decide. I have feelers out all over trying to track these people down. If they're still in the area, let's take care of them first before you go after her."

"Every minute she's out there by herself, she could be in danger," Darryl insisted as he stuffed toiletries into his bag. "I'm not going to take that chance."

"From what everyone tells me, she more than held her own against Dutch. She sounds like a tough lady."

"She is, among other things. The problem is Dutch is a sore loser. He won't let her walk away, getting the best of him. Next time he'll kill her. You and I both know that."

"Have you thought this through, Darryl?" Conor asked. "You're putting yourself in danger. And how are you going to get there? It's not like you can just waltz into Newark Airport and buy a ticket to Montserrat for whatever time you want. Do you even have a passport?"

"I do... somewhere," Darryl answered. "I don't know if it's expired or not, and I don't really care. I'll figure it out."

"TSA will figure it out for you when they deny you access to a flight. You can't do this, Darryl."

Darryl zipped the duffel bag and slammed it onto the bed.

"What the fuck am I supposed to do, Conor? Just leave her there? Forget about her and hope she's okay? If it was Maeve or Aoife, you would be doing the same thing. So don't bullshit me."

Conor sat back in the chair and chuckled.

"You're in love with this woman then," Conor replied.

"So what if I am?" Darryl barked. "That just makes it more important to me. I thought part of what we did was protect, Ceannaire. That's what I'm trying to do. I don't mean any disrespect, but if you're not going to help me, then let me be so I can sort this out."

Conor arose from the chair and struggled with his cane as he moved toward Darryl.

"Do you remember when I asked you to join the Sandhogs, Darryl? And then the Cosantóir?"

"I do," Darryl nodded. "It was the best thing to happen to me since Annie was born. I needed a new job and direction, and you gave me both."

"You know it's not easy for an outsider to get into either," Conor reminded him. "Most Hogs are descendants. There's no one else crazy enough to do what we do. Sandhogs and the Cosantóir, they're both brotherhoods. We look out for each other and help when it's needed. I knew you were like that the day I met you. You have always been someone I could count on, good or bad. So I'm not going to turn you out now."

"Thank you," Darryl said humbly.

"Let me make a couple of calls," Conor said, patting Darryl on the back. "I may be able to get you on a private charter."

"So I won't need my passport?"

"I didn't say that," Conor answered. "But I know someone who can help us with that too. I'm going to need a few hours to pull it all together. Catch your breath, and don't forget to pack your inhaler."

Darryl did a double-take as Conor moved slowly to the doorway.

"How did you know about that?"

"I'm old, not stupid, Darryl," Conor laughed. "I know the signs of silicosis. Lots of guys from my era deal with it. How long have you known?"

"Not long," Darryl admitted. "They still have more tests they want to do. I think it will be alright."

"Don't take it lightly, Darryl," Conor warned. "I've seen too many guys do the same thing and end up badly. You're a young man with a lot to live for."

"Thank you, Ceannaire," Darryl told him. "For everything."

"Don't thank me yet," Conor told him. "I said I would try. Sit tight. I'll be in touch."

Darryl sat on his bed, staring at the duffel bag at his feet.

I'm not sure how long I can wait, he thought.

The emerging sunlight danced on the stained glass suncatcher perched in the window, splaying a rainbow across Rose's eyelids. Her eyes fluttered open, and she caught her breath, unsure of just where she was. The simple bed she slept on in the sparsely decorated room gave her a start. She swung her feet off the bed, placing them on the small, worn area rug so she wouldn't stand directly on the cement floor. The box fan in the window turned slowly, attempting to move the hot, dry air around the room with little success.

Rose shuffled across the room and tugged open the worn wooden door that led to the rest of the tiny house. She guided herself automatically to the small bathroom on the left and reached into the pitted cast iron tub to turn the shower on. Rose disrobed and showered under the trickling water, doing her best to wash while the hot water held out well so she could rinse the previous day's travel off her body.

Once she was done, she tied her hair up to keep it off her neck in the already sticky air. She padded back to her room and dressed quickly, putting on the t-shirt and shorts she had borrowed from Annie. While the fit was a little awkward, Rose made it work by tying the t-shirt off to bare her midriff before she walked out of the bedroom again and toward the kitchen.

Rose recognized her mother's distinct hum whenever she worked in the kitchen. Memories flooded back as she thought about her childhood days of going into the kitchen with her mother to make breakfast before she would walk to school.

Rose angled into the tiny kitchen and sat at the folding table pressed against the wall as she watched her mother humming and cooking. The smell of saltfish curing and cooking on the stove permeated the air. Rose looked on as her mother deftly tossed the onions and peppers before adding a healthy portion of Scotch bonnet pepper to the dish.

"Easy on the peppers, Mama," Rose warned, causing her mother to spin around.

"Good morning!" Margaret Boyle announced, turning her attention back to tossing the vegetables. "You used to have no problem with bonnets when you were a little girl."

"That was a long time ago," Rose laughed.

"Your tastebuds got weaker in Ireland," Margaret muttered. "I blame that on your father."

"Daddy never cooked much," Rose said as she walked to the stove to grab the kettle of hot water. "I did most of the cooking there, even when I was a little. I learned from the best."

Rose gave her mother a kiss on the cheek before turning to the two teacups placed on the table. Steam climbed from each cup before Rose plucked two teabags and sank one into each mug.

Margaret portioned the saltfish breakfast onto plates before moving one over in front of Rose. Rose immediately went to dig in before her mother halted her.

"Rose! Manners. We say Grace first in this house still."

Rose smirked as she folded her hands and bowed her head while her mother prayed aloud.

"Dear Lord, thank you for this food we are about to eat. We are grateful you have provided so much for us, and we ask that You bless this food and continue to guide our family along Your path. And thank you for bringing our sweet Rose home to us to take part in our bounty. In the name of Your son, Jesus. Amen."

Rose added 'Amen' after her mother finished. She dipped her fork into the fried egg that sat atop the saltfish and vegetables, getting a little bit of everything in one bite. The pepper's heat crept up on her, but she dutifully enjoyed the morsels.

"Just like I remember it," Rose said. "Maybe a little bit spicier."

"Bah," Margaret waved. "American food and Irish food. You haven't had a good meal since you were seven."

Margaret passed a basket of fresh johnnycakes to Rose. Rose helped herself to two, putting them on the edge of her plate. Margaret looked at her with a raised eyebrow.

"What?" Rose asked as she tore a piece of the bread off and popped it into her mouth. "You make the best johnnycakes on the island. Always have."

Rose picked at her plate, enjoying her breakfast until she noticed her mother wasn't eating but watching her.

"What's wrong, Mama?" Rose asked as she took another forkful of fish.

"Oh, I don't know. My daughter, who I haven't seen in two years, shows up on my doorstep in the middle of the night without explaining why she is there. It does raise some questions, Rose."

"I told you, I just needed to see you for a bit," Rose answered, going back to her breakfast.

"Hmmm," Margaret replied, crossing her arms. "And where did that shiner around your eye come from? What's really going on, Rose? Don't try to lie to me. You've never been good at it."

"I'm not lying to you," Rose asserted.

Margaret got up from the table, taking her empty plate and reaching for Rose's while Rose sipped her tea. Instead of taking Rose's plate, Margaret placed her hand on Rose's cheek, rubbing her thumb just under the tender bruise.

"What happened? Who hurt you enough to make you run home?"

"Mama, it's complicated," Rose insisted, standing up from the table to wash the dishes.

"I may not have a Trinity College education, but I think I can figure this out," Margaret told her. Rose picked up the sponge in the sink and began to wash the plates while Margaret grabbed a dish towel. "Who is he? Never mind. I don't need to know who he is. If he hits you, he isn't worth the air you breathe."

"It's not that, Mama. He would never..."

Rose clipped the conversation short.

"So there is somebody," Margaret nodded. "It's not Walter, is it? I never liked him. He always put on that fake attitude when you would have me on speaker phone."

"No, it's not Walter," Rose admitted. "Darryl is very different from Walter."

"Oh, so the mystery man has a name," Margaret added. "So if he didn't do this, why wasn't he there to protect you when it happened? Doesn't sound like much of a man to me."

"There's a lot to this you don't know."

Rose went to work on cleaning the cast iron pan that always sat on her mother's stove.

"Make sure you do that right," Margaret chided. "That was my—"

"I know. It was your grandmother's," Rose interrupted.

"And someday, if you're lucky, it will be yours," Margaret told her.

"I have a cast iron pan at home, Mama."

"Not like this one," Margaret said as she hoisted the pan with one arm and began to dry it. "This one has been seasoned perfectly over decades. I can cook anything on it, and it's better than any of those new-fangled non-stick pans. And you know what? This one has a legacy—memories—that you won't find on Amazon."

"Fair enough," Rose said, turning off the water and drying her hands.

"So, if you're not going to tell me why you are here, I hope you're prepared to do some work. I've got laundry to hang and chickens to tend to, and then I have work to do."

"You can't relax for one day?" Rose asked.

"Relaxing doesn't pay the bills, honey. How else can I afford this palace?" Margaret laughed.

"Mama, I send you money every month. If you need more..."

"You think I'm just going to sit here and live off your money? Put my feet up and watch TV all day long? All the neighbors will think I'm rich and come begging.'"

"You're being ridiculous," Rose waved off. "If you need something, get it or let me know."

"I'm doin' just fine," Margaret crowed. "I take care of myself. I pick up odd jobs here and there, babysitting, mending, selling eggs, etc. I even cook dinners for a few people on the street and deliver them. It gives me enough to line my pockets. It's all good between what you send and what I get from your father. Damn, maybe I am rich!"

Margaret belly laughed at the thought.

Rose went about the rest of the day, helping her mother as she did when she lived in Montserrat as a young girl. It returned the fond memories of Rose's youth on the island, though just one glance up provided her with a harsh reminder of what forced her away from her home in 1995. Looking skyward toward Soufriere Hills, plumes of smoke emanating from the volcano against the blue sky, appearing more like clouds than potential danger.

When the first slight tremor from the daily tectonic earthquake rumbled under her feet, Rose was thrown for a loop, dropping the freshly washed sheet she held in her hands to hang on the clothesline. Margaret didn't miss a beat, humming along and placing items as if nothing went on.

"You lost your legs for it," Margaret laughed as she spotted Rose stumble.

"I haven't dealt with it for a long time. It doesn't scare you at all?" Rose asked as she lifted towels onto the line to dry in the warm sun.

"It's been there my whole life, darling, and it will still be there long after I'm gone. It gives me an excuse to shake and dance a bit."

Following an afternoon of collecting eggs from the chickens, Rose sat on her mother's house's modest concrete front porch, putting her feet on an old steel milk jug that her mother seemingly had forever. Margaret appeared with glasses of lemonade for each of them before joining Rose.

"You look exhausted," Margaret quipped as she swirled her frosty glass.

"I've lived in New York for the last ten years, Mama," Rose said as she wiped the sweat from her brow. "It's not eighty degrees in March there. Hell, we just had snow not that long ago."

"Don't swear in my house, Rose," Margaret said sternly. "You might be thirty-four, but you are not too old for a mouth of soap."

Rose giggled at the thought of Margaret chasing after her with a bar of Ivory as she did when Rose was a child. It was always more of a game than a punishment since Margaret threatened but never followed through.

"Are you ready to talk about it yet?" Margaret asked as she looked out upon the clear sky.

"Nope," Rose said swiftly.

"Okay," Margaret nodded. "Take a two-minute break, then come help me in the kitchen. I have a couple of meals to make. I hope you're still good at chopping vegetables."

Rose waited a few moments, finishing her lemonade and thinking about what might be happening with Darryl. She envisioned him still in his jail cell, awaiting the chance to get out. Rose fretted about him making bail and seeking her out with her nowhere to be found. She gripped the burner cell phone she got before leaving New York as it sat in the pocket of her jean shorts. The temptation to call him was great, but she knew the trouble that might cause.

Once her glass was empty, Rose moved back to the kitchen, where her mother was already hard at work. The familiar smell of the goat meat sizzling in Margaret's Dutch oven pot flooded Rose's senses and brought an immediate smile to her face. In Rose's youth, many days passed as Rose learned to peel and chop vegetables while her mother made her famous goat water.

"Go grab some thyme and spring onions from the garden," Margaret bade.

Rose moved out the back door to the gardens in the backyard. She plucked sprigs of thyme and some spring onions from the ground before returning to the kitchen. She passed the herbs to her mother and set to work chopping green and red peppers and onion before reaching for the ceramic bowl on the counter that always housed the Scotch bonnets.

"Careful handling that," Margaret warned. "You're out of practice."

"I remember what to do," Rose replied, grabbing the small wooden cutting board reserved just for the spicy peppers used in the house.

"Here," Margaret said, handing Rose latex gloves.

"I don't need them," Rose insisted.

"Put them on, Ms. Rose," Margaret scolded. "Glendon Hospital is a hike from here, and finding someone with a car to take you this time of day will be impossible."

Rose begrudgingly put the gloves on before handling the sweet-smelling peppers, chopping them into yellow and orange strips before leaving some roughly chopped. Rose gathered garlic bulbs, Scotch bonnet, peppers, and onions and scanned the kitchen counter.

"What are you looking for?" Margaret asked as she stirred the browning goat meat.

"You have a blender or food processor?" Rose asked.

Margaret let out her deep laugh.

"You're too funny, girl," Margaret chortled. "Why would I have those when I have these?" Margaret wiggled her fingers.

"Because it would save you a lot of time prepping," Rose added. A deep sigh escaped her lips as she placed the items back on the cutting board.

"Use this," Margaret said, pulling out her heavy stone mortar and pestle and sliding it over to Rose.

"Jesus, Mama, how do you lift this thing?"

"Strike two with the swearing," Margaret chastized. "I don't stay in such great shape sitting around watching movies on Netflix. I'll stop moving around when I'm dead."

Rose grunted through making the paste before passing it to her mother. She watched Margaret work her magic, adding ingredients without measuring yet knowing what was just right to create her desired flavors. Finally, Margaret covered the dish and stood back.

"Now we wait," she smiled, starting to wash the utensils she used while Rose dried.

Rose placed the dish towel down and moved toward the living room to rest on the couch for a minute. Margaret followed her in and stood next to the sofa, arms crossed.

"Ready to talk now?" Margaret asked.

"Mama, please," Rose pled, resting her head on the back of the couch.

"It's fine," Margaret nodded. "Come help me make cassava to go with the goat water."

"Mama, really?" Rose whined.

"Yes, really," Margaret said, pulling her daughter off the couch.

"Please tell me you have cassava flour, and I don't have to grate and squeeze for an hour," Rose complained as she stepped back to the kitchen.

"Of course I have it!" Margaret exclaimed before following Rose to the kitchen.

Rose got all the ingredients out and pulled an apron off the nail in the kitchen.

"What are you doing?" Margaret asked.

"I want an apron on so I don't get flour all over me."

"That's my apron."

Rose looked down and the red and white striped apron and smiled, remembering when she made the apron as a young girl to give to her mother for Christmas. She smiled at it before going back to the nail to hang it up.

"You can wear it," Margaret responded, taking it back down and placing it over Rose's head. She tied the knot in the back for Rose before moving in front of Rose. She looked into Rose's eyes as she smoothed out the apron for her. Margaret delicately placed her hand on Rose's face, just under her mark.

"I'm so glad to see you," Margaret said softly. "No matter what the reason is."

"Thank you, Mama," Rose replied, choking up.

"Now get to work on the cassava bread," Margaret waved. "I want to see if you remember how to do it."

Rose fumbled through the recipe at first, getting guidance from Margaret with small noises she made to let her know when she did something correctly.

Once the bread was done, Margaret helped herself to a piece to taste test. Rose watched as her mother picked up the still-hot bread and tore off a bit to chew. Margaret got up from her seat and walked toward her pantry, pulling a jar off her shelf. She popped the preserve jar open and spread homemade papaya jelly on a portion before popping it into her mouth.

"Very nice," Margaret offered as she wiped her mouth. "We can serve this with the goat water."

"I'm so glad," Rose said sarcastically as she removed the apron.

"I want to make sure people are happy with what they get, Rose. My reputation around here matters."

"I know, Mama."

Rose barely had time to catch her breath before Margaret was packaging up portions of goat water and grabbing her picnic basket to place items in.

"Let's go," Margaret said as she grabbed her sun hat from the old coat rack by the door.

"Where are we going?"

"I have to get these to people while the meals are hot, Rose. Get your walking shoes on."

Rose took a scarlet scarf from the top of the bureau near the door and used it to tie her hair in a ponytail before taking the picnic basket from her mother and making her way down the road alongside Margaret.

The day's heat abated slightly, and Rose's skin glistened with sweat when they reached the first tiny house they were visiting.

Margaret knocked on the screen door before letting herself into the modest home.

"That you, Margaret?" a voice echoed from the back room.

"It's me, Dean," Margaret yelled back. "I've got your dinner."

An older man in a t-shirt and jeans walked his way out with the help of a wooden cane. He smiled at Margaret and took her hand gently as he walked her back to the kitchen.

"Sit, sit," he insisted to her. "And who's this pretty one?" Dean asked as he turned to Rose.

"Easy, Dean, that's my daughter you're talking about," Margaret warned.

"This is little Rosie?" Dean said with surprise. "I haven't seen you since you were this high," he said, holding his hand against the fridge's wall halfway up.

"Rose, do you remember Dean Lynch?"

"I do," Rose nodded and smiled. "Mr. Lynch had the general store for a long time, right?"

"I did!" he exclaimed. "I used to give you a watermelon Jolly Rancher when you came in."

"I remember that," Rose grinned.

"What you don't remember is I used to pay him to do that so you would tolerate shopping with me," Margaret added.

"Oh, come on now, Margaret," Dean chuckled. "She wasn't bad at all. Always smiling."

"Thank you," Rose gloated.

"Okay, let's get moving," Margaret said as she rose from her seat.

"You're leaving already?" Dean asked. "Sit and have a drink. I can make us some mules. I just made ginger beer the other day."

"Uh, next time Dean," Margaret rushed as she moved to hustle Rose out the door. Rose moved ahead of her mother, glancing back to see Dean working to take hold of Margaret's hand while Margaret continually brushed it away.

"Thank you for dinner," Dean said politely as he reached the porch. "How long are you staying for Rose?"

"I'm not quite sure yet," Rose added.

"Well, I hope to see you again," Dean smiled. "It's nice to have two pretty faces to visit me. You look like sisters walking along here."

"Stop buttering us up, Dean," Margaret shot back. "See you tomorrow."

Rose walked along down the street as her mother caught up to her.

"How much do you charge him for cooking him dinner?" Rose asked.

"What?" Margaret said as she shuffled.

"For Mr. Lynch's meal," Rose added. "I didn't see you ask him for any money."

"Oh. Dean usually pays me at the end of the week. I'm sure he'll pay me tomorrow. He was probably just embarrassed about it in front of you."

"Uh-huh," Rose said skeptically. "You know, I think maybe he's a little sweet on you, Mama."

"Don't be ridiculous," Margaret scoffed, stepping up her pace.

"It's okay if he is. Daddy's had girlfriends for years. You're allowed to have a boyfriend."

"What your father does is his business, not mine," Margaret answered. "I'm too old for boyfriends."

"Mama, you're only fifty-five. I think it's cute."

"Let's move along. Miss Eileen's meal is getting cold with all this wind your yapping."

Margaret ambled up to the next house and rang the bell rope hanging by the front door. A woman about Margaret's age and height greeted both women with a grin.

"Hello, Miss Eileen," Margaret beamed, giving Eileen a hug.

Eileen held the door open as Rose walked in behind her mother, carrying the picnic basket.

"They get the other two dinners," Margaret directed Rose, pointing her toward the kitchen as her mother sat in the living room.

Rose entered the kitchen to see a young, slender woman feeding a toddler in a highchair some mashed fruit.

"Here are your dinners," Rose said, smiling at the baby as she placed containers on the counter.

"Oh, thank you," the young girl said. "Let me get those. Can you give her a little fruit while I get plates?"

"Um, sure," Rose added, sitting down in front of the toddler, gripping a spoon, and tapping it on the tray. The youngster babbled a bit as Rose scooped up a bit of mashed mango and fed it to her.

"Are you new helping Margaret?" the woman asked as she took the tops off the containers and poured the goat water into deep ceramic bowls.

"Oh, I'm her daughter, Rose," Rose answered as she fed the toddler another spoonful. "I'm just visiting her for a bit."

"I'm Brigid, Eileen's daughter," she smiled as she grabbed the cassava bread wrapped in a towel, "and this cutie here is Brianna."

"Hello, Brianna," Rose cooed, eliciting a giggle.

"I was hoping you were local," Brigid said as she moved the goat water bowls to the table. "There aren't too many people around my age here to talk to."

"That has to be tough," Rose lamented.

"Don't get me wrong. I love my mother and her friends," Brigid said as she set a place for her mother. "It would be nice to have someone to hang out with once in a while."

Rose guided the spoon to Brianna's mouth as she laughed once more.

"What are you two gabbing about?" Eileen asked as she ambled in and sat at the kitchen table.

"I'm just telling Rose that I was glad to see a different face around," Brigid said as she pushed her mother's chair in.

"You mean a young, pretty face," Eileen laughed as she grabbed a spoon and helped herself to her meal.

"You're as pretty as anyone around town," Brigid added.

"Back in the day, Margaret and I would turn all the heads when we walked into the pub, right?"

"True enough," Margaret said with flair, making everyone laugh.

"You two should go out somewhere and do whatever people do nowadays," Eileen remarked.

"Are you gonna watch Bri while I go out?" Brigid asked.

"Of course, I will."

Brigid turned her eyes hopefully toward Rose.

"Do you want to? It's been so long since I went out anywhere. We could just go to Sunny's down the street for a drink or two."

"I don't know," Rose said with trepidation.

"Go out and relax a bit," Margaret told her daughter. "Or you can stay at home with me all night. I'm sure I can find some more chores I've been putting off for you to take care of instead."

"Please, Rose," Brigid whispered.

"Sure," Rose caved. "I guess going out would be okay."

"Thank you!" Brigid squealed. "I have to figure out what to wear and do my hair. What time do you want to go?"

"How about eight?" Margaret added.

Rose spun her head around to look at her mother.

"Just a suggestion," Margaret shrugged.

"I guess eight works," Rose added, rising from her chair so Brigid could sit back down.

"Oh, I'm so excited!" Brigid shrieked.

Rose and Margaret made their way home, taking their empty picnic basket with them. Once they were down the road, Rose turned to her mother.

"You were quick to volunteer me to go out," Rose chided. "I didn't really want to go anywhere."

"You could have said no," Margaret told her as she walked. "I'm not forcing you to do anything. It can't hurt for you to make a new friend while you're here, for however long you're planning on staying."

"You trying to get rid of me already?' Rose asked. "You said you were glad I was here."

"Of course, I'm glad you're here, but I have a life here. I do things."

"I see that," Rose laughed as she caught her mother staring at Dean's house as they moved past.

"Hush!" Margaret scolded, slapping at Rose's shoulder.

Rose dished out what was left of the goat water and cassava bread so that she and Margaret could have dinner. Once the meal was plated, Rose dutifully waited to eat while her mother said Grace, bringing a slight grin to Margaret's face.

One spoonful of the flavorful stew had Rose experiencing the sweet heat of the Scotch bonnet peppers through her body.

"Whoa!" she exclaimed, grabbing her glass of lemonade and drinking it down quickly.

"Goat milk will calm the heat better," Margaret said as she ate calmly.

Rose sprang up from her chair and grasped the glass bottle of goat's milk, pouring herself a glass and gulping it.

"You'll get used to it again," Margaret laughed.

Chapter 25

Darryl finished packing and carried his bag downstairs with him. He and Annie sat at the kitchen table eating pizza from Marina's while discussing all that was going on.

"So the police are involved in all this?" Annie asked, aghast.

"Not all the police. Just one bad cop," Darryl corrected.

"What a shock," Annie added. "I didn't like that guy from the moment he showed up at the door with that warrant. He was up to something, and the way he kept eyeing me up and down…" Annie shivered.

"Hopefully, they track him down, and Gemma Quinn too, and then we can put all this behind us," Darryl added as he ate the last of the crispy crust in his hand.

"And what about Rose?" Annie asked.

"I'm going to get her back," Darryl said earnestly. "As soon as I hear from Conor about a flight and passport, I'm out. Liam promised to have brothers here to watch out for you just in case. Annie, you should know that if anything happens…"

"I'm not even going there, Dad," Annie said, holding up her hand to halt the conversation. "I've spent my whole life worrying about where you are and what's happening to you. So I know the drill, even if I don't want to think about it."

"Okay, but you should know where everything is."

"I know," Annie spoke. "It's all in the floor safe under your chair. You really shouldn't have made the combination my birthday."

"How did you know about that?"

"Please, Dad. It wasn't hard to figure out. I've known for a long time. Whenever I move your chair to vacuum and move that nasty throw rug there, you can see the cutout on the floor. I just pop the panel off, and there it is. Which reminds me—"

Annie rose from the table and headed to the living room, Darryl following behind her closely. He looked on as Annie pushed his recliner out of the way and kicked at the area rug. Annie knelt and pulled the faux panel from the floor, revealing the safe door. She quickly spun the combination and unlocked the safe, pulling the Ziploc bag out from within.

"Rose left this and told me not to give it to anyone, but I figured you should have it."

Darryl saw it was the bag containing the invoices, keys, and the emerald. While examining the bag, Darryl realized what his next step needed to be.

"I have to go, baby girl," Darryl said, hugging Annie tightly. "I'll keep you posted, I promise. Just stay put if you can, please. It will be safer. I love you."

"Love you, too," she replied, choking back tears. "Please be safe, and hug Rose for me when you see her. Wait."

Annie broke the embrace and reached back into the safe, pulling out an envelope.

"Is this enough, or do you want another one?"

Darryl glanced in to see the wad of hundred-dollar bills.

"Part of that is to pay for your wedding someday," Darryl answered. "I'm not just hoarding cash."

"Whatever it's for, you need it now. Use cash so no one can trace you."

Darryl tucked the money into the inner pocket of his leather jacket before kissing Annie on the forehead and heading out the door. He paused as he sat on his motorcycle, using his phone to look up the address of Thomas Quinn's house.

Driving along through Monroe, Darryl pondered what he would do if he were confronted by Myers or Dutch at Quinn's house. While both seemed unlikely, he prepared himself for the possibility of a confrontation without a weapon.

He reached Old Mansion Road, traversing past the imposing building lights of Mediacom, before beginning his descent down to a stretch of flat road. He slowed as he reached the mailbox with the number 81 and a reflective shamrock. He ducked into the driveway, noticing just one vehicle present there, and parked before making his way to the front steps. He peered through the living room window and spotted Riley leafing through photo albums. He lightly tapped on the window with his index finger, startling the girl but gaining her attention. She walked toward the front door, where Darryl greeted her.

"Are you alone?" he whispered as she opened the door.

"Of course," she said as Darryl entered the house. "What are you doing here? When did you get out? Have you heard about my mother? How's Rose?"

"Slow down, Riley," Darryl stated, trying to calm her.

"I can't believe all this," she said, sitting on the love seat. "First Detective Myers and my mother come and search the entire house, and then the police show up and do the same thing, asking me all kinds of questions and looking for my mother. Did she really do all those things? Would she have killed my grandfather, her father?"

"I wish I had all the answers for you, Riley, but I'm still piecing things together myself. Do you know if your mother and Myers found what they were looking for?"

"I doubt it since they were cursing and swearing the entire time. Mom and Myers went through Grandpa's room and office, tossing everything, and looked behind, into, and under whatever they could. What is everyone looking for?"

"These," Darryl said, holding up the Ziploc bag.

"A bunch of papers? What are they?"

"Invoices for a million dollars worth of emeralds that your grandfather bought."

"What? But Mom went through the safe in his office. There wasn't anything like that in there."

'Can you take me to his office?" Darryl asked.

Darryl followed Riley down the hall as she opened the door at the end and switched the light on. Darryl entered the office and saw it had been gone through with a fine-tooth comb.

"Mom went through it the day Grandpa went into the hospital, and then after he died, she came back with Detective Myers. Then the police came here and did the same thing. I haven't even bothered to look through and straighten up."

Darryl reached into the plastic bag and pulled out the key they discovered in the jewelry store office. He checked Thomas's desk without finding any locked drawers or false bottoms. The safe revealed little and nothing that a key could be used for. Darryl sat back on the edge of the desk, stumped.

"There's got to be something that this key fits."

A glow appeared through the bay windows behind Thomas's desk.

"What's that?" Darryl said, alerted.

"The motion lights in the backyard," Riley said. "The deer set them off all the time."

"Let's just make sure it's deer," Darryl said as he eased out of the office and made his way toward the back door.

"Are there any weapons in the house?" Darryl asked quietly as they moved.

"I don't know," Riley said, panicked. "Grandpa never said anything about guns."

"Never mind," Darryl added. He peered out the door in the kitchen before slowly opening it and stepping out onto the back patio. He took two steps out onto the polished stone before spotting many deer suddenly staring back at him. The deer quickly departed further back into the woods.

"See?" Riley said, pointing as the deer escaped from view.

Darryl looked out onto the expansive backyard as the lights illuminated the area.

"Wow, you've got a lot of space back here," Darryl admired.

"Yeah, Grandpa loved the yard here," Riley smiled. "We would sit out here almost all year long, no matter the weather. I would still use the tire swing on the enormous tree back there. I always begged him to build me a treehouse there when I was little, but he said the tree was too special to do that with."

Darryl looked closely at the silhouette of the tree. Even without a trace of any leaves on it, the maze of branches and twists in the tree, along with the size, let him know it was old.

"Is that an oak tree?" Darryl asked.

"I think so," Riley shrugged. "The squirrels and deer love it for the acorns every year."

"Damn," Darryl said softly. "You crafty son of a bitch."

Darryl trekked out onto the lawn, crunching leftover bits of ice.

"What are you doing?" Riley yelled before following behind Darryl.

Darryl reached the tree's base and looked around for anything that might stand out.

"It's freezing out here, Darryl," Riley said, crossing her arms.

"Do you have your phone on you?" Darryl asked as he pulled his out.

"Yeah," Riley answered, taking her phone from her jeans pocket. "Do I need to call the police?"

"No!" Darryl shouted. "Don't call anyone. Just turn your flashlight on."

Riley and Darryl both shone lights at the tree.

"What are we looking for?" Riley asked.

"Anything that looks out of place," Darryl said, scanning high and low.

"It's a tree, Darryl," Riley said as she moved. "It all looks out of place to me."

Darryl walked over toward the shadow of the tire swing as the light wind moved it slightly. His eyes followed the rope it was tied to up to the higher limb where it all began.

"How tall was Thomas?" Darryl asked as he searched.

"I don't know," Riley said, exasperated. "5'10" maybe. I never asked him."

Darryl calculated about that height and stared at the tree. He spied a knot in the tree that protruded slightly and approached it. Clearing some of the ice off of it, he looked more closely.

"Shine your light here," Darryl pointed as he put his phone in his pocket. Riley moved near Darryl and spotted her light for him. Darryl gripped the knot between his two hands, attempting to pull it off. When it didn't budge, he used his large palms to twist the knot and felt it give. He turned the knot several times before it pulled off in his hands.

"Light here," Darryl ordered as he saw the gap in the tree. Riley's light flashed over and shined on steel.

"What is it?" Riley asked as Darryl pulled the strongbox out. He removed the key from his pocket and placed it into the lock, opening the box. Inside was a green velvet bag with a note attached. He pulled the paper out and gazed at the words:

Roisin,

Ádh mór agus grá.

Thomas

Darryl opened the bag and poured the contents into his palm. The light from Riley's phone danced across the green gems that fell.

"Holy shit!" Riley said.

"You said it," Darryl replied. He poured the jewels back into the bag and closed it before walking back toward the house.

"Should we call the police now?" Riley asked as she closed the back door.

"Let's leave them out of it for now," Darryl warned. "We don't know if Myers has other people involved that might get back to him about it. For now, I think you need to sit tight and stay safe. If it's okay, I will have one of the brothers come here to protect you until all this is ironed out."

"And what are you going to do?" Riley questioned.

"I'm going to get Rose and finish all this. Thank you, Riley."

Darryl left Riley's house and sped back toward Harriman to Conor's place.

Darryl pulled down the long driveway leading to Conor's home and parked his bike. The motion lights illuminated his way to the front porch, where Darryl knocked lightly.

Conor opened the door and stepped out onto the porch, closing the door quietly behind him.

"Maeve's asleep, and if Jameson sees you, he'll start barking and want to play," Conor said in hushed tones.

Conor handed over a packet to Darryl. Darryl began to go through, examining the flight voucher and his passport.

"The flight leaves White Plains at 11 PM and lands in Montserrat at around three-thirty in the morning. You'll get there around four. Do you know where you're going from there?"

"Haven't a clue, but I'll find her," Darryl said confidently.

"I don't want to know how much this cost, do I?" Darryl inquired.

"No, you don't," Conor assured. "I had to call in many favors for this one."

"Thank you, Ceannaire," Darryl replied sincerely.

"Demon, be careful, okay?" Conor said, shaking Darryl's hand. "If Dutch and this detective are involved, you don't know what they are capable of doing. Watch your back."

"Will do," Darryl nodded.

"She's worth it, right?" Conor shouted as Darryl approached his motorcycle.

"No doubt about it."

Darryl took off toward the New York State Thruway, wending his way down to Westchester Airport before finding the location for Fand Charters. Darryl parked his bike in the private lot and headed to the small office next to the airplane hangar. He swung the door open and was greeted by a young woman behind the counter.

"You must be Mr. Garvey," she said as she looked at her computer screen.

"How did you know?"

"You're the reason I'm open now," she laughed, punching in information on her computer.

"Do you need to see my passport?" Darryl asked, reaching for his packet.

"You're Darryl Garvey, right?"

"Yes, Ma'am," he answered politely.

"That's all I need to know," she said, turning back to her computer. "You can head out to the plane if you want. The pilot will be out in a minute. Is that the only bag you have?"

"That's it," he said, holding up his duffel bag.

"A man who travels light. I like it," she grinned.

Darryl made his way out to the hangar where the Learjet 75 sat majestically with its stairs out, awaiting his arrival. He walked up the steps to look at the luxury interior before selecting one of the eight seats. Darryl placed his bag on the seat next to him and pulled the green velvet bag from his jacket. He felt the slight weight of the gems in his palm.

"So this is what a million dollars feel like," he said softly.

Footsteps echoing across the hangar floor to the metal steps of the plane had Darryl hurriedly place the emeralds out of sight again. The woman from the terminal climbed on, carrying a bag with her.

"You're working for the flight, too?" Darryl asked.

"You bet," she said, storing her bag. "My name's Lucy, Lucy Kerwin," she said, presenting her hand to shake Darryl's.

"Darryl," he nodded. "Is the pilot ready to go?"

"She sure is," she remarked, closing the exit door and walking up to the cockpit.

"You're flying the plane?"

"I'm flying MY plane, yes, Darryl," Lucy replied. "My other pilots weren't available on such short notice, so you get to ride with the boss tonight. I hope that's not a problem."

"Not at all," Darryl spoke. "I'm just surprised a bit, is all."

"I didn't get to restock much, but there are drinks at the bar if you want anything. We'll be taking off in a minute or two. So just relax and enjoy."

Darryl buckled his seatbelt before the plane rambled onto the tarmac before heading toward the runway to take off. Impressed by the smoothness of the ride, Darryl rested his head back, thinking more about his actions once he reached Montserrat.

"You can turn music on if you want," Lucy shouted from the cockpit. "It won't bother me a bit."

"I'm good, thanks."

"I've got to tell you, you don't look like my typical client," Lucy laughed. "It's usually guys in three-piece suits or rappers with an entourage of women hanging all over them."

"I'm sorry to disappoint you," Darryl smiled.

"It's refreshing," Lucy sighed.

"If you just want to lay back and sleep, I can leave you alone," Lucy said. "I had one too many cups of coffee tonight to keep me hyped."

"I may close my eyes for a few minutes if that's okay. It's been a bit of a rough week," Darryl added.

"You're the boss."

A bit of turbulence jostled Darryl in his seat. He flung his eyes open and coughed a bit, reaching for his inhaler in his pocket and taking it out for a puff.

"You okay back there?" Lucy asked.

"I'm good," as Darryl's cough subsided.

"Sorry about that. We hit a little stormy stuff, but we should be past it now. It looks like smooth sailing the rest of the way. We've got about an hour left before we're there."

"Wow, I slept that long?" Darryl said softly.

"You even had a nice little snore, too," Lucy laughed.

"I apologize," Darryl added.

"I've heard much worse coming from back there," Lucy told him. "If the cockpit door is still open, you know you're good."

Before long, the jet began its descent as they neared John A. Osborne Airport. Lucy touched the plane down safely and taxied to the private hangar without incident.

"Welcome to Montserrat," Lucy said as she brought the plane to a stop. "The sun won't be up for another couple of hours, but it's out there."

Darryl unbuckled and waited for Lucy to open the hatch for the door before descending the stairs.

"Sorry I wasn't better company," Darryl apologized as he stood at the bottom of the airplane steps.

"You were fine," Lucy said as she put her backpack over her shoulder.

"Are you flying right back?" Darryl asked as they walked toward the terminal.

"No, I'm spending the night here, and I'll head back tomorrow," Lucy replied. "How long are you staying for?"

"I don't really know," Darryl said as he stopped walking. "I don't even know where I'm going or staying tonight."

"So you plunked down all that money to fly down here on a moment's notice, and you don't know why you're here or where you're going? Must be nice."

"It's not exactly like that," Darryl said. "I did come for a reason, but—"

"Who is she?" Lucy said as she looked at her phone.

"What's that?" Darryl asked.

"The woman you came here to see. I've learned that men are motivated by very few things, which usually boils down to money and sex."

"It's not either of those. Not really, anyway," Darryl admitted.

"Ahh, so it's love then," Lucy joked. "Very romantic, Darryl. I'm sure she'll be over the moon to see you."

"Maybe. Rose doesn't know I'm coming, and I have no idea where she is."

"Something tells me there's more to this story than you're letting on," Lucy remarked.

"There's a lot more, unfortunately," Darryl sighed.

"Well, you can tell me more about it on the way," Lucy said as a car pulled up to the curb.

"On the way, where?"

"You said you didn't know where you're going. So I booked a place at Tropical Mansion Suites. You can stay there with me and then find your lady love in the morning."

Darryl stood back while Lucy climbed into the back seat of the Uber.

"Are you coming?" she asked.

With no other immediate options, Darryl got in the back seat next to Lucy.

Darryl stared out the window into the island's darkness as the driver took them to Sweeney Road before pulling in front of Tropical Mansion Suites. He piled out of the car with his bag while Lucy dashed out and into the hotel to check-in. Darryl arrived at the front desk just as Lucy was confirming everything.

"Lucky for you, they had the Deluxe room still available for you," Lucy smiled, passing a key to Darryl. I'll be in one of the standard rooms."

Lucy walked past Darryl toward the room locations. Darryl followed behind, stopping short just behind Lucy.

"This is me," Lucy grinned. "You're just down at the end of the hall."

"Thanks," Darryl stated. "I wasn't sure what the arrangements were going to be."

"Darryl, you went on about coming here to find a woman you're in love with. Did you really think I would try to lure you into bed with me after all that?"

"No, I mean, no! Of course not," he said, flustered.

"Relax, Darryl," Lucy said, putting her hand on his arm. "I'm just teasing you. Besides, no offense to you, Darryl. You're an attractive man and all but not my type. Too many of the wrong parts for me."

"Huh?"

"Bless your heart," Lucy said with condescension. "Think about it, Darryl. We can talk more over breakfast if you want."

Lucy unlocked her room and entered it, leaving Darryl standing in the hallway pondering for a moment before the light bulb in his head turned on.

"I got it!" Darryl shouted as he laughed and moved toward his room.

Lucy laughed heartily from within the room.

"Good for you!" she shouted.

Even with his body exhausted, Darryl barely slept. The king-sized bed proved millennia more comfortable than the jail cot he used recently, but all his thoughts were consumed with finding Rose. Once the sun rose fully, Darryl showered and dressed, grabbing his bag and walking out the door and down the hall toward Lucy's room. He saw her door was ajar and knocked.

"Hello?" he asked.

"I'm out on the patio," Lucy yelled as Darryl walked through the room to the small patio outside that overlooked the gardens and pool. Lucy sat at the table there, drinking a mug of coffee.

"Good morning," she asked. "Sleep well?"

"Not really, but it was better than I expected," Darryl added as he sat in the empty chair next to Lucy.

"So, what's the plan, Darryl?" Lucy asked. "I see you have your bag with you, so you must have some idea of what to do."

"I'm still working on all that," Darryl told her. "I know Rose's last name, and her mother lives on the island, but I have no idea where that is or what her mother's name is."

"It's a starting point," Lucy answered, sipping her coffee.

"I really appreciate all you've done," Darryl replied. "I'm sure this disrupted your plans and all. When are you returning to New York?"

"I can leave this morning," Lucy told him. "I might linger for a little bit before I go, though. Soak in the sun for a few hours, and have a good meal. How long are you staying?"

"I don't know. I'm hoping to go back as soon as I get Rose."

"You better look at the airline flights," Lucy warned. "There aren't a ton of flights in and out of here each day, and you usually have to go to Antigua first before coming here. That's the nearest commercial airport."

"You got here without a problem," Darryl noted.

"Private charters can get away with stuff like that. You're paying extra for the service."

"Well, do you think I could convince you to stay another day so Rose and I can fly back with you?"

"That's a tall ask, Darryl," Lucy told him.

"I'll pay you, of course," Darryl told her.

"Do you know how much it was for this trip? But, you weren't the one that paid the tab, so I'm guessing whoever fronted this trip has deep pockets you can turn to again?"

"Not really," Darryl admitted. "But I think I can help you out."

Darryl reached into his leather jacket and pulled out the green velvet bag. He placed his fingers in and delicately pulled out one of the more giant emeralds and presented it to Lucy.

"Is it real?" Lucy asked skeptically.

"According to the experts, it is," Darryl responded. "That one stone is at least $100,000, probably more."

"Darryl, I don't want to get involved in anything illegal. If you stole these, that's on you. I'm not taking hold of smuggled gems so you can impress a woman."

"They aren't stolen. Scout's honor," Darryl crossed his heart. "They belong to Rose, and I found them for her. She'd be okay with using it for that."

"How long have you known her?"

"A month or so,"Darryl admitted.

Lucy gazed at the emerald and then turned back to Darryl.

"I'll give you three days to get it all together," Lucy said, putting her sunglasses on and stuffing the gem in her pants pocket. "I'm out of here on day three, though, with or without you. And you have to pay my expenses while I'm on the island."

"Sounds fair," Darryl nodded.

"Well, then let's go get breakfast and find Rose," Lucy said, slapping her palms on her knees before standing up.

Rose walked down to Brigid's house with the warm breeze against her face. Since the only clothing she had was what she had borrowed last minute from Annie, Rose stuck with the t-shirt and shorts she wore for most of the day. Her sandals kicked away a few stones on the road before she reached the front porch of Eileen and Brigid's place.

Before she could knock, Eileen greeted Rose at the door.

"She's just about ready," Eileen said as she opened the door.

Rose entered the house and paced around, looking at some of the pictures on the wall. Old black and white photos were balanced with newer, color pictures, including several of Brigid holding what Rose assumed was a newborn Brianna.

"Thank you for agreeing to go out with Brigid tonight," Eileen said in hushed tones. "She doesn't get out much since Brianna was born."

"Oh, it's fine," Rose answered. "It will be good for me, too. I could use some fun right about now."

Brigid emerged from one of the back bedrooms, clad in a tank top and short floral skirt. She gave a quick twirl before dancing into the living room.

"I'm all set," she said excitedly. Brigid turned to Eileen and gave her a hug.

"We won't be too late, Mom," Brigid answered.

"Take your time. I've got the little one covered. Enjoy yourselves and be careful."

"Yes, Ma'am," Brigid said politely before grabbing Rose's hand and rushing out the door with her.

Sunny's was a short walk from the house, and the music emanating from the bar had Brigid swaying her hips before the two women even entered the establishment. The Caribbean music blared loudly once the door was opened, and Rose was surprised at the size of the crowd for a weeknight. Naturally, heads turned when they walked in, and many prying eyes followed Rose and Brigid as they walked up to the bar.

"Brigid!" the bartender said as he came down and wiped the space where the girls sat. "Quite a surprise to see you tonight. You look... wow."

"Thanks, Mark," Brigid blushed lightly. "This is my friend Rose."

"Pleasure to meet you, Rose. What can I get you, ladies?"

"I'll have one of your famous rum punches, Mark. How about you, Rose?"

"A Guinness for me, please," Rose told the bartender.

"Coming up," Mark said, slapping the bar.

Rose scanned the small bar, noticing some locals laughing and drinking while a couple of older men played darts in the far corner. The cut-out square for the dance floor had a few couples moving to the music.

"Let's dance!" Brigid said enthusiastically, grabbing Rose's hand again and dragging her to the dance floor.

The two danced and giggled, drawing the attention of more than one male patron in the place. The first song blended right into the next at a faster pace. Before Rose knew it, she had worked up a sweat and was glad when the second song ended. Rose steadied her way over to her bar stool with Brigid garnering applause and curtseying to the crowd.

"You looked amazing out there," Mark said as he slid the rum punch in front of Brigid. Brigid wasted no time putting her mouth to the straw and sucking down almost half the glass.

"Thanks," she grinned at Mark before he moved off to serve one of the other patrons.

Rose gently sipped her Guinness before leaning next to Brigid.

"I think Mark is sweet on you," Rose said in her ear.

"You think?" Brigid said, taking another sip of punch. "We've known each other since we were kids in school."

"He's definitely interested in you," Rose asserted. "It's all over his face whenever he talks to you."

"Mark is nice," Brigid began, looking at him, "but I don't know. Sometimes I just wish there was a bad boy around to just take control and... you know... do whatever he wants to me."

Brigid sighed and then laughed before finishing her rum punch and placing her glass down. In seconds, Mark was back.

"You want another?" he asked.

"Please," Brigid said, batting her eyelashes as she reached over the bar to hand the glass to Mark.

Mark smiled and went off to craft another cocktail while Brigid sat back.

"Having the bad boy isn't what it's cracked up to be," Rose advised. "At some point, you want the nice guy to be with every day."

"Hmmm, I guess I haven't reached that point yet," Brigid added. "Have you?"

Rose took another sip of Guinness, pondering the question.

"I'll let you in on a little secret," Rose said. "I think I have the best of both worlds."

"Bad boys can't be nice too, Rose."

"Maybe not. But nice guys who know what they're doing can make you feel like you're with a bad boy."

"Ohhh! Do tell!" Brigid squawked as Mark passed a fresh drink to Brigid.

Rose grinned just at the thought of Darryl and what he made her feel and think.

"Darryl is definitely special," Rose sighed. "On the outside, he looks mean, really mean. He's tall, dark, rides a motorcycle, has tattoos, and works a difficult job. But inside, he's caring, thoughtful, funny, and gentle."

"He's gentle all the time?"

"Well, not always," Rose gushed, warmth spreading over her body.

"That's what I'm talking about!" Brigid howled, draining her rum punch and slamming her glass on the bar.

Rose and Brigid laughed as Brigid polished off another punch, and Mark reappeared at their end of the bar holding two more drinks.

"Compliments of the gents at the table," Mark told the ladies.

"Oh hoh," Brigid laughed, looking over at the men smiling in their direction.

"I haven't had a man do that for me in a long time," Brigid said, swaying on her stool. "You must be my good luck charm, Rose. Let's invite them over."

"Brigid, no, I really don't want to…" Rose began, but it was too late. Brigid had already signaled that they were welcome as the two waltzed over to where Rose and Brigid sat at the bar.

Both men were tall and lean, dressed finer than the other male patrons in the place, clean-shaven, and walking confidently.

"Good evening, ladies," the one man began as he stood next to Brigid. "My name is Samuel, and this here is George."

"I'm Brigid," she said, "and this is Rose. Thanks for the drinks."

My pleasure, Brigid," Samuel grinned. "It's nice to have two fun, attractive ladies here."

"Yes," George said to Rose, leaning closer to her so that Rose could detect he was wearing too much cologne. "I haven't seen either of you in here before. Are you new to the area or just visiting tourists?"

"Oh, I live nearby," Brigid said, pointing wildly while she sipped her punch. "Rose here is just visiting from..."

"Brigid, they don't need to know everything about us," Rose said warily. "I'm in town visiting family. Thank you for the drink."

"Of course," George answered politely. Rose's radar was up as she felt George stare at her. She looked over at Brigid, swaying on her stool and giggling at everything Samuel said to her. Rose noticed Brigid's hand go up toward her mouth, covering it as if holding something back.

"I think my friend needs the restroom," Rose said as she attempted to squeeze past George.

"I think she's okay," George said, glancing at Brigid before trying to stop Rose. But, instead, Rose pivoted past the man and took Brigid by the arm.

"Let's go freshen up," she said to Brigid, pulling her off the barstool.

"But he was just telling me—" Brigid began as she belched, covering her mouth again. She then hurried alongside Rose to the bathroom.

Brigid pushed her way through the bathroom to one of the stalls, and Rose heard the loud retching sounds go on for a minute before stopping.

"You okay in there," Rose asked.

"Not really," Brigid groaned before vomiting again.

Rose entered the stall and held Brigid's hair back as she kept expelling rum punch. Rose gently petted Brigid's head, using toilet paper to wipe her forehead and then her chin once she was done.

"I'm sorry, Rose," Brigid burped.

Rose recoiled a bit from the smell before helping Brigid stand up straight.

"It's okay," Rose answered. "I think maybe our fun is done for the night."

"But I'm having such a good time, and those guys..."

"Trust me, there are better guys than them around," Rose said, flushing the toilet before leading a stumbling Brigid over to the sink. Rose brought Brigid's face closer to the running water so she could splash cold onto her before washing her hands.

Leading Brigid out of the bar, she saw George and Samuel still standing close by where the girls had sat. Once George spotted the ladies nearing, he elbowed Samuel to get his attention.

"Everything okay?" Samuel smiled.

"I think my friend has had it for the night," Rose told them.

"Oh, come on," Samuel complained. "At least finish the drinks we bought with us."

Samuel and George both pushed drinks toward the ladies. Brigid instinctively reached for hers before Rose moved it away.

"No more for you," Rose scolded.

"Well, surely you can finish yours, then?" George asked, handing Rose her pint glass. Rose spotted the exchanged looks between the two men and put down the glass.

"I think I'm done, thanks," she answered. "Hey, Mark!" she yelled, getting the bartender's attention. She pushed the glasses toward Mark.

"We didn't even touch them," Rose said. She spied George and Samuel whispering to each other and then leaned closer to the bar.

"I don't trust them, and I need to get Brigid home. Can you keep them here while we slip out?"

"Is she okay?" Mark asked.

"Too much fun in one night. She'll be fine if I get her out of here without trouble."

"You got it," Mark answered, coming around the bar.

Mark assisted Rose in getting Brigid from the stool to the front door.

"Rose is right," Brigid said, turning to Mark. "You are very nice, Mark," Brigid said as she placed her hand on Mark's cheek. "Do you have any bad boy in you?" she whispered and giggled.

"What?"

"Never mind her," Rose said as they stepped out of the bar. "Thanks, Mark."

"Sure," Mark said, turning around and spotting the two men walking toward the front door. Mark blocked their exit long enough for Rose to get Brigid up the street and to Brigid's home without incident.

Rose got her friend into the house and the couch, where Brigid immediately lay down.

"I'm staying right here," Brigid insisted, kicking her sandals off and placing her head on a pillow. Rose reached over and grabbed a throw blanket to put over Brigid. "Thank you, Rose," she mumbled.

"You bet," Rose smiled before tiptoeing out the front door. Rose stepped off the porch and paced back to her mother's house, looking over her shoulder to ensure she wasn't followed. Then, she walked in, closing the front door behind her and locking it.

"Back already?" she heard her mother yell from her bedroom. Rose paced down the hall and found her mother sitting up in bed, the dim light on her nightstand lit while her mother sat knitting.

"Why are you still up?" Rose questioned. "It's late."

"I just wanted to make sure you got home," Margaret added, placing her knitting aside.

"Mama, I'm a grown woman," Rose stated.

"That doesn't matter. You're still my daughter. I didn't get to sit up waiting for you when you went out with friends or on a date when you were younger. Indulge me now."

Margaret patted the empty space on the bed next to her as Rose came around and sat next to her mother.

"Did you have fun?" Margaret asked.

"Brigid went a little overboard, but we had a good time, thanks."

"Nice. It's nice Brigid has a friend," Margaret said, patting Rose's hand. Margaret let her hand linger on Rose's before Rose intertwined her fingers with her mother's to hold it. They sat silently for a moment, listening to just the slow rocking of the ceiling fan.

"Mama?" Rose asked, staring straight ahead before turning her head toward her mother.

"Yes, honey?"

"I'm ready now," Rose spoke as she placed her head on her mother's lap.

Margaret stroked Rose's hair as Rose closed her eyes.

Chapter 26

Rose awoke with a start, bolting up in bed with a gasp. She had slept soundly in her mother's bed, Margaret holding her as she told her story regarding everything that had happened with Thomas Quinn, Darryl, Gemma Quinn, Dutch, and the police. Tears were shed, and her mother never passed any judgment, listening to all Rose had to say before Rose was spent and fell asleep.

The fresh aromas of bacon filled Rose's nostrils as she climbed from bed and went to the kitchen. When she reached the room, Margaret turned and smiled at her daughter.

"Good morning," she offered, pointing to the table so Rose would sit.

"Can I help with something?" Rose yawned.

"I've been doing it myself for a long time, Rose. I can manage, thank you."

Rose sat back before Margaret looked her way again.

"You can pour us some tea," Margaret pointed to the porcelain teapot.

Rose dutifully tended to the tea while Margaret plated eggs, bacon, and fresh fruit. Rose suddenly was ravenous, polishing off her over-easy eggs and crisp bacon while dunking her bread in what was left of the yolk on her plate.

"What's going on today?" Rose asked as she reached for the last piece of bacon.

"Not all of us are on vacation, Rose," her mother responded. "I do have chores to do around here."

"You know I can help you, Mama," Rose answered. "Just let me take a shower, and I can do whatever you need to be done."

"Are you sure you can do this? It's not like standing behind a jewelry counter dressed all pretty. It's labor."

"I think I can manage," Rose challenged.

"Good!" Margaret answered. "After your shower, you can do the dishes and then tend to the chickens. After that, I need to go to the market and get a few things for dinner tonight. Then, when I come back, we can work out in the garden."

"Will you stop off to see Mr. Lynch on the way?" Rose said as she got up from the table.

"Don't be fresh," Margaret chided.

"That wasn't a no," Rose laughed as she moved toward the bathroom to shower.

The cool shower proved refreshing, and Rose dressed in a pair of capris and a yellow blouse that she tied off at the bottom. A yellow scarf to keep her back completed her outfit as she emerged and went back to the kitchen. A note from her mother read:

Dishes, chickens (check for eggs, feed, and don't forget to close the gate), sweep the front porch. Be back soon.

Rose laughed at the note left, wondering if her mother did stop off at Dean Lynch's place on her way to the market in town. The dishes took mere moments to wash, dry and put away, and Rose grabbed the basket by the back door and walked out to the small chicken coop her mother kept just to the right of her garden.

Rose spread the feed for the chickens to get them moving this morning while she went to collect the eggs. The surprise occurred with the bounty discovered, filling the basket quickly, and providing her mother with plenty that she could use and sell. However, when she emerged from behind the coop, she spotted the gate open just enough for several chickens to have slipped through.

Rose raced out, shutting the gate to keep the rest of the brood inside before she corraled two nearby and deposited them back where they belonged. She heard the telltale cluck of one that clearly wandered further off, and she made her way to the side of the house. Rose spotted one, grabbed it, tucking it under her arm before it could escape, and returned it to its rightful place. She noticed another turn the corner and head to the front of the house.

Rose dashed around to the other side, expecting to cut it off when she reached the front yard. But instead, she saw a man standing there, holding the chicken in his arms.

"Oh, thank you," she said, expecting he passed by, and grabbed it. "He got away from me." When the man turned, she recognized the face of George, one of the men from Sunny's.

"No trouble at all," he smiled as he petted the chicken.

"I... I didn't realize you lived nearby," Rose said tentatively, looking around but seeing no one else out and about.

"I don't really," he added, stepping toward Rose. "I was looking for you."

"I appreciate you helping me, but—"

Rose reached for the chicken, but George turned slightly to the side.

"I wish you hadn't run off like that last night," George said, staring down at the bird in his hand. "It would have been much easier if you had stayed for that drink."

"I need to get inside," Rose said as she slowly stepped closer to the house. She could see the screen door and figured she could make a run for it and get inside before George would reach her. "Maybe we can meet another time. My mother will be back any second."

"I doubt it," George smiled. "She looked pretty cozy at Mr. Lynch's on the front patio drinking lemonade."

Fear sprang through Rose's body as she ran toward the front door, getting inside and shutting the door before George could get there. She locked the door and went to her room to grab her purse and phone. She got to the room, but her bag was nowhere to be found.

"Looking for this?" a voice echoed from the hall as Dutch emerged from the shadows, his face gnarled with scars and burn marks, holding her cell phone.

Darryl had little luck in attempting to track down Rose's whereabouts. There were plenty of Boyles listed in Montserrat, but he had no idea if Rose was related to one of them or if that was even the name her mother went by anymore. With no town or location to work with, the search could take days, time Darryl did not want to waste.

"This will take forever," Darryl said, closing Lucy's laptop.

"Hey! Careful with that, or you'll be getting me a new one," she chastised. "I think we're going about this all wrong. We need to plan better. You said Rose left the island after the eruption."

"Sure, her and thousands of other people," Darryl responded.

"And how old was she?"

"Seven."

"Was she born here?" Lucy asked.

"I think so," Darryl replied. "So what?"

"So if she was born here, there are records somewhere, right?"

"Maybe, but who knows where those might be? After the volcano, it sounds like everything went to hell."

"She never mentioned anyone that might be able to help us?"

Darryl's gaze shot up and stared at Lucy.

"You're brilliant!" he shouted, grabbing his phone.

"Thanks, but what did I do?" Lucy said, confused.

"Rose never told me about anyone here, but I know someone who can help us." Darryl scoured through his phone before realizing he had no information on Liz.

"Damn it! I don't have her number!"

"Whose number?" Lucy asked.

"Rose has a roommate back home. They've been friends since they were kids. So she should know where to find Rose's mother. I never spoke to her on the phone, though. I don't have her number."

"Did you think about any of this stuff before coming here?" Lucy complained.

"Look, you don't know the whole story of what's going on, so you don't understand the mess."

"Maybe it's time for you to enlighten me if you want my help," Lucy shot back.

Darryl watched as Lucy stormed down the street, ducking into a pub on the right.

Darryl paced after her, tucking his phone away, before finding Lucy seated at a wicker bar drinking.

"What are you doing?" Darryl asked, watching Lucy take hold of her glass.

"You obviously don't need me to do anything right now, so I'm having a drink and relaxing. So you can go do whatever it is you need to do. I'll have my drink, go back to the hotel, gather my things and go home. Or you can start being straight with me. Your choice."

Darryl's eyes shifted from Lucy to the bartender and back to Lucy again.

"What are you drinking?" Darryl asked.

"Moscow Mule."

"Two more, please," Darryl indicated to the bartender. He waved Lucy over so they could sit at a table tucked at the back of the bar.

"What I tell you stays between us, right?" Darryl asked softly.

"Of course," Lucy nodded. "Pilot-passenger privilege and all."

The bartender arrived, placing two glasses on the table before staring at Lucy.

"He's buying," Lucy indicated, pointing at Darryl. Darryl reached into his pocket to pull out cash and passed it over to get the bartender to leave. He sipped the drink, bringing the freshness of the lime juice and cold vodka to the back of his dry throat before he went into the tale of the last several weeks.

When he was finished, Lucy had finished her initial drink and started on the second one.

"Did you read all this in a book somewhere, or is this the truth?"

"No, it's all too real. Now that the police know it wasn't me, I want to find Rose and bring her back. But, now we have to find Liz Harrison, too."

Lucy pulled her cell phone out and dialed, bringing the phone to her ear.

"What are you doing?" Darryl asked.

"Now you'll see why I'm a good businesswoman," Lucy smiled.

Darryl sat back with his cocktail, watching Lucy go to work on her phone. He got half the conversation as he listened to Lucy talk to someone she worked with.

"I need the info ASAP, Andrew," Lucy added. "Rose Boyle has the potential to be a huge client for us."

"What? She works in a jewelry store," Darryl whispered before Lucy waved him off.

"Right. I need Ms. Boyle's contact information in the US and anywhere else, and I needed it five minutes ago," Lucy spoke. "Just text me numbers and email when you have it. Thanks, Andrew. I'll see you in a few days."

Lucy hung up and placed the phone on the table before reaching for the rest of her drink.

"Well?" Darryl asked.

"Andrew will have it in minutes. We perform background checks on people all the time. So Andrew can find out all we need to know about Rose so we can locate her mother."

"Why didn't you just mention that before?"

"I didn't know you had literally nothing to go on here, Darryl, or how dire the situation might be. So now we can get moving."

Darryl had barely finished his cocktail when Lucy's phone buzzed. She plucked it from the table and smiled.

"Margaret Boyle lives in Woodlands on Hibiscus Drive. She's been there since the volcano eruption in 1995. Let's get a cab and go."

Darryl walked to the bar to speak with the bartender.

"Is there a taxi service you know of?" Darryl asked.

"Of course!" the bartender laughed. "Charles Flannery. He's the best driver and guide in the area. Knows the island like the back of his hand."

"Great. Do you know if Charles is available or where I can contact him?"

"Yes, I do," the bartender answered, smiling back at Darryl but not saying anything.

"Oh, for God's sake Darryl, tip the man!" Lucy groaned as she stood next to Darryl.

Darryl handed over twenty dollars and looked at the bartender, raising his eyebrows as he waited for an answer.

"Well?" Darryl said impatiently.

"Thank you for contacting Sunny Island Tours. My name is Charles. How can I be of service to you today?"

"You've got to be kidding me with this," Darryl grumbled.

Darryl fought the urge to reach across and throttle the older man standing across from him.

"Charles, can you give us a ride to Hibiscus Drive in Woodlands?"

"It would be my pleasure, sir," Charles beamed. Charles tossed aside his bar apron and grabbed a straw hat underneath the counter.

"Donny!" Charles yelled as a younger man in a stained white apron emerged from the kitchen. "I've got a taxi service. You or Sheila have the bar until I'm back."

Charles led Darryl and Lucy out to the front of the bar and to the beat-up Jeep stationed there.

"This is your taxi?" Darryl asked.

"Roads here are not the easiest to maneuver all the time, sir," Charles said as he opened the door for Lucy. "This Jeep has seen me through under all kinds of conditions. I guarantee a safe ride."

Darryl begrudgingly climbed into the front seat next to Charles as he started up the Jeep and took off, kicking dirt and dust up behind him.

"You know where you're going, right?" Darryl roared over the noise from the vehicle.

"Of course!" Charles laughed as he made a sharp turn. "I've lived on the island for over forty years, long before the volcano made it famous. So I know every inch of this place before, during, and after the explosion. Besides, I have family and business in Woodlands. So I'm an entrepreneur, you might say."

"I bet you are, Charles," Lucy chuckled.

The windy road, up and down hilly areas and across narrow strips of what barely could be considered roadway, had Darryl hanging on to the roll bar of the Jeep as they moved along. He caught a glimpse of the street sign marking Hibiscus Drive as Charles maneuvered onto it. Darryl swore the Jeep was on two wheels as he made the turn.

"What house address do we need?" Darryl asked, turning to Lucy.

"You don't need a number," Charles interrupted. "Just tell me who you are seeking. I'll get you there."

"Margaret Boyle," Darryl stated.

"Margaret!" Charles laughed. "Every long-timer knows her. You should have told me you were her friends. I've known her since we were children in school."

"Of course you have," Darryl responded with an eye roll.

Charles sped up as they moved down the street, avoiding the stray animals or pedestrians along the way and honking and waving at friends.

"I own that bar too," Charles said as they went past Sunny's.

A short ride later, Charles pulled the Jeep in front of a small white house surrounded by a picket gate.

"Here she is," Charles answered, grinning. "We made it no time at all."

Darryl hopped out of the Jeep immediately and assisted Lucy from the back seat. He handed forty dollars over to Charles, who gratefully stuffed the bills in his shirt pocket.

"Thank you, sir," he nodded. "If you two need a ride back soon, I'll stop at my pub and check on things there. You can walk down and meet me, or here is my card so you can call my phone."

"Thank you so much, Charles," Lucy said, taking the car.

"My friends call me Sunny," he smiled at Lucy, holding her hand for a moment and kissing it as she took the card.

"Yeah, thanks, Sunny," Darryl added.

"Tell Margaret Sunny said hello," he waved as he made a u-turn just before another vehicle came down the street.

Darryl opened the gate and marched up to the front porch, rapidly knocking on the screen door.

"Hello?" he asked, peering through the screen.

"Maybe they are out back," Lucy said. "I'll go look."

Darryl waited impatiently by the front door before Lucy reappeared.

"Nothing back there but chickens," Lucy spoke.

Darryl tugged on the screen door and saw it was unlocked. He glanced at Lucy before walking in.

"Darryl, what—" Lucy had started, but Darryl was already in the house.

"Rose? You here?" Darryl yelled. He walked into the kitchen and saw nothing out of the ordinary. When he moved back to the living room, Lucy was standing there.

"We shouldn't be here if no one's home," Lucy admonished. "Maybe they went out to the store or for a walk."

"Maybe," Darryl said. "But I need to know if she is even here."

Darryl moved toward the bedrooms. He looked in one room where the bed was neatly made before heading to the other at the end of the hall. It was there he stopped short.

"What's up?" Lucy asked.

"Look at the door," Darryl said, pointing. The door had obviously been damaged, with a boot print toward its bottom. Darryl squatted to get a closer look. "Someone kicked it."

He moved inside and saw the bed holding Rose's handbag with its contents emptied out. He walked over and saw her wallet there, her passport, and the strip of photos they had taken at the arcade bar.

"Something bad happened," as Darryl stormed out of the house. He went out the gate looking for signs of anyone milling around that he could speak with. When he saw no one, he began to march down the middle of the street. It took effort on Lucy's part to catch up as Darryl made his giant strides.

"Darryl, you don't know for sure..."

"Where the fuck are all the people in this town?" Darryl roared. "Someone must have seen something."

Darryl spotted Charles sitting on the front porch with two older residents halfway down the street. He walked right over to where Charles sat.

"I was just talking about you," Charles said. "I told Margaret I just dropped two people at her house looking for her. I should have known she would be here with Dean," he said with a sly grin.

"Hush, Sunny," Margaret scolded as she looked at Darryl. "Do I know you, son?" Margaret asked, looking up at Darryl's form.

"Mrs. Boyle, no, you don't know me. We've never met," Darryl said, sweat dripping. "I'm a friend of Rose's."

Margaret got up from her wooden chair and stared up at Darryl.

"You must be Darryl," she said softly.

"Yes, ma'am, I am. Do you know where Rose is? I need to find her."

"She's back at the house," Margaret answered. "She was tending to chores while I went to the market, but I got a little... sidetracked," she said, glaring over at Dean Lynch.

"No, ma'am," Darryl said. "I was just at the house. No one was there, and Rose's bag was spread over her bed. It also looked like someone else might have been there with her."

"Oh no," Margaret answered. Darryl noticed the older woman's face grow ashen as she struggled to sit down. "Do you think they found her?"

"Did Rose tell you everything that was going on?"

"Yes, last night," Margaret admitted. "She was hesitant to mention anything about it, but I knew something was wrong when she arrived here. She told me about the break-in, Mr. Quinn, God rest his soul, the notes, everything. Even about the attack and you."

"I don't know who found her, but I can promise you whoever is involved will be sorry about it when I get her back," Darryl vowed.

"Should we go to the police?" Margaret asked.

Before Darryl could answer, his cell phone began to ring. He pulled it from his pocket to see if it was Annie or one of the Cosantóir. Instead, it was shown as a private number. He answered quickly, thinking it could be Rose.

"Rose? Is that you? Are you okay?"

Silence on the other end gave way to a familiar voice.

"I heard you were out of jail. I give that old man Jackson credit for figuring out I was involved."

"Myers?" Darryl asked. "Yeah, I'm out. Don't worry. I'm making sure that misery in your life is a top priority for me."

"Hah, I'll bet you are. Anyway, this isn't really a social call for me. I caught up with your girlfriend, and it seems she doesn't have what I need or am looking for. I thought you might want to help me out with that."

"You do one thing to her, and I will cut your fucking heart out, you know that, right?"

"I won't have to do anything to her if you can give me the information I want," Myers responded.

"I can do more than that," Darryl answered. "You can tell that bitch Gemma that I found the stones."

"You're full of shit. You have one emerald and the keys. That's enough to get me started."

"Believe what you want, but I have the entire lot of them. Quinn was smart. I guess his daughter didn't get those genes."

"Prove it," Myers demanded. "Send me a picture."

Darryl waved Lucy over and asked her to hold out her hands. He then poured the contents of the velvet bag into her palms and snapped a photo before sending it.

"Believe me now?"

"Well, perhaps we have something to work out," Myers said snidely.

"Where is Rose?" Darryl demanded.

A moment later, an image was sent to Darryl's phone. He opened it and saw a picture of Rose standing next to Dutch. Dutch held a switchblade under Rose's chin as he grinned maniacally at the camera.

"I have to admit, Demon, she's more challenging than I imagined. She really did a number on poor Dutch. He wants nothing more than to run at her and get even."

"You want your fucking gems, then you need to let her go. I'll bring them to you," Darryl snarled.

"Problem is, my friend, that we're not in little old Harriman anymore. Rosie tried to run away while you were in jail, so we needed to come and get her. I can't promise you she'll be okay by the time you get here."

"I know where you are, asshole," Darryl answered. "I'm already on Montserrat looking for her. Just tell me where and I'll be glad to get her."

"You're smarter than I give you credit for, Demon," Myers laughed. "Tell you what. I'm getting us settled here. I know exactly where we can meet.. You bring the emeralds, and Rose can walk away with you."

"Really?" Darryl said skeptically. "There's no catch to that at all?"

"Nope. I don't give a fuck. The police are already after me. I have a plan, and I can see it through and disappear with the emeralds. Now, Dutch here might feel a bit cheated. I can't say what he might do, so you better make sure you listen to me."

"We'll be in Plymouth at around 11 PM. I'll call you then and guide you to where you can find Rose. So leave the gems, take her, and be on your way and we'll be square. Got it?"

"Right," Darryl agreed.

"Don't mess with me, Darryl," Myers warned. "You know how Dutch can be."

"Let me talk to her, Myers," Darryl insisted.

"What?"

"I want to talk to Rose, so I know she's okay."

"Sure, why not," Myers said.

Darryl listened as he heard some shuffling and a door open and close.

"Someone wants to speak with you," a muffled Myers voice spoke.

"Hello?" Rose's voice quavered.

"Rose? Are you ok?"

"Darryl! Oh, thank God. I'm scared. Where are you?"

"I'm close by," he said. "I'm coming to get you."

"You need to find my mother and make sure she's alright. They told me they would hurt her if I didn't go with them, and they haven't said anything else."

"She's fine, Rose. I'm with her right now."

"Put me on speaker, so I can talk to her," Rose pled.

Darryl obliged and brought the phone nearer to Margaret.

"Mama?" Rose stated.

"I'm here, honey. I'm fine," Margaret said shakily.

"Mama, I'm glad you're fine. I love you. Don't forget to close the gate, so all Miss Birch's goats don't wander down to the beach."

"That's more than enough," Myers was heard barking. "Now that the love fest is over, be ready for a call at 11."

Darryl's phone beeped when the call disconnected. He turned and looked at Margaret as she sat, holding Dean Lynch's hand.

"Why is she bringing up Helen Birch's goats?" Sunny asked.

"Because she was telling me where she is," Margaret stated. "I used to tell her that constantly because our goats shared the pasture with Helen's. Rose would go feed and play with them when she was little. She's near our old place in Plymouth."

"So let's go get her," Darryl stated.

"It's not that easy," Sunny said seriously. "That's the strictest exclusion zone. You can't get in there without government permission, and even then, it's only during daylight hours. So people don't just walk in and out of there. It can be dangerous."

"So how do we get government permission? Who do we have to ask?"

"Darryl, asking might not be the best move," Lucy interrupted. "You think the government will just say okay when you tell them the reasons you need to get there? They'll say no, send the police, and all hell will break loose. Who knows what would happen to Rose after that."

"There has to be something I can do instead of just waiting around all day," Darryl said with frustration.

"I can get you there," Sunny told Darryl.

All eyes turned in Sunny's direction.

"I'm accredited as a guide into the exclusion zone," Sunny replied. "No one will question us going into the area during daylight. I can get you pretty close to where Rose is if they are near the old house."

"How much?" Darryl asked.

"I'm not taking your money for that. These people are my family. We help each other. Just let me make a couple of calls."

"Thanks," Darryl said, patting Sunny's shoulder.

Sunny moved off to make his calls as Darryl moved over toward Lucy.

"You should go back to the hotel," he advised.

"Why?"

"Because it's dangerous. I don't know what Myers or Dutch will do, or if they have anyone else with them, what weapons they have, or anything like that."

"I'm invested in this now, Darryl," Lucy told him. "I want to see it through. Besides, I can take pretty good care of myself. There's a lot you don't know about me. I'll be fine. Let's go get Rose."

"I don't want to be responsible if something happens or if you can't keep up—" Darryl began.

"Stop right there," Lucy ordered. "You're not responsible for me. That's my job. You worry about yourself and whether you can keep up with me. Got it?"

"Fair enough," Darryl nodded.

Sunny walked back over to Darryl, stuffing his phone in his pocket.

"We're all set," Sunny said. "We'll stop at the pub on the way out to pick up some provisions."

"Darryl," Margaret spoke, approaching him. "Bring her back safe."

"I promise you I will," Darryl replied, taking Margaret's hand.

Rose sat back against the wall, grass growing through the floor of the room she resided in. The house Myers and Dutch chose to bring her to had survived the volcano structurally. The doors and floors were mostly intact, but the place was overgrown in every direction.

Rose had not seen this part of the island since she fled the volcano many years ago and didn't look back. Once Dutch took her from her mother's house and bound her hands with a zip tie, all she could do was stare out the car's window as they drove along. When she spotted they were heading into Plymouth, she hoped the police or government officers would stop them. However, George was in the vehicle with them and talked and bribed his way through so they could access the exclusion area without any trouble or notice.

A stroke of luck brought them to the area nearest the beach where Rose lived as a youngster. They drove past her old home, buried under feet of ash and hardened lava, leaving Rose aghast at the devastation she saw. The pasture Rose played and worked in with the goats, sheep, and other animals was destroyed and filled with overgrowth. When she had the chance to talk to Darryl and then her mother, she realized dropping that clue would help point Darryl in the right direction to where she was.

George swung the door to her room open and stood at that doorway, staring intently at her.

"Do you think I could get some water?" she asked.

"Why?" George responded.

"Because I'm thirsty," she said.

"Mr. Myers said not to speak with you about anything."

"Then why did you even bother to open the door? Just leave," Rose added with disgust.

"You know, if you and you're friend had just gone along with us at the bar, this would have been so much simpler," George said.

"I'm sure it would have. You would have drugged us, doing God knows what, and two of us would be here instead of just me. How is that simpler?"

"You're too smart for your own good," George spat out.

"Or you're too ignorant to know you're getting used," Rose shot back. "I don't know what Myers promised you or paid you, but if you really think he's going to give you more out of this, you're nuts."

"What's the problem in here?"

Rose spotted Dutch standing next to George now.

"She's asking for water," George griped.

"Just give her a bottle of water to shut her up," Dutch complained.

"Myers said not to."

"It's fucking water, man, not the keys to the car. Just go," Dutch ordered, pushing George out of the way.

Rose watched as Dutch entered the room with her, drawing closer to where she sat. He squatted down in front of her, giving her a better view of the damage she had inflicted on him back at her apartment. Burn marks and blisters covered the right side of his face.

When he reached out to brush his fingers on the stray strands of hair across her face, she cringed with revulsion.

"Oh, don't be that way," he laughed. "I'm getting you water. You could show some appreciation."

"Go away. I'm not that thirsty."

"Damn. I get what Demon sees in you. You are a fine-looking woman and ballsy too. If you had just given me what I wanted, things would have been different."

"I don't know what fantasy world you and that other moron live in where you think being an asshole is a turn-on for women. If you honestly believe I would do anything with you willingly, you're insane."

Dutch squinted as he peered at Rose.

"I never said anything about willingly," Dutch answered, running his hand on Rose's leg. "Whatever way I want, it would work."

"You're disgusting," Rose said as she pulled her legs closer to her body.

"Maybe, but I'll be rich and disgusting," Dutch gloated.

"You're as dumb as your friend there," Rose nodded toward the door, where George appeared with two water bottles. "Myers is using both of you. Once he has what he wants, do you think he will give anything to you? Someone has to take the fall for all of this, and you can be sure it won't be him or Gemma Quinn. They'll be laughing it up in South America while the two of you rot in jail cells. You're the one that killed Thomas. He's going to let you hang for that. You'll never see a dime of what he promised you."

"Is she right?" George asked as he handed the water to Dutch.

"She's just fucking with us," Dutch said. "She doesn't know shit. Myers gave me money to do the job and promised the rest when it was done. So we'll get our shares."

"Right. Keep telling yourselves that," Rose told him. "You can write letters to each other from prison telling each other how well it's all worked out."

"You're in no position to be so mouthy," Dutch said as he grabbed a bottle of water and held it in front of Rose's face.

Dutch unscrewed the cap and placed the bottle close to Rose's dry lips. Two drops trickled out as Rose took them, but Dutch pulled the bottle away before she could get any more. He took a big swig of the water, grinned, and let out a satisfied sigh.

"Nice," he told her, holding the bottle up so Rose saw the beads of cold sweat dripping down. "Want some now?"

"I don't want anything that's been near your mouth," Rose growled.

"Fuck you," Dutch grunted, forcing the bottle to Rose's lips and pouring water into her. Rose choked as the water reached her, and she held as much as she could in her mouth, spitting it all back in Dutch's face when he pulled his hand away.

"Right back at you," she shouted, water flowing from her mouth onto Dutch and down her body. George cackled at the sight.

"Shut your fucking mouth!" Dutch roared as he stood up and punched George on the head, knocking him to the ground. Dutch stepped back toward Rose, lifting his hand to hit her. Rose never flinched, staring back at him.

"You already did it once. You think I won't retake it?"

Dutch moved closer and lifted Rose to her feet, pinning her against the wall.

"I can't wait to have my way with you," he hissed at her. Dutch moved to press his lips against Rose. Rose pulled back, and the moment she felt his lips touch hers, she opened her mouth and bit down as hard as she could. She gnashed her teeth through flesh, clenching her teeth tight.

Dutch howled and could not pull away until he pressed his hands on the wall behind Rose, pushing fiercely to free himself from her jaws.

Dutch stepped back, and Rose huffed and breathed heavily, a portion of Dutch's lower lips hanging from her mouth. Dutch's hand reflexively went to his mouth, covering the gap where his lip was, as Rose saw his palm filling with blood. She spat the flesh from her mouth and wiped the blood off on her arm.

George sat stunned at the action as Dutch continued to cry out in pain. The commotion had Myers dashing into the room.

"What the hell is going on in here?" he shouted. He looked over at Dutch, hunched over an ash-covered wood table. Dutch turned toward Myers, giving him a view of the damage Rose caused.

"She bith my fuckin' lipth off!" Dutch lisped.

"For Christ's sake, Dutch, what are you doing? All you idiots have to do is keep her here until tonight. Is that too much to ask?"

"Are you going to leave us hanging on everything?" George asked as he stood up. "I ain't taking the fall for all this fucking mess. I want my money."

"Where is this coming from?" Myers asked. "I gave you $500 to get the girl last night, and you didn't do that right. You'll get what's coming as soon as I have the gems. That was the deal."

"Yeah, but she said—" George began pointing at Rose.

"Why the fuck are you listening to her? Of course, she will say anything that she thinks might save her ass. Just do your job."

Rose eyed Myers, who stepped cautiously toward her.

"You've been nothing but a thorn in my ass from the start of all this," Myers told her. "Gemma told me you would be a problem, but I never imagined all this hassle."

"Serves you right for listening to her," Rose said as she spat blood in Myers' direction.

Myers sidestepped the fluid and walked over to where Dutch stood, groaning. He plucked the black bandana from Dutch's back pocket and closed in on Rose. Rose kicked wildly to keep him away before he shoved her to the floor. Rose's head thumped on the hardened floor, stunning her and allowing Myers to move on top of her. He grasped the bandana and shoved it into Rose's mouth, quickly tying it behind her head to gag her.

"Keep quiet now. This is the only time I'm warning you. No talking, biting, or whatever else you're thinking of doing. All this can't get over fast enough. You give me more trouble, and not only will I make sure Darryl and your mother get killed, but I'll let Dutch do whatever he wants to you. I can guarantee you that he has some pretty nasty thoughts running through that pea brain of his."

"Hey!" Dutch yelled, still working to stem the blood flow on his face.

"Just get the fuck out, Dutch, so we can clean you up. George, if she so much as grunts at you," Myers stood up and pulled a knife from the sheath on his back, "cut her however you want."

Myers led Dutch out of the room as George sat in an old beach folding chair across from Rose. She spotted the knife glistening in the sun streaming through the broken window. She sat back against the wall, getting her heart rate and breathing back under control as she stared ahead.

Please hurry, Darryl, she thought.

Chapter 27

Darryl sat in the front seat of the Jeep as it idled in front of Sunny's. His foot tapped rapidly on the floor as his impatience grew as they waited for Sunny to reappear.

"What is taking him so long?" Darryl said, reaching over to honk the horn.

"I'm sure he'll be out shortly," Lucy reassured. "It's going to be okay."

"Every minute we're just sitting here is one more that Rose could be in danger," Darryl gruffed, pressing on the horn again.

Sunny finally appeared, holding two backpacks that he placed in the back seat with Lucy.

"What's the hold-up?" Darryl rushed.

"I had to make sure we had everything we might need," Sunny insisted. "Besides, I got a little more information while I was there. Mark, my nephew, said Rose was in last night with one of the local girls. They had a couple of drinks before two guys came over to them, starting a conversation. He had never seen either of them before, and he said Rose had her radar up. She left and had Mark stall them so they could get out safely. She knew something was up. Mark said the guys left as soon as they could get past him."

"So we know there are at least four of them if you include Dutch and Myers," Darryl reasoned.

"I can't imagine they would have more than that. You can't just sneak a big group of people into the exclusion zone without raising some interest in what's going on," Sunny told him as the Jeep pulled away from the pub.

"We can stick to the main roads until we're inside the zone. After that, I can get us close to where they should be, and we can walk the rest of the way. Sound good to you?" Sunny proposed.

"Whatever you think is best," Darryl answered. "Just get me where I need to be."

Most of the ride passed in silence as Darryl contemplated steps he might have to take to make everything work in his favor. He considered sending a text message to Annie or Finn to let them know what was going on but changed his mind, not wanting to put anyone else on edge.

Darryl barely noticed under the cloudless blue sky when they pulled up to the checkpoint leading into Plymouth. Sunny broke into hustle mode, giving the officer his speech about taking American tourists through the zone for a tour.

"It's a nice day for it," the officer said as he looked over Sunny's credentials. "Good views of the hills and volcano right now for pictures."

The officer looked over at Darryl and then at Lucy.

"They know the rules?" he asked Sunny, pointing.

"Oh yeah, I made sure I let them know. No touching anything, no taking anything. It won't be an issue."

"We've had problems lately," the officer reiterated. "Remember, it's only until dusk. So don't make us come get you."

"It's never a problem with me, sir," Sunny smiled before the officer waved them through.

"Will they really come looking for us?" Lucy asked as they pulled away.

"I'm not sure," Sunny answered. "I've never been here after dark, but I've heard they do."

"Let's hope we're in and out of here before it's an issue," Darryl said, staying focused.

Sunny wended his way slowly along the roads he could traverse, his tour guide sense taking over as he pointed areas out to Darryl and Lucy. All the while, Soufriere Hills loomed in the distance, pillows of smoke drifting along, seemingly harmless.

"Here," Sunny indicated as they made their way down what Darryl thought was a paved road but was actually a strip covered in ash and lava. "This will lead us down where we can leave the Jeep."

Sunny pulled off into an area with high grass and reeds, allowing the vehicle to disappear from view before he came to a stop. Lucy hopped out of the back seat as Darryl climbed out, stomping down some of the overgrowth so he had space. Sunny got out and handed one of the backpacks to Darryl before putting the other on his back.

"What are you doing?" Darryl asked him.

"I'm coming with you," Sunny indicated.

"I don't know if that's a good idea," Darryl told him.

"You two have no clue where to go," Sunny said. "I can take you right into where they should be and lead you back out. Trust me, you need me."

"I can't have anyone getting in the way... either of you," Darryl said, looking at Lucy and Sunny.

"I don't think he has much faith in us, Sunny," Lucy smirked. Lucy reached behind her back and pulled out a 9 mm Beretta M9.

"Where did you get that?" Darryl said.

"I spent five years in the military," Lucy said. "I told you there's a lot you don't know about me. I'll be fine."

Darryl's gaze shifted to Sunny reaching into his backpack. Sunny removed and opened his foldable machete, wielding the blade in front of him.

"What?" Sunny asked. "It's for cutting tall brush as we move. And anything else that might get in my way."

Sunny led the way as they moved along. Telling the difference between streets, forest, and overgrowth became impossible at points as they walked along. The group had reached a particularly steep incline, and the trek became more difficult for Darryl. His breathing began to labor a bit as he lagged behind Sunny and Lucy. At one point, he stopped and put his hands on his knees, working to inhale and exhale before he pulled out his inhaler.

He took a quick puff and held it in before breathing and noticing Lucy staring at him.

"You okay?"

Darryl nodded as he took a second puff and held it.

"You have asthma?" Lucy asked.

Shaking his head negative, he let his breath out.

"Silicosis," Darryl said as he took a few steps forward.

"Shit, Darryl, you shouldn't be hiking like this," Lucy told him.

"I'm not stopping. Just get moving."

Sunny took steps back to find Darryl and Lucy.

"What's going on?" he asked.

"Nothing. Let's go," Darryl said as he glared at Lucy and moved forward.

Darryl worked to keep pace until the trio had reached a bit of a clearing. Finally, the view down to the beach became visible.

"Here's the pasture," Sunny told them as he gave a bottle of water to each of them. "You can see remnants of the busted fence there," he pointed. "It leads straight down to the beach. Margaret's old place is just up around the bend there, so they could be anywhere from here."

"So, how do we find them?" Lucy asked Darryl.

"It shouldn't be too hard," Darryl answered. "Just listen."

The trio fell quiet as Darryl moved his head around.

"All you can hear are the birds. If there are any noises, even a twig breaking, you would hear it for yards. Once we're close to them, we'll have to be on alert."

Sunny passed out a couple of energy bars to Lucy and Darryl as they sat and got their bearings. Darryl had just unwrapped his and taken a bite when rustling in the bushes nearby started. Everyone stopped moving, and all heads swung in that direction. Lucy had already pulled her Beretta out, pointing it in the direction of the noise as Darryl readied himself for the attempted ambush.

"It could be-, " Sunny whispered before Darryl hushed him.

The rustling moved closer until a dark head popped through the thickets. Lucy hesitated a moment before pulling her gun down when she heard the dog panting.

"Jesus," she said as she sat back down.

The light brown dog emerged from the brush cautiously, examining the group.

"Strays are all over the place in the exclusion zone," Sunny added.

"The poor guy looks pretty hungry," Darryl answered. He peeled the wrapper off the rest of his energy bar and held out a piece. The animal looked at Darryl warily, sniffing the air, before taking tentative steps toward Darryl. The dog gingerly took the part from Darryl's hand and chomped it quickly, happy for the morsel. Darryl held out the rest, and the dog moved in, taking it from him and laying on the ground next to him as he ate.

"We'll never be able to shake him now," Sunny lamented.

Darryl allowed the animal to partake of his water, with the dog lapping happily as it poured into its mouth.

Darryl let the dog smell his hands before attempting to pet the pit bull. The dog enjoyed the scratches under his chin and on his belly.

"No collar or anything," Darryl noticed. "Who knows how long he's been here."

"Darryl, we need to get moving," Lucy spoke.

Darryl nodded and stood, stashing the other water bottle in his pack. Sunny led the way with Lucy right behind him. Darryl brought up the rear and heard the movement of paws, first behind him and then alongside him.

"We can't bring him," Sunny said in hushed tones. "He'll give us away."

"I didn't invite him," Darryl replied. "Just keep moving."

They traversed the barely discernable path toward the ruins of homes, with Sunny cutting back overgrowth with his machete. Finally, Sunny brought them to a halt as they reached the edge of what used to be the village, peering around the corner.

"There," Sunny pointed, indicating one lone man standing outside a ruined house, smoking a cigarette.

"How do we do this?" Lucy asked.

"I have an idea," Darryl added, huddling close to Sunny and Lucy.

Sunny burst out first, walking and laughing with Lucy close behind him. Sunny went into his guide spiel, pointing out ruins up and down the street as they drew the smoker's attention.

"That building there," Sunny pointed, "is where George Martin had his recording studio. Paul McCartney, George Harrison, Sting, and stars came down here to record albums and vacation."

"Oh my," Lucy fawned, snapping photos with her phone as she walked.

"Hey!" the man shouted, snuffing out his cigarette. "What are you doing here?"

"Just taking this pretty lady for a tour," Sunny smiled. We're walking through."

"You need to leave. Now," the man added, walking toward them.

"But I wanted to go in there," Lucy whined. "We'll just be a minute. I thought you said we were allowed to be here?" she looked at Sunny.

"Look, friend," the man said, moving his open shirt to the side to reveal the knife he wore on his hip, "it's not a good idea for you to be here right now. Take her down to the beach and then be on your way, got it?"

"Absolutely," Sunny agreed, backing off. "Come along, miss."

"Can we just get two more pictures?" Lucy asked.

"Make it fast," the man snapped.

Lucy turned and snapped off a quick photo before moving closer to where the man and Sunny stood. She handed her phone to Sunny.

"Just take one of him and me," she said, standing next to the man. Lucy had made sure to pull her tank top down more to reveal her ample cleavage. "You don't mind, do you?" she asked, cuddling up to him.

"I-I-" the man stammered, glancing down Lucy's shirt.

She turned toward Sunny and smiled, putting her arm around the man.

Lucy hugged his right hip before deftly snatching the blade from him and holding it against his groin.

"Move one inch or make one noise and I'm walking out of here with a souvenir from you, got it?" she growled.

She poked the blade's tip against his crotch so he knew how serious Lucy was before he simply nodded.

Sunny let out a whistle as Darryl emerged from his hiding spot behind the building.

"Where are they?" Darryl asked.

"Who? I'm just—" the man started.

"You're just nothing," Darryl interrupted. "Standing in the middle of a ruined town smoking for no reason? Where are Myers and Dutch?"

"I don't know who—" the man said, trembling.

"Cut his balls off, Lucy," Darryl said, turning in disgust. Lucy poked the blade into his thigh, drawing a quick response.

"Wait!" the man said fearfully.

"They're in one of the houses just through the other side of the village, I swear!"

"Is the woman with them?" Darryl asked, stepping next to him.

The man nodded frantically.

"How many people are there?"

"Four. Myers, Dutch, George, and the woman. That's all. Please, don't—"

Darryl looked at Lucy and nodded as she drew the blade back, cutting through the khaki pants he wore and drawing blood from his thigh with just the tip. The man started to howl before Darryl approached him and took him into a wrestling sleeper hold. He gripped tightly, cutting off the blood flow and oxygen as the man struggled before slumping to the ground.

"Wow, that really works, huh," Sunny said, surprised.

Darryl scanned forward as he watched the dog move to the edge of the village, ears perked up.

"He spotted something," Darryl said. He dragged the unconscious man into the nearby building, leaving him against the wall.

Darryl and the group moved stealthily toward the edge of town where the dog stood, sniffing the air. Darryl pointed toward the two buildings there, both set back under the shade of a group of tall trees.

"I just saw a shadow moving in that building there," he indicated to the one with the door closed. A loud noise had Darryl pull back as he peered and watched another unknown man pop open one of the shutters of a far window, sending it crashing to the ground. It was then that Darryl saw Myers appear from the other building, wearing sand-colored shorts and a tropical button-down shirt.

"What the hell are you doing?" Myers yelled into the open window.

"She was complaining it was too hot in here, so I opened the window more," the man replied.

"I don't give a fuck what she wants," Myers yelled back. "It's bad enough I have to put up with Dutch's whining. Just keep her still and quiet, George!"

"I'm trying," George answered. "It is hot in here, though."

"Deal with it while I get him fixed up!"

"I'm going in there to get Rose," Darryl said.

"You don't know what kind of weapons any of them might have," Lucy replied. She removed the knife she had taken from the first kidnapper and handed it to Darryl.

"Is there an easy way to go around the back of those houses?" Darryl asked Sunny.

"There's no straight path if that's what you mean," Sunny answered. "They back up against the forest with a slope. So you'll have to work at it and be careful."

"I'll manage," Darryl added confidently. "If you see anyone that's not Rose or me, come out of that building, shoot him, and then get out of here."

Darryl crept around toward the rear of the buildings, staying on firm ground for as long as he could before he was forced into the overgrowth. He stepped lightly when he reached the first building, staying as close to it as possible to avoid slipping down the steep slope and deep into the forest. His vantage point gave him a view through one of the damaged shutters. He saw the hulking form of Dutch with his back to Darryl as Myers stood in front of Dutch before stepping back, tossing blood-soaked gauze onto the floor.

"Christ, man, she did a number on you," Myers said, almost laughing.

"No kidding," Dutch spoke, muffled. "Don't fucking laugh about it."

"Relax, Dutch," Myers said, sitting down in the chair opposite Dutch. "By tonight, you'll have enough money to go someplace else where no one cares what you look like."

"Just make sure I get one more crack at her before Demon gets here," Dutch snarled. "I want her broken to pieces when he gets here."

"Easy, you'll get your chance," Myers answered. Darryl spied Myers pouring himself a glass of whiskey, and held it up. "I'd give you some, but it might burn a little, and I don't think you could handle it," Myers laughed.

"Fuck you," Dutch spat.

Darryl carefully moved on, knowing he had to go quickly to ensure Rose's safety. He slid past the first building, walking in the empty space between the two before nearing the second. He saw little to no firm ground to move on, pressing himself as close to the outer wall as possible. Halfway along the wall, his left foot slid, and he lost footing.

"No, no," he groaned as his body fell forward and skidded down the slope uncontrollably.

As much as Darryl attempted to brace himself, his feet tore through the earth and underbrush while his hands tried to dig in or hold on to something, anything that might prevent him from falling further. Then, finally, the heel of his right foot caught a tree stump to halt his progress.

His movement halted, Darryl lay face down, catching his breath. Tightness filled his chest again as he began to cough. Darryl looked up the incline to see the base and wall of the house well above him now. He also heard scrabbling noises coming through the woods adjacent to him. He reached for the knife he had placed at his side, only to feel it wasn't there any longer. Glancing, he saw it positioned about five feet further up the hill from where he landed.

The movement got closer as he attempted to pull himself to his knees to be ready to fight, only to see the pit bull walk up next to him and begin to lick his face.

Darryl exhaled and patted the dog on its head.

"Thanks, dude," he said as the last licks hit his cheek. "I don't suppose you know how to fetch knives, huh?"

The dog tilted his head at Darryl as if pondering the question before his ears perked up, and his gaze went up the hill.

"What the fuck was that?" Myers could be heard yelling. "George, check it out!"

Darryl flattened himself out as best he could, considering his enormous size, hoping to avoid detection. He heard footsteps above him as George inched his way along the rear of the house to get a look. Darryl peered over and saw the dog's hackles going up and a low growl beginning in the pit bull's stomach.

"Quiet, dude," Darryl whispered, reaching out for the dog but unable to grab him. Instead, the dog began barking and moved in front of Darryl, inching up the hill to conceal Darryl's presence.

The dog began barking fiercely when it spotted George, causing the man to freeze in his tracks and recoil.

"It's just a dog," George yelled. "And a mean-looking SOB at that. Easy, fella."

Darryl lifted his head slightly as he saw George put his hands up in front of him. The dog let out a guttural growl and bark, pushing George firmly against the house wall.

"Fuck this," George muttered and left the scene, leaving the dog barking. Once George disappeared, the dog stopped and trotted back down the hill, positioning himself in front of Darryl and licking Darryl's nose.

"Thanks," Darryl said, petting the dog's short, dark coat.

Struggling to his feet, Darryl slowly worked toward the knife, placing it at his hip, before moving right, using trees and rocks to steady himself along the way until he saw he was clear of the rear of the house. Again, he strained to get up the incline, finally making it and collapsing on the ground at the far side of the structure.

He patted the left pocket of his dirty and stained pants, feeling for his inhaler to make sure it was still there. Darryl stood, peering through the slats of the ash-caked blinds covering the window. He spotted Rose in the far corner, hands bound in front of her, against the wall. He watched as George pulled up a chair in front of her and sat down to begin whittling a stick with the knife he had in his hands.

Just a few feet separated Darryl from the front of the house. Unable to discern what Myers and Dutch spoke about in their location, he moved to the front corner and peeked. Then, he looked across to where Lucy and Sunny stayed positioned, giving Lucy a thumbs up before the dog moved over to stand next to Darryl. Lucy pointed, questioning, but Darryl could only shrug, knowing there was little he could about his newfound companion at that point.

Darryl reached into his pocket and pulled out another energy bar, unwrapping it quietly. He fed a piece to the dog before tossing another part so it neared the front doorway. The dog sprinted after it, laying down in front of the access, chewing his prize.

"You again?" George was overheard. "Go away!"

The dog ignored his pleas, munching the treat before lifting his head and growling. George had moved closer to the door, and Darryl saw him waving his hands to shoo the pit bull away. The second he spotted George cross the doorway's threshold, Darryl sprung into action.

He ran full speed at George. The man was caught off guard, his mouth opening but no noise coming out as Darryl's body violently collided with his. Darryl put all his weight into the block, sending George sprawling into the door frame. The distinct sound of George's head thudding against the jamb echoed before Darryl watched the man's eyes roll as he crumpled to the floor.

Darryl pivoted and saw Rose, a shocked look on her face, struggling with the zip ties on her wrists and ankles. Darryl leaped into the room, grabbing his knife and heading toward Rose. He made short work of the ties digging into her body, freeing her so she could stand. She quickly embraced Darryl hugging him tightly.

"Darryl," Rose wept uncontrollably.

"Rose," Darryl said, taking a step back. "We need to move. Now."

"What's going on now, George?" Myers spoke as footsteps neared where Darryl and Rose stood.

Darryl shoved Rose to the side, so she was on the other side of the door frame when Myers reached the house.

"Fuck," Myers was heard as Darryl recognized the sound of a gun clicking. He saw the gun cross through the frame, and Darryl chopped it down, sending the weapon skidding to the floor as Myers attempted to react. Next, Darryl brought his fist down rapidly to Myers' chin, knocking the detective to the ground. Then, Darryl planted a swift kick with his right boot to the midsection of Myers, eliciting a loud gasp as the air left Myers' body.

Darryl reached down, plucking Myers off the ground by his shirt collar. He lifted the smaller man up and slammed him violently against the wall, spreading ash clouds all around them. Myers gasped again, unable to mount a defense.

"I should just tear your arms off and beat you to death with them," Darryl roared, slamming Myers into the wall again, cracking the space behind Myers' body. Myers attempted to raise his right hand toward Darryl's face. Instead, Darryl placed his left forearm under Myers' throat while grabbing the trembling right fingers moving toward his face.

"I don't think so," Darryl stated. He took Myers' fingers in his right palm before bending them back as far as possible. The sickening bone cracks were followed up by Myers's gurgling as he attempted to yell out in pain.

It was only out of the corner of his eye that Darryl saw someone moving toward him. A quick hit sent his body and Myers tumbling to the floor. Darryl rolled, hitting the table and toppling it to the ground. He saw Myers gasping for air while gawking at his mangled right hand. A glance up showed Dutch looming over Darryl.

A poorly placed bandage covered what was left of Dutch's bleeding lower lip while the one covering the gash on Dutch's head flapped freely.

"Who hit you with the ugly stick?" Darryl said as he squatted before launching himself at Dutch, sending both men grappling on the floor.

Finally, Darryl got on top of Dutch, punching him with his left hand below the ribcage.

"You're fucking girlfriend has been a pain in my ass," Dutch grunted. Then, he punched at Darryl's side, landing and knocking Darryl to the floor.

Dutch had rolled to the side, and as Darryl looked over, preparing for his next move, he was blinded. Dutch had tossed a handful of ash into Darryl's eyes and face, preventing him from seeing. Darryl staggered, thumping against the wall as he attempted to clear his eyes. The blurry vision of Dutch came through just as he was struck by a wooden chair, knocking Darryl to the ground. Dutch immediately followed that move with a series of kicks as Darryl protected his head and took punishment to his arms and stomach.

Darryl frantically wiped at his eyes, feeling the familiar tightness in his chest.

"Not now," he muttered, feeling for his pocket. Unfortunately, the inhaler wasn't there.

"You looking for this?" Dutch laughed. Darryl squinted, barely able to make out Dutch holding the plastic inhaler in his hand. "Looks like you're in a little bit of trouble, Demon. Did you need some help?"

Dutch squeezed the inhaler rapidly, sending mist into the air several times.

"Stop, please!" Rose begged, rushing to Darryl's side. Darryl felt Rose press her face to his.

"Just slow down and breathe," she whispered into his ear. "Breathe. I got you. I'm here."

"You've caused enough trouble," Dutch yelled.

Darryl blinked quickly, tears coming from his eyes as he attempted to get his breathing under control. He realized Dutch had yanked Rose to her feet and away from him. He made out Rose's form as she struggled in Dutch's arms.

"Just lay there, Demon," Dutch laughed. "You'll have a good view of me taking care of your woman for you before I cut her throat."

Darryl struggled, crawling across the floor as he spied Dutch pulling out his knife and bringing it down toward Rose's shirt. The blade tore through the fabric of her blouse as Dutch cackled again. Darryl scooted closer, seeing Dutch lift Rose up and throw her onto the wooden table. She kicked at his hands and face violently as she screamed.

Another pair of shoes came into Darryl's view as he looked up and saw Myers looming over him. Myers had his gun in his left hand, shakily pointing down at Darryl while holding his right hand close to his body.

Myers stepped on Darryl's right hand, pressing down with his weight and causing Darryl to grimace.

"I should do the same thing to you," Myers growled.

"Don't kill him yet," Dutch yelled as he worked to fight off Rose's defense. "I want him to hear all this."

"I'll just shoot him in the spine so he can't move and dies slow," Myers cackled, cocking his gun.

Darryl closed his eyes, awaiting his fate before a ruckus broke out in the room. A deep growl followed by howling disrupted the action. A gunshot rang through the air, followed by shrieks. Darryl had expected to feel a bullet, but nothing happened. He opened his eyes again to see Myers lying on the floor next to him, screaming, as the pit bull gnawed on what was left of his right hand.

Rose was at Darryl's side now as he was tugged away from Myers' body. Sunny rolled Darryl to his side, allowing Darryl to spot Rose huddled next to his face, holding out the inhaler for Darryl to use. She administered three puffs into Darryl's throat as he began to cough and breathe.

Darryl's view turned to the doorway where Lucy stood, her pistol aimed at Dutch as he sat bleeding against the far wall.

"Call him off! Please!" Myers repeatedly yelled as the dog had turned his hand and wrist into ground beef.

"Sorry," Lucy answered. "He won't listen to me."

Darryl sat up, his racing heart becoming more controlled. Sunny opened a water bottle, pouring it into Darryl's eyes to clear out the ash and dirt before wiping his face.

Darryl turned his head and saw Rose, her face covered in dirt and tears.

"Can you hear me?" Rose said as Darryl focused his vision.

"Always," Darryl coughed, leaning his forehead against Rose's before she took his face in her hands and kissed him.

The dog released his grip on Myers when he heard Darryl's voice and walked over and lay next to Darryl. The pit bull proceeded to lick its paws and lips, washing the blood off its body as Myers groaned in agony.

"You okay?" Lucy asked as she squatted in front of Darryl.

Darryl nodded as he put his arm around Rose, cradling her.

"He dead?" Darryl asked, nodding toward Dutch.

"He's breathing right now," Lucy said. "I got him in the shoulder. I had the other one in my sights until your friend jumped in and took him down. I fired and got that asshole instead. My aim is rusty. I wanted to get him in the head."

Darryl struggled to his feet, with Rose trying to stop him.

"Don't get up," Rose said, holding his hand.

"I need to do this," Darryl said as he forced himself up. He stepped over Myers's prone body as it slowly wriggled on the floor until he reached where Dutch sat against the wall. Blood oozed from the bullet hole under his shoulder blade.

Dutch forced a grin to his mouth, unveiling gums and teeth exposed by where his lower lip once was as he coughed blood in Darryl's direction.

Darryl reached over and pressed his thumb into the gunshot wound, causing Dutch to cry out.

"Fuck!" Dutch sputtered, eyes closed.

"Give me one reason why I shouldn't kill you," Darryl uttered, pulling his knife out and pressing it to Dutch's neck.

"Don't have one," Dutch spat. "Do what you gotta do. I'm telling you now, Demon. You let me live, and I'll find you—both you and that bitch—and I'll torture you until you beg me to kill you."

Darryl pressed his thumb deeper inside, causing Dutch to moan and struggle. Finally, Darryl flicked the knife tip over to the bullet wound.

"I could dig out for you if you want, Dutch," he said. "Fingers or blade?"

"Fuck you," Dutch winced.

"Have it your way," Darryl added, positioning the knife over the wound.

"Darryl, don't," Rose implored. "You're better than him."

"I'm really not, Rose," Darryl said, fighting himself. "I can be just as bad... even worse right now. After what he did to you and tried to do to you," Darryl pushed his thumb in deeper as Dutch howled.

"Nothing he did to me will change how you feel if you kill him," Rose pled. "Let him rot in a cell for the rest of his life. That one too," she added, pointing to Myers.

Darryl tensed, staring deep into Dutch's eyes, before looking at Rose and pulling his hand away. He got up and moved toward one of the chairs in the room, sitting down before Rose came and sat on his lap, flinging her arms around his neck.

"Thank you," Rose said, her voice muffled as she had her head on his shoulder.

Darryl sighed, closing his eyes as he held Rose. He heard the commotion in the room, and his eyes flung open as he heard Lucy yell out.

"Darryl!" she shouted.

He opened his eyes, spotting her pushed to the floor as Dutch rushed toward Darryl and Rose, his knife poised high above his head as he moved to strike down. Before he could, the whoosh of a blade hit the air as Darryl sat, stunned, staring at the large knife protruding from Dutch's belly.

Dutch's eyes fixed on Darryl before looking down at his stomach and then back at Darryl. The blade eased out as Dutch collapsed to the floor, leaving Sunny standing there holding his machete with a trail of blood on it.

Rose clung tightly to Darryl, burying her head next to his neck. He held her close as Lucy moved over to check the vital signs of Dutch. A large pool of blood had already formed underneath him and began to spread across the floor. Lucy looked up and shook her head at Darryl when she found no signs of life.

"We should get out of here," Lucy said, standing next to Sunny.

Darryl stood up, took Rose's hand, and walked over to where Sunny paused. The older man stared at his machete, still dripping blood.

"Sunny?" Darryl spoke softly.

"I'm okay," Sunny replied, coming out of his daze. "Let's go."

"What do we do about him?" Lucy asked, pointing at Myers on the ground and weeping.

Myers gazed up at Darryl.

"I need a hospital," he implored. "Don't just leave me here."

Darryl squatted down next to the detective, plucking the gun within his reach off the floor to avoid further incidents.

"You expect me to take pity on you now, Myers? After all this?"

"I'll bleed to death if you leave me here like this!" Myers shouted.

"Nah," Sunny spoke. "Odds are the local wild boars will find you when they are out looking for food. They will come for you if you're lying on the ground like that."

"Fuck! Please, Darryl, Rose..."

Darryl glanced over at Rose as she approached. She grabbed a closed water bottle from the window sill and placed it on the floor next to Myers's body.

"We'll let the officers know you're here," Rose said stoically. "If you survive until then, maybe they'll feel sorry for you and get you help."

"That's it? The guy kidnaps you, threatens to rape and kill you and your family, and you'll leave him here alive?" Lucy yelled. "He's getting off too easy. What's to prevent him from getting up and running away?"

"Nothing," Rose added."Taking his life won't make me feel better. Besides, I don't think he's in a condition where he can do much. Even if he runs, he'll never be able to navigate the woods or the roads with his hand like that. He'll pass out from pain and blood loss eventually."

"Well, I'm not taking any chances," Lucy barked. She approached Myers, gun in her hand, as he winced in fear. Instead of shooting him, however, she simply knelt down and undid the laces on his boots, pulling them off his feet.

She held up the footwear for all to see.

"Now he's not going anywhere, and he'll have to worry about snakes and insects. Good luck, asshole."

Darryl took Rose's hand once more and led her out of the house, with Sunny and Lucy following behind.

"Wait! Wait!" Myers yelled, but Darryl kept moving forward with the others.

The group passed through the village and back toward the hidden Jeep with few words passing. Darryl occasionally looked over at Rose to see how she was doing. It was only when they neared the vehicle that Rose began to speak up.

"Is Mama okay?" she asked softly.

"She's fine," Darryl answered. "She told me to make sure I brought you back safely. I promised I would."

Rose nodded and gripped Darryl's hand tighter.

"Good. You don't want to disappoint her," she uttered thoughtfully, forcing Darryl to smile slightly.

"Who's your friend?" Rose asked, indicating the pit bull following close at Darryl's side.

"Oh, yeah," Darryl said, glancing as the dog paused when they reached the Jeep. "He just showed up out of nowhere. He's the real hero."

"Does he have a name?"

"He doesn't have a collar or tags," Darryl answered as he placed his backpack in the back of the Jeep. "I don't know what to call him, but he saved our lives."

Darryl stood next to the vehicle as Rose bent down and held out her hand for the dog to sniff. The animal walked over to her, smelled, then licked her hand before she pet him.

"How about Conlaoch?"

"Huh?" Darryl asked.

It's pronounced Kawn-lay," Rose laughed. "It's Irish Gaelic for hero. He's a famous warrior from mythology. What do you say?" Rose asked the dog.

Darryl positioned himself in the back seat as Rose climbed in and sat next to him. She waved the dog in, and he immediately jumped aboard, placing himself between Rose and Darryl. Darryl pulled the velvet bag from his pocket and passed it to Rose. He watched as she opened it, reading the note from Thomas Quinn.

"ádh mór agus grá," she said softly.

"What does it mean?" Darryl asked.

"Best of luck and love," Rose answered, reaching over to take Darryl's hand while she examined the emeralds.

"So this is how it's going to be, huh?" Darryl asked, looking into Conlaoch's face. "I guess he's part of the family now."

"What family?" Lucy asked from the front seat as Sunny started the Jeep and backed out to pull away.

"Ours," Darryl added proudly, reaching over Conlaoch's head to take hold of Rose's hand.

Epilogue

"So, how are you feeling?" Finn asked as he sipped his coffee, looking back at Darryl.

"Better," Darryl admitted. "No broken bones or anything for anyone, and we're recovering physically and mentally. So I'd say we're getting there."

"Glad to hear it," Conor added, arriving at the table and sitting next to Finn with his own hot mug. "Where does all the legal stuff stand?"

"Well, after we directed the cops on our way out of the exclusion zone, they picked up Myers and the two locals helping him. Myers was damn lucky he only lost his hand. He's facing charges in Montserrat on kidnapping, assault, and half a dozen other things, on top of the murder for hire in Monroe. I think his days on the outside are long over."

Conor nodded, sipping his beverage before he turned to Finn.

"And what about all the stuff with the shop and the emeralds and such?"

"Legally, it all belongs to Rose," Finn added. "Thomas Quinn laid it all out in his will. So there's nothing to contest, especially since Gemma Quinn has her own troubles."

"What about her?" Darryl inquired.

"No one knows where she disappeared to," Finn replied. "She has access to enough money and methods where she could just disappear if she wanted to. The police are still looking into it, but who knows if or when they will track her down. I don't think you'll have to worry about her turning up soon."

"So what about you?" Finn asked Darryl.

Darryl eased back in his chair and sipped his drink, putting him out of frame on the laptop's video camera before sitting up straight.

"What about me?"

"When are you coming home?"

Darryl sighed deeply.

"I'm not," he announced to Finn and Conor.

"What do you mean you're not?" Finn said, shocked.

"I mean, I'm not—actually, Rose and I aren't—coming back to Harriman, at least to stay," Darryl stated. "After the doctor's diagnosis, I've decided to put my papers in and retire on disability. I can't keep working with the Sandhogs if I want to have a life. So we're going to live here, in Montserrat. Rose can be near her mother, we can get a nice home here, and the weather is ideal for me and my condition. Rose even has a spot picked out where she can open her own jewelry shop, and I have an idea what I might do here."

"What's that?"

Darryl leaned over and petted Conloach on the head, the dog squinting from enjoyment.

"A dog sanctuary," Darryl answered. "There are many strays here that need a place to call home, just like me."

"What about Annie, your house, and the Cosantóir?"

"I already spoke to Annie," Darryl reassured. "I asked her if she wanted to come down here to live or stay in New York. Right now, she wants to stay. The house is paid for, so she has no worries about that. I'll take care of her, and Conor assured me that the brothers would watch out for her. As for the Cosantóir..."

"You'll always be a brother, Darryl, no matter what," Conor interrupted.

"You knew all this already and didn't tell me?" Finn asked his father.

"Boy, I don't have to tell you everything going on as soon as it happens," Conor scolded.

"This is what's best for me, Finn. It's been a long time since I did anything for myself. I know this is right. We'll be back in a week to finalize retirement and make arrangements for our things to be moved, like my bike."

"What's this about a bike?" Rose's voice echoed behind Darryl. Rose walked up and draped her arms over Darryl's shoulders, kissing his cheek. "Hi, Finn," Rose said, waving into the camera.

"My motorcycle," Darryl told her. "I'm bringing it down here."

"You can just ride a scooter," Rose said, drawing looks of shock from all three men. "I'm kidding. Relax, gentlemen."

Rose stood up and looked at Darryl.

"I just wanted to let you know things are starting," Rose said before looking at the camera again. "Sorry, boys. Darryl's done playing with you for now. He's mine."

"I'll talk to you soon," Darryl spoke to the screen, waving his big palm to Conor and Finn.

"Bigi sona!" Conor spoke.

Confusion crossed Darryl's mind before Rose put her arm around him.

"He told us to be happy," Rose said softly in his ear.

"Thank you, Ceannaire, for everything," Darryl added sincerely.

"My pleasure. We'll talk soon."

Darryl shut the laptop and turned to face Rose. He bent down and placed his lips on hers, putting his hands on her hips as he did. Reggae music blared in through the windows and down the street.

"The parade is going," Rose said as she pulled her lips away from Darryl's.

"I hear," Darryl replied, staring into Rose's eyes. "Do we have to go right now?"

"Well, Mama is down with Mr. Lynch watching from his front porch," Rose purred.

Darryl lifted Rose, causing her to shriek as she wrapped her legs around his waist. He walked with her, smiling, as they reached the hall and went toward her bedroom.

"You said the St. Patrick's Day festival runs for two weeks," Darryl said as he pushed open the bedroom door with his foot.

"That's true," Rose added as Darryl placed her gently on the bed. "We have time," she grinned.

"We have a lifetime," Darryl said, pushing the door closed as he paced back to the bed to be with Rose.

Acknowledgments

T here are always many people to thank before, during, and after I write, and this book is no different.

I always thank Scarlet Lantern Publishing for standing by me through the writing process. Not only are the publishers the best, but the team of editors, cover artists, social media managers, and the wonderful fellow authors all provide me with constant help, support and encouragement. They are the best to work with throughout.

A large portion of this book was written at Meadow Blues Coffee in Chester, NY. It doesn't get done without the constant support of the owner, Gina Stafford, for plying me with coffee and treats, encouragement, and plenty of laughs that helped me from start to finish. The book never gets done without her pushing me along.

My faithful beta readers have seen me through several books now, keeping my story on the straight and narrow as I work on each novel. Thank you so much to Chrissy Hauser and the real Liz Harrison for guiding me and letting me know what makes sense to others besides me!

Hudson Valley Scribes is the best group of fellow authors and friends you can have as a support group. All of the constant encouragement, critique, insight, and education the group provides for me helps make me better each day, and without all of you, I don't think I would still be at this.

My friends and family can never get enough credit for their role in my work. To my brothers and sisters—Kevin, Kerry, Don, Lauren, and Kate—and my fantastic Mom, wonderful nieces and nephews, aunts and uncles and cousins, friends I've had for over forty years, or those that have recently come into my life, you all inspire me in one way or another. Thank you for your constant love and support.

Finally, the books never happen without Michelle and Sean. They are my rocks and true rockstars that have seen me through everything. My alpha readers, my biggest cheerleaders, and the best two people in the world. Saying thank you for all you both do is never enough.

Until the next book—ádh mór agus grá.

Also By M. Geraghty

The Cosantóir MC

Small Town, Biker Romances

Finn

Preacher

Liam

Demon

The **Home Stand** Series

Small Town, Sports Romances

Change Up

Spring Fever

The Sweet Spot

The **Celtic Sisters** Series

Small Town, Dark Romances
A Calm in the Storm

Standalone Romances

For What It's Worth

A Christmas, Rockstar Romance

www.ingramcontent.com/pod-product-compliance
Lightning Source LLC
Chambersburg PA
CBHW020932020726
47495CB00002B/461